Copyright © 2025 J

All rights reserved

The characters and events portrayed in this book are fictitious. Any similarity to real persons, living or dead, is coincidental and not intended by the author.

All brand names and product names used in this book are trademarks, registered trademarks, or trade names of their respective holders. J Frances is not associated with any product or vendor in this book.

No part of this book may be reproduced, or stored in a retrieval system, or transmitted in any form or by any means, electronic, mechanical, photocopying, recording, or otherwise, without express written permission of the publisher.

No part of this publication may be used or reproduced in any manner for the purpose of training artificial intelligence technologies or systems.

Cover design by: Get Covers

CONTENT WARNING

This book is meant for mature audiences and contains content that may be triggering for some readers - including sex, profanity, drug addiction, mental health issues, infant loss, grief, domestic violence and references to suicide.

If you or someone you know is contemplating suicide then please call the helpline on 116 123 or go online to www.spuk.org.uk.

If you are the victim of domestic violence then please reach out to the National Domestic Abuse Helpline on 0808 2000 247 or go online to www.nationaldahelpline.org.uk.

If you are struggling with drug or alcohol addiction and need help, then please go online to www.mind.org.uk.

SONG LIST FOR RECLAMATION

Dancing Queen - Abba
Empire State of Mind – Alicia Keys
Addicted - Jonny Houlihan
Memories - Maroon 5
Everybody Hurts - REM
The Scientist - Coldplay
Talk – Coldplay
Princess of China – Coldplay featuring Rihanna
Dukebox - Cyberius (from the first nightclub scene)
Fortnight - Taylor Swift feat Post Malone
Only Love Can Hurt Like This - Paloma Faith
Ink - Coldplay
This Love - Maroon 5
Kiss Me - Ed Sheeran
Pour Some Sugar on Me - Def Leppard
Lose Control - Teddy Swims
I Got You Babe – Sonny and Cher
River Deep - Mountain High – Ike and Tina Turner
Photograph - Ed Sheeran
The Drugs Don't Work - The Verve
Run - Snow Patrol

About the Author

J Frances is in her early forties and is a hopeless romantic who is addicted to books. Her love for books started as a young girl when she used to read book after book, forever visiting the library either with school or with her mum.

With a vivid imagination and a clear passion for writing, she began writing stories on her beloved typewriter until eventually finding the time in her life in her early thirties to write her first ever novel back in 2013. J Frances lives in Lancashire with her husband, two sons and pet dog Milo.

Her first novel, A Leap of Faith, is also available to purchase on Amazon Books.

For Those In Need of Help

Writing this series of novels put me on one hell of a journey, and whilst I loved writing this story, the difficult parts that came with the story did really affect me.

I am therefore dedicating this novel to all those people out there who need that help. To all those who are suffering with their mental health, have suffered a bereavement and are struggling with their grief, to those who have lost loved ones to suicide and to those who are struggling with drug or alcohol addiction. Please never give up hope. Please seek help and talk to somebody.

If you take anything away with you after reading this series of books, then I truly hope that it is the light. A bright light shining in the darkness. A beacon of hope. Because if you think you have nothing else left in the world, you always have hope.

Thank you for reading this book, and to those who are struggling right now, I truly hope that this story helps and inspires you to find the light.

Love to all........J xx

Prologue

Manchester – November 2004

"Can you feel it moving yet?"

I turn my head to look into the dark brown eyes of my boyfriend and smile up at him. "Hmm, not quite yet, baby, but I'm eighteen weeks pregnant now so I'm sure we won't have to wait for much longer."

He smiles back at me, rubbing his nose up against mine, those come to bed brown eyes of his gazing deeply into my blue ones. "I hope not, because Daddy here is becoming impatient." Giving my tummy an affectionate rub, he says, "You sure you can't feel anything at all? Not even a few butterflies?"

God, he can be so sweet sometimes, sweet as well as incredibly hot, one hell of a combination that's for sure. "I'm already feeling butterflies from you, baby," I murmur.

He arches an eyebrow, looking surprised at my confession. "Even after four years of being with me, you still get butterflies when I touch you?"

I bite my lip, said butterflies now well and truly taking flight in that tummy of mine, and not from the baby. "Oh yeah, and not just when you touch me."

His eyes gain heat, suddenly going from soft and tender to dark and dangerous within the space of a few seconds. "That's good to know, and you do realise that you still have exactly the same effect on me but in an entirely different way, don't you?"

"Mmm, what way might that be then?" I tease, rubbing my bottom up against his crotch. As I'm sat in his lap with his arms snaked tightly around me, it doesn't take much to realise what he's talking about, but I enjoy teasing him anyway.

"You know damn well what way, Lauren Whittle, it's always been the same. That's why we've ended up with that little bean of ours in your tummy in the first place, all because I just can't keep my hands off you and never have been able to."

This, I am proud to admit, is true, and four years into our relationship, nothing has changed between us. What started out as a young, teenage journey of firsts for the both of us soon turned into something so much more than that. Something deep and meaningful, intense at times and wildly passionate. And Jonny is just so unpredictable and sexy, so completely sexy. With his jet black hair, dark brown come to bed eyes and tattoos, Jonny is my ultimate bad boy with the added bonus of being completely and utterly sweet, because he loves me to the moon and back. He has a huge heart and would literally do anything for me, a fact which sometimes scares the shit out of me. Speaking of which…

"We should tell your mum and dad soon…" I hesitate, not really wanting to say the next bit. "And my dad…maybe."

That kills the moment between us, Jonny briefly turning away from me before turning back again, his eyes suddenly angry. "Number one, your dad isn't fit to be called that title and I've told you before to stay away from him, I don't want you or our baby anywhere near him. And number two, it's none of their fucking business, Lauren, we're nineteen years old for fuck's sake and we live together, we can do what the fuck we want when we want. When have you and me ever been any different?"

Typical Jonny, always immediately on the defensive whenever I mention the dreaded P word. Whilst Jonny's mum and dad can be over bearing at times, his dad more so than his mum, they know just how musically talented their son is. They want to put those musical talents of Jonny's to good use but as much as Jonny loves music, he prefers to do things on his terms and he doesn't like being told what to do, hence the current disagreement between them.

His mum and dad want him to cease a huge opportunity over in the States that has recently come his way. It's a massive opportunity actually, so massive that I insisted he take it, but he flatly refused, saying he wanted to look after me and our baby, our little accident that couldn't have happened at a worse time, as bad as that sounds. I was all set to go to the States with him, until I found out I was pregnant.

When Jonny told his parents no to the amazing opportunity without giving them a reason, all hell broke loose. Jonny hasn't spoken to them in four weeks and still refuses to, not wanting them to know anything about the fact that he is going to become a father. Add to that Jonny hating my dad's guts for reasons I won't go into just now, you could say we're in a little bit of a dilemma, well, I am anyway.

"Jonny, I still think…"

He shakes his head, his eyes determined. "Don't, Lauren, we're not discussing that again."

"But you're so talented, Jonny, the songs you've written, your singing voice, the music you write, not to mention the instruments you play…"

"Look, when you finish working at the pub to go and have the baby, I'll carry on playing the pub circuit like I told you I would, it's kept us going up until now. I am not leaving you to chase some stupid dream that probably wouldn't even work out anyway and if you think I'm dragging you over to the States when you're carrying my baby around with you then you can think again. I love you, Lauren…both of you."

He slips his hands underneath my top and places his palms flat against my tummy. I can't help but smile as he begins to affectionately rub my tummy again. I can feel the rough edges of his fingertips graze against the sensitive skin there. I get goosebumps. I love the rough feel of his fingers on me. I have Jonny's many years of playing the guitar to thank for that.

I lose the will to bother fighting with him anymore as he starts to sing softly into my ear. It's a song of his I know so well and love so very much, a song he once wrote especially for me, about me. I close my eyes and lose myself in his voice and his touch, the lyrics of *My Angel* taking my mind to another place entirely.

As Jonny continues to caress me with his voice alone, his hands suddenly leave my body and I feel instantly cold, my eyes fluttering open in surprise. But I soon warm up again when I see his hands moving to the keyboard in front of us, his adept fingers starting to play the notes in time with his voice. That beautiful, heart wrenching, all-consuming singing voice of his that gives me tingles down my spine every time I hear it. As his fingers play out every note to perfection, I reach my own fingers up to caress his cheek and he turns his mouth into my palm, the lyrics all but lost as he kisses my hand softly.

I start to sing the lyrics for him and he smiles down at me, his eyes soft and tender once more. He loves my singing voice as much as I love his but I still think he's a far better singer than I am. The occasional duets we sing together have always gone down well with the small audiences in our local pubs, our love of music as well as our love for each other spilling out from within.

Music is our connection, it's what binds us together and always has done. Music is Jonny, music is me, music is us. I'm more of a dancer than a singer though, always have been and always will be. The A level in dance that I achieved at college is proof of that but finding work afterwards has been really hard. It's a tough business to get into, as is the music industry, which is why I want Jonny to grab any opportunity that comes his way. Convincing him of that though is proving to be extremely difficult at the moment.

We finish the song together and Jonny wraps his arms around my waist again. He nuzzles his nose into my neck and inhales me deeply. "God, I love you, Lauren, so fucking much it hurts." He sounds a little sad when he says that, almost wistful, it makes me worry.

"What's wrong, baby?" I ask gently.

He sighs heavily against my cheek. "I just don't want our little bubble to burst when news of the baby comes out. Which it will…inevitably. I know you want to tell them sooner rather than later but I don't because I know what will happen."

Now I am worried, and all because Jonny is worried. He normally says fuck the world and to hell with everybody else but this time, I can see something is really bothering him. "I can come to the States with you, Jonny, we can live our dream together with the baby, I'll follow you wherever you go, you know that. I know you want to go, Jonny, I can see it in your eyes."

"No, Lauren."

"But it's our dream, remember? You going over there with your musical talents, me following my dream of becoming a professional dancer in the theatre on Broadway one day. Once the baby gets a little older we can sort something out, I swear we can do it."

He's gritting his teeth now and I know he wants to shout holy hell at me like he normally does but since finding out about me being pregnant, he's been holding back from arguing with me for fear of causing stress to the baby. He's more than a little over protective to say the least but I think it's sweet, I think he's sweet. "This is all on my dad's terms, Lauren, *not* ours. Don't make me say out loud what you already know to be true."

I know exactly what Jonny means and I have to bite the insides of my mouth not to burst into tears. Pete Mathers, Jonny's dad, doesn't want me to go to the States with them. That isn't part of the deal and never has been. Pete hates my guts and always has done. For some reason he thinks I'm a bad influence on his son. He says that I've done nothing but distract Jonny from the word go and even though Jonny is more than a little distracted by me in more ways than one, he still works really hard on his music and even has his own little recording studio set up in the spare bedroom of our flat.

I've done nothing but encourage Jonny's musical talents over the last four years, because to me, that's what makes Jonny who he is. Pete fails to see that and also fails to see just how madly in love we are and I know it's all because of the fact that he thinks I'm just not good enough for his only son. In some ways I can see why he thinks that, considering my lousy upbringing and rough background. And that's without him even knowing about my dad being a violent alcoholic.

Neither of Jonny's parents know about my dad's violent ways and we intend to keep it that way. It's a lot easier to keep a secret these days as things with my dad have now calmed down. Before meeting Jonny, my dad used to raise his fists to me on a regular basis but once Jonny came into the equation and got involved, my dad backed off a whole lot more.

Two years ago I left home and moved in with Jonny, finally ridding myself of the man who'd made my life one constant misery. I admit that I have paid him the occasional visit every now and again to help him out with money, because of course, he doesn't work either. Jonny hates this and has told me repeatedly to stay away from him, especially now that I'm pregnant. So far I've stuck to my promise and stayed away because to be honest, I don't want our baby anywhere near the man who used to not only beat his own daughter, but his wife too.

My mother, the woman I barely remember. She slit her wrists and killed herself when I was just five years old, so I didn't really know her at all. My first ever memory is of finding her lifeless body led on the bathroom floor in a pool of her own blood. Something I'd rather forget about but can't. How I didn't get moved into care after that I really don't know but either way, I feel a whole lot happier now than I have ever done, and it's all thanks to Jonny. And his mum. She's lovely.

Judy Mathers has been the complete opposite to Pete, welcoming me into her home with open arms, much to Pete's annoyance. I was getting on pretty well with Judy, up until four weeks ago when Jonny fell out with the pair of them.

"You don't have to say it out loud, Jonny, because I already know your dad hates my guts but the fact is, if you really want to go over there and take me with you, he can't stop us. Since when do you give a shit about what your dad thinks anyway?"

He shakes his head, sighing heavily. "I don't give a shit what he thinks and if I wanted to go, I would fucking well take you with me, but I am not giving in to his demands, Lauren. My mum's getting as bad as he is these days as well. She used to be the one fighting my corner but now she's wading into the argument along with him. The last thing I need right now is for you to take their side, I thought I could at least rely on you to support my decision."

Feeling suddenly guilty, I unwrap his arms from around my waist and stand up. There's just enough space between the keyboard and Jonny to turn around. Jonny frowns up at me, wondering what on earth I'm doing. He's probably thinking I'm about to storm off to our bedroom, but that's not my intention. I know what Jonny needs right now and I'm going to give it to him. I wrap my arms around his neck and sit back down in his lap, straddling him this time. His frown soon vanishes when I start to rub myself up against his crotch. I feel him harden beneath me instantly.

"I'm sorry, baby," I whisper against his mouth. "Let me make it up to you." I wind my fingers into his hair as I pull his mouth against mine, and I already know I'm forgiven.

"That's more like it," he murmurs, his hand reaching into my top to cup my breast. I moan softly as those musically talented hands of his start to work their magic on me this time.

"I love you, Jonny," I say, "I love you so much."

Jonny sighs against my mouth, his hands now moving around my body more urgently than before. "You and me against the world, baby," he whispers. "Just you and me."

"Just you and me," I say, repeating his words back to him. "Always."

CHAPTER 1

London – July 2015

"Oh my god, Lauren, he's here, in London! Jonny Mathers is somewhere here in London! Arghhh!"

Bless my best friend Stacey, she's more than a little enthusiastic about most things, but this is ridiculous. Mostly because she's been talking non-stop about the fact that Reclamation, one of the biggest rock bands in the world at the moment, will be performing at the O2 arena in London to close off their European tour next week. But that's not why it's so ridiculous. What's so ridiculous is the fact that she has absolutely no idea that the lead singer of the band, Jonny Mathers, is the man I once spent four and a half years of my life with. Four and a half amazing years.

It seems like a lifetime ago now, almost like a dream. But it wasn't a dream, it was real. So real in fact that I can still barely breathe whenever I hear his voice. That voice that made love to me and me alone once upon a time. Now, that beautiful voice of his makes love to every other woman in the world on a daily basis thanks to their chart topping success over the last nine years. I can barely go a few days without hearing a song of his on the radio or seeing his beautiful face being splashed about in the tabloids. And that's the part I hate the most, seeing his private life laid out completely bare for every man and his dog to see.

I try to ignore the papers and just live my life but it's difficult, considering that I still love Jonny just as much as I did back then, when I left him, ten years ago. Yes, that's right, I left him. A long and painful story that I won't go into just now but let's just say, I somehow ended up down here in London and even though Jonny and I are now worlds apart, it doesn't mean I don't think about him every single day.

I've got every single, every album and every DVD release by Reclamation, the rock band that Jonny and his dad formed together over in the States. And what a formation it is. They aren't heavy rock. More alternative rock, similar to the likes of Coldplay and Snow Patrol. Coldplay have always been a massive influence on Jonny over the years because, like them, Jonny doesn't just sing a song. He writes it, breathes it, lives it. He creates the music and the lyrics, bringing a song to life with his hands as well as his voice. He is one of the finest musicians to ever grace the earth in my opinion and I know that may sound a little biased on my part, but tell that to every other Reclamation fan around the globe.

Jonny's acoustic piano numbers are the ones that really get to me, the way his fingers move over the keys when he plays to his audience, the way he sings into the microphone like he's singing to you and you alone. The thing is, he did once sing to me and me alone, just me and nobody else. And now, here I am, several years later, sitting in the kitchen with my best friend who's all excited about going to see them next week while I'm secretly dreading it.

I could hardly say no when she asked me six months ago about buying front row tickets to go and see them. I had no feasible excuse to saying no to Stacey, considering I'm a massive Reclamation fan myself. But I wanted to say no, because it will be the first time in ten years that I'll be seeing him in the flesh and I don't know how I will cope with it, if I will cope with it at all.

"Yes and I'm sure one of the first things he'll be doing is

popping in to see you, Stace," I say, idly flicking through my fashion magazine. She sits herself down at our dining room table opposite me and folds her arms, waiting for me to look up. When I do finally look up, she's giving me the 'are you for real?' look. "What?" I feign innocence, but she just rolls her eyes and sighs.

"Considering you're a massive fan of Reclamation, you're not very enthusiastic about the fact that Jonny 'Sex God' Mathers has just arrived in our city! God, what I would give to be his microphone." Her face takes on a sickeningly dreamy look and I shake my head at her.

"Yeah, you along with every other woman on the planet." I turn my attention back to my magazine and try to push away all images of Jonny and his many women. He's a renowned womaniser these days and eats women for breakfast but I suppose it's to be expected, considering his rock star status. It doesn't make it any easier for me though which is why I try *not* to read the papers.

"Yeah but not every other woman on the planet does what we do for a living, babe, you more so than me. You'd have him eating out of the palm of your hand with those long, naturally curly blonde locks of yours and your sexy dance moves, not to mention your beautiful singing voice." Not so sure that Jonny would like what I currently do for a living actually, considering our history together.

"Stace, can we talk about something else please?" I'm beginning to feel uncomfortable now and I just want to talk about something else, or nothing at all. Either way, I don't want to talk about Jonny for a minute longer.

"What's wrong, Lauren?"

My eyes flick back up to meet hers and she looks genuinely concerned for me, her perfectly plucked eyebrows and beautifully made up face searching mine for an answer. An answer I'm not prepared to give to her right now, if ever. Best friend or not, I don't want her to know anything about me and Jonny. I've never spoken of him to anybody because what we once had together was personal and private. It was a time when I didn't have to share him with anybody else. Now, he has to share himself with every single person out there and whilst he seemingly copes with it pretty well, he's had the occasional wobble along the way, his angry outbursts at the paparazzi and his drunken bust ups at parties to name a few. I don't want to add to any of that and so, I swallow down the truth and once again, lie to my best friend.

"Nothing's wrong," I say, "it's just, since you mentioned work, you've suddenly got me all nervous about our new routine tonight, that's all."

She rolls her eyes at me and starts to play with her flawlessly straight, styled to within an inch of its life, long auburn hair, wrapping the long strands around her perfectly manicured fingers. My best friend is as preened and well-groomed as I am, something that is a necessity in our job.

"Oh, stop with all the worrying, the new routine that you've put together is hot stuff, we'll be pulling in the big tips tonight, girl, you'll see." She grins and winks at the same time and I just sigh in response.

Unlike me, Stacey loves the job that we do. It's how I met Stacey actually, and whilst it pulls in the money, I am not proud of my job, not one little bit. I only do it so I get to be up on a stage, singing and dancing, just like I dreamed of doing one day. The trouble is, once the singing and the dance routine is done with, I then have to take my clothes off for complete strangers, because unfortunately, my job as a lap dancer requires me to.

I hate the job title. Lap dancer. But that is what I am. A lap dancer at a prestigious London club called Carnal Desires that is so famous, celebrities are even on the guest list there. It's as tasteful as you can possibly get for a lap dancing club as well as being discreet, but that doesn't change the fact that men go there to see women cavorting around in all their naked glory.

Like I said earlier, Jonny and I are now worlds apart from where we once were. So far apart, I wonder if our worlds will collide together ever again....

CHAPTER 2

I'm just adding the finishing touches to my makeup in the dressing room of Carnal Desires when I suddenly hear the familiar yell from Frankie that I'm due on stage in five minutes. Five minutes. Shit. I don't feel ready to perform a routine tonight at all, let alone the new one I've only just put together with the other girls this week.

I feel more nervous tonight for some reason and I have no idea why. You'd think after working here for nine and a half years that I'd be used to taking my clothes off in front of men by now but I don't think it's that. And it's not as though I'm nervous about the new routine either, even though I told Stacey earlier on that I was. I think the discussion about Jonny and his band has sent me off kilter for some reason. Knowing that the love of my life is currently staying in the same city as I am but not knowing exactly where he is, is making me anxious, which is ridiculous, because it's not as if he hasn't visited London before.

He's done two UK tours up to now but we failed to get tickets for either of those tours as they sold out within the first hour of going on sale. This time, because the band added two extra nights on to their original three night stint in London, she managed to get two *front row* tickets for the opening night. Not many bands play five shows in a row but due to such high demand, they decided to do it for their fans.

I have to admit to feeling a little antsy and nervous about

seeing him in the flesh next week for the first time in all these years. And the front row? *What if he sees me from the stage?* Yeah right, like he's going to see *my* face amongst the thousands of other screaming women who want to get into his bed. Oh god, what if I bump into him after the show or see him leaving the arena with hordes of women? How would I cope with that? I wouldn't cope with it which is why I shouldn't be going!

"Lauren!" Frankie, the club's manager and a complete asshole, is now standing in the doorway of my dressing room looking extremely impatient. He's in his mid-fifties, wears a mousy brown toupee although he says it's his real head of hair - yeah right, the entire thing moves whenever he's unfortunate enough to be standing in a draught - and he also looks like he's been tangoed. Yes, my manager is the man from the Tango advert but he really thinks he's something special, which he isn't. Some of the other girls laugh at his jokes and play along with his stomach roiling attempts at flirting but I don't, and he hates that.

"There's a whole club of paying punters out there and you're sat in front of the mirror fucking well daydreaming! I don't pay you to sit on that juicy arse of yours, Lauren, I pay you to show it off. Now for the last time, you're on!"

I'm only thankful for one thing at the moment. That I have my own dressing room. The other girls have to share one but as I'm Frankie's "Star Attraction" these days, he's given me my own dressing room. At least I can get dressed in peace now without his leering gaze and wandering hands all over me. The other girls just put up with it but I don't and never have done. Frankie knows that I pull in the big money for him thanks to all the hard work I put in to all the dance routines and so he leaves me well alone. Well, apart from the constant nagging at me of course, but that, I can put up with.

I rise from my seat, checking my reflection in the mirror one last time. I'm wearing one very sparkly, hot pink, sexy leotard tonight, complete with sheer gloss tights and silver high heels. I've taken my inspiration from Kylie Minogue's outfit when she performed at the Sydney Olympics a few years ago. I'm even wearing the huge plume of pink feathers on my head to complete the look.

The other girls are wearing the exact same attire as me, apart from the head gear. As I'm the main singer, Frankie always likes me to wear something that makes me stand out from all the other girls. Some of the girls hate it and it's led to some very catty bitching going on behind closed doors but I'm used to it now and I always have Stacey fighting my corner, thank goodness. I don't know what I'd do without her sometimes.

"Okay, let's do this," I say to myself, swallowing down a sudden bout of nerves. Shit, what is wrong with me tonight? If I fuck up my routine then the shit will really hit the fan so I really need to get my head together.

"The girls are waiting side of stage for you, Lauren, don't keep the men out there waiting any longer. You are up to this tonight, aren't you?" Frankie's frowning at me now. He's sensing my anxiety and I really don't want him to see me like this. I haven't felt this anxious or nervous about going on stage for a long time and I'm not about to go back to feeling how I felt when I first started this job all those years ago. No, I've got this. I will be fine. I am fine. Shaking my anxieties away, I pull my shoulders back, straighten myself up and rise to my new height of six foot, thanks to my five inch killer heels.

"I'm always up to it, Frankie, you know that."

He breathes a sigh of relief and holds his arm out, taking a step backwards into the brightly lit corridor. "Your audience awaits, my girl."

Eurgh, I hate it when he refers to me as "his girl." I'm not his girl and never will be. I've only ever been one man's girl and that man is now a world famous rock star, completely out of my reach.

"Dancing Queen here I come," I say, stepping out into the corridor. That's the song I will be singing tonight, still in keeping with the Kylie theme I mentioned earlier. I only hope that I look more confident than I feel right now. I still feel really off but it's too late now as I approach stage side. I'm greeted by ten perfectly made up women with false smiles looking right back at me. Well, nine false smiles actually, Stacey's beaming smile is genuine, that much I do know.

"Let's do this, ladies!" I try to inject as much enthusiasm into my voice as possible, and it works. I'm greeted by whoops and claps from every single one of them. Oh well, no more stalling, here goes nothing. It's show time!

****

"What the fuck was that, Lauren?!"

Frankie is standing behind me in my dressing room looking really angry, and I honestly don't know why. It's four hours later, I've performed the routine to perfection along with my girls and I've given the men out there exactly what they want in terms of showing them my bits so I don't know what his problem is.

As I'm practically naked, apart from the tiny pink g-string that's currently wedged firmly between my bum cheeks, I really don't want Frankie in my dressing room, but he's not for leaving just yet, not by a long shot. I reach for an old top of mine from a drawer somewhere and I throw it on as quickly as possible. I'll wear a bin liner at the moment if it means covering up from him.

"What was what?" I snap, arms folded in defiance. I'm not in the mood for an argument right now. After feeling off earlier on, this is the last thing I can be bothered with and I swear if he pushes me tonight, I will storm out, never to return ever again. Yeah right, like I haven't said that to myself so many times before!

"Sex, Lauren, they want sex out there. That's why they come to the fucking club in the first place!"

I must look confused because he's scratching his face impatiently now, his overly brown fingernails from years of plastering on fake tan showing up in the brightly lit confines of my tiny dressing room. Eurgh, this man really does make my stomach churn sometimes.

"They got sex, Frankie, I performed the routine and then eleven hot girls took their clothes off. You can't get more sexual than that!"

Frankie is about to shout back but Stacey suddenly arrives in my doorway looking more than a little annoyed. She must have heard our raised voices from down the corridor and Stacey, bless her, is quick to defend, even if it is Frankie we're going up against.

"What's going on?" she asks, walking into the room to stand next to me. She folds her arms along with me and we stand there, shoulder to shoulder, defiant against this pathetic excuse of a man.

"What's going on?" He looks shocked, exasperated even. "You lot need to pull your fucking fingers out that's what's going on. Audience feedback is shocking tonight! Most of the men out there felt like they were being subjected to some cabaret act from a Butlins holiday resort!"

Now I am angry, really bloody angry. "It is cabaret, Frankie!

We put on a show two nights a week before we get our kit off. We sing, we dance, that's what cabaret is!"

He slams his palm down on to my dressing table, his face reddening by the second. "And that cabaret is supposed to be the foreplay before the main strip show, Lauren, not some fucking musical from Broadway! I mean, Abba? Dancing queen?!"

Stacey is about to protest but I grab her arm, pulling her back. This is my battle and I will fight this one, tooth and nail if I have to. "You liked it enough in rehearsals this week and you agreed to the song choice so don't stand there now and pretend you didn't. Just because a few choice men don't like it, *you* suddenly don't like it. You're so full of it, Frankie, so full of it!"

He steps forward, pointing an angry finger between both Stacey and me. "You better watch your mouth, Lauren, because you are replaceable. You may not think you are, but you are. All of you girls are fucking replaceable. If the audience don't like it, I don't fucking like it, and that means the big fucking boss at the top doesn't like it either. Now you lot better get a new act together for tomorrow night and fast. I want sex and lots of it, and if I don't get the sex on stage tomorrow night, you'll be out on your ear. Do you understand me?"

His voice is low now, threatening. Frankie doesn't normally intimidate me but for some reason, his threat is really getting to me tonight. Even though I would love nothing more than to tell him to stick his poxy job, I really need the money and the buzz of singing on stage and so, I swallow down my pride and reluctantly agree to his request. Stacey has other ideas though.

"Just how are we supposed to come up with a new routine in less than twenty-four hours, Frankie?"

Frankie takes a step backwards and shrugs his shoulders. "Not my problem, girls. It's Lauren's problem now, not mine."

And just like that, the orange idiot storms out of my dressing room leaving me to wonder what on earth I'm supposed to do next.

I sigh heavily and sink down into my chair, head in hands. Stacey walks over to the door and slams it shut then sinks down on to the floor to sit next to me. "He's such a wanker, Lauren, don't take any of what he said to you just now to heart. That routine was amazing tonight, *we* were amazing."

She places a reassuring hand on my knee and I look up, my eyes already glistening with tears. God I really am losing the plot tonight. Since when have I been so bloody sensitive? *Since realising I'm going to be seeing Jonny next week in concert, that's when.* "Hey, don't cry, Lauren, he's not worth it."

I shake my head and push back my tears. I won't cry over the Tango Man, I won't allow myself to cry over him. "I'm not crying, Stace, I won't cry." And I don't, thankfully.

After about a minute of silence, Stacey speaks up again, her tone soft. "So, what are we going to do then for tomorrow night?" Shit, it's Saturday tomorrow, the main night of the week and I've got no routine to perform. I'm really going to have to pull something out of the bag this time. Talk about last minute.

"I don't know, Stace. I'll sleep on it, see what tomorrow morning brings. There's nothing we can do now anyway." She nods, her hand still on my knee. Bless her, she's so supportive and sweet, unlike the other girls. I bet they'll be bitching non-stop about me once Frankie's had a word with them. They'll love every minute of me screwing things up tonight but I won't be beaten, not by Frankie and certainly not by them.

"Okay," she says, "let's go home then, I think we both need a stiff drink after tonight, I've got a bottle of vodka stashed away in the cupboard somewhere." I smile at her suggestion and I like her thinking. A lot.

"Vodka is the answer to all my worries right now, Stacey Kerr, let's go home and get pissed."

"Erm, I think pissed is off the menu tonight, girl, we have a new routine to put together tomorrow morning, remember?" She's right, we do, oh well.

"I'll just have the one drink then," I sigh, standing. She stands up and pulls me in for a hug.

"Don't worry, chick, it'll be fine, we'll have something sorted in no time. We'll all pull together tomorrow morning, you'll see." I only hope that the other girls will all pull together or, come tomorrow night, I will be totally and utterly screwed.

CHAPTER 3

I'm having the morning from hell. I'm back at the club with the girls, batting ideas around about coming up with something for tonight and so far, not so good. I've come up with a few suggestions unlike anybody else in the room but the girls aren't for agreeing to anything I have to say. As predicted, things have turned bitchy and they're all laying into me for landing them in the deep stuff with Frankie last night. All except Stacey of course, who is currently trying to salvage the situation, but she's losing the battle as I'm slowly losing the will to live.

"It's all about the Lauren show these days." Kelly, the queen bitch from hell and the worst of the bunch is just sitting on the stage admiring her nails, a look of pure disinterest on her face. She's the stereotypical lap dancer, absolutely stunning but a complete and utter bitch to almost everybody around her, apart from the people she thinks are worthy of talking to her of course. Apparently, I'm not worthy of talking to her. Not that I'd want to. She does nothing but bitch about all the other girls behind their backs and likes to stir up shit so she can sit back and watch the results.

Standing at five foot eight, Kelly is slender, and with her long luscious locks of dark brown hair, almond shaped eyes and full pouting lips, she's the typical beauty that most men lust after. I'm as tall as she is but in contrast to her perfectly proportioned figure, I'm curvy. Really curvy. I have a big bottom and large breasts but, without wanting to sound like I'm overly confident, because I'm really not, I do have a great pair of legs that go on for miles. Jonny used to tell me repeatedly how he loved my long legs being wrapped around him constantly. He also used to go absolutely wild for my curves, my big bottom and large breasts gaining lots and lots of attention from him once upon a time. Anyway, back to my hellish morning....

"Kelly, if you don't have anything constructive to say or any ideas of your own to put forward then don't say anything at all," I say, desperately trying to keep my tone light. But it's difficult, she's making it really difficult. She lets out an overly dramatic sigh, still admiring her nails.

"What's the point of suggesting anything? You only do what you want to do anyway. Isn't that right, girls?"

The girls all start to murmur some sort of response, shrugging and looking between themselves, not sure what to say or who to side with. Kelly looks up then, her hazel brown eyes locking with my blue ones in silent combat, her mouth curling up at the corners. She's nothing less than sly and she's trying everything in her power to get a rise out of me and if she's not careful, she'll be getting more than just a rise out of me this morning. Stacey is quick to defend though.

"Back off, Kelly, we all put ideas in and Lauren just pulls it all together, if you actually had any ideas of your own then we might actually consider them but as you don't, keep all further opinions to yourself."

Kelly throws her head back and laughs loudly, tossing her ridiculously shiny hair over her shoulders. Her laugh sounds more like the cackle of a witch. Quite appropriate for her really, considering that's exactly what she is. "Oh spare me the best friend act this morning, it's getting really old, Stacey. 'Miss Perfect' over there needs bringing down a peg or two. I am not risking my job again all because she wants to pretend she's some award winning actress on Broadway!"

Kelly pushes herself up off the stage and stands up, pointing towards the exit over in the corner. "If you want to be in the theatre, darling, I suggest you walk out of this place and head across the city towards something more up your street, say, Her Majesty's Theatre perhaps? I hear they're looking for new props."

Her hateful words burn into me like acid. Pure acid. I suddenly feel tears threatening to fall from my eyes and then I hear Stacey launching into a tirade of abuse against Kelly while I just stand there and say nothing, glued to the spot like a statue. I want to shout back at her. I want to slap her, pull at her hair and throw her around the room, but I don't.

One minute I'm standing there, listening to the girls screaming and shouting at one another, and the next, I find myself standing outside on the pavement. And then I'm running away, as fast as my legs will carry me. But where I'm running to I honestly don't know. All I know is that I have to get away from there because I can't stand it for a minute longer. I don't care where I end up as long as it's as far away from there as possible and right now, I really don't want to have to go back there ever again.

****

Now I really am torturing myself. I'm sat in a Costa coffee house drinking a latte while reading a newspaper. But it's not just any newspaper. Oh no, this one is a tabloid, something I never ever buy, but as today's tabloid has an overly large photograph of the most beautiful man in the world splashed across the front page, I found myself unable to resist buying it.

Through my blur of tears and my sprinting marathon across London earlier on, I somehow ended up coming to a complete stop outside some newsagents. And all because Jonny was looking right back at me. I only wish he had been looking right back at me but I'll have to settle for him looking back at me from the front page of a newspaper instead.

He looks sad on the photograph and it makes me feel sad to see him that way. His expression looks similar to how it looked when I last saw him, before I left Manchester, before he went into rehab to fight his cocaine addiction. Little did we know then that that would be the last time we ever saw each other. He was in such a bad place after....

My eyes begin to glisten with tears at the painful memory and I find myself unable to resist running my fingers over the inky image of him. I begin to trace the outline of his face with the tip of my index finger, taking in everything I ever loved about him. I drink in those long dark lashes and those deep and meaningful brown eyes of his that I used to get lost in so easily. Even though he's sad, he still looks beautiful. So beautiful. Heartstoppingly so.

He's turning backwards in the photograph as though he's looking around at something or someone. Probably another photographer if the expression on his face is anything to go by. His jet black hair is gelled into its trademark style, all ruffled up and messy in a complete want to run your fingers through his bed hair kind of way. He's wearing a v-neck black t-shirt with some rock band logo on the front and stone washed black denim jeans. Add to that his biker boots and the sleeves of tattoos on both arms, he is the epitome of bad boy rocker and I sigh out loud without even realising I'm doing it. Until I get a funny look off some woman sitting across from me at another table.

I ignore the woman and get back to reading about the love of my life and it's only when I start to read the article that I realise why he's looking so sad. His mum is ill. Really ill by the sounds of it. It doesn't say what she's ill with and it certainly doesn't go into too much detail thank goodness, but it sounds serious.

So serious that his dad is still in the States with her. That's a first for Pete Mathers. As he's their manager and co-owner of their very own record label now along with Jonny, he literally accompanies Reclamation everywhere. The fact that he isn't with them now tells me that the tabloid isn't making this up, although I suddenly wish they were.

The article goes on to say that Jonny didn't want to disappoint his legion of fans in the UK and that his mum is doing okay, despite what other sources are reporting. She apparently told him to finish his European tour before returning home to the States ahead of his US tour, starting next month. This is all hearsay of course but there must be some truth in it for them to print something so personal in the first place. It's not as though it's an article about his bed hopping antics this time. It's an article about his mum, and his mum is his whole world. They may have clashed a little bit towards the end of my relationship with him but Jonny idolises his mother. He used to clash with his dad on a daily basis but he always got on really well with his mum, and so did I.

Judy was always warm and welcoming to me, like the mother I never had. She used to talk me to death about Jonny's escapades as a youngster and how his love for music came about. It's only a shame that I didn't get on with Pete just as well but then, Pete always hated me, although I think he would have hated any girl who'd taken the heart of his son at a time when he thought Jonny should have been going places. All Pete wanted was for Jonny to follow in his footsteps and achieve what he failed to do in his own band. Global superstardom. Well, Jonny has certainly achieved that and he's now filthy rich as a result, no doubt something else that Pete Mathers wanted for his son, and himself.

I'm only thinking what Jonny used to tell me himself, that all his dad wanted to do was to re-live his youth through

Jonny. Getting Jonny to achieve everything that he didn't. That's what made Jonny want to constantly run in the opposite direction, anything to defy his overbearing father who, thanks to none other than me, got his own selfish way with his son eventually.

I can't help but wonder how things might have been had I not upped and left Manchester all those years ago, but then, I can't ever imagine a world without Reclamation in it. Jonny deserves to be where he is now and I would never want to take that away from him, despite the pain I still feel at not having him in my life anymore. Which brings me to think about the pain he must be in at the moment with his mum being really ill.

Having your life splashed about on the front pages must be difficult for anybody to have to deal with, but I know Jonny and I know him well. He doesn't deal with bad things happening to him very well and I can't help but worry for him, worry that he'll end up down that dark, self-destructive path again somewhere, all helpless and alone. The dark path that I feel solely responsible for. The one that he ended up on because of me. Me and my bastard of a dad.

I'm starting to get upset again and I try desperately to push back my tears as painful memories begin to surface in my mind. We were so happy together. Deliriously happy. And the baby we "accidentally" made together cemented what we had back then. Our baby. Our little boy.

That's it, I can't think about it any longer and so I throw back the rest of my latte, intent on leaving the damn newspaper on the table for somebody else to read. But just as I'm about to leave, Jonny's face looks up at me one more time from the front page and I suddenly feel bad about leaving him there in the middle of a coffee house, his private life on show for the entire world to see. It may seem silly but I suddenly feel the over protective need to shield him from any more pain. I grab the newspaper and throw it in the nearest bin. It may only be one less tabloid in the world today but if it means that one less member of the public gets to read about Jonny's private life then that thought alone makes me feel a little better.

Back out on the streets of London I try to steer all thoughts away from Jonny and his mum, trying to focus on what the hell I'm supposed to do with that bitchy lot over at the club. And it's not until I'm passing a travel agents and I see *Reduced Flights to New York* plastered across the window that I get a brain wave. I think about Kelly's bitchy words from earlier, something about Broadway and theatres.

I come to a stop outside the travel agents and pretend to be looking at holidays when all I'm thinking about right now is my new routine for tonight. Bright lights. Broadway. New York. Dreams. So many dreams. I sigh heavily. If only I was that lucky, I'd be over there in an instant. That was my dream once upon a time, my dream with Jonny, and whilst I know that the girls will probably think that my idea is all about me again, I suddenly don't care. If they've come up with any better ideas in the meantime then that's fine but I think I'm on to something here and hopefully, they'll agree.

The song I have in mind for tonight is a corker. It's slow and soulful but with a sexy edge if performed correctly. I know I can sing it because I sing it to myself all the time in my apartment. It's a favourite of mine, as is the singer. I need somebody to play the piano on stage for this song and it is a slow one but I think a slow number is what we need after the fast paced cheesy dance disaster that was last night. We'll need to dress in dark colours and wear dark sultry makeup to pull this one off. The dancing will be slow and sexy which will give Frankie and his audience of complete perverts exactly what they want. Add to that a grand piano to dance and cavort around, I think it will go down a storm.

Mind made up and keen to share, I sprint back off to the club hoping against hope that we can pull the damn routine together in time for tonight, because I only have the last few hours of the day left to do it in. I only hope I can.

CHAPTER 4

Well, it's happening. We're about to go on stage and perform something we've pulled together in just a few hours. It's the first time ever that we've done this and surprisingly, the girls agreed to my idea straight away. Well, apart from Kelly of course, but she got overruled by everybody else. Thankfully. The whole New York and theatre dreaming theme went down well and I couldn't help but throw a snide remark over at Kelly, telling her that some of what I'd come up with in my mind had come from her.

I thanked her wholeheartedly for contributing to the new routine which led to her huffing and puffing before storming out of the club this afternoon. Stacey had been trying to ring me all the time I'd been out wandering around London, worrying about me, wondering where on earth I'd got to. By the time I got back to the club, they were all pretty desperate to come up with anything, and so my New York theme was born.

And here we are, dressed to kill in our sexiest black lingerie with smoking hot makeup and high hair. It's all about the sex appeal this evening, and we all made sure we arrived at work earlier than normal, wanting to spend longer on our hair and makeup. We've really vamped ourselves up for tonight and with the resident pianist now taking centre stage at the grand piano and the lights dimming down in readiness, our last minute number is about to begin.

I'm just about to take the first step up to the stage, when

Stacey tries to pull me back to tell me something. Typical Stacey, arriving at the last minute. Again! She's nearly always the last one to arrive at stage side, usually having to make one last dash to the loo before the performance. She insists that it isn't nerves but I think it is, it happens far too often for it not to be.

She's just about to whisper something into my ear when Frankie yells out my name on stage and so I quickly turn away and walk up the steps, desperate to do as I'm told tonight. I pissed Frankie off good and proper last night and I don't want to do it for a second time. He's a complete wanker but it's not just my job that's on the line tonight, it's all the other girls' jobs as well. I owe it to them to make things right and that's what I'm going to do. Right now.

I gulp back my last minute nerves and slowly step into the spotlight. I'm greeted instantly by wolf whistles and whoops from all the men in the place and even though I can't make any faces out because of the bright lights, I can tell that it's packed. It's Saturday night, our busiest night of the week, and I'm about to perform something that is so last minute, my mouth has suddenly gone dry. No, I can do this. Tonight is no different than any other night. I know the song off by heart. Once I get started and the other girls gradually join me on stage, I'll be fine. I hope.

I strut over to the piano in my usual model like manner, swaying my hips from side to side, smiling widely at the audience, microphone in one hand, other hand on hip. I'm met with a few more whistles and cheers as I reach the piano, standing there like some over confident fashion model just waiting for the pianist to start up.

The thing is, I'm not confident at all. Far from it. In fact, I suddenly feel intimidated about the size of this place even though I've performed on this stage many many times, and it's nothing compared to the size of a theatre or stadium, somewhere where I dream of performing in one day. *Yeah right Lauren, like that's ever going to happen.* I'll just have to make do with a lap dancing club for now. The lap dancing club that I've now worked in for nine years. The one that is suddenly looking larger by the minute and even though I am exaggerating ever so slightly because of my highly anxious state, Carnal Desires is *the* biggest lap dancing club in London.

It's on two levels and it's all very flashy and modern. Sexy but not distasteful, unlike some of the other places in other areas of London. The stage itself is huge with a long walkway running right down the middle. The walkway then eventually breaks off into five single podiums. At the end of each podium is a pole and I can tell you that this place charges an absolute fortune for a table that is lucky enough to be seated at the end of one of those five podiums. They are, of course, the seats with the best view in the house and are highly sought after, as are the VIP rooms.

The VIP rooms or, "curtained off" areas as they're sometimes referred to, are situated on the level above me with a spectacular view of the stage. Not that men go up there for a view of the stage of course. They go up there for an entirely different view, a very up close and personal view which again, men in their droves pay a fortune for.

The number of celebrity men and MPs we've had in here over the years is sickening but it's all discreet and above board, all legal. The private dances are what bring in the big money for women like me and I'm ashamed to say it that yes, I do the private dances as well. I don't like doing them but I get paid a hell of a lot for it and you can't work in a club like this and not do them. You either do everything or nothing in this business, it's that simple. There's no touching though, that's the main rule of the house. Any touching and they're out on their ear for good.

Okay, time to belt out some high notes I think. I nod to the male pianist and he starts to play. Oh how I love the sound of a piano, my favourite instrument in the whole wide world. The sound of a piano playing instantly makes me think of Jonny. I could just sit back right now and watch Jonny playing on the piano for hours. Once upon a time, I did sit back and watch him play on the piano for hours. Before we moved into our flat of course. We could hardly take a grand piano to our tiny flat, much to my disappointment. It wasn't just the piano playing I missed either. It was the hot sex that went with the piano playing that I missed. I lost count of the number of times we almost got caught having sex on said piano when Jonny lived with his parents. He was such a bad influence. Those were the days….

Anyway, back to the song. The pianist has now done his lengthy introduction and now it's my turn. Oh well, here goes nothing. "Ooooo, New York." I'm singing Empire State of Mind (Part II) Broken Down by Alicia Keys, and while I have to hit the high notes with this chart topping number, I've become well practised with my vocals over the last few years. I'm more confident with my singing voice now than I ever was.

I smile at my audience, I sing like I've never sang a song before in all my life and then, when I arrive at the middle of the song, I hop up on to the piano and lie down on my side. This is met with cheers and standing ovations from some of the men in the club as the pianist tries his absolute best to concentrate on his music, bless him. He's doing well I have to say but then, his professionalism is what he's paid for after all.

God, I love this song, it's so powerful and sexy and I feel better now than I've felt all week. My nerves are long gone and I'm belting out the high notes like never before. I love the buzz of being on stage, the glare of the lights shining down on me, the sound of the music playing in my ears, the cheers and the whistles from the audience. I lap up every single minute of my performance tonight and just before the song ends, I leap down off the piano and run over to join all the other girls who have just appeared on stage to join me.

As I close the number off, the other girls, one of which is Stacey, start to strut their stuff around the stage. Stacey looks more excited than usual. Probably because she knows, like I do, that we've pulled it out of the bag, thank goodness. Frankie will be rubbing his hands together I should think, considering the applause we're now getting. I've now finished the song, the pianist has taken his bow and exited off stage and it's time for me to walk forward and take my curtsy. Right before I take my kit off. The bit that I really hate. Oh well, my moment in the spotlight had to end, right? Looks like the stripping is about to commence!

I toss my mike to Frankie who is busy leering at me and giving me the thumbs up from the side of the stage. Leering aside, the thumbs up is definitely a good sign. All eleven of us are lined up and ready to go now. The music from the speakers starts up and that's it, we're off, doing what we do best, strutting our stuff and working that stage.

I'm busy removing my bra, disposing of it in as sexy a way as practically possible when I catch Stacey's eye from the other side of the stage. She's discreetly nodding towards the front of the stage, and I frown. She knows I'm giving her the "what the fuck?" look because she rolls her eyes in response before nodding again.

I really think my best friend is losing the plot tonight and I don't have time to try and interpret secret messages right now. I'm still on a high from my New York routine and I'm trying my graceful, sexiest best not to lose focus and so I turn away from her and head towards the middle podium.

Hand on hip, breasts out for all to see, I'm wearing nothing more than a black lacy g-string and silver high heels. I can hear an overly loud man at the table in front of me getting more than a little enthusiastic already as I strut seductively towards him and his mates. Great, a pissed up loud mouth is just what I need tonight. He'll be out on his ear if he gets any louder, that's for sure.

From a distance, I can't make out the faces of the men due to the bright lights above me but as I get closer, I make sure to avert my gaze elsewhere. I make it my own rule to never make eye contact with any audience member, not even for a second. I think it's asking for trouble, like you're connecting with them on a much deeper level. I don't want to connect with any single one of them on a deeper level and so I tend to look into the distance when I work the pole. I try to adopt a sexy dreamlike gaze and try my absolute best to concentrate on what I'm doing.

"Oh yes, that's it, baby, just like that! What an ass!" Great, the pissed up loud mouth is now throwing suggestive comments my way. That's all I need. And he's American. So, we have Americans in the house tonight, do we?

As I continue with my moves, he starts to mutter more suggestive remarks at the top of his voice, and that's when I start to feel uncomfortable. Most men in the club tend to just leer at me and whistle, with the odd comment thrown in every now and again, but this asshole is loud, as are his friends, one friend in particular actually.

"Shut the fuck up and back off."

I'm trying my best to concentrate really hard on what I'm doing but I can't help but notice something familiar about the male voice I heard just now. The second one. The one that sounds completely pissed off with his overly loud friend. The one who was quick to defend me.

"Oh come on, Jonny, that's why we're here in the first fucking place, to feast our eyes on some hot, juicy ass. What's eating you tonight anyway? You've been quiet from the minute the show started. You normally love all this shit."

Jonny? *Oh shit.* The name is the same but surely it can't be him. No way. I'm too scared to look. I can't look. I'm carrying on regardless. *Just work the pole, Lauren, work the pole.*

Another suggestive comment from his friend leads to the all too familiar voice to speak again. "I said shut the fuck up."

The only thing that isn't familiar to me about the voice is the American lilt. Apart from that, it's really familiar, so scarily familiar that I already know it's him. Please no, don't be him, not now, not here. Of all the times I wanted to see him again. Of all the ways I imagined seeing him again, this wasn't how I imagined it at all. Surely not, surely....

I pause mid-spin on the pole because my eyes do something they never ever do when I'm up on stage. They look up and make eye contact. They look up mid-spin and make bloody eye contact, and now I'm frozen to the spot because looking right back at me from below the stage, with a look of uncertainty plastered across his beautiful features, is him. Jonny. My Jonny.

"Lauren?"

He already knows it's me, that's why he was defending me against his friend just now, and yet, he's saying my name as though it's a question. As though he doesn't believe that it's actually me, just like I don't really believe it's him.

I let go of the pole and take an unsteady step backwards, making some feeble attempt at trying to cover up my breasts with my arms. I'm shocked and I really don't know what to do. I can't speak. I literally cannot form the words to speak and I wouldn't know what to say anyway. I feel as though the world has stopped turning.

While all the other girls are still shaking their booties around the stage, I'm standing here completely naked apart from a barely there g-string and Jonny Mathers, world famous rock star and one time love of my life, is staring right back at me. Oh fucking hell my world has just ended. My world has just come crashing down around me and I'll never get it back ever again.

His band mates are slowly starting to realise that something is going on and I'm now receiving some boos and catcalls from other customers on surrounding tables. They're clearly wondering what the hell is going on and from the look on Jonny's face right now, I'd say he's wondering what the hell is going on as well. The loud one, the one who's been making suggestive comments to me for the last five minutes, makes some unwelcome attempt at breaking the icy atmosphere that has suddenly descended between me and Jonny, and he fails, spectacularly.

"What? You know this hot piece of ass, Jonny? Someone you actually went back to more than just the once? That's a first."

He laughs loudly but Jonny turns to him, grabbing him roughly by the t-shirt. "I said shut the fuck up! Nobody speaks about Lauren like that. Nobody. Not even you, dickwad." He shoves the man I now recognise as Ben Anderson, a renowned womaniser and the band's bassist, backwards, leading him to stumble.

One more hurtful glance up at me and Jonny storms away from the table, two burly looking men in hot pursuit behind him. They're definitely not club security either, they're obviously Jonny's personal bodyguards who've been watching the entire scene unfold.

I'm still frozen to the spot and I'm devastated, totally

and utterly devastated. I back slowly away from the three remaining band members, Ben dusting himself off after the altercation with Jonny. They all look so familiar to me now. Hell, I've followed the band closely for the last nine years so they should be familiar to me.

They all start to move away from the table to presumably go and find Jonny but their presence doesn't go unnoticed by everybody around them. No doubt every single person in this room knew about Reclamation gracing them with their presence tonight. Everybody except me.

As I turn my back on the audience and return to the main stage, I catch Stacey's eye again and she's looking at me with questioning eyes. It suddenly dawns on me that that's what she was trying to tell me about earlier on, just before I went on stage. She was trying to tell me about Reclamation being in the building. She must have found out at the last minute when she went to the toilet but by the time she found me, it was too late.

If only I'd have waited just thirty more seconds before going on to that stage, this wouldn't have happened, because I wouldn't have gone on knowing Jonny was out there. No way. But now, as I take centre stage once more, for fear of losing my job as well as the love of my life all over again, I feel numb. I feel lifeless and numb, because everything I once had with Jonny is now tainted. Tainted because of this, because of what I've become.

Those eyes of his that once looked at me with love and tenderness have now disappeared. Only to be replaced by shock and disgust, and really, I can't blame him for looking at me that way. Not one bit. The girl that he did all of his firsts with, the girl who he fell in love with so madly, so deeply, is now nothing more than a woman who gets her kit off for other men while cavorting about the stage in all her naked glory.

I can see myself so clearly now whereas I couldn't before. I've actually led myself to believe that what I've been doing in this club for the last nine years is okay, when actually, it's far from being okay. But, regardless of how I feel, I carry on for the rest of the night, and there's only one reason why I carry on doing what I'm doing. Because I've already lost him. And this time, I think I've lost him for good.

Any hope of ever reuniting with Jonny is now gone. Finished. I'm not looking forward to getting home later on and having Stacey in my ear either, all excited about my encounter with the world famous rock band that we're supposedly going to see together next week. I can't go and see them now. Not after this. It's too painful. Far too painful. I don't think I'll ever come back from this.

CHAPTER 5

"Lauren, what happened? Have you got a world famous rock band fighting over you, or what?"

It's almost 2.00 am, I'm still in my dressing room at work, and Stacey's already starting her interview with me. I'm trying my best efforts to get dressed as quickly as possible so that I can get the hell out of here and pretend that tonight didn't happen but Stacey's making it difficult, really bloody difficult.

"Nothing happened, Stace," I mumble, throwing on a tank top and jeans.

"That's not what that lot are saying out there." Stacey still isn't dressed so she's standing here, in the middle of the dressing room, arms folded over bare breasts in a g-string, and she's not for moving any time soon if the look on her face is anything to go by.

I so don't want to get into this right now and after the ear bashing I got from Frankie just now, I'm tempted to walk out of the place altogether and never come back. That wouldn't bring Jonny back to me though. Not now. It's too late for that. The damage has already been done.

"I don't give a shit what anybody is saying. One of the men from the band got gobby, the other one didn't like it. They came to blows and left. End of story. Why Frankie's blaming me for losing him lots of money as a result of them leaving, I really don't know. I know I had a momentary lapse of concentration up there but at least I carried on with my dancing afterwards. I did nothing wrong but as usual, Frankie wants to point the finger at me, well he can go and fuck himself for all I care. The whole damn place can go and fuck itself. I'm done."

I grab my bag and head for the door but Stacey pulls me back by the arm. She grabs my shoulders and spins me slowly around to face her. She's got that worried look on her face again and I know that she doesn't buy anything I've just told her. She knows me too well. Too bloody well. "What is it?" she asks softly, looking concerned. "You can tell me, Lauren, I'm your best friend, remember?"

She is my best friend. She's the most wonderful best friend in the whole wide world and yet, I can't tell her about Jonny, especially after tonight. It's too raw and painful and even after all these years, I still can't think about what happened back then without wanting to curl up in a corner and scream loudly in pain. I physically ache when I think about what led to me leaving Manchester, leaving Jonny. I can't talk about it yet, I just can't.

"I'm just over tired, Stace. Tired and wired. I just want to be by myself for a bit, get some air. Is that okay?"

She shakes her head, eyes determined. "If you think I'm letting you walk home on your own at this unearthly hour of the morning then you're mistaken. I'm coming with you."

I roll my eyes, shaking my head at her this time. "Stace, I walk home on my own when you're not here. I'm fine, and I have my phone on me. Please…I just need the walk home to clear my head. I'll text you as soon as I get in and then, tomorrow morning, we'll talk."

Or not talk. But right now, I'll promise her anything just so I can get some time on my own. Anything so I don't have to talk to anybody about the mess that is tonight. She eventually nods and I feel a surge of relief wash through me. Thank god for that, I thought I was about to have a huge fight on my hands. Stacey can be rather stubborn at times. Stubborn but lovely. So lovely.

I reach over and give her a kiss on the cheek. "Thanks, Stace. I'll see you in a bit, yeah?" She nods again but her face is serious.

"You will, and I'll be right behind you, Lauren, once I've got dressed that is."

I cease the opportunity to lighten the mood between us when she says that. "Wouldn't want to go giving a glimpse of that body of yours away for free on the streets of London now, would we?"

That makes her grin and I get a slap on the arm for that remark. "Cheeky cow."

"I am a cheeky cow but you love this cheeky cow," I jest.

She rolls her eyes and starts guiding me towards the door. "I do, now get out of here before I change my mind." I don't need telling twice, I'm out of there in a flash, my best efforts of not being seen by Frankie again actually paying off this time.

I step out on to the pavement into the cool night air and close the front door of the club behind me. Breathing a sigh of relief that my night from hell is finally over with, I turn to my left and start my walk of shame along the pavement.

"I watched your performance tonight, Lauren."

I stop in my tracks, momentarily glued to the spot by a male voice coming from behind me. That masculine, sexy, achingly familiar voice that I heard earlier on in the club. Oh my god, he's here. I can't believe it. He waited for me. After storming out of the club earlier on, I thought he'd left for good, never to be seen by me ever again. And now he's here, standing right behind me on a dimly lit pavement in London at 2.00 am, waiting for me to turn around and face him.

I'm frozen to the spot again by fear and nerves and all I want to do right at this very moment is run away. Run away so that he can't look at me with disgust all over again. I don't want him to look at me ever again if I have to see that look on his face. I can't bear it. And yet, I feel compelled to turn around and look at him. I can't not look at him. He's like a magnetic force to me, drawing me into him without even realising he's doing it.

He always was, and still is, it seems, my addiction. My drug. My fix. And right now, I simply have to give in to that pull, even it means that I only get to speak to him for five minutes. Hell, I'd give my right arm to have five minutes of Jonny. I know that the five minutes I'll be getting from Jonny won't be the five minutes I used to dream of getting after all these years apart though. The romantic whirlwind of a reunion that I constantly used to daydream about is now well and truly gone, that's for sure. Okay, enough stalling, I have to turn around and face him.

It's only when I do turn to face him that I wish I hadn't. God, he's beautiful, even more so in the moonlight. I drink in his silhouetted form in all its glory, his ruffled black hair, those dark brown eyes that I'm already feeling lost in. I notice that he's added plenty more tattoos to his collection. Of course I knew that already from seeing him in the newspapers but seeing them in the flesh, seeing *him* in the flesh, is a different thing entirely. His arms are completely covered in them which only adds to the appeal for me.

Jonny had his first tattoo done when I had mine done. Another first together, one of many. I wonder if he still has that first ever tattoo. He had my name tattooed on to his inner right forearm. He always used to tell me that I'd got under his skin and in his blood. Quite appropriate that he literally burned me into him really, as I did with him. I've still got his name tattooed on my right ankle. It's only small and discreet but Jonny thought it was sexy. I stuck to the one while he quickly became addicted to the art. Ten years later, here he is, my tattooed bad boy. Well, he's not mine anymore. I only wish that he was.

"Jonny..." I start to speak but I can't find the words. His eyes are burning into mine and I can't move, can't speak. Those beautiful brown eyes of his are filled with hurt and uncertainty, regret even. Maybe he regrets waiting for me now. Now that he's seen me, faced me. All manner of images from earlier on in the club are probably flashing through his mind. Images that I wish I could take away from his mind but can't. I want him to remember me how I used to be, before he walked into that club tonight. Not now, not like this. I never wanted this.

"I know that I looked shocked when I saw you earlier on, Lauren, but the truth is that I watched you from the very beginning of your performance tonight so I knew it was you strutting up to that podium before you even got there. When I heard your name being called out I thought it was just a coincidence but then...there you were."

He's speaking softly to me at the moment but I know it won't last, it can't possibly last. "I wanted to leave, Lauren. I wanted to leave there and then because I couldn't bear the thought of what was to come next but..." He pauses, swallowing hard, his eyes still fixated on mine. "I couldn't leave because I was mesmerised." Now I am shocked at his confession. "Mesmerised by you and your beautiful singing voice, your dancing. I was frozen to the spot by an angel...my angel."

Oh god, I can feel tears brimming at the back of my eyes. He's calling me his angel again, even after seeing me up there on that stage doing what I was doing, he still thinks of me as his angel. It's our song, my song, the song he wrote for me. He blows out a breath from between his lips and places his hands around the back of his neck. He lets them hang there for a moment as his eyes flick down to the pavement, and then he shakes his head in disbelief.

"Not many women can sing a song like Alicia Keys can, but you did. You hit every note to perfection and yet, I'm now standing here wondering how the fuck you can belt a song out like that but somehow end up here." He gestures towards the club behind us, his face suddenly darkening. "Working in some seedy, slimy shithole, getting your kit off for a load of fucking perverts?!"

And we're off. Jonny has done the softly softly approach with me and now he's all guns blazing. Some things never change. "Jonny…" I start to speak but he cuts me off.

"What the fuck happened, Lauren? Why you? Why?"

I shake my head and try desperately to force back the tears that have been threatening to fall for the last few minutes but it's no use, they start to flow from my tear ducts anyway, whether I want them to or not.

"Don't…" I start to speak again but then some movement in my peripheral vision makes me stop in my tracks. I look over Jonny's shoulder across the road and see a man standing there watching us. He's standing at the driver's side of a brand new, top of the range, black Range Rover with tinted windows. He's dressed in a black suit and tie and he's built like a brick shit house. When Jonny notices that my eyes aren't on him, he turns around but then turns back to me just as quickly.

"Don't worry about him, Tony's with me."

He turns back to the big hulk of a bodyguard called Tony and nods his head. Tony then turns and gets back in the car.

He clearly heard Jonny's raised voice and was quick to react. I was almost beginning to wonder if Jonny had really come to find me all on his own. When you're a world famous rock star I expect you're rarely on your own when you've got fans and paparazzi mobbing you every few minutes. Even at this early hour of the morning.

Jonny's angry gaze is now back on me but the distraction has given me that little bit of time I needed to compose myself. I sniff loudly and look away from him. I can't bear to look at him for a minute longer. I don't want to do this.

"Jonny, I can't do this with you, it's too painful." It takes all my effort to say anything at all, my voice almost cracks with emotion, but it's all I can muster up to say to him at the moment.

"Oh, you are going to do this with me, Lauren. Right. Now."

I shake my head, determined. "No!" I blurt out, before turning away. And that's when he touches me. For the first time in ten years, he's touching me, pulling me back by the arm to face him again, and I stumble into him as he grabs a tight hold of my arms, shaking me.

"How the fuck did you end up here? Like this! What made you end up here? Answer me, Lauren! Fucking well answer me!"

A surge of anger suddenly courses through me like never before. Freeing myself from his grip, I push him backwards, shoving at his chest angrily while he looks on at me, shocked.

"How dare you come back here tonight and demand that of me?! Ten years, Jonny! Ten bloody years and you stand there and judge me?! I've had to endure years and years of watching you live your life in the limelight! In the papers! On the television! And while I tried not to read most of it, I admit to reading some of it! I've watched your highs and your lows, and the women…" I scoff, shaking my head in disgust. "Don't even get me started on your women! What was it your fellow band member said to you tonight? You normally love this shit! Oh and I bet you do, don't you? I bet you bloody do!"

I felt sorry for him before, felt bad for him seeing me on that stage cavorting around, but now I'm angry. Angry that he's judging me and questioning me. Like he's got some god given right to judge me after some of the things he's done over the last few years. And now that I've started to lay into him, I find myself unable to stop.

"I bet you'd be shagging one of the other lap dancers right now up some darkened alleyway somewhere if you hadn't seen me in there tonight! That is what you went in there for after all, isn't it?!" I shove at his chest again and he stands there in shock, completely speechless.

Well good, I'm glad he's speechless. Now he knows what it feels like to be on the receiving end of a good stripping down. I bet nobody even dares to strip him down these days, unless it's some woman stripping him of his clothes that is. God, I really am angry now, but then, so is he.

"I really don't know how you expect me to react after seeing what I saw in there! You're not just *some* other woman that I fucked around with and disposed of afterwards! You're not just *some* woman I spent one fucking night with, Lauren! You're my sweetheart. My girl. My everything! Well, you were my everything, until you fucked off and left me without so much as a goodbye, without so much as a fucking explanation!"

I knew that one was coming, him sticking the knife in and twisting it, twisting it to the point of excruciating pain. Pain I just don't want to deal with. Not again. I can't do this again.

The tears are falling again now and my anger is retreating. My emotions are raw and open and I wonder how much more I can stand of this. "Leaving you was the hardest thing I've ever done, Jonny, don't think that it wasn't."

"So fuckin' hard that you did it anyway. My heart bleeds for you, Lauren, it really bleeds."

I don't know what to say to that and so I say nothing. I can see the pain in his eyes. I can see all the hurt, all the anger, a full flurry of emotions whirling around in them.

"If I could turn the clock back then I would but I can't, Jonny…" I gulp back a sob, "I can't."

We've only been standing here for five minutes but it feels like an eternity to me and I'm suddenly conscious of the fact that Stacey will be leaving the club very soon. She said she wouldn't be far behind me. I really don't want her to witness this scene but I really don't want to have to say goodbye to Jonny either. I want to hold on to him for as long as possible. Hell, I don't want to let him go ever again. I shouldn't have let him go the first time round, but I did. Something I'll regret for the rest of my days.

"Why did you leave me, Lauren?" he suddenly asks me, his sorrowful eyes desperately searching mine for answers. Answers I'm not prepared to give to him. Not now. Not ever. Jonny's been through enough pain and anguish in his life because of me and I will not hurt him or his family anymore. If I tell Jonny the reason for me leaving him all those years ago then all hell would break loose and I cannot and will not let that happen. Which is why I decide to bid him a quick farewell.

"Goodbye Jonny," I whisper, my voice at breaking point. I turn away from him and start to walk slowly along the pavement. Surprisingly, he doesn't reach out to pull me back and press me for an answer to his question, but he doesn't quite let me go either.

"My girl shouldn't be walking home on her own at this time

of night. Let me take you home, Lauren."

I stop walking, close my eyes, and bite down hard on my bottom lip in the hope that the pain will stop me from breaking down completely at hearing his kind words. Even now, after everything that's passed between us tonight, he still thinks of me, cares about me, wants to make sure I get home safe.

"And then what?" I ask quietly, afraid of the answer.

Jonny is offering to take me home and I want to believe that he's offering so much more than that to me right now. I want him to do a whole lot more than just take me home. I want him to scoop me up into his arms and tell me it's all okay. I want him to tell me that he doesn't care what he saw in the club tonight because he still loves me. I want him to forget all about the fact that I left him all those years ago without ever saying goodbye to him. I want him to forget all the bad memories and remember the good ones. I want to make new memories with him, a whole host of new memories. If only he would give me that chance.

"And then I drive away knowing that you're safe."

There it is, the answer to my question, and it's like a stab in the heart, the final, fatal blow that I simply can't deal with. He doesn't want me anymore after what he saw in there tonight. He doesn't feel the same way as he used to and it breaks me, shatters me. He. Doesn't. Love. Me. Anymore.

Of course he doesn't love me anymore. It's been ten years. Ten long years. So much time has passed, feelings change, people change. I haven't changed though, not really. I still love him. More than he'll ever know, and that will never ever change. I only wish that I'd never asked that question just now. I should have just carried on walking away. Well, I'm walking away now. Far away. And I'm never looking back.

"Goodbye Jonny," I repeat, my tone firm.

It's only as I walk that little bit further away from him that he finally says something in response to my farewell. "At least you said goodbye to me this time."

And that's the last thing he says to me. He doesn't run after me and plead with me. He doesn't shout and yell at the top of his voice down the street to get me to turn around and go back. He just lets me go, and I know that this time, he's letting me go for good.

CHAPTER 6

I'm lying in the bath. It's the morning after the night before and I've been in the bath for two whole hours now and I haven't moved a muscle. I haven't moved because I'm numb inside. Lifeless and numb. Stacey's been shouting at me through the bathroom door for the past half an hour wondering what the hell is going on with me and I haven't answered her. I don't want to speak to anybody. I don't want to leave my apartment ever again after last night. My life is over. I may have spent the last ten years without him but at least in those ten years there was still a glimmer of hope that I might eventually reunite with him again. Now, I don't even have hope to cling on to. I just want to curl up into a ball and die.

I'm even considering letting myself freeze to death in this damn bathtub. Anything to take away the agonising pain that I'm currently in. That's how truly devastated I am. How could he let me walk away from him like that? After everything we ever went through together.

I'm willing to look past all of his faults. The drinking, the drugs, the women. So many women, so many notches on that overly large bedpost of his. God, I hate them, every single one of them, for having a piece of Jonny. My Jonny. I have to stop saying that to myself because he isn't *my* Jonny anymore and he hasn't been mine for a very long time. Rock star Jonny can't look past what I've become. He now sees me as one of those whores he chases around. One of those women that he loves to get into his bed, fuck them into next week and then kick them back out of bed again the following morning. He's such a hypocrite, and he's a man whore. A complete male slut. God, I'm so angry with him. So bloody angry I could scream out loud right now but instead, I swallow it down and remain silent. So very silent.

I start to poke my perfectly pedicured toes into the taps at the end of the bath as I stare into space, wondering what the hell I'm going to do next. Do I really want to go back to that sleaze pit of a place and get my tits out again for all and sundry? No. Do I have to go back to that sleaze pit to get my tits out again for all and sundry? No, but I need the money and I'm qualified for absolutely nothing else. Do I want to go back to that sleaze pit and get my tits out to all and sundry again just to spite Jonny? Hell yes, that's exactly what I want to do. In fact, that is what I really need to do. Not that he'll ever know about me going back there of course. I won't be seeing him again after last night, that's for sure, but it'll make me feel better, like I've got one up on him somehow.

If he thinks I'm a slut merely for working as a lap dancer then that's what I'll be, a slut. But I'm not a slut, and it hurts that he thinks I've turned into one, because I've never slept around and I never will. I also hate how he assumes that all lap dancers are an easy lay, because that isn't the case at all either, and it's just so stereotypical of the Jonny he has become.

Most of the lapdancers I have worked with were just desperate for the money at the time or found themselves in a situation whereby they felt they couldn't get a job elsewhere. Just like me. Little old me, who has only slept with the grand total of two men since I left Jonny over ten years ago. And those two men weren't one-night stands either. Oh no. I don't do one night stands. Never have done, never will. They were relationships, and both of those relationships fell apart because of one reason and one reason only. Jonny. Jonny bloody Mathers!

He stole my heart when I was just fifteen years old and he never gave it back to me. Until last night. He gave it back to me last night and then pierced a knife right through it. Spoiling me, ruining me for every other man. I was already ruined by him though. There could never be another man for me after him. There's only one Jonny, and that Jonny is now a complete and utter asshole with no regard for women or anybody else around him. He's a diva actually. A big rocker diva who gets what he wants with a click of his fingers. Lucky him.

God, I've turned into a right bitch since last night. I don't like bitchy Lauren. In fact, I hate bitchy Lauren. Bitchy Lauren only comes out to play when she's jealous and upset and I'm both of those things right now and all because of *him*.

"Lauren, will you talk to me please? I'm getting really worried now. I swear if you don't say something to me in the next thirty seconds then I'm breaking down the door!"

I almost jump out of the bath when I hear Stacey's booming voice coming from the other side of the door. God, I really need to get a grip of myself and get back into the real world. I'm even starting to scare myself, never mind her.

"You'll never break that door down in a million years," I say, finally breaking the silence. I hear her breathe a sigh of relief.

"Well thank god for that, I thought you'd bloody well drowned yourself in there! What the hell is going on with you, Lauren? Is this about last night and what happened at the club? I'm your best friend, Lauren. Talk to me…please."

So many questions from Stacey and rightfully so. If the tables were turned then I'd be asking the very same questions. In fact, I would have broken the bathroom door down by now. She deserves better than this, better than me. Maybe I should tell her the truth, finally get it off my chest and relieve myself of everything that is Jonny. She's my best friend and I trust her with my life and the only reason why I haven't told her about him before now is because of how painful it is to speak about the events that led up to me walking away from him. Why I walked away from Manchester. His dad. My dad. The baby.

I slowly stand up in the bath and lean over to grab my towel from the towel rail. Once I've stepped out of the tub, I wrap the bath towel firmly around my naked body which is now looking more than a little shrivelled up thanks to being in the murky bath water for far too long. I unlock the bathroom door and finally, after two long hours, I open it.

Stacey is standing on the other side waiting for me. But she doesn't stay standing there for long. She reaches over and pulls me into a hug. And then it happens. I start to cry. And when I say cry, I mean really cry. It's a really good bawling session actually and it's just what I need right now. Stacey is what I need right now. And there we stand, outside our bathroom, two best friends hugging each other for how long I don't know. I don't care either. All I know is that Stacey is here for me no matter what. That's what best friends are for after all.

****

"I don't believe it. I still don't believe what you've told me. I mean obviously you're not lying to me but..."

"You don't believe it?" I finish Stacey's sentence for her. She's said she doesn't believe it about ten times up to now so she's starting to get a little repetitive to say the least.

"But..." she hesitates, "all those times that I said I wanted to get into his pants and you've...already been there, and you loved him. He loved you. You were teenage sweethearts and...I don't believe it."

I roll my eyes and throw myself against the back of the sofa. We're in the living room eating a box of chocolates and between the two of us, we've almost destroyed said box of chocolates already and we only opened it half an hour ago.

I have to admit that I haven't told Stacey everything about me and Jonny. I've only told her snippets of information. That we were together for four and a half years and how his dad always hated me. I haven't told her anything about my dad's violent ways and I haven't told her about the baby either because both of those things are just far too painful to share. The only other thing that she does know about is why I left Manchester. Something that Jonny doesn't even know about himself. And there's only one reason why I left Jonny and one reason alone. His dad.

"If you say 'I don't believe it' one more time, I swear I'm going to kill you!"

She huffs loudly and then folds her arms. "Well I don't know what you expect. You've just told me that you once had a serious relationship with one of the most famous rock stars in the world. A rock star that I've drooled over for the past nine years while you've sat back and said nothing! God, if I'd have dated him and you'd have been going on about wanting to get into his pants, I'd have said something to you, that's for sure."

"He's not mine to get jealous over anymore." I sigh. "And anyway, you're my best friend, I'd rather you got into his pants instead of any one of those other women he's fucked around with over the last few years, believe me." She turns her head to look at me and raises her eyebrows in shock. "What?" I shrug.

"Oh come on, Lauren, like you'd ever want to share *him* with any other woman!"

"Like I said, he's not mine to share anymore and his hordes of screaming women are more than welcome to him and his manhood."

"Speaking of his manhood..." She pauses briefly to curl her legs up on to the sofa, reaching for another chocolate in the process. "Let's get to the really interesting part about your relationship with bad boy rocker." I stop her before she even gets started.

"Let's not, I'm not spilling anything about what went on between me and Jonny in the bedroom, or out of the bedroom, depending on where we were at the time." Her eyes widen at that remark and she breaks out into a knowing smile. A suggestive bloody smile.

"Oh I bet he was a right goer, wasn't he? I bet he's pure filth in bed, isn't he? Oh come on, just answer the one question that I've been wondering for the last nine years. Please make all my fantasies about him come true."

Oh god, as much as I love Stacey, this conversation is getting into a weird area for me, but it's to be expected I suppose. I've always known about Stacey's massive fan crush on Jonny. She's no different to every other woman on the planet so her fantasising about a former boyfriend of mine because he's so famous shouldn't really bother me, but it does, just a teensy weensy bit. However, because it's Stacey and because I love her so damn much, I decide to finally put her out of her nine year misery.

"Okay," I sigh, "I'll put you out of your misery. Yes, he's pure filth in bed, but don't forget that we were only young teenagers at the time, Stacey. He was my first and I was his first, and what started out as a sweet, teenage romance eventually turned into something far more deep and meaningful than either of us ever expected. The older we got and the more time we spent together and the more firsts we encountered as those two loved up teenagers, the more intense and passionate our relationship became. We were…wild together, completely reckless and hopelessly in love. So in love." My voice trails off as a lump forms in my throat. God, I miss him. I miss him so very badly.

"Sorry, I didn't mean to upset you, Lauren." Stacey reaches out and places a reassuring hand in mine and I smile softly. "Although I'm glad you've finally given me the answer I've been longing to hear, lucky cow. Don't worry though, any further fantasies of Mr Mathers and his guitar are now well and truly buried." I can't help but burst out laughing when she says that, she always manages to cheer me up somehow.

"I'm not even going to ask," I say, and she chuckles in response.

"So…he doesn't know why you left Manchester then? Why you left him?"

I shake my head. "No, and…as much as I wanted to tell him when I saw him last night, I didn't because…well, if I tell him that his dad was the reason for me leaving him then Jonny will go on the warpath with him, because that's what he does, and he really doesn't need that at the moment, what with his mum being ill and everything. According to the newspapers she is anyway. It'll just stir up more trouble for him and I really don't want that, despite how angry I am with him right now. And anyway, I don't think I'll be seeing him ever again after last night."

"Erm, well you will be seeing him again, next week, at the concert."

Oh shit, the concert. "No, Stace, I can't go now, I can't face seeing him again."

"And just who am I supposed to take with me if you don't come along?" I get up from the sofa and make my way over to the kitchen to try and avoid the question but she gets up and follows me. "Those tickets cost a fortune, Lauren, and they're on the front row. You can dress up really really hot and make him sweat. He's bound to notice us on the front row."

I fill up the kettle and click it on, sighing loudly. "Stace, I don't want to see him ever again, he thinks I'm nothing but a slut just because I'm a lap dancer and he made it quite clear that he wants nothing to do with me ever again. Haven't you been listening to a word I've said?"

She places a hand on her hip and gives me that "are you for real?" look that she always gives me when she's pissed. "Number one, he didn't call you a slut, he was just shocked and upset to see you standing there on a stage almost completely naked and therefore got over protective and jealous over you and I can't really blame him for that, you two have a massive history. Number two, he defended you from his overly flirtatious bassist who clearly liked what he saw and I have to say, I can't blame him."

I roll my eyes but she carries on regardless. Once Stacey starts on at me, that's it, there's no stopping her. "Number three, he offered to drive you home and was probably being all gentlemanly by not pursuing anything further than that. You've just seen each other for the first time in ten years and trying to get you into bed the first chance he gets is sending out the wrong signals even though he probably did want to fuck you senseless, and again, I can't blame him for wanting to, you're hot stuff..."

"Stacey!"

She cuts me off to finish her lecture. "And number four, I really really want to see them in concert and as your best friend who supports you no matter what, I think you owe me that much at least."

It's time for me to place my hand on my hip this time. "Have you finished with the lecture?"

She shrugs. "Only if you agree to come to the concert with me next week. It's our first night off work together in ages and

I'm absolutely desperate to spend some girly time with my best friend. I know it'll be hard seeing him again, on stage, in the flesh."

She pretends to fan herself with her hand as though she's too hot, and I find the nearest thing to me, which happens to be a wet dishcloth, and hurl it at her. She catches it and throws it right back at me, the cow.

"You're such a bossy cow sometimes, Stacey, and you drive a hard bargain."

"I know, but I've made you smile as a result." She winks at me, and it's only then that I realise she has made me smile, and laugh. I feel so much better than I did earlier on and it's all down to her.

"Okay," I sigh. "Anything for a quiet life, but if I get the wobbles or freak out then we're leaving. Agreed?"

She rolls her eyes but agrees with me anyway, extremely reluctantly I might add. "Fine, but you won't get the wobbles as we're downing the vodka before we go. I'm making a proper night of it and so are you." She gives me the look and I sigh once more, turning away from her and back to the kettle that's just boiled.

"Fine, we'll down the vodka before we go to the concert, but for now, we'll stick to coffee. Fancy a brew?"

"Oooh, I thought you'd never ask."

CHAPTER 7

I can't believe it. It's Wednesday night and we're here. At the concert in the O2 arena! The first night of Reclamation's five night run. We're on the front row, right in front of the main stage. The stage that also happens to have rather a long walkway attached to it. God, I can't wait to see Jonny strutting his stuff up on that stage with his guitar, and from where I'm standing, I'm going to get one hell of a view, that's for sure!

I'd be lying if I said I wasn't just a teensy bit excited. Okay, I'm really excited. I'm beside myself actually. This will be the first time I've ever seen Jonny and his band playing live, and I'm already feeling the atmosphere in the arena beginning to build as the lights dim down and the place fades into darkness.

The crowd of twenty thousand people are going wild for them to come on and Stacey and I are right there with them. Tonight is just what I need to cheer myself up as I haven't felt at my best these last few days, and Jonny hasn't been in touch. Not that I expected him to be but, I kind of hoped he might have come to see me again. Not that he knows where I live, and he doesn't have my phone number, which doesn't help, but he knows where I work, and...well, a girl can dream, can't she?

Anyway, putting all that shit to one side, I really want to enjoy myself tonight, and the four large vodkas I had before we left home earlier on are already working their magic. I feel relaxed and excited and Stacey is literally almost peeing herself right now, she's *that* desperate for them to come on.

We're wearing our best rock chic attire tonight. I'm dressed in skinny black jeans and a white tank top with *Rock Star* printed on the front of it in black letters. I'm wearing black knee high boots over the top of my jeans and I've scrunched my natural blonde curls with mousse to give it more of a messy look. I've also gone really heavy on the makeup. I love black eyeliner at the best of times but I've really gone to town with it tonight. Black smoky eyes and bright pink lip gloss are the way forward and it's all part of the theme. As are the many silver bangles adorning both my wrists. Stacey went out today and bought them especially for tonight. They're not real silver, obviously, just some cheapies from Claire's Accessories, but I thought they were a good idea and they complete our look.

Stacey looks as smoking hot as I do. She's wearing the same gear as me but her tank top is bright pink. She always likes to stand out from the crowd does Stacey. I'm sure she chose the colour on purpose so that she can catch the attention of a certain lead singer. Can't blame a girl for trying, especially when she's doing it for me, bless her.

Right, enough talking, something is happening because the twenty thousand screaming fans have just started to scream a whole lot louder, as has Stacey. I swear I'll be deaf by the end of tonight but it'll be worth it. *He's* so worth it.

The sound of an electric guitar suddenly fills the arena but the place remains in complete darkness. Oh my god, it's him! It's Jonny! Playing solo on the electric guitar! Could I be any more excited? I so need to get a grip. Oh to hell with it, I'm a Reclamation fan too, just like the rest of them.

The crowd are going absolutely mental right now and are starting to chant his name. All I can hear is "Jonny! Jonny! Jonny!" being screamed around me. Women are jumping up and down waving god knows what in the air and the men are imitating playing the guitar. God, this feels so surreal to me. These people are chanting the name of the man I knew long before he graced the world with his presence, but it feels wonderful and I feel proud. So very proud.

The long guitar intro ends and then…a huge bang echoes around the arena and suddenly he's there, with his back to the crowd, standing on a platform bathed in light, like an angel. My angel. He's in his best rock star pose, right arm up with his hand balled into a fist as if he's punching the air and his left hand on the neck of his guitar. He's dressed completely in leather and if my knickers weren't wet before, they certainly are now!

His leather jacket is turned up at the collar and he's had his name emblazoned diagonally across the back of it. The silvery letters sparkle under the spotlight and even though he still has his back to the audience, the man just oozes sex. Complete and utter sex. Nobody can wear leather quite like Jonny. He has lovely slim hips and a perfectly shaped bottom. A bottom you just want to sink your teeth into, or grab hold of, whichever you prefer. I've done both but we won't go there.

Stacey turns to me and screams something into my ear but as every other person in the arena is currently screaming at the same time, I have no idea what she's saying to me. I just nod and scream back, as well as jumping up and down on the spot and clapping of course. I'm so getting into the spirit of the concert and it hasn't even started properly yet.

It's about to start now though because Jonny suddenly jumps down off his platform and on to the main stage. He starts to run up the walkway to his crowd of fans straight away. Yep, that's Jonny. Always thinks of his fans first. I've seen it on the DVDs. He always runs to his audience first.

I turn to the side to drink him in in all his glory as he sprints right to the end of the walkway. I've got a perfect view of the main stage from here but I now find myself having to look up at the large screens above us to see him properly. His face is already hot and sweaty but his dark brown eyes are alive with the buzz of the atmosphere around him. He's biting his bottom lip and punching the air with both hands and his fans are going nuts. And then….

"Hello London!" That sexy, masculine voice echoes loudly around the arena and the fans start to chant his name again. He's clapping along with them now, and smiling, but he's still biting that lip. Damn him, I love it when he does that. It's sexy. He's just so bloody sexy.

"Are you ready?!" The crowd shout yes. "Are you ready?!" The crowd scream even louder this time. Jonny puts his hand to his ear as if he can't hear them. "I said are you fucking ready?!" Typical rock star and typical Jonny, he always did love the F word.

Stacey is screaming yes at the top of her lungs along with me and everybody else and finally, after teasing his audience to the point of madness, something that Jonny loved to do with me once upon a time, the music finally starts.

The drum and bass sound from the main stage and the rest of the band suddenly come to life, the other three members of Reclamation now in full view. Lights and lasers fill the arena as Jonny starts to go mad on the guitar. He's still on the walkway strumming away and the fans closest to him at the moment are already head banging to the deep rocky rhythms of Reclamation's first ever number one single, Blazing Inferno.

My eyes are fixated on the large screens above me as I watch Jonny run back down the walkway and on to the main stage to get to the microphone. How he manages to continue to play the guitar as flawlessly as that whilst running along a stage, I'll never know.

I have the perfect view of Jonny now as he's back on the

main stage and I've just noticed his bare chest under that snug leather jacket of his. I'm so bloody close that I can make out two large tattoos on his pecs, as well as a few smaller ones underneath. Well, they're new to me because he didn't have any tattoos on his chest when we were together. Shit, I want to touch them and trace my fingers around them as well as my tongue. In fact, I'm pretty sure that if I stretched myself out far enough, I could actually touch him, and his tattoos. God, I want to touch him but then, so do all the other women in the arena around me, including Stacey. She's elbowing me in the side and grinning at me like a loon.

After an extended rocky intro, Jonny finally takes to the mike and starts to sing in that rough and rocky way he always does when he sings an upbeat number. I watch him intently as he loses himself completely in a song that has *very* suggestive lyrics. Everybody likes a bit of controversy and whilst it's not overly rude, any fully grown adult will know what the song is about. I for one know *exactly* what it's about. Mainly due to the fact that the song is about me and him. Well, I'm ninety-nine percent sure it is anyway.

It may sound presumptuous of me to think that but Jonny used to put nearly everything about himself and his life into his songs. Discreetly done of course, but that's his talent. And that's what I think he's done with Blazing Inferno because everything in this song is me and him. What we did together, what he did to me, what I did to him. He used to talk sex to me all the time and the effect I had on him and so I know from those things that he put a lot of that into this song.

To everybody else in this arena, it's just a song about hot sex between two people. To me, it's about the hot sex between us. And I love it. In fact, just seeing him standing there right in front of me, belting out this sexy rocky number is really getting me going. Those knickers of mine are definitely getting wetter, I can feel it.

The first few songs they play are all upbeat numbers, Jonny running back and forth on the stage with his electric guitar while the others really go to town on the rhythm guitar, drums and bass. They're loud, wild and seriously rocking this place tonight, but the faster numbers are about to be put to bed for a bit as the stage goes into complete darkness for about a minute.

The crowd are screaming, waiting all too impatiently for what may come next. And what comes next is Jonny taking centre stage on the grand piano. Oh wow, Jonny on a piano, now I am in trouble. I'll be launching myself at the stage in a minute if I'm not careful.

He's lost the leather jacket and is now dressed in a black t-shirt, much to my disappointment. I'd rather he wore the leather jacket but he still has the leather pants on I see. A small consolation I suppose. The grand piano is positioned in the middle of the stage and he's so close to me right now that I swear he would be able to see me, if only he looked up.

He isn't looking up though, he's looking down at the keys as he starts to play a song called Fragmented. The screams from the crowd die down a little bit as they watch their idol get to grips with the piano, one of the most beautiful musical instruments in the world to me. And all because Jonny is playing it. This slow paced little number about love and loss is a favourite of mine. Another number one hit I might add. It's the complete opposite to his rockier rhythms and I love the fact that he is so versatile with his music. You can't put Jonny's music into any one category really because he has such a wide variety of different sounds. He loves to use different instruments whenever possible and he loves the fast paced songs as much as the slower ones.

He's so into the song right now, closing his eyes as he sings softly into the microphone, his fingers hitting every chord on that piano to absolute perfection. His voice sounds even more beautiful echoing around an arena as large as this. He's certainly come a hell of a long way from the small confines of a pub in Manchester, playing small gigs to pubs full of customers all by himself. Well, with a little help from me of course.

This is so much better than I ever imagined it to be, seeing him up there in the limelight, all eyes on him. I feel like I'm falling in love with Jonny all over again tonight. And just as that very thought is going through my mind, Jonny suddenly looks up from the piano and his gaze hits mine. And there it is, instant recognition.

His eyes seem to grow softer, more tender, something that just this afternoon, I feared I may never see again. It's as though he's re-connecting to me through his song, through his lyrics. I can feel Stacey's eyes on me now but I don't turn to her. I can't. I'm transfixed, utterly mesmerised by him and his performance. And his gaze doesn't leave mine, not even for a second. My heart is beating so fast that I swear it's going to jump out of my chest and smash right into him.

As he eventually brings the song to a close, the crowd start to scream once more, and it's only then that he finally looks away from me, breaking our connection instantly. I still can't believe that he saw me from the stage. I'd obviously hoped that he would see me but I'm still in shock that he did. I turn to look at Stacey and she's giving me that knowing smile of hers. I just shrug back at her and receive a rolling of the eyes in response.

That sizzling performance on the piano and the fact that our eyes locked together for a long moment has left my stomach doing somersaults but Jonny is now strutting along the stage once more, all calm and collected, mike in hand, clapping along with his screaming fans. The spotlight above the piano slowly fades to black and I wonder what's to come next.

After about a minute of smiling that sexy ass smile of his,

Jonny wanders over to the rest of the band behind him. They start to chat between themselves for a moment as the audience continue to chant loudly. I'm surprised they can even hear each other over the deafening roar in this arena.

A Mexican wave has just started doing the rounds as well, along with lots and lots of foot stomping. All four band members seem to be exchanging nods with one another and then, Jonny finally turns back towards his audience, walking slowly towards the edge of the stage once more.

"So, which one of you lucky lucky ladies out there wants to get up on this stage tonight and sing along with me then?!"

And I'm officially deaf. Seriously, the screaming from all the women has now reached a ridiculously phenomenal level and as much as I would love to be screaming right along with them, I'm not. Not one bit. I can't believe that he's honestly going to get some crazed female fan of his up there on the stage to sing along with him. Surely not. He doesn't normally do things like this. Or does he? Not on any DVDs I've ever seen but then, they're just one-offs. Jonny's been doing tour after tour around the world for the last few years so he probably does this sort of thing all the time.

Throngs of women around me are literally throwing themselves at the stage to try and reach out and grab hold of him. I bet his security team are having kittens right now. Typical Jonny, never ever plays by the rules. He makes his own rules, and right now, every female in this arena wants to break those rules right along with him. Stacey is nudging me in the ribs and jumping up and down on the spot but I'm not. I don't want to see this. I don't want to see Jonny working his absolute best on another woman, even if it is just for the show.

He's scanning the front row now, smiling that sex hot smile of his he always wears when he really wants something. The really arrogant one. The one he knows full well the effect it has on the knickers of any woman. Me included. And just when he couldn't tease the women in this arena any more, he then starts to run along the edge of the stage, touching the many pairs of women's hands that are reaching out to grab him from the front row. All except mine. My hands are well and truly by my side, and they're staying there. As much as I'd love to reach out and touch Jonny, I don't fancy being the one to be pulled up on to that stage to sing in front of twenty thousand people. I know I've always dreamt of doing that, but no. They're just daydreams that will never ever happen. Never. They're not real. Not real. Not real….

Oh shit, Jonny's eyes have stopped roaming the front row for the woman of his choice. And they've stopped roaming the front row because they've landed on me! They're locking with mine in that familiar heated way they always used to. The way they did just moments earlier when he first saw me in the crowd, gazing down at me from the stage as I gazed up at him. No, surely he won't choose me. Unless he's doing this deliberately to get me up there with him, but why on earth would he want to do that after our angry exchange the other night? After everything he saw me doing in that strip club?

Either way, from how he's looking at me right now, I'd say he clearly does want to get me up on to that stage with him. To sing a song together. Like we used to. Shit. This isn't some dingy back room in a pub in Manchester. This is an arena. The O2 arena. In London. Where twenty thousand fans are now screaming at the top of their lungs for their idol to pick them. But he's already made his choice. And that choice is me.

"I think I've found my lady for the evening!" he shouts loudly into the microphone, his eyes never leaving mine. "Would you like to come up here and join me in a sing song?"

Oh fuck. I am *the chosen one* and I'm now speechless, frozen to the spot. I only wish Stacey would bloody well freeze on the spot along with me because she's now jumping madly and throwing her arms around me. I'm fairly conscious of the fact that a lot of women are now glaring at me for being *the chosen one*. I'm also conscious of the fact that I can't say no because who would say no to getting up on that stage with Reclamation? Me, apparently.

Jonny planned this deliberately. I know it. I can feel it. It's too much of a coincidence to me that straight after he's seen me in the crowd, he's now doing something like this. Oh hell, I can't get up there. But I have to. Speak Lauren, speak. React. Move. Something. Anything.

"Is the lady shy?"

Jonny's voice echoes loudly around the arena and I'm vaguely aware of the women around me now screaming things such as "I'm not shy, Jonny, pick me!" "If she doesn't want to do it then I will!" "I love you, Jonny!"

'No you don't love him!' is all I want to scream back at them, but I don't. Instead, I swallow down my nerves and shake my head at him, smiling. He smiles back at me, and I swear my heart almost explodes with emotion. It's his beautiful smile. The one I used to see so often and loved so very much. The smile he only ever reserved for me. The one I used to see every morning when I woke up next to him. The one I used to see after he had made slow, passionate love to me. That smile I saw when I first told him I was pregnant, despite it being a huge shock to both of us at the time. Oh how I love that smile, and I love him. So much. Even now. Even after all this time.

"Apparently the lady isn't shy after all. Put your hands together for the lovely lady!"

Screams, claps and god knows what else ensue but I'm not really listening to all the white noise that's going on around me anymore. I'm just focusing on the fact that I'm now being escorted away from the crowd of insane fans and on to the stage by two very burly looking security men who have suddenly emerged from nowhere. This is surreal, completely and utterly surreal.

When I do finally get on to the main stage, Jonny is right there waiting for me, extending his hand out to me, still smiling. Shit, he's extending his hand out to me, the hand I haven't held on to for a *very* long time. I suddenly feel like that giggly fifteen year old girl all over again. The one that kept catching his eye from across the road while he waited for his school bus as I waited for mine. The girl that kept turning up her school skirt just that little bit shorter every morning in the hope that he would eventually come over and talk to her. And he did. After two weeks of wolf whistles and giving me the eye.

So many years ago now since we first met and yet here we are, all these years later, about to sing together in front of thousands of screaming fans. Shit, I'm nervous, even more so now that I'm under his close scrutiny. Jonny can undress a woman with his eyes alone and I suddenly feel completely naked under his gaze. I can feel his eyes moving over every single inch of me as if he's touching me, undressing me, like only he can. My heart is thumping in my chest, my knickers are definitely wetter than they were before and every nerve ending in my body is coming alive for him. Alive to the tune of his song.

It's like a lightning bolt to my hot core when Jonny finally takes hold of my hand, threading his fingers through mine, the familiarity not going unnoticed by me, or my hormones. I can feel the rough edges of his fingertips grazing softly against my skin, a sensation that used to drive me nuts. And it's driving me nuts now. Almost to the point of making me forget where I am, until Jonny finally looks away from me, turning his gaze back to his audience. And that's when I suddenly realise what I'm about to do.

My gaze follows his and I'm met with the most wonderful sight I've ever seen in my entire life. Twenty thousand people screaming for the man standing next to me, camera flashes and that all important Mexican wave still going strong. I feel alive just from standing up here with him. No wonder he loves doing the live shows so much. This beats everything that I've ever done and I'm silently thanking Jonny for picking me. If I never get to be up on a stage like this ever again, I don't care. This is it. My one chance. My one moment to shine. And Jonny is making that happen for me. Right now.

"Time to put a name to the face of this beautiful lady standing next to me I think!" Now I'm blushing. Jeez, I so need to get a grip. Jonny turns back to me and smiles. "What's your name, sweetheart?" *You know my name!*

Still, it would look kind of suspicious if he suddenly let on that he knew me already. The women in this arena would definitely be gunning for me then, that's for sure. I clear my throat nervously, tucking a loose strand of curly hair behind my ear with my free hand. Mouth aimed directly at the microphone, I speak into it.

"Erm…Lauren, my name is Lauren." My voice sounds really odd echoing around the arena, something I am definitely not used to, that's for sure.

"That's a beautiful name," he says, his face suddenly serious. Fuck, he's giving me the serious look this time. The familiarity over already knowing my name as well as knowing everything else about me is clearly going through his mind right now. "And where are you from, Lauren?" *The same place as you.* I swallow past the lump that has suddenly formed in my throat and speak nervously into the microphone once more.

"I live in London now but…I'm originally from Manchester."

A light smile creeps across his lips and his eyes are beginning to look a little mischievous. God, I wish I knew what he was thinking. "What a coincidence," he shouts into the microphone, "so am I."

The crowd go wild for him again, all knowing full well where their rock star icon originally came from, Jonny never forgetting his roots. "Now, as all our fans in this arena know, Reclamation have never recorded a duet with anybody and so, for the first time ever tonight, I'm going to sing a cover. A cover of your choice, Lauren."

Oh. My. God. Now I really am shitting myself. What the hell am I supposed to choose to sing along with him? When Jonny used to perform his gigs around Manchester, he did it all by himself. He wrote his songs, played the guitar, the keyboard, the piano. Basically, any musical instrument that he could get his hands on. It was only every now and again that I used to take to the stage along with him. And whenever I did sing with him, it was cheesy stuff, typical duet stuff. Duets that people in pubs like to hear, not people in vast arenas. People who have come here tonight to hear rock music. Well, alternative rock music anyway.

Reclamation are well known for their versatility in the music world, which suddenly brings to mind another favourite band of mine. Coldplay. Jonny's influence from our early days. If he wasn't playing his own songs to me then he was playing theirs. The Scientist is a particular favourite of mine, one which Jonny used to play to me on the piano quite a lot. That isn't a duet though and this is not helping me one bit. Think Lauren, think.

And then all of a sudden it hits me. A few years ago, Coldplay did a duet with the lovely Rihanna. A great duet. Now, I may not look or sound as hot as Rihanna but I can sing the song and I really like the song. That's it. That's what I want to sing, if Jonny agrees of course. "How about...Princess of China by

Coldplay?"

I see the flicker of recognition in his eyes, and then he smiles. "You like Coldplay?" God, he's good at the pretence of apparently not knowing me. I nod, blushing. "What do you think, boys?" He turns toward the rest of the band behind us. "Can you manage to rustle up some Coldplay for us?" They give him the "what the fuck do you think?" look and then nod.

Jonny turns back to me. "Coldplay it is!" His grip around my hand tightens as he leads me further on to the stage. We're standing right in the centre now and I'm beginning to shit myself. Jonny must sense my sudden pang of nerves because he turns to me and winks, squeezing my hand gently.

"London, may I introduce you to the next Rihanna. A beautiful lady from Manchester who is about to rock your world...and mine along with it!" Why does he have to keep saying things like that? I am literally trembling right now and not just from the nerves about singing. The nerves over him and what he does to me.

No time to be nervous for a minute longer though as some stage hand suddenly appears from nowhere to hand me a microphone of my own. As Jonny is about to sing with me, Will Parker is standing in on the lead guitar for Jonny. As well as providing the backing vocals for the group, Will is the band's rhythm guitarist. He also plays the keyboard and a whole host of any extra instruments that the band require him to play. Will certainly looks ready to rock with Jonny's electric guitar strapped tightly around his front.

And rock he does when he suddenly kicks in with a guitar intro from a song he's never ever played before. How do bands do that? Turn their hand to playing anything and everything? Jonny was always doing that. He could literally play anything I ever asked of him without even reading the music. A talent that is well beyond me. Anyway, back to the song. The intro is now over with, the drum and bass have kicked in and now… time for the lyrics.

Turning to me, his heated gaze fixated on mine, Jonny starts to sing. "Once upon a time somebody ran, somebody ran away saying fast as I can, I've got to go, I've got to go!"

The lyrics seem suddenly inappropriate, or appropriate, depending on how you look at it. I bet Jonny's thinking that's exactly what I did. Ran away from him as fast as possible. I hope he isn't thinking that though because it couldn't be further from the truth. "Once upon a time we fell apart, you're holding my hands the two halves of my heart, ohhhhhhh, ohhhhhh."

He's giving me that heated look again and I can feel him gripping my hand tighter than ever, as though he's trying to talk to me through the song, the lyrics seeming to be telling our story. Thank god the entire arena doesn't know our story, that's all I can say.

Anyway, my turn now. I take a deep breath, waiting for my moment. And then…. "Once upon a time we burned bright, now all we ever seem to do is fight, on and on, and on and on and on…" More appropriate lyrics for us and more screaming. A hell of a lot of screaming coming from the crowd and I have to say, I'm loving it. Every minute of it.

I start to smile with excitement as my nerves begin to melt away and before long, I'm moving my hips in time with the music. Jonny then starts to move his hips along with me. And there it begins. Our foreplay. In front of twenty thousand screaming fans, Jonny and I are partaking in a foreplay we know so well.

This is our connection to one another, through singing, through dancing. In the bedroom, out of the bedroom. It never mattered where we were as long as we were doing this together. Jonny taught me a hell of a lot more about how to dance and move my body than I ever learned at college, just as I taught him everything in return. In the bedroom.

He suddenly lets go of my hand and snakes his arm around my waist, pulling me against him, all the while his heated gaze on mine. As he takes the lead with the lyrics once more, I lick my lips as I watch him undressing me with his eyes. With every lyric that comes out of his mouth, it's as though he's touching my naked body with his fingers, his mouth, his tongue. The lower halves of our bodies are now pressed against each other, grinding together in unison with the music.

As we hit the high notes, our bodies start to pick up pace, writhing together in the sexy, sweaty way they always used to. Clothes or no clothes, I feel like Jonny and I are completely naked up here. I'm vaguely aware of the crowd but I suddenly don't care that twenty thousand people are watching us get down and dirty together. And Jonny doesn't care either. Because it's still there. Even after all this time. The connection to each other. The invisible rope that binds us together so completely. I feel almost suffocated by my depth of feelings for him.

Our voices begin to meld together as our lyrics become one, the outro of the song building up to our very own crescendo. A crescendo of epic proportions. I don't want the song to end. I want the song to carry on. I want Jonny to carry on doing what he's doing to me right now. I can feel the rough edges of those fingertips again through my top, grazing against the skin on my lower back in the most spine tingling, erotic way.

As we finally finish the song, the crowd going absolutely berserk, Jonny leans in and kisses me on the cheek. But before he pulls away, I feel his hot breath against my ear and I swear I nearly pass out from the sensation. "Come backstage after the show, Lauren," he says, "I need to talk to you."

Holy shit, he needs to talk to me. Just a few days ago, I feared I may never see Jonny ever again and now, not only has he just pulled me up on to this stage to get me to sing with him, now he wants to talk. I'd be lying if I said I didn't want more than just to talk to him but it's progress, right?

Or maybe I'm reading too much into it, maybe he just wants to say goodbye to me properly, instead of leaving things like we left them the other night. But before I can even start to think clearly about what he's just said to me, I find myself now being forced to take a full on curtsy in front of the arena.

"I think we have a future Rihanna on our hands here London! Everybody hear it for Lauren!"

Jonny now has his stage mask firmly back in place and he wears it well. Time for my mask to slip back on I think. I smile, I curtsy, and then, after Jonny places yet another kiss on my body, on my hand this time, I am then escorted off stage as quickly as I was escorted on to it just a few minutes ago. My moment in the spotlight finally over with.

CHAPTER 8

Okay, so this is really happening. To my surprise and absolute delight, security let me and Stacey backstage straight away, which is promising, because I know how tight they are on security when it comes to famous people.

Famous people. Shit, I still can't get used to saying famous in the same sentence as Jonny. It just doesn't feel real to me at all. I still feel like I'm dreaming at the moment, floating down the white glossy corridors of the O2 arena towards Jonny's dressing room. We're being escorted by that burly looking man from the other night, the man Jonny referred to as Tony. The man I assume to be Jonny's personal bodyguard, or one of them anyway. Like I said, surreal doesn't even cover what I'm feeling right now.

Tony is even bigger than I first thought. In fact, he's massive. But I suppose he needs to be, considering the risky job he does. He's tall, hefty, bald, a little scary looking and I'd say from the way he's strutting down the corridor in front of us right now, he's most definitely a force to be reckoned with.

We finally reach Jonny's dressing room, Tony coming to an abrupt stop in front of the door. "If you'll just wait here a minute, ladies," he says.

Both Stacey and I watch as Tony slips into the dressing room, the door closing gently behind him. It's only then that I look up and notice Jonny's name on the door. *Jonny Mathers Dressing Room 10*. It's only a temporary sign of course but still, it's yet another reminder to me of just how different our lives are now.

"Oh my god, I can't believe I'm about to meet the lead singer of Reclamation," whispers Stacey excitedly, "you are the bestest best friend in the entire world, Lauren, you do know that, don't you?" I can't help but smile when she says that and I'm just about to respond, when the door opens. Out comes Tony, smiling. He looks friendly when he smiles, I think he should smile more often.

"In you go, ladies." He holds the door open for us and we step inside, giving him our thanks along the way. He's quite the gentleman is Tony, I'm warming to him already. But I'm warming to the other gentleman in the dressing room a whole lot more, because Jonny is sitting there in his chair waiting for us, looking all hot and sweaty from his performance just fifteen minutes ago.

Under the soft glow of the dressing room lights, his tattooed arms look even more sexy to me, as well as his post show messy hair and dishevelled black v-neck t-shirt. I notice he's changed out of his leather pants but the stone washed black denim jeans he's currently wearing look just as sexy on him. He's also wearing some black leather bands on both of his wrists, similar to the ones he used to wear in our early days. Mmm, he is just so comfortable in his own style, all bohemian and rocky whilst being completely and utterly yummy. Okay Lauren, get a grip, he's asked you to come down here to talk to him, nothing more, so talk.

"Hey you," I say to him, smiling.

He smiles and then stands, reaching over to kiss me on both cheeks, the sheer proximity of being so close to him giving me goosebumps. When he pulls back I can't help but notice that familiar gleam in his eye, the one I saw earlier on stage.

"Hey to you too," he says, his gaze locked firmly on to mine.

In an attempt at breaking the overly long eye contact that

seems to have developed between us, I turn to Stacey. "Jonny, may I introduce you to my best friend, Stacey." Jonny turns and flashes her his most panty wetting smile, leaning in for a kiss. Stacey's cheeks are now a similar colour to her top, bright pink.

"It is soooo amazing to finally get the chance to meet you." And she's off. "I've got all your albums and DVDs and the show tonight was just amazing. I mean truly amazing…"

Stacey is still talking and Jonny is just smiling away at her, biting that deliciously sexy bottom lip of his and listening intently to every word she is saying. He's probably experienced this many times before with over the top excitable fans but as this over the top excitable fan is my best friend, it's up to me to stop her from babbling any further. I give her a quick elbow in the ribs and she stops mid-flow.

"What?" she asks innocently.

Jonny chuckles softly and then says, "Well, it's lovely to meet you, Stacey. It's because of fans like you that I'm still in a job."

Well, that compliment goes down very well with her, she's now blushing bright pink again. And finally, now that Stacey is quiet, I have an opportunity to speak to him. Trouble is, I don't know what the hell to say to him! Shit, I'm beginning to think I'm slowly turning into one of those fans who forget how to talk when they're in the presence of somebody famous. Which is ridiculous, because I know Jonny. Well, I did know him, once upon a time. I only wonder how much of the old Jonny I once knew is still in there. I'm sure it is, but that isn't helping my brain freeze right now. Thankfully, Jonny breaks the awkward silence that seems to have descended.

"We're having an after show party tonight at Infusion in central London. I have a few interviews and some shit to do first but I was wondering if you two wanted to come along?

The rest of the band will be there and it's all paid for by my label. It's my way of saying thanks to all my staff for their involvement with the show and all the hard work that's gone into bringing it to the stage. What do you say?"

Jonny's eyes are now back on me and I can feel Stacey almost peeing herself with excitement standing next to me but in all honesty, I'm not really sure about whether I want to go to the after show party or not. Jonny asked me to come down here to talk to me and so far, we've barely said two words to each other. I realise that Stacey being here isn't really helping but I didn't want to leave her on her own. "I'm not really sure, Jonny…" I start to speak but Stacey cuts me off.

"Of course we'll be there! Infusion is *the* place to be in London." She bumps shoulders with me, glaring. Shit, now I'm feeling railroaded. If I could just have five minutes alone with Jonny then that would help matters. "In fact, I think I best pay a visit to the ladies room before we go," she says, clearly getting the hint, "can you point me in the right direction, Jonny?"

Jonny soon latches on to her thinking and nods, leading her towards the door. He opens the door and wanders off down the corridor. He returns just ten seconds later with Tony in tow. "Tony will direct you to the toilet, Stacey, it's a bit of a maze out there so stick with him or you might get lost."

"I'm sure you wouldn't mind if I did got lost," she quips.

I almost die when she says that but before I can kill her with my eyes, she disappears into the vast corridor, taking the infamous Tony along with her. Closing the door, Jonny then turns to me, a look of uncertainty crossing his features.

"I'm sorry if I've pushed you into coming to the after show party. I just thought…" He blows out a breath. "Oh shit, I don't know what I thought to be honest, Lauren." I'm confused.

"So, you don't want me to come to the party after all?" And now, so is he.

"What? No, of course I want you to come to the party, I just meant…" There he goes, sighing again.

"Look, what do you want to talk to me about, Jonny? In fact, what was all that dragging me up on stage all about earlier on?" Not that I minded of course. I mean, I was a little bit embarrassed about it at first but then once I got into the swing of the song and into the swing of Jonny looking at me, touching me….

"Because I saw you in the crowd and just had to get you up there with me. I couldn't quite believe it was really you at first to be honest, I thought I was dreaming. I thought surely I had to be dreaming." He swallows hard, his eyes fixated on mine. "Look, I'm sorry for getting you up there but I…"

"Don't apologise, Jonny, I enjoyed it. It was a little surreal but I loved it. Thank you…for doing that for me." He nods, his eyes suddenly distant.

"You belong on a stage, Lauren." I assume by saying I belong on a stage, he definitely does not mean the stage I currently perform on.

"No, Jonny, you're the one who belongs on a stage. You were amazing tonight, truly amazing. It's the first time I've ever seen you and the band performing live and I'm so glad I came to watch you. You've made such a success with the band, you deserve to be where you are now." And I mean that, with every fibre of my being I mean it.

"I'm sorry for what I said to you the other night," he suddenly blurts out. "I was angry and in shock and…" I hold my hands up to stop him.

"It doesn't matter."

"It matters to me. I shouldn't have said those things to you and I shouldn't have let you walk away like that but…no matter how hard I try, I just can't get the image of seeing you in that club out of my head, Lauren. I just can't."

"Are you ashamed of me?" I finally dare to pluck up the courage to ask that question, because from the way he's talking right now, I'd say that he is. He shakes his head at me, frowning.

"Don't say that to me, I could never be ashamed of you. I just can't bear the thought of you working in a place like that. Why do you do it?" I shrug, feeling suddenly defeated.

"Not everybody gets their dreams handed to them on a plate, Jonny. Not everybody has parents like your parents. I didn't."

He looks at the floor and sighs. "No, I know you didn't, Lauren. I'm sorry, I didn't mean…" He lifts his gaze back up to meet mine, his eyes sorrowful. "I'm sorry," he whispers.

"No, Jonny, I'm the one who's sorry, for everything."

Shit, how did we end up here? Like this. We were happy, so ecstatically happy, and now, ten years later, we can barely hold a proper conversation with one another. On stage it was as though we were a couple again, singing together, touching, dancing. Now, here we are, back to reality again and I hate it. I hate that I've lost those years with him. I hate that I can't just talk to him like I used to be able to. We used to talk all the time, we used to laugh until we cried and we used to cry together until we laughed. This just isn't us. This isn't how we are together. I hate this.

Jonny must sense my spiralling emotions because he suddenly takes a step closer to me. Reaching slowly forward, he moves his hand up to caress my cheek with the tips of his fingers and I find myself drawing breath at his touch.

Jonny looks as emotional as I feel and I can't help the little butterflies that are beginning to take flight in my tummy right now, the skin on my face tingling under his touch. I close my eyes and nuzzle my cheek against his calloused fingertips, past memories of Jonny touching my damp, naked body beginning to surface in my mind.

"Oh, Jonny…" I whisper, wanting more. So much more.

And then it's over in a flash, Stacey suddenly bursting back into the room at the most inconvenient moment. Jonny instantly pulls his hand away, his eyes now firmly on the door behind him. I try to look casual but it's difficult, considering how emotional I'm feeling right now.

"Better?" I ask Stacey.

"So much better, and my word, I've just met Ben, the bassist, he so wants us to go to the party tonight." *Oh, I bet he does.*

Jonny turns back to me. "Look, if you don't want to come, then…"

"I'll come," I say, suddenly changing my mind. After our little "moment" I don't think I'm ready to say goodbye to Jonny just yet. He looks relieved.

"Okay, that's great. I've got some shit to do first but I'll get Andy to drive you both over in the Range Rover."

"Andy?" I thought his bodyguard was called Tony. He smiles at my confused expression.

"Andy's another member of my security team, Lauren. He'll take good care of you both, don't worry."

Hmm, I'm suddenly looking forward to being taken good care of by one of his bodyguards, as well as having a ride in that sleek new Range Rover I clapped my eyes on the other night. My mood is improving already. Perhaps a party is just what I need. "Sounds good. You ready, Stace?"

She rolls her eyes at my sudden mood change. "I've been ready for the last five minutes, girl!"

Jonny laughs. "Lauren always was fickle."

"I wasn't!" I protest.

"You so were."

I pull a face and then head towards the door. "I really don't know what you mean," I say, although I do know what he means, I know exactly what he means. And just for that one brief moment, it feels like we're the old "us" all over again.

CHAPTER 9

Well, unbelievably, we are here! At Infusion! One of the most exclusive nightclubs in London. And this exclusive club is currently home to Reclamation, thanks to Jonny and his label securing the entire VIP area for their private party. And so far, what a party it is.

I've never seen such a large VIP area in a club in all my life. It's all very sassy and modern with a huge dance floor on the level below us, but it's the bar area that is a particular highlight for me, and yes, it's simply because the alcohol is free for the night. Yes, I'm that shallow. But I don't care. Jonny's label is paying for the entire thing tonight and as his guests, it's up to Stacey and I to utilise that privilege as much as possible. So far, we've had two cocktails each so you could say we're already on our way to being a little tipsy, especially after the vodkas we downed earlier on at home and throughout the concert. Oh well, I'm allowed to enjoy myself.

So far though, no sign of Jonny. I'm thinking he must still be at his interviews or whatever it is you do after a concert. I just want him to be here, standing next to me, talking to me or touching me. I would definitely prefer the latter but I don't think that's going to happen somehow, although I do think Jonny felt the same way as I did earlier on. At least, I think he did. I'm just so confused at the moment with everything that is Jonny. He seems angry with me about my job one minute and then upset about it the next. Then he seems to just want to talk like we're friends and then he's touching me and looking at me in ways that are just so not fair. I want him back. So much it hurts.

"They're here, Lauren!" Stacey is suddenly elbowing me in the ribs, shouting at the top of her voice. I notice some other guests standing nearby, looking in our direction.

"Yes I think everybody in the club heard you, Stace, although I hardly think they need an announcement if the cheers from the entrance over there are anything to go by."

Jeez, this is so weird, watching Jonny and his band entering the VIP area as if they're royalty. Well, I suppose they are royalty in the eyes of their devout fans, the royalty of the music world. I've got a great view of the entrance from my standing position at the bar and I drink in Reclamation in all their glory.

Jonny is smiling that cocky smile of his as he shakes hands with people standing near the entrance, the ones that are dying to get just a minute with him. The other three band members follow suit, followed by a whole team of people from security men to people with clipboards and mobile phones and then…a woman.

My heart leaps into my throat as I take in her stunningly attractive six foot figure. Her long raven black hair is so straight and shiny that it looks as though it has been straightened with an iron. She also has that dazzling model like smile about her that most men would drool over. Basically, she is a model, but she's wearing an expensive looking designer suit and is clutching a clipboard, which tells me she's definitely an employee.

But now, she's reaching over and placing an affectionate hand on Jonny's arm, and he's smiling. He's smiling at her. Oh no, I can't handle this. She isn't an employee after all. She's his girlfriend. Jonny has a girlfriend and he didn't say. Jonny has a secret girlfriend and the papers don't know about her? How could he not tell me about her? After everything that seemed to pass between us earlier on and after asking me here tonight, knowing full well what seeing him with another woman would do to me.

I'm just about to launch into a bitchy tirade with Stacey but then I stop dead. Jonny has just noticed me from across the room and his eyes are now locking with mine in that heated way they just shouldn't do. Not when he has a girlfriend.

Shit, my legs are turning to jelly and my stomach is doing somersaults because he's coming over. He's coming over and I can't handle it. Shit. "He's coming over," mutters Stacey, stating the obvious.

I turn away from Jonny and decide to look at the bar instead. My stomach is in knots right now and I just don't know if I can handle an entire night of this. Of him. With her.

"I see you made it here in one piece then?"

Okay Lauren, he's speaking to you so get a grip. Get a grip and turn around. In fact, say something casual and sarcastic, that should work. Throwing back some more of my cocktail first in the hope that it gives me some new found confidence from somewhere, I then turn around. And now I am in trouble because it isn't just Jonny standing there. Oh no, it's the entire bloody band. All four of them. And for the first time ever, I notice Stacey is silent right along with me.

"Erm…" I start to speak but mess up straight away. Jonny smiles that beautiful smile of his and then turns to the other three band members standing either side of him.

"Will Parker, Zack Miller, Ben Anderson, meet Lauren, or should I say, meet the new Rihanna." He winks and then I blush bright red. I can't help it. How bloody embarrassing is he? Cute, but embarrassing.

Turning to Stacey, he speaks again. "Boys, this is Stacey, Lauren's best friend. Stacey, meet the band."

Stacey turns a similar shade of red to me when Jonny winks at her and the other three lads then reach out and shake hands with us. I really cannot believe that this is happening! That the entire line up of Reclamation are now exchanging handshakes with us first before going over to anybody else in the club, apart from the people around the entrance before us of course, but I'm not counting those! Wow, I think for the first time in my life, I'm coming over all fanlike myself. Maybe Stacey isn't the only crazy fan out of the two of us after all!

"Hey, sexy, we meet again." That's Ben, the overly perverted bassist from the club the other night, the one who's already receiving daggers from Jonny I notice.

Now that I'm getting the chance to meet him properly, Ben actually looks a little different to the photographs I've seen of him and he's slightly shorter than I imagined him to be. I'd say he's about five foot ten. He has dark blonde spiky hair with the most piercing blue eyes and even though he isn't the most attractive of men in my opinion, there's something a bit rough around the edges about him. Something no doubt that women go nuts about. He reminds me a little bit of a surfer with his rugged facial features and rough stubble. The tattooed arms and ear piercings complete his look, in typical rock band fashion.

I notice he's already moving on to Stacey, that familiar cheeky twinkle in his eye making Stacey instantly turn to mush. Oh dear, as much as I love Stacey, she does pick them. Usually the wrong ones, but then, so do I, if my last two relationships are anything to go by.

Next up is man of many musical talents and master of the rhythm guitar, keyboard, and basically any other instrument going, Will Parker. Will is the other looker of the group in my opinion, second in line to Jonny of course. He's the tallest one in the band, about six foot five, and with his unruly brown hair, golden skin, chiselled jawline and deep blue eyes, he's every woman's dream. Except mine. We all know who my dreamboat is but we won't get into that just now.

"Nice to finally meet the woman who's sent this one next to us into a tailspin since he saw you the other night. Great performance tonight too." Will winks at me and then smiles. Wow, he really is hot, and lovely, really really lovely. So complimentary. And he said that I sent Jonny into a tailspin? Well, not so sure about that considering the model like girlfriend of his that he strutted in here with just a moment ago. *Oh come on, Lauren, get a grip, now is not the time to start being bitchy.*

"Hey," says Zack, extending his hand. Zack Miller, the drummer of the band, is now saying hello to me and he definitely is your typical drummer with his shaggy, shoulder length dark brown hair, hazel eyes and grungy look. Out of all the band members, he is the one most famous for his many piercings, and not just on his face…apparently. I shake his hand and smile back.

"Hey, it's so lovely to finally meet you all," I say, looking at each one of them in turn. Well, all except Ben, who is now chatting up Stacey for England and is going to have absolutely no trouble getting into her knickers whatsoever. "Great show tonight," I continue, "and thank you for giving me the opportunity to sing with you all. It's something I'll never ever forget."

I look at Jonny when I say that and I notice the muscle in his jaw tick, his eyes seeming to flash with something although I'm not entirely sure what. Or maybe it's nothing at all. Maybe I'm just imagining it.

"Hey, we may just have a fifth member of Reclamation here, Jonny," says Will, nudging his band mate in the side. Jonny's face remains expressionless, his lingering gaze still firmly on me. Shit, does he really have to keep looking at me like that? No wonder I'm confused. He simply nods in response and then gestures towards the bar.

"Can I get you a drink?"

I turn behind me to pick up my cocktail. Raising my glass I say, "I'm good for now, thank you. Thanks for the two cocktails I've already had though, they were yummy."

Jonny breaks out into a knowing smile at that comment, shaking his head. "Some things never change," he murmurs.

"What?" I ask.

"You always did love a good drink."

I'm just about to protest when he suddenly slips in to stand next to me at the bar. He then proceeds to order himself a bottle of beer, as well as a vodka and coke with lots of ice and a slice of lemon for me. Just how I like it. Oh well, looks like I *will* be having another drink after all, courtesy of Jonny, my protests of not wanting another one clearly falling on deaf ears.

"You remembered what I like then?" I ask, taking a sip of my current drink, the cocktail.

Jonny turns around. Leaning his back against the bar, he folds his arms and says, "Oh, I remember everything you like, Lauren." *Oh my.* Flushing pink at his suggestive remark, I turn back towards the bar.

Will and Zack begin to notice the sudden tension developing between me and Jonny and are quick to slope off elsewhere, telling us they will see us later on. Stacey and Ben are now wandering away from the bar as well, hand in hand, heading off towards the dance floor. Well, he didn't waste any time with her, did he? Still, if Stacey has a great night then what the hell. At least Stacey knows what Ben wants from her. I just don't have a bloody clue what Jonny wants at the moment. Talk about mixed signals.

Time for small talk I think. "So…how were your interviews or whatever it was that you were doing before coming here?"

He shrugs, appearing disinterested. "I don't like doing interviews but as far as interviews go, they were okay I suppose."

Okay, so that didn't work. Time to down the rest of the cocktail and start on my vodka. I relish the last few drops of my 'Sex on the Beach' and then reach for my vodka and coke. And that's when Jonny turns back towards the bar. He reaches for my hand and links his fingers through mine, stopping any attempt at me picking up my drink. My pulse is now going through the roof and my heart is thumping in my chest because not only is he holding my hand in public, he's now giving me *that* look again.

I clear my throat nervously. "Jonny, what are you doing?" I ask quietly. An entire party being held in their honour is going on around us and yet he's standing here at the bar with me.

"I'm holding on to what's mine," is his reply. *Erm, what? Where the hell did that come from? You hate that I'm now a lap dancer and you have a girlfriend!* I snatch my hand away from his and pick up my drink.

"I don't think your girlfriend would be too happy if she saw you holding my hand." Shit, did I really say that out loud? I've clearly had too much to drink.

"What?" He looks confused and if I'm not mistaken, a little pissed off.

"Oh come on." I turn around and with a nod of my head, gesture towards the raven haired beauty who's currently in deep conversation with several people standing around her, mostly men I notice. "You can't keep that model like beauty a secret for much longer, Jonny, I saw you with her on the way in, all touchy feely and intimate." God, now I'm sounding a little bitchy, but Jonny doesn't even turn around to see who I'm talking about I notice, because, it seems, he doesn't need to.

"If you're talking about Lara, she's my PA, an employee of the label."

"Lara?" I ask in mock surprise. "Beautiful name as well as beautiful looks, *and* she works for you as well? She really must be the whole package, Jonny." I turn back towards the bar and slurp at my drink. Why the hell did I just say all of that? Oh well, too late now.

"What the fuck is wrong with you, Lauren? I said she works for me, that's it."

"Like her working for you would make any difference if you wanted to get into her knickers." And I'm off. Jealous, bitchy Lauren is making an appearance already and that took...five minutes.

Leaning in closer, hot breath against my ear, he mutters, "There has never been and never will be anything between me and Lara. As much as she would have loved there to be, believe it or not, I don't fuck around with my employees."

I make the mistake of turning my face towards his, my lips brushing with his in a fleeting moment. I quickly turn away again to break the dizziness of being so close to him. "Since when do you give a shit about breaking the rules?" I snap. Oh my word, I wish my mouth would stop already!

"I don't, but then...most of the rules I ever broke were the ones I broke with you." He always has to say the right thing doesn't he? Smooth talker. "Anyway, what's with all this jealousy shit all of a sudden? It's a bit rich considering what you do for a living, isn't it?"

And there it is again, his hatred of my job rearing its ugly head and I suddenly feel like I've just been slapped in the face. Again! I throw down the rest of my vodka and coke and turn to leave.

"Fuck you, Jonny," I mutter under my breath.

He comes after me, grabbing my arm. "Where are you going?"

I shrug my arm away from his grip and glare at him. "To go and find my best friend, Stacey, who, by the way, is also a lap dancer. I trust you'll no doubt give her a good dressing down while you're at it. Why stop at just me?"

"Lauren," he mutters, as if in warning.

"Just leave me alone, Jonny. Just stop with all this bullshit and leave me alone."

Before he can respond, I quickly walk away. That's it for me. I've had enough of Jonny and his judgemental attitude. I've also had enough of his mixed signals. I'm done. Totally and utterly done. Time to go and find Stacey and leave I think.

****

It's half an hour later and I'm still here. I'm still here at the after show party and it's all thanks to Stacey who did not want to go home due to being so loved up with Ben.

After threatening to go home on my own, she finally managed to tear herself away from the wandering hands of Ben to spend some time with me. Jonny didn't follow me after I stormed away from him and I'm glad, because I'm now busting some moves with Stacey on the main dance floor downstairs, well away from the VIP area, well away from the party, but most of all, well away from Jonny.

I just can't believe him. I honestly can't believe what he said to me earlier on. He's so up and down, and has been since we first bumped into each other at the club the other night. So much so that it makes me wonder if he's back on the drugs again. God, I hope he isn't. It was a living hell the first time round when Jonny became addicted to drugs and I'd hate to see him go down that self-destructive path all over again.

I shudder at the memory of finding him lying unconscious on our living room floor after his accidental overdose. Our coffee table was covered in remnants of white powder, used straws and tatty rolled up bank notes. Jonny was so desperate for his fix by that point that he'd literally use anything and everything just to get that high.

That was the final nail in the coffin for me and that was why he ended up in rehab. I was so desperate to get him better again that I had no alternative but to go to Jonny's parents and beg for their help. Little did I know that that would inevitably spell the end for us. As soon as Jonny's dad saw an opportunity to prise me away from his son, he took it.

Not wanting to delve back into that painful part of my past for a minute longer, I manage to pull myself out of my deepest, darkest memories. No, I don't think Jonny would be foolish enough to get addicted to that shit again. No, I just think he's finding the fact that I'm now a lap dancer really hard to accept. He seems to want me one minute and then snap at me the next, his anger seeming to bubble to the surface at the sheer mention of my job. A job I suddenly wish didn't exist.

That being said, he is far from being perfect himself and I know I've said this before but it's true. He is such a hypocrite and I hate that. How he can even dare to stand there and say those things to me when he's probably shagged his way through I don't know how many lap dancers in his time, I honestly don't know. Yes, I understand that it's because it's me who is now one of those lap dancers but that doesn't mean I'm the same as all those other women, although he seems to think it does. Well, fuck him. Fuck him and his stupid band. I'm going to enjoy myself tonight, even if it kills me.

And I'm certainly enjoying myself right now as Stacey and I strut our stuff together on the dance floor. Stacey is grinding her hips against mine, the pair of us boogying on down together to some upbeat dance tracks. We're attracting more than a few stares from the males in our vicinity but in my opinion it's completely harmless. Stacey and I have always enjoyed clubbing together, spending the vast majority of any night out on the dance floor. We're young, free and single and we enjoy a good boogie so I see no harm in what we're doing whatsoever. Until some utter tosspot thinks it's his god given right to start touching me up from behind.

I give Stacey the look and she backs away a little bit, giving me some extra space. As I move forward in an attempt at stepping away from the wandering hands, they move along with me. In fact, they're not just around my hips now, they're slowly moving down my thighs, and that's when I snap. I whirl around to face whoever it is and am met by some stoned looking, bedraggled man who clearly does not want to take no for an answer. Reaching for me again, he makes a grab for my waist this time and I try to back away but he's having none of it.

"Oh come on darlin', that's not very friendly now, is it?"

Instead of responding to him, I avoid any further eye contact and try to walk past him but he blocks my path. As the dance floor is pretty crowded, I can't make a quick exit in any other direction either so I turn around and Stacey turns around with me.

I start to follow her in a feeble attempt at pushing our way through the crowd but I suddenly find myself hauled backwards and into the arms of an overly eager stranger who clearly wants more than just a drunken dance. "Not so fast darlin', I only want a dance with you." *Yeah right!*

"Get off me!" I scream, trying to prise myself away from his vice like grip.

Due to the loud music, Stacey has only just noticed that I'm not following her and is quickly trying to get back to me, but all the other clubbers seem to be blocking her path, completely oblivious to what is happening around them.

The pervy drunk starts to whisper disgusting things into my ear, crushing my back against his chest, and that's when I really start to panic. Fear wraps itself around me, the club and all the people in it suddenly becoming a complete blur to me.

Oh no, not now. Please, not now. I can't have a panic attack now, not after all this time. Blood rushes in my ears and my heart almost thuds itself out of my chest, it's beating so hard. So fast. With fear. And panic. *No Lauren, don't have a panic attack, you haven't had one for a very long time, you can do this. This man isn't your dad! This man isn't your dad!*

"Get the fuck away from her, asshole!"

One minute I'm worrying about the onset of a panic attack because of almost being crushed to death by some perverted stranger, the next, the pervert is releasing me from his grip and turning towards the angry male voice, only to receive a punch to the face by none other than Jonny. I stumble backwards in shock as Jonny then launches himself at the man amidst shocked onlookers. *Holy shit.*

"Mother fucker!" Jonny takes another swing at the man but

thankfully, Jonny's bodyguards arrive on the scene just in time and are on him straight away, pulling him back. But he's wild with fury, like an uncaged animal intent on putting down whoever stands in his way, and that's when I suddenly burst into tears with shock. I hate seeing him like this. I've seen Jonny like this before and it's all because of his overwhelming need to protect me from other men. And that was for one reason and one reason alone. My dad.

Jonny was angry and devastated when he first found out about my dad hitting me. I somehow managed to keep it hidden from him for the first two years of our relationship. When he did eventually find out, he went crazy and stormed round to my dad's house, threatening to report him to the police, amongst other things. My dad just laughed in his face and squared up to Jonny. Jonny only being a teenager at the time decided not to challenge my violent father and so, he instead turned his back on my dad and took me along with him.

About a week later, Jonny found us a cheap flat to rent somewhere and that's when we officially moved in together. After that, Jonny became a lot more over protective of me, but in a nice way. Most of the time. We did have the occasional heated row over his over protective ways but they always got resolved one way or another, mostly through the steamiest of sex sessions. The last time he saw my dad though, the pair of them came to blows, after what my dad did....

Quickly pulling my mind back to the present, I notice the man is now goading Jonny, suggesting they finish off what Jonny started, but Jonny isn't having any of it. Wrestling against his own bodyguards, Jonny tries to break free from their grip. "Don't you ever touch Lauren again!" he shouts at the man, "do you hear me?!"

The man just laughs and attempts to walk towards Jonny in a

cocky like manner but is quickly stopped by club security who proceed to walk him away from the scene and throw him out on his ear.

Stacey is now at my side, her arm around my shoulders, comforting me, calming me. I look on at Jonny and feel so grateful to him for arriving when he did. I hate that he got into a scuffle because of me but I am so relieved he turned up at that moment otherwise I most probably would have been in the middle of having a panic attack right about now.

"Jonny…" I start to speak, wanting to give him my thanks for protecting me, but he cuts me off.

"You see what you've done?!" he yells. "You and your fucking dancing around poles and getting your kit off has done this, Lauren! No doubt he was a former customer thinking he could get that little bit extra from you! Is this what you want? To be the subject of perverts groping you every five minutes?!"

Oh my god, he couldn't be more wrong, and the fact that he thinks it's to do with my job, hurts, really hurts. My bottom lip starts to wobble as I fight to contain my emotions but it's no use, I can't contain them for a minute longer. Jonny's words have hurt me more than my dad's fists ever did and it takes everything within me not to hurl a barrage of abuse at him.

The only thing stopping me is the crowd of spectators surrounding us, people whispering and looking on in shock that Jonny Mathers, world famous rock star, has been fighting in the middle of a dance floor over a woman. A lap dancer. Yes, a lap dancer who deserved every bit of that groping I got just now, because that's what I am.

"Well, I guess that's what you would think, Jonny."

That's all I manage to say to him, and then I turn and walk away. And right now, all I want to do is carry on walking, because I really don't care if I never see him again.

****

It's the following morning and both Stacey and I are sat in front of the television eating a bacon sandwich. Stacey went out to get us one due to the fact that our fridge is looking a little bare at the moment. Bacon sandwiches weren't the only thing that she came back with though. She also came back with a newspaper tucked under her arm. A newspaper that tells the entire story of what went on at the concert last night. Yes, it's true, both Jonny and I have made the front pages of the tabloids this morning! A huge photograph of me and Jonny belting out our duet together on stage is plastered across the front page with a headline that reads:

A girl from Manchester meets a boy from Manchester. Sizzling chemistry on stage gets fans in a frenzy!

Even though I'm mortified at my face being put out there for the entire world to see, the article is actually quite nice. It's very complimentary of our performance but also makes suggestions about us possibly knowing each other. Which we do, obviously, but I don't want the entire world to know that.

I have a feeling that the entire world are going to know absolutely everything about me and Jonny in the not too distant future though. If our duet is already in the papers this morning, it's only a matter of time before word gets out about his altercation in the club with that man last night. Reporters are everywhere and even though I do feel a little sorry for Jonny having to live his life constantly in the limelight, I still feel angry and bitter because of his stinging verbal attack against me last night. His words were like poison to me and I'm still finding it hard to erase them from my mind.

It's only now that I'm looking at this newspaper article that I feel really sad. We were in a good place when we performed this duet together, almost like we were a couple again. Jonny got me up there to give me a chance to perform in front of thousands and he did it without even a second's thought. And then, after apologising to me, he went on to throw my career choice in my face. Again! I just don't get it and it seems that Stacey doesn't get it either but that hasn't stopped her from defending him. Oh no, she's been trying to make excuses for Jonny all morning, as well as going on and on about Ben the bassist.

It turns out that Stacey exchanged more than just a few snogs with Ben last night. Apparently, they exchanged phone numbers and even though Ben is a renowned womaniser, if the bleeping on Stacey's phone this morning is anything to go by, I'd say he was rather keen on my best friend. They've been texting each other back and forth for the last two hours and I know she is trying to be her best supportive self with me but I can see her mind is elsewhere. And I don't blame her. I'd be fed up of me by now as well.

"Right, that's it, just go and bloody well meet him and get it over with." I sigh, shoving my now empty plate on to the coffee table in front of me. Curling my legs back up on to the sofa, I turn to look at my friend who is, as you can probably guess, still texting.

"And leave my now famous best friend to reach the depths of depression all over again after the state you were in last night? I don't think so, Lauren, nice try."

"Look, I'm fine. I've been through a whole lot worse, Stacey, believe me." If only Stacey knew just how much shit I've been through in my past. The less said about that though, the better. When Stacey doesn't respond to me due to being in "Ben world", that's when I finally snap.

"Look, Stacey, you're away with the fairies anyway so just go and meet Ben for crying out loud and do whatever it is you two want to do to each other and leave me in peace!" Okay, so that came out a little harsher than I wanted it to but her stubbornness about not leaving me on my own is beginning to get on my nerves. And it works, because she finally looks up at me.

"Are you sure?" Wow, she really is in dream world this morning. The Stacey I know and love would definitely have snapped back at me for sure.

I roll my eyes and turn my attention back to the television. "Yes," I sigh. "Just go and get laid and then come back and tell me how good he is." That gets a reaction, because she shoves me on the arm.

"Don't be so sure that's what we're going to be doing, Lauren Whittle!" I give her the "do you think I'm stupid?" look and shake my head.

"This is Ben the womaniser we're talking about here, Stace. The one who was saying all sorts of stuff to me at the club the other night. I'm kind of thinking that you're not going to be going out for a coffee with him if you get my drift."

"Well, coffee is over rated anyway," she replies. I can't believe it when she says that, the little minx.

"You little harlot, Stacey Kerr, don't go telling Jonny about what you plan on getting up to with Ben today, he may start giving you a lecture on sex before marriage." I can't help but stick that snide comment in. The way Jonny is going on at me at the moment, nothing would surprise me.

"I'm sure he could write a book on sex before marriage, Lauren Whittle, and no doubt three quarters of that book would be about the four and a half years he spent giving you the good stuff, as well as the filthy stuff."

I pick up the nearest cushion and swipe her across the arm with it. "Piss off!" I chuckle.

She dodges my next swipe with the cushion by leaping to her feet and getting out of the way. "Friend beater!" she retorts, backing away towards the hallway.

"Finally going to get ready for the rough and ready Ben then are we?" I ask in a silly voice.

She winks and then wiggles her hips. "Absolutely!"

CHAPTER 10

Well, I'm still curled up on the sofa in the living room of my apartment with my pyjamas on, feeling completely sorry for myself. Stacey left to go and see Ben just over an hour ago and even though I practically had to force her through the door to get her out of here, I must admit that I am now missing her company. Yes, it's now mid-afternoon and yes I should be keeping my mind occupied on other things. In fact, I should probably go out and do some food shopping, but I can't be bothered. I even got bored of the television not long after Stacey left. I'm now trying desperately to get into a new thriller I'm in the midst of reading on my kindle but it's no use, I can't follow that either.

I could go and have a long soak in the bathtub I suppose but even that seems like too much of an effort at the moment. Shit, what is wrong with me? Up until seeing Jonny last Saturday, I was fine. Completely and utterly fine. And then, without warning, he re-appears in my life like a bolt of lightning and just fucks everything up. I was content and settled and even though I still harboured feelings for him and found it hard watching his life being played out in the press, I coped. I don't know how I coped, but I did. But now I'm not coping and from the way Jonny was behaving last night, I'd say he isn't coping with it very well either.

We were always volatile though, and even though we're no longer together, that hasn't changed. Jonny's fiery personality used to clash with my strong headed stubbornness quite often and he always hated the fact that I used to stand up to him so damn much. It made for some interesting rows but then we always made up afterwards, passionately so. And all because we loved each other so much.

I sometimes think we loved each other too much but then, how can you love each other too much? Is it possible to love each other too much? I honestly don't know. But we did, I'm certain of it. And I'm pretty certain that's why Jonny's dad wanted me out of Jonny's life so badly, because of the extreme lengths that his only son was prepared to go to just to look after me, protect me, love me. Like I said last night, Jonny's impulsive need to protect me all stems from me having a violent father and that is something I cannot change, as much as I'd want to.

A sudden knock to the door of my apartment interrupts my thoughts and I bolt upright on the sofa. Who could that be at this time of the day then? I'm not expecting anyone as far as I know and Stacey didn't say to expect a delivery. She is partial to ordering things over the internet though and I suddenly wonder if it's that. But I have no makeup on and I'm still in my pyjamas with my hair piled up into a messy bun so I'm hardly in any fit state to answer the door. I pride myself in my appearance and Stacey is the only person to witness me looking like shit.

I do not want some hot delivery guy witnessing me looking like death warmed up. Hell, I don't even look warmed up! Another, more impatient knock to the door comes next and I find myself reluctantly standing up. Placing my kindle on the coffee table, I slowly saunter out of the living room and into the hallway.

As I get nearer to the front door, I suddenly start to feel a little apprehensive about answering it. What if it's somebody from the press about the fight in the club last night? What if it's somebody asking questions about my relationship with

Jonny after seeing us in the newspaper this morning? Oh shit, reporters can get hold of addresses so easily and now I really am starting to panic. I don't have a peep hole in my door either so I can't spy out the lay of the land first. Another knock confirms to me that whoever is standing on the other side of that door knows full well that I'm in. And whoever that someone is, they're not for moving.

Right, fine, let's open the door and get it over with then. Clearing my throat, I slowly unlock the door. Turning the handle, I notice my palm is sweaty. Shit, get a grip Lauren, it's probably some idiot with the wrong address. Or some persistent postman waiting on the other side with a package for Stacey. Yes, that's who it will be. Then why the hell do I feel so nervous?

It's only when I do take the plunge to open my front door I realise why I feel so nervous. Standing on the other side of it, dressed in the exact same clothes from the night before and looking almost as bad as I do, is Jonny. My former boyfriend and now famous rock star is standing in a corridor outside my poky little apartment in the middle of London. Oh hell, I knew I shouldn't have answered the door. My gut feeling was telling me not to answer this door and now I know why. I can *feel* Jonny's presence without having to see him.

He's wearing that pained expression on his face that knocks the wind out of me every time I see it. I've seen it so many times before and I don't want to see it again. My knee jerk reaction is to slam the door in his face and even though every thought in my head is telling me to do the exact opposite of that and just hear him out, I don't. I attempt to slam the door but of course, Jonny has other ideas, pushing his hand firmly against the other side, stopping the door from going any further. My feeble attempt at shutting him out seems suddenly pointless.

"Lauren, just hear me out please." His voice is low but firm and I can tell from the determined look on his face that he won't be sent away easily. Jonny is more than a little persistent and when he sets his sights on something, he *always* gets it. Well, he *used* to anyway.

I take a step back from the door and fold my arms. If he thinks I'm letting him into my apartment then he can think again. "Say what you have to say and then go." I try to make my voice sound as emotionless as possible because the last thing I need right now is to appear vulnerable to him.

"Can I at least come in?"

"No!" I snap.

Jonny looks a little taken aback by my quick reply. Well good, he deserves it, every bit of it. He slowly pushes the door a little further open and even though I'm trying my best efforts to keep my eyes on anything else other than him, I can still feel his eyes on me, raking over every inch of my pyjama clad body. I get goosebumps. I can't help it. I feel naked whenever he does that.

Okay, Lauren, get a hold of yourself and remain firm. You can do this. "How the hell did you find out where I live, anyway?" I ask that question even though I'm fairly sure I already know the answer. There's only one way Jonny could have found out where I live. Stacey.

"I saw Stacey arrive at the hotel earlier on to meet Ben and I admit it, I grilled her about telling me where you both live."

I can't help the small chuckle that escapes from my mouth when he says that. Grilled Stacey my ass, Stacey would have openly told him where we live just to get him to come over here and sort things out with me. She was practically defending him this morning.

"And you just strolled over here all on your own then, did you?" I can tell he's already becoming impatient with my sarcastic manner but I don't care, I want him to see how much he upset me last night. And not just last night. Every other time he's seen me since being in London.

"Tony's waiting for me downstairs."

"Of course he is," I sigh.

"Oh, just cut the bullshit, Lauren," he snaps. That gets my attention. My gaze now firmly locked on to his, I suddenly see the anger in his eyes. Shit, his glare is practically pinning me to the spot. "That man from last night? Who was he?"

Erm, what? Where the hell did that come from? Here we go again. I begin to massage my fingers into my temples in an attempt at trying to calm myself down, but my patience with him is slipping.

"If you'd have bothered to hear me out for yourself last night instead of throwing hurtful remarks at me in front of a nightclub full of people, you would already know that I have no idea who that man was and he didn't have a clue who I was either! He was just some pervert in a club who was trying his luck with the first female who happened to bump into him on the dance floor! He didn't know I was a lap dancer and was not a former customer of Carnal Desires! Happy now?!"

He slowly nods his head, still glaring at me. "Oh, I'm ecstatic, Lauren."

"So, you aren't even going to apologise for the nasty things you said to me in the club last night then? If not, turn around and go back to your hotel room, Jonny…"

"Look, I am sorry for what I said to you, okay? Of course I'm sorry for that. I shouldn't have said any of those things, I was well out of line, but I'm not sorry for defending you, Lauren.

That man attacked you! It may not have looked much to the people dancing around you but I know how it looked and it looked bad..."

"I know how it looked, Jonny, and as grateful as I am to you for coming to my rescue last night, I can take care of myself. The last thing I want is for you to get into trouble all over again because of me..."

"Not gonna happen, Lauren. If you're in trouble or being hurt in any way then I step in to protect you, end of."

"That man didn't hurt me last night, Jonny. He was just some overly drunk or stoned pervert looking for a quick grope on the dance floor, and anyway, I've managed to protect myself just fine for the last ten years without you in my life so you can rest easy now knowing I'm strong enough to fight my own battles."

Jonny frowns. "I never said you weren't strong enough. Lauren, you're one of the strongest people I've ever met. I just came by here today to apologise for what I said and also to make sure that you're okay after last night. Are you okay?"

I nod. "I'm okay, Jonny, honestly I am."

"You swear?" Jonny doesn't look convinced that I'm telling him the truth. I'm going to need to reassure him that little bit more I think. Without breaking eye contact, I take a step towards him.

"I swear." I never intended to whisper those words to him, but somehow or other, I did. And now, with our eyes still locked together across the threshold of my apartment, I'm suddenly aching to reach out and touch him, because maybe, just maybe, there is still a chance for us. A chance for us to be together again.

Mustering up the courage to finally do it, I slowly reach out my hand towards his face. My fingertips just about brush the soft skin of his left cheek before he suddenly pulls away from me, leaving me feeling foolish and well and truly rejected.

"Don't, Lauren," he says quietly, looking away from me. Flushing pink with embarrassment, I start to stutter my way through a pathetic apology.

"I'm sorry," I mumble, "I just thought that...maybe..."

Sighing heavily, Jonny says, "Thought what?" And just like that, I'm annoyed with him all over again. Annoyed with Jonny and his never ending mixed signals!

Taking a step back from him, I say, "Jeez, I don't know, Jonny, maybe I thought that you actually came over here this afternoon because you still care about me? Or maybe it's due to the fact that you said you were holding on to what's yours in the club last night – that something being me! Maybe it's even because you hauled me up on to that stage last night in a sing song in front of twenty thousand fans! Not to mention that moment we had in your dressing room after the show! Or maybe I imagined all of it, Jonny! Maybe you just don't care about me after all! How the hell should I know?!"

A look of disbelief washes over Jonny's face when I say that. "Care about you?" He almost laughs. "Lauren, didn't you hear anything I just said to you? Shit, I fucking loved you once upon a time!" he shouts at the top of his voice. "I loved you from the second I laid eyes on you when we were only fifteen years old so don't talk to me about caring about you!" he snaps. I notice he refers to the loving me part as being in the past tense, something that cuts deep with me. So deep to the point of pain. Physical pain.

"So you loved me once upon a time but not now?!" I shout back at him, "after everything we ever went through together and our love is now *past tense* to you?!"

"I don't know what the fuck you expect?!" he bites out.

Pointing an angry finger at me, he finally lets me have it, the last ten years of bitter resentment spewing out of him in all their horrifying glory. "You left me, Lauren! You fucking left me in that shitty rehabilitation centre in Manchester and you didn't even say goodbye! You just fucked off and went, like I meant *nothing* to you! Like everything we ever had together meant *nothing*! Do you know what that was even like, Lauren? Well? Do you?"

I shake my head at him, tears now pricking at the back of my eyes. I feel so ashamed of myself for doing what I did. If only he knew the truth, he might think differently. Maybe he wouldn't. Who knows. All I do know is that I cannot and will not tell him why I left.

"You clearly didn't love me enough, Lauren," Jonny says sadly. "Nowhere near the depth of love I had for you. Nowhere fucking near."

"That's not true," I say, shaking my head, "I loved you more than life itself…I still do."

"Nobody who loves somebody that much abandons them in their hour of need…nobody."

"I'm sorry, Jonny, really I am."

"I don't want to hear sorry from you anymore, Lauren. I just want an explanation as to why you left me, I think I deserve that much at least."

Shrugging my shoulders in defeat, I can't even seem to find the words to say anything at all, let alone lie to him. "Did it really all become too much for you, Lauren? The grief? What your dad did to us? My drug addiction? Did it really all become so fucking much for you that you just felt the need to run off and leave all of it behind and me along with it?"

After a brief moment of silence, I finally speak. "Yes," I lie, my voice wavering slightly. "I couldn't cope with any of it anymore." Lie. "You turned to drugs in your hour of need. Mine was to run away." Another lie. "And I'll forever live in regret, Jonny." Truth. "Because I've never stopped loving you…and I never ever will." Truth.

Shaking his head, he starts to back further away from me into the corridor outside my apartment. "Well, it's a bit late for that, Lauren. Actually, it's a lot late. About ten years fucking late," he mutters.

Sighing heavily, I say, "If that's what you think then you really shouldn't have come here today."

Jonny nods his head in agreement. "You're right, I shouldn't have come here today, but you know what? That's the fucking problem! You!" He points over at me once more. "You get under my skin and in my head and I just can't get you out of there! It's driving me crazy! You're driving me fucking crazy!"

Storming back over to me in a blind rage, he then slams his hands on either side of the door frame, his eyes blazing down at me. Lowering his voice, he says, "You are dangerous to me, Lauren, and you always were."

Looking up at Jonny right now, at his darkened eyes, aflame with both passion and anger as he goes to war with himself, his ragged breathing as he tries desperately to show some sort of restraint around me, I can't help but suddenly feel intensely turned on. Because this is the side of Jonny I went absolutely wild for. The side of Jonny that, back in the day, I wanted so desperately at times, I would literally do anything to get it. Which is why Jonny is one hundred percent correct. I really am a danger to him. I always was, and I always will be.

"You're right, Jonny," I say quietly, still holding his penetrating gaze, "I am dangerous for you, and I always was. Which is why you should leave. Leave and never look back."

Jonny begins to nod furiously. "I should leave, Lauren…I really should." Stepping over the threshold into my apartment, he finally closes the space between us. "But I won't," he says firmly, before suddenly grabbing at my face, taking me completely by surprise. "Because I can't." The painful expression from earlier returns to Jonny's face, his restraint finally slipping. "And I hate that I can't."

I open my mouth to respond but before I get the chance to speak, Jonny's mouth is crashing into mine at a hundred miles an hour, and finally, after an entire decade without him, I'm getting to touch him, smell him, taste him. Oh, the taste of him. He tastes of whisky and aftershave and cigarettes and everything Jonny. So much Jonny. God, I just want to dive into him so I can feel him everywhere. Absolutely everywhere.

Holding him firmly against me, I kiss him back with the force of a thousand kisses, telling him in my own way that I'm sorry for doing what I did to him all those years ago. For just upping and leaving him without ever saying goodbye.

Taking that as an invitation for more, Jonny begins to slowly back me into my apartment. Kicking the door shut behind him, I then plunge my fingers into his hair, pulling him further on to my mouth. Jonny responds with a low growl before shoving me up against my hallway wall. Quickly reaching my hand down, I start to fumble in desperation for the zipper on his jeans but to my disappointment, Jonny suddenly pushes my hand away.

"No, Lauren…wait…" he mumbles in protest, before wrenching his lips away from mine. Taking a step backwards and completely breathless, he shakes his head at me. *What the hell?*

"Jonny?" I reach out to touch his face but he takes another step back, shaking his head once more.

"Don't," he whispers, almost as if he's in pain, "please don't."

I don't think I've ever seen Jonny like this ever before. In all the years we were together the first time round, I never saw him looking so...torn. Hell, is this what I've reduced him to? Is this what my leaving has really done to him?

"Jonny," I whisper, feeling wretched. So wretched. And because I feel so wretched, I find myself unable to say anything else to him.

Well, actions speak louder than words sometimes. And this is one of those times. Reaching around the back of my head, I pull out the hair tie that's holding my messy bun together, my riot of blonde curls suddenly cascading around my shoulders, right down to the middle of my back. Jonny glances down at my curls before frowning up at me.

"Lauren, what are you doing?"

Pushing my hair tie over my hand and on to my wrist, I then reach for my pyjama top. Pulling it up and over my head in one swift movement, I toss that to the floor and then reach for my pyjama shorts.

Shaking his head at me, he mutters, "Don't."

Ignoring his protest, I hook my thumbs into the waistline of my pyjama shorts, slowly pulling them down my legs, making sure I keep eye contact with him the entire time.

Standing gloriously naked in front of him for the first time in ten years, I watch as Jonny slowly appraises my every inch, because, in spite of his protests, in spite of everything, he still wants me.

"You're...bare down there," he says, his voice coming out all gruff. Yes, I am bare down there. As a requirement of my job, I *have* to be, but I never used to be, which is why Jonny is having real trouble tearing his eyes away from the most intimate part of my body.

Eyeing the bulge in his jeans, I can't help but pass comment. "And you clearly like that I'm bare down there because you can't hide your desire for me, Jonny." Closing the distance between us, I gaze up into the now blazing eyes of the man I love. Pressing my mouth up against his ear, I whisper, "And you never could." Jonny clears his throat nervously but says nothing.

Pulling back slightly, I take a hold of his right arm. "You know, in all the years we were apart from each other, I always wondered if…"

"If what?" he asks quietly, his face deadly serious.

Glancing down at his arm, I whisper, "Whether you'd kept it? Kept the tattoo of my name on your arm?"

Holding up his right forearm, I soon get my answer. There, etched into his skin, is the first ever tattoo he got when he was with me. My name. *Lauren.* Swallowing back my emotions, I whisper, "You kept it." Our eyes lock together once more, Jonny's eyes lingering on my face for a long moment, the muscle in his jaw ticking madly.

"Of course I kept it," he whispers, "it was the only part of you I had left."

Letting out a breath I didn't even realise I was holding, I then reach for his face. He doesn't pull away this time, instead gently nuzzling his cheek into the palm of my hand. "I kept mine too," I whisper, referring to the tattoo of his name on my right ankle. Jonny's eyes close on a sigh, his lips finding the palm of my hand as he places a kiss there. "Take me to bed Jonny," I plead, "please take me to bed."

Jonny stops kissing my hand, instead placing his hand over

mine and linking our fingers together, the familiarity between us from long ago making my stomach flip. "Then show me the way," he finally whispers.

Feeling more relieved than I've ever felt in my life, I try not to show how nervous I am, instead tugging gently on Jonny's hand, leading him down the hallway to my bedroom. Pushing open my bedroom door, I then turn to watch as Jonny closes it behind him. And then he looks over at me, standing at the bottom of my double bed in the middle of my bedroom, waiting for him. I've been waiting for him for the last ten years and right here, right now, in this moment, I feel as though I need to pinch myself to believe that this is real. That he really is here, standing in front of me, stripping himself naked.

And what a sight it is. Jonny's tattoos on his chest are the first thing I notice, every single one of them on his torso all shiny and new to me. Not to mention sexy as hell. Jonny wouldn't be Jonny without his tattoos. The sleeves of tattoos he has on both arms have also been added to over the years. Jonny is literally a walking work of art, in every sense of the word.

Finally divesting himself of his boxer shorts, a naked Jonny slowly saunters his way over to me by the bed. Feeling suddenly overcome with emotion and almost dizzy like in his presence, I find myself having to grab on to him to make sure I don't fall. But boy am I falling. Falling for him all over again. And hell does he catch me.

Lifting me up from the floor by my thighs, Jonny then captures my mouth with his, kissing me with such gentle tenderness, I feel I might weep. Wrapping my hands around the back of his head, Jonny then slowly lowers me on to my bed. Crawling on top of me, he continues to kiss me, his tongue brushing gently with mine in soft strokes, his fingers now beginning to explore my body.

There isn't a part of my body that Jonny doesn't touch with his fingers or worship with his tongue. From the top of my head, all the way down to the tattoo of his name on my right ankle, he takes his time over me, caressing me, touching me, pleasuring me. Oh, the pleasure this man can give, his magical fingers working overtime as they play me to perfection to the tune of his song.

His breath whispers across my skin leaving goosebumps in its wake, every single part of my body tingling from head to toe, Jonny's slow, teasing build up with his tongue resulting in an almighty climax. An orgasm to end all orgasms. A sheet clawing, eyes rolling into the back of the head, seeing stars kind of orgasm. An orgasm the likes of which I haven't felt in a decade.

I then take the time to pleasure him in return, re-acquainting myself with his tattoos whilst saying hello to his new ones. I kiss him, take care over him, love him. I love him with my mouth and my fingers, kissing every single naked inch of his skin I possibly can. To the point where Jonny can no longer handle it.

Suddenly flipping me over so that I'm flat on my back, Jonny braces himself above me, his eyes wild with passion. "I'm done with the foreplay, tell me you want me," he breathes.

Reaching slowly up to caress his cheek with the tip of my finger, I whisper the words, "I want you."

Letting out a ragged breath, Jonny then whispers, "Tell me you need me."

Running the tip of my finger back and forth across his bottom lip this time, I whisper, "I need you…I've always needed you, Jonny."

Placing his forehead against mine, his eyes close for the

briefest of moments. "Oh, Lauren," he whispers, his words barely audible. And then suddenly his mouth is on mine, bruising and passionate, a no holds barred kiss that has me writhing against him in desperation.

"Make love to me," I beg, "please."

Suddenly wrenching his lips away from mine, he frowns down at me. "Lauren, we need to be careful, we should use a condom."

Brushing a hand through his hair, I say, "I'm on the pill, Jonny, and I'm clean…and…I want to feel you, skin to skin."

He still looks a little uncertain. "Are you sure? I'm clean too, but we'll only do this if you're sure."

Smiling up at him, I say, "I've never been more sure about anything in my life." Reaching up, I kiss him softly on the lips and he sighs against my mouth.

"God, I've missed this…I've missed you," he whispers.

Bracing himself above me once more, he gently parts my legs with his knees as I guide him slowly inside. I can't help the anguished cry that escapes my lips as Jonny gently thrusts himself into me, filling me completely.

"Fuck," he bites out, "oh, Lauren, you feel fucking amazing. You always felt so amazing."

Jonny starts to move inside me, slow at first, the gentle rhythm kissing my insides, bringing about all sorts of emotions within me. Jonny showers me with kisses all over my face and neck, and I cling on to him, kissing him back, pulling him further into me, urging him to go faster, to move inside me harder.

"Harder," I moan, "I need it harder."

Jonny growls at my request, upping his tempo as he surges

into me over and over and over again. But it still isn't enough for me. With Jonny, I could never get enough. "I need more," I pant, "let me ride you."

Jonny doesn't need telling twice. Taking me with him, he rolls us both over so that he's flat on his back on the bed and I'm on top, straddling him. Threading my fingers through his, I slowly sit myself up, Jonny still buried deep inside of me.

Placing his hands on my hips, I then start to ride him. I ride him fast and hard. And deep. So very deep. In fact, Jonny is so deep rooted within me right now that I don't know where Jonny begins and I end. We are one now. One frenzied, tangled mass of fire and passion, love and anger. So much anger still there. I can see it in his eyes, I can feel it in his grip, his fingernails practically digging into the skin on my hips. But I want it this way. I need it this way. And so does he.

Leaning over, I continue to ride him as I grab at his face, kissing him passionately. He responds with a growl, his teeth clacking together with mine as we begin to surge towards our climax together, Jonny's hands relentless in their quest to get himself in and out of me as fast as possible. And that's when I feel it. The oh so familiar sensation building inside me all over again.

"Oh god," I moan against his mouth.

Jonny groans. "That's it baby," he breathes, "come for me now and take me with you."

I finally reach my climax, wave after wave of pleasure hitting me head on like a freight train. I cry out loudly against his lips, shouting out to God and the heavens as Jonny slams into me one final time before flipping us over again. Pressing my hands into the mattress above my head, he drives me back into the bed and continues to fuck me hard, chasing his own climax whilst drawing out mine. I watch in a hazy blur of pleasure as he throws his head back, groaning my name loudly, his body juddering against mine as he floods my womb with his release.

When he's given me absolutely everything, he falls limp against me, his hot sweaty body sticking to mine, his breathless pants in my ear. I want to stay in this moment with him forever. I feel so ecstatically happy about our reunion that I simply don't want to move away from him ever again. Jonny though, for whatever reason, seems to feel differently.

Pulling out of me far earlier than I would have liked, he then rolls away from me on to his back, instead staring up at the ceiling. Turning to look at him, I feel a sudden chill run through me. He looks…uncomfortable. I start to wonder whether I'm just being overly paranoid, until he sits himself up at the end of the bed without saying a single word to me. He's turning his back on me and I don't know why.

"Jonny?" I say, daring to break the silence that's suddenly descended between us. "Are you okay?"

I'm met with a sigh, swiftly followed by him tugging his boxer shorts back on. Oh, I get it now. I see what's going on here.

"You're regretting me already?" I ask, my voice quivering a little. I can't help it. I'm gutted. Devastated, in fact. And after the earth shattering sex we've just had together? It doesn't make any sense. Sitting up on the bed, I continue to press him for an answer. "Well?"

Jonny sighs at me once more. "Of course I don't regret you… I…"

"You what?" I snap, quickly becoming impatient with him.

"Look, I'm fucked up, Lauren!" he snaps back at me. "My head is well and truly fucked and honestly? I don't know what I want anymore."

"You wanted me just a few minutes ago," I bite out, "but not now?"

He frowns. "This has nothing to do with not wanting you, Lauren. Of course I want you. I still…" Looking suddenly uncomfortable again, he instead reaches for his jeans from the floor. Standing up, he pulls them back on. "I just don't think I can trust you ever again."

"But…we can re-build that trust together, Jonny. I can rebuild that trust with you…if you let me. I swear it's my biggest regret. I would never leave you ever again."

Doing up his zipper, he then fixes me with a long stare. "And what if things get tough between us again? What if I start doing drugs again? And I can't promise that I won't because I've been in and out of rehab so many times over the last ten years that I've now lost count. I still have trouble fighting that addiction, Lauren, even now. The life I lead these days is…well it's a world away from the life we once had together in Manchester. I'm constantly surrounded by temptation and when it comes to drugs, I'm weak, and I always will be."

Standing up from the bed, I quickly reach for my satin dressing gown from the back of the door. Wrapping it tightly around me, I then turn back to Jonny. "I want to live that life with you, Jonny. It'll take some getting used to on my part but I want to be with you no matter what. And if things get tough again then I will be right there with you this time, where I belong."

Jonny's face darkens when I say that to him. Yanking his t-shirt back on, he then scowls over at me. "You should have been there the first time, Lauren, but you weren't."

I shake my head at him. "You sound so bitter."

Sitting back down on the end of my bed, Jonny starts to pull on his socks and boots. "Bitter doesn't even cover how I feel at the moment," he mutters.

Feeling exasperated at being unable to somehow get through to him, I start to get angry again. Angry and accusatory. Not a good mix.

"So, what was this afternoon then, Jonny? Huh? Just an afternoon of you getting your end away? Or maybe it was your way of revenge? Getting me back for walking out on you all those years ago? Making me believe that we could make another go of it together when in actual fact you had no intention of ever giving me another chance!"

"Don't be so fucking ridiculous!" he shouts.

"So what was it then?!" I yell back at him, "I deserve a bloody answer at least!"

"It was nostalgia!" he snaps.

"Nostalgia?!" I almost laugh at his pathetic excuse. "Really, Jonny? Nostalgia?"

Sighing heavily, he gazes up at me from the bed, his eyes lingering on mine for a long moment. "And memories." Swallowing hard, he says, "I wanted to erase the hatred I felt towards you after you left me, and I wanted to replace that hatred by remembering our happiest times. I haven't been able to get my head to remember the happy stuff, Lauren. Every time I see you I just feel so…angry all the time. But in spite of all that anger, I still want you. Badly. So badly that we ended up in bed together and…it was amazing, so fucking amazing that at one point, when I was still inside you…I felt like we were back in Manchester again. Back to how we used to be. But then it all ended and reality quickly set in and unfortunately, so did my anger."

"So, that's it?" I ask impatiently. "you're just going to give up on us because you're still *so* angry with me?"

Standing up from the bed, he glances down at the floor before looking up at me again. "I'm not saying that, Lauren. I just need time to think because whenever I'm around you I feel like I'm suffocating, like I can't breathe, like I'm drowning in you."

"It's called love, Jonny," I bite out, "because that's exactly how I feel whenever I'm around you!" I jab my finger into his chest when I say that to him.

He sighs. "I just need some time, Lauren, that's all I'm saying."

"Well, you can have all the time you need, Jonny, because if you want space, you need to leave. Right now."

"Oh, you want me to leave right now?" he snaps.

Reaching for the door handle, I yank open the bedroom door and look away from him. "Right now," I mutter. "And close the front door on your way out."

He doesn't close the door on his way out. He slams the door. On me. On us. Maybe forever.

CHAPTER 11

"So, let me get this straight, you and Jonny went to bed together and then he just…upped and left you afterwards?" asks a shocked looking Stacey. I let out a heavy sigh. It sounds even worse when said out loud.

"He said he doesn't know whether he can trust me again, Stace, and you know what? I can't say I actually blame him really. I mean, would you trust somebody again after they just abandoned you at the worst ever time in your life?"

She shakes her head at me and starts waggling her finger in mid-air. "Oh no, don't start with that shit. You had no choice but to leave him! His dad gave you no choice!" she yells at me from across the kitchen table.

"He doesn't know about his dad's intervention though, does he?!" I yell back at her.

Shit, even we're arguing with each other now! Stacey has been back in our apartment for barely ten minutes after spending the entire afternoon with Ben, and we're already at each other's throats. Something I dreaded might happen. Especially as I've suddenly gone on the defensive about Jonny and his actions earlier on this afternoon. And probably because I spent the last couple of hours after he left, all on my own. Thinking. Thinking that Jonny is right to distrust me. Thinking that yes, he does need some time to think things over about his future with me. It's only a pity that he didn't think about his future with me before he took me to bed.

Still, I didn't exactly discourage him this afternoon even though I could see he was reluctant. He initially pulled away from me in an attempt to stop things from going any further and I just turned it around and used his weakness against him. That weakness being me standing in front of him with no clothes on whatsoever. Yes, this is my fault. I started something that I wanted Jonny to finish. I just didn't expect it to finish with him telling me he had to re-think things.

"Look, Stace, he just needs time to think…"

"You should tell him, Lauren!" Stacey shouts, "you should tell him everything!"

I shake my head at her. "No way, I can't tell him, I won't do that to him and his family."

She screws up her face in anger. "So? What? Jonny's dad wins again? Just like he won the first time round?"

"It isn't about Pete Mathers winning!" I snap, "it's about me protecting Jonny from himself! I've told you this before, Stace, if Jonny found out his dad was the sole reason for me leaving then he would go ballistic, and that's putting it mildly."

"Jonny needs to know the truth, Lauren," Stacey urges, "regardless of the consequences."

Letting out an exasperated sigh, I say, "It would drop a bomb on his family unit and his music career and…he would most likely go off the rails again into drugs and god knows what else and I can't be the one responsible for wrecking his life again, Stace. I won't. And as my best friend, you must promise me that you will say nothing and stand by my decision."

Folding her arms across her chest in annoyance, Stacey huffs loudly. "I don't stand by your decision, Lauren, but I promise I won't say anything to Jonny…or Ben. I'm your best friend, even if I want to kill you right now for being so stupidly stubborn."

I shrug my shoulders in defeat. "Stupidly stubborn I may be but…I promise you it's for the best for all concerned and…you never know, once Jonny has cleared his head properly and had time to think, he may want to try again after all. I just have to be patient and give him some space."

Stacey rolls her eyes at me. "Give you some space?" she scoffs, "hell, Jonny practically made a beeline for me almost as soon as I stepped over the threshold into that hotel to see Ben this afternoon. He couldn't get to see you quick enough. And now he's suddenly telling you that he needs some space?" She shakes her head at me. "I'm sorry, Lauren, but that's unfair."

Placing my forehead in my hands, I sigh. "I know that's how it looks but…Jonny's head seems to be in a bad place at the moment and to be honest, mine isn't in the best place either. We have huge history together and our reunion seems to be dragging up nothing but the darkest memories of our time together. We were so happy together, until…"

"Until?" questions Stacey, her voice calmer than it was before.

I look up into the soft, pleading eyes of my best friend. A best friend desperate for answers. Answers that, since finding out about my past relationship with Jonny, she's never probed me for. And probably never will. Because Stacey knows deep down that something bad happened to me. Something so bad that I can't even bear to say it out loud, never mind think about it.

"I know that you don't want to tell me the full story about your break up with Jonny," she says quietly, "but if you do ever feel the need to tell me about it then…I'm here for you, Lauren, as and when you need me. Okay?"

Feeling a little teary at her heart-warming gesture, I reach over for her hand. Knotting my fingers through hers, I say,

"One day, Stace, I will tell you everything…I promise." She smiles, and I take that as an opportunity to finally change the subject. "Anyway, that's enough depressing talk for now, why don't you tell me all about your afternoon with Ben instead?"

Stacey's demeanour completely changes at the sheer mention of Ben, her dazzling smile almost blinding me. "How long have you got?" she asks, wiggling her eyebrows suggestively.

Glancing over at the clock on the kitchen wall, I say, "Not long, we start work in an hour."

Grinning like the cat who got the cream, she says, "I better talk fast then."

****

It's a long shift at work that night, my mind whirring with thoughts of all things Jonny. It's only a relief that it's a Thursday night and not a show night. At least when I'm just pole dancing, I can do it without thinking. The men in the audience get what they want while I get to lose myself in my own thoughts for a short while. It's only a pity that said thoughts are upsetting ones.

Stacey did her best to cheer me up earlier on though, telling me all about the intimate details of her afternoon with Ben. And when I say intimate details, I mean seriously intimate. In fact, I'm surprised that girl is even walking straight tonight, never mind pole dancing. Ben doesn't have a reputation with the women for no reason so it's no wonder that Stacey can't stop smiling.

The trouble with Stacey though is that when a man comes along who she really really likes, she falls hard for them. She wears her heart on her sleeve and hides nothing when it comes to her feelings and emotions. You always know where you stand with Stacey. I just hope that Ben doesn't break her heart.

I also hope that Stacey is going into this thing with Ben with her eyes wide open because she also told me earlier that he wants to see her again. A first for him apparently. I just hope I'm not the one having to pick up the pieces of her broken heart afterwards. Mind you, at this rate, I'll be picking up the pieces of my own broken heart right along with hers.

I breathe a sigh of relief when 2.00 am finally rolls round, both Stacey and I retiring to my dressing room together after the last customers leave the club. I notice that Stacey is still looking bright eyed and bushy tailed whereas I feel completely deflated. Miserable in fact.

"You okay?" asks Stacey, pulling me out of my depressing reverie. Glancing up into the dressing table mirror, I see Stacey standing behind me, a look of concern now plastered across her pretty features.

I manage a small smile. "Yeah, I'm fine. I'm just tired and it's been a really long day so a good night's sleep will do me the world of good."

"You sure?" She doesn't look convinced.

Turning around, I fold my arms in defiance. "Yes, I'm sure. Now stop worrying about me, will you?"

"You know that's never going to happen, right?" she says.

I smile at her. "Right."

She smiles in return. "See? I just made you smile." She flashes me a cheeky wink before starting to get herself dressed.

"That's because you're magic, Stace."

Chuckling to herself, she says, "That's what Ben said to me this afternoon." We laugh, and then finish getting ourselves dressed before leaving the club.

Pulling the front door closed behind me, Stacey and I step out onto the pavement. The cool night air hits my face and I inhale deeply, enjoying the crisp like freshness after being stuck in a stuffy, sweaty club for the last few hours. It may be July but in typical UK fashion, the night air still feels a little cool and for once, I am grateful for it. Stacey begins to chatter away to me as we slowly make our way along the pavement.

Out of the corner of my eye, I suddenly notice a black car parked alongside the pavement, just a little further down from the club. As we get nearer, I notice it isn't just any black car, it's a black Range Rover, just like the one me and Stacey travelled in after the show on Wednesday night.

My stomach flips in excitement. Could it really be Jonny? No, surely not, not after everything he said to me this afternoon about needing some space. But it's his car, I'm certain of it, it has blacked out windows and everything.

Hope starts to rise within my chest, my heart fluttering as I see the back door of the car being flung open. I swear my heart stops entirely as I see a black boot stepping out onto the pavement. I grab a hold of Stacey, stopping her mid conversation.

Looking over at the car, she soon latches on to the fact that this car is clearly waiting for us. And the man stepping out of that car and onto the pavement is none other than…Ben?

Well, as happy as I am for Stacey right now, I have to admit that I'm bitterly disappointed that the boot doesn't belong to Jonny. Unless Jonny is in the back of the car as well? *Here's hoping Lauren, here's hoping.*

Stacey looks at me excitedly, her eyes swimming with happiness as she releases me to go and run over to her rugged looking bassist. Ben grins at her wickedly, scooping her up into his arms as he plants one hell of a smacker on her lips.

"You miss me?" he asks, grinning down at her.

"Hell, yes!" she squeals, kissing him back.

Great, yet another public display of affection. Still, I shouldn't get jealous. Stacey deserves to be happy, and more.

Slowly approaching the two lovebirds, I manage to sneak a quick peek in the back of the car without them noticing. The back seat is empty. *Of course it's empty.* My stomach drops to the floor as realisation finally dawns on me that no, Jonny isn't with Ben after all. I was stupid to even think it. Stupid stupid stupid!

"Hey Lauren," says Ben, pulling my attention from the empty car seat. Turning to look up at him, I'm met with a huge grin. "If you're looking for Jonny, then…"

"I'm not looking for Jonny," I say, immediately going on the defensive.

Ben nods his head, his grin slowly fading. "Okay, fair enough."

Knowing that Jonny is a touchy subject, he quickly turns his attention back to Stacey, smiling down at her like a loved up school boy. Right, time for me to leave I think.

"Okay, well, I'll be heading home then. I'll see you tomorrow, Stace."

Brushing past the pair of them, I am all set to walk home alone, when Ben calls me back. "Hey, where do you think you're going?"

Turning back round, I frown over at the pair of them. Holding out my arms, I say, "Erm…home?"

Ben shakes his head at me. "Not on your own you're not. I came here tonight to give you two lovely ladies a chauffeured lift home with me and Tony, and a lift home you'll get. Now get in the car."

Stacey raises an eyebrow at him. "Bossy much?"

He breaks out into a mischievous grin, his eyes twinkling wickedly. "I thought you loved me being bossy."

Biting down on her bottom lip, she says, "Mmm, I guess I do." She giggles. *Oh, to hell with this.*

"Right, fine, I will get in the car."

Walking back past them, I am just about to get into the back of the car when Ben says, "There's one condition attached to this lift, you know."

Rolling my eyes, I say, "And what's the condition?"

"That you allow me to stay over at your place tonight?"

Turning back round, I raise my eyebrows at him in surprise. Stacey I notice looks as shocked as I am. "You want to stay over at mine?" she asks in complete disbelief, "with me?"

Grinning down at her once more, he says, "Yeah, baby, I wanna stay over with you…if that's okay with boss lady over there of course?" Hmm, that'll be me then!

"You want to stay over at our place when you're currently renting out a penthouse suite in a swanky mid London hotel that's bigger than our entire apartment?" I ask.

He shrugs. "I know you may find this hard to believe, Lauren, but I actually wanna see where Stacey lives. I also just wanna escape the glare of the fans and the press by avoiding the hotel for a little bit."

Ah, sweet. And shocking. Deeply shocking really, considering what Ben's supposed to be like. Hmm, maybe there's more to Ben than I originally thought. Perhaps I shouldn't be so judgmental and maybe give him a chance.

"Fine," I reply.

"You won't regret this, Lauren," he says, flashing me a cheeky wink.

"Hmm, I hope not. Oh, and the condition to you staying over is that you keep the noise down."

Flushing pink with embarrassment, Stacey shies away from Ben's reaction by burying her face into his leather jacket.

Grinning, Ben says, "Well, I can't make any promises to you on that front, darlin', but I can promise you that I'll at least try. And I'll try *really really* hard."

Rolling my eyes once more at the suggestive idiot, I put an end to the conversation by slipping into the back seat of the Range Rover. Nodding a quick hello in Tony's direction, I then sink into the luxurious leather car seat and strap myself in.

Well, Jonny may not be here right now but at least Ben came in his place. And I know he only really came for Stacey but in a roundabout sort of way, he's taking care of me too. By making sure I get home safe. And for that simple act of kindness, he can stay over for as long as he wants to, because if Stacey is happy, then I'm happy, and right now, I'll take any shred of happiness I can get.

****

Surprisingly, and thankfully, I don't hear any noise coming from Stacey's bedroom at all during the night. In fact, it's only upon waking up the following morning when I first hear something, and even then it's nothing rude.

Lying back in my bed, I smile to myself as I hear Stacey giggling like mad through the wall, Ben most likely carrying out some sort of playful attack on her as they roll around in bed together. I can hear the murmuring of Ben's voice every now and again and Stacey's muffled laughter and I can't help but start to feel sorry for myself all over again.

Hearing those two this morning just reminds me of what Jonny and I used to be like. Loved up teenagers fooling around together without a care in the world for anything or anybody else. Hell, we were like that all the time. I hardly remember a morning when we weren't giggling together in bed, wrapped up in nothing else but each other.

Some days, we spent nearly all day in bed, only getting out every now and again to grab something to eat or to go to the toilet. Jonny would sometimes strum on his guitar and sing to me for hours and hours, me fixated on him, him on me. We had no television, hardly any money, and not much in the way of material possessions, but boy we were happy. Money may make the world go round for a lot of people but really and truly, it can't buy you happiness, as Jonny has since found out himself.

Some time later, I decide to finally haul my sorry ass out of bed and go for a shower. Dressed in my pyjamas, I grab a bath towel from my drawer and head out into the hallway towards the bathroom.

Walking into the bathroom, my mouth drops open in shock when I'm met with a full on rear view of Ben. Stark bloody naked! Standing under the shower in the bath tub. My bath tub!

Glancing over his shoulder, Ben is seemingly unaffected by my being there, instead grinning at me from ear to ear whilst continuing to soap himself up good and proper.

"Hey, Lauren, if you wanted a threesome, you only had to ask for it." He laughs. Shaking my head at him, I slam the door behind me and head down the hallway, towards the kitchen.

Stacey is already in the kitchen putting on a pot of coffee and humming happily to herself. She smiles up at me as I approach her. "Hey, Lauren, you okay?"

"Well, I was okay, until about thirty seconds ago when I walked into the bathroom and saw your new boyfriend showering in the nude."

Stacey bites down on a smile. "Oops, sorry."

I can't help but smile back at her. "He suggested a threesome, you know?"

She frowns. "He what?"

I burst out laughing. "Oh come on Stace, he was kidding…I think."

She rolls her eyes. "Well with Ben, you never know."

"Never know what, ladies?"

Both of us turn to see Ben strolling into the kitchen. Fresh from his shower and dripping wet, he's wearing nothing more than a white bath towel wrapped tightly around his waist. Normally, Ben wouldn't be my type with his blonde spiky hair and rugged facial features, however, I reserve judgment on that this morning looking at the body on him.

He has a six pack to die for and one hell of a V. He also has a huge tattoo of some sort of dragon adorning the entire left side of his body. Starting just under his armpit, it snakes itself all the way down towards his abdomen, dipping right into the waistline of his towel. Hmm, I wonder where that dragon ends? I'll have to ask Stacey.

"Never mind what we were talking about," says Stacey, reaching up to kiss him.

"Hey, baby," he says, grinning down at her.

"Hey," she replies, kissing him again.

"Seriously, you two need to get a room."

"We have one," says Stacey, smiling over at me.

I roll my eyes at the pair of them. "Well stay in it and bloody well use it then," I say, chuckling.

"You coming with?" Ben asks me, raising a suggestive eyebrow.

Stacey pokes her index finger into his ribs. "Hey you, enough with all the flirting and the whole threesomes thing!"

Holding up his arms in the air, as if in defence, he says, "Just kidding." Grinning, he then flashes a cheeky wink in my direction. "Maybe."

Reaching for the tea towel from the kitchen worktop, Stacey takes a swipe at him with it, forcing him to make a run for it. Stacey gives chase, the pair giggling again like they were this morning.

I then hear a bedroom door slamming shut. About a minute ticks by before I finally realise that they won't be coming back out of the bedroom any time soon. Turning back to the coffee that Stacey had made a start on, I decide to take over where she left off. Looks like I'll be making coffee for one then.

****

Some time later, the lovebirds emerge from their newfound love nest, the pair of them looking a little giddy and somewhat dishevelled as they re-join me in the living room.

Curled up on the sofa reading my kindle, I can't help but make a quip. "There's still some coffee left in the pot, although I think it might have gone cold by now."

I glance up at them. Ben pinches Stacey's bum before wrapping his arms around her waist from behind. She squeals in surprise before smiling up at him in adoration.

Honestly, as happy as I am for my best friend, these constant public displays of affection from the pair of them this morning are really starting to make me feel sick. And only because I'm jealous. Jealous of something that I no longer have with Jonny. Which is why I need to distract them. And fast.

"Hey, Stace, how about you go and put a fresh pot of coffee on and leave me to get properly acquainted with your new boyfriend?"

Switching off my kindle, I place it on the coffee table and smile up at them both. She narrows her eyes on me, as if silently berating me for something. I don't know whether she's telling me off for suggesting she make the coffee or for insinuating that Ben is her boyfriend but either way, it works.

"Fine," she says, pulling out of Ben's grip, "I'll go and make the coffee."

Stacey heads over to the kitchen as Ben perches himself on the end of the sofa. Placing his right ankle over his left knee, he rests back against the cushions and looks over at me.

"So, you wanna get to know Stacey's new boyfriend do you?"

Rolling my eyes at him, I say, "Enough with the suggestive comments already. I mean, can you ever be serious? Even for a minute?"

He scowls over at me. "Hey, I can be serious, sweetheart."

"Then be serious by answering something for me," I say, deliberately lowering my voice.

Ben glances over at Stacey who's now busying herself in the kitchen with the coffee. Looking back over at me, he fixes me with a serious stare.

"You're worried I'll break her heart," he says quietly.

"Should I be worried?" I ask, trying to keep my voice down.

He shrugs. "Lauren, Stacey knows where she stands with me. She knows what I am and what I do and we're having a lot of fun together. Where's the harm in that?"

With a heavy sigh, I say, "I just don't want her heart getting broken, that's all."

Ben glances over at Stacey in the kitchen once more, his eyes softening slightly as she innocently goes about her business, completely unaware of the serious conversation we're having over in the living room. For the first time ever, I think I see a different side to Ben in that moment, a tenderness that perhaps lies beneath all that bad boy, man whore, bravado like image that he impresses upon people.

Turning back to me, he says, "I really like her, Lauren, and…I'd never intentionally hurt her…okay?" The serious expression on his face and the genuine look of honesty in his eyes tells me all I need to know. That he's telling me the truth.

With a nod of my head, I say, "Okay."

He nods back at me before turning his attention back to Stacey who is now walking over to join us again, this time with a tray in her hands.

"Coffee's up," she says, placing the tray of cups down onto the coffee table.

"Service with a smile eh, babe?" says Ben, "I love it."

She beams down at him before sitting herself onto his lap. He pulls her in for yet another kiss and the lurch in my stomach is so strong this time that I find myself unable to hold back from commenting.

"Jeez, can't you two come up for air for even a minute?" Oops, I never intended for it to come out quite like that but, nevertheless, it works. Pulling apart, the pair of them look over at me in surprise. "Sorry, I didn't mean to say it like that but...well..." I try to stutter my way through some sort of apology but thankfully, Ben comes to the rescue.

"No need to apologise, Lauren, we have been a bit...full on this morning." Stacey giggles as Ben nuzzles his nose into her neck.

"Just this morning?" I ask, unable to keep the sarcasm from my voice.

Ben's mouth pulls into a wide grin. "You know something, Lauren? You are one smart ass woman with one hell of a smart ass mouth to go with, I can see why Jonny likes you."

Huffing loudly, I reach over for my coffee. "I don't think Jonny likes me very much at the moment." Blowing over the surface of my coffee, I then take a quick sip.

"Doesn't like you?" scoffs Ben, "jeez, Lauren, Jonny is fuckin' crazy about you."

Unable to keep the shock from my face, I look over at Ben to see both him and Stacey staring at me as though I suddenly have two heads.

"What?" I ask, genuinely surprised.

Stacey rolls her eyes at me as Ben continues. "Seriously, Lauren, I've never seen Jonny so out of his mind crazy over a female to the point where he can't even fuckin' function."

Trying to act all nonchalant and unaffected by Ben's words, I simply say, "Well, that's of Jonny's own doing, not mine."

Taking another sip of my coffee, I then notice out of the corner of my eye, Stacey staring down at Ben, her eyes growing larger by the second, almost like she's urging him on to say something else. Something more. "What?" I ask them, suddenly curious, "what is it?"

Glaring up at Stacey, Ben suddenly looks uncomfortable. "It's nothing," he mutters.

"It isn't nothing," says Stacey, "now tell her what you told me this morning."

"Tell me what?" I press, beginning to feel worried.

Sighing, and clearly annoyed, Ben reluctantly decides to tell me. "Look, I know Jonny's being difficult with you at the moment but, you coming back into his life when his head was already all over the place beforehand has just sent him reeling. He's got a lot of shit going on in his personal life right now so just…go easy on him." Great, now I am worried. Really worried.

"What sort of shit?" I ask, desperate for answers.

Looking between both Stacey and me, Ben says, "Look, I'm not supposed to say anything about any of this, Jonny will fuckin' kill me."

"Well, perhaps you should have thought about that before telling Stacey this morning," I snap, "now tell me what's going on."

Sighing, Ben slumps back against the sofa in defeat. "I only told Stacey because she said that Jonny's behaving like a complete shit with you at the moment."

"He is behaving like a complete shit with me," I say, "but considering our past together and how I left him, I can sort of understand it, but if there's more to what's upsetting Jonny then I want to know. I *need* to know."

Taking a deep breath, Ben finally tells me what's wrong.

"Jonny's mom is terminally ill with cancer," he says quietly, "she…got the original diagnosis over a year ago and started treatment straight away, but unfortunately the cancer has since spread and now it's terminal. She got the news that it was terminal literally days before we came over to the UK to finish our European leg of the tour, so Jonny couldn't even be there with her. He's absolutely devastated, as you would imagine."

"Oh my god," is all I can muster up to say to him, "the papers were right."

Looking over at Ben, and then at Stacey, I suddenly find myself unable to breathe. Judy Mathers, the woman I once looked upon as a mother like figure, the woman who believed in me and Jonny when nobody else did, is dying.

Oh god, I don't think I can cope with this horrific news. When I first read about it in the newspaper the other day, I was hoping that maybe it was all hearsay or at least, not as serious as what the papers had perhaps made it out to be. But it's worse than that. So much worse.

"I need to see Jonny," I whisper.

Standing up from the sofa in a rush, the room suddenly starts to spin around me. Feeling panicky, I try desperately to focus in on the now blurry faces of Stacey and Ben reaching out for me, but it's no use, I can't see them. They're talking to me I think, but I can't hear them either. Apart from the loud ringing in my ears, I can't hear anything. And then I see darkness. Nothing but darkness.

****

"Lauren?" I think I hear Stacey calling me, but from where, I'm not sure. "Lauren!" Yes that is definitely Stacey's voice. So why can't I see her? "Oh for god's sake, why can't I wake her up?! Maybe you should call an ambulance!"

An ambulance? What the hell? And then suddenly, I can see Stacey standing over me, her face one of complete and utter panic. "Lauren? Oh, thank god for that! Can you see me? Ben, she's awake!"

"Stacey," I try to speak but for some reason, the words won't come out properly.

"Sssh, it's okay, Lauren, don't worry, you're fine now. Just stay calm, I've got you."

"Where am I?" I ask, still feeling confused.

"You're at home, Lauren, you passed out on the sofa. Thank god. If it had been anywhere else, I dread to think..."

And then I suddenly remember what happened. I panicked. When Ben told me the news about Jonny's mum, I went into full blown panic mode and blacked out. "How long have I been out?"

"Only for a couple of minutes, but, Lauren, it felt like an eternity. I was about to get Ben to dial for an ambulance and then you woke up. Maybe I should still dial for one."

"No," I say firmly, "I'm fine. I just panicked, that's all."

"But, Lauren, you haven't had a panic attack in years and this was weird because you didn't seem to panic all that much before passing out."

With a heavy sigh, I say, "Can you help me up please?"

Stacey calls Ben over for assistance and together, they sit me up on the sofa. Propping me up with a load of cushions, Stacey then heads over to the kitchen.

"I'm getting you something to eat and drink, and then I'm going to ring the doctor."

"No need, I'm fine now." And I am fine now. I still feel a little woozy and tired but other than that, I feel okay.

"Lauren, I'm ringing the doctor whether you like it or not. Tell her Ben."

Looking a little uncomfortable, Ben sits himself down on the coffee table in front of me. "That best friend of yours is one bossy female but, as bossy as she is, she's right, Lauren. You should get checked out by a doctor. You scared the shit out of her just now. And me. Plus, it's my fault that you blacked out in the first place. I knew I shouldn't have told you about Jonny's mom..."

I shake my head at him. "Don't blame yourself, Ben, I made you tell me what was going on with Jonny and anyway, you weren't to know how I'd react. I've suffered with panic attacks since being a teenager so it's nothing new to me."

Stacey struts back over to me, a glass of water in one hand and a cereal bar in another. "Right, I want you to drink that and eat this," she says, referring to the water and the cereal bar.

"Fine," I sigh. Reluctantly, I take the glass of water and start drinking.

"And when you've finished, I am putting you to bed to get some sleep and then I'm calling the doctor. Deal?"

Jeez, Stacey can be as bossy as hell sometimes, but her heart is in the right place, which is why I don't bother to put up a fight on this occasion. "Deal," I say.

CHAPTER 12

I hear his voice cutting through the darkness, saying my name over and over again, urging me to wake up. But I don't want to wake up. Not if waking up means that he isn't really here. If this is a dream then I want to stay in it forever.

"Lauren, please wake up," he says again, sounding more worried than before, "please just wake up." Hmm, maybe he is really here, maybe this isn't just a dream after all.

Finally forcing my eyes to give in to the pull of his voice, I slowly begin to open them. Blinking madly because of the brightness and unable to fully focus, I think I've made a mistake at first, thinking that it really was all a dream after all, until finally, after the longest few seconds of my life, I see him. I see him looking over me, his face etched with worry, his eyes filled with concern.

"Lauren?" asks Jonny, his hands now touching my face, inspecting me, checking that I'm okay. "Lauren, are you okay?"

Still wondering whether or not I'm dreaming, I smile up at him anyway. "I am now," I whisper.

Relief floods his face, his eyes closing for the briefest of moments. "Thank fuck for that."

Still a little unsure about whether I'm still asleep or actually awake, I reach up to touch him. Caressing his cheek with the palm of my hand, I am surprised to find that I can actually feel him. That this isn't a dream after all. Jonny is really here with me. In my bedroom.

"You're really here," I whisper.

"Of course I'm here, Lauren. When Ben rang me to tell me that you'd had a panic attack, I came straight away…"

"Ben rang you?"

He nods. "Of course he rang me. Why wouldn't he ring me?"

I frown, remembering the events of yesterday. "Because of what happened between us yesterday?"

He lets out a heavy sigh, an uncomfortable silence suddenly descending between us. I decide to be the one to break that silence. "And what about your mum, Jonny? When Ben told me the news, I just…"

"Panicked?" he asks, his concerned eyes searching mine. I nod. "Look, Lauren, you don't need to worry about any of that for now. We can talk about my mum another time. Okay?" I love how he still refers to her as his mum and not mom. The slight American lilt in his accent and the fact that he's lived over in LA for so many years still hasn't changed that about him I notice.

"Okay," I say, reluctantly.

Jonny is just about to say something else, when the door to my bedroom suddenly opens and in walks a male I've never seen before, followed by Stacey.

"Oh good, you're awake," says Stacey, "this is Dr Williams, he's a locum doctor from our surgery. Our usual doctor is away on holiday but Dr Williams agreed to come out to you straight away after I explained what happened over the phone."

I nod my thanks. Jonny moves away from the side of the bed so that Dr Williams can get in to take a look at me. He's a friendly looking man in his mid-forties with greying hair. He places his large bag on the floor by the side of my bed and then proceeds to pull all sorts of things out of it.

I slowly sit myself up in bed so that he can get on with his checks although in my opinion, him being here at all is completely unnecessary. "Look, Dr Williams, is this really necessary? I mean, I'm fine now. It was just a panic attack. I've had them before, I know all the signs."

Ignoring my polite protest, Dr Williams takes a firm hold of my wrist, feeling for my pulse. "You say you've suffered with panic attacks previously?"

"Yes."

"How long ago was the last one?"

Trying desperately to think back to when I had my last panic attack, I soon realise that it was quite some time ago. A few years in fact. Probably longer than that actually.

After I left Jonny in Manchester, I suffered with them for quite a while afterwards, so much so that Stacey had to help calm me down before I started any of my shifts when I first started working at Carnal Desires. The thought of pole dancing used to make me feel so anxious, I'm surprised I ever got over that feeling. But, thanks to Stacey, I did get over it. And I've never had a panic attack since then. Until today.

"I'd say it was about seven or eight years ago since I last had one. I had a slight panicky moment the other night when some drunken pervert was giving me some unwanted attention in a nightclub but, thankfully, it came to nothing." I glance over at Jonny who now looks cross with me.

"You nearly had one the other night when we were at Infusion? When that man tried to..." Feeling upset with myself for inadvertently upsetting Jonny, I look away from him. "Lauren, why didn't you tell me?" he asks.

I shrug. "It didn't amount to anything so I said nothing."

Dropping my wrist gently on to the bed, the doctor then proceeds to wrap a blood pressure monitor around the top of my arm. "Did you always black out following your panic attacks?" asks Dr Williams.

"Yes," I say, with absolute certainty. I don't even need to think about that one. That's why I hate them so much. Not only do they cause me to panic but they send the people around me into a panic as well.

The doctor nods his head at me. "Okay, well, your blood pressure is looking good however your pulse still seems a little fast so I'd like you to rest up for a while, certainly for the rest of today at least. I'd also like to test your urine so if you could pee into a pot for me and get your friend to drop the sample into the surgery later on today, I'll then get your blood sugar levels tested. I also want you to get plenty to eat and drink this afternoon to boost your fluid intake and raise your energy levels so you feel less woozy. Something sugary is probably best for that." He smiles at me. "You have a good bunch of people around you to take care of you, Miss Whittle. I suggest you lie back and accept the help." He nods his thanks to both Jonny and Stacey and then leaves my bedroom.

"Well, he's certainly thorough," I say.

"He needs to be bloody thorough after what happened. Bloody hell, Lauren, you gave me one hell of a fright today," says Stacey, looking worried again.

"And me," says Jonny quietly. Turning to Stacey, he says, "Stacey, would you mind giving Lauren and I some time alone? I think we need to talk."

Nodding her head, Stacey says, "Sure, no problem." Reaching for my hand, she gives it a gentle squeeze. "I'll be back in a bit to check on you."

I smile. "Thanks, Stace."

Stacey closes the door behind her, leaving Jonny and I well and truly alone. And now that we're alone, I suddenly feel awkward. About yesterday and our current situation and now this big heap of a mess I've somehow managed to get myself into after hearing the news about his mum.

"Jonny, I know you said not to right now, but please tell me about your mum, how..."

"Sssh," says Jonny, hushing me.

"But..."

Sitting himself down on the side of my bed, he takes a hold of my hand and sets me with a serious stare. "Like I said before, we don't need to talk about that at the moment..." I start to protest again but he cuts me off. "Hey, we can talk all about that later on or tomorrow, but for now, I just want you to calm down and focus on the here and now."

I suppose Jonny is right. It's no good getting myself all worked up again about the very thing that caused me to have a panic attack in the first place. "Yes, you're right. We'll talk about it another time."

Jonny nods, his face still serious. And then, from nowhere, he suddenly says, "Lauren, you scared the shit out of me today."

Feeling weary from being told off for something I had absolutely no control over, I say, "Yes, so people keep telling me."

"This isn't a joke," he snaps.

Feeling surprised at his angry outburst, I snap back at him, "I never said that it was. Jeez, Jonny, I can't control having a bloody panic attack although I really wish that I could."

Looking suddenly guilty, Jonny sighs. "Yeah, I know, I'm sorry, I didn't mean…" He sighs once more. "Shit, Lauren, I'm not dealing with this very well I know, but…when Ben rang me to tell me that you'd had a panic attack and blacked out as a result, I almost lost it. It reminded me of all those other times from our past when you suffered so badly with them because of what your dad did to you. And then, because your dad popped into my head, my morbid mind then zoned in on the time you were in the back of that ambulance, when you nearly died, after…"

Jonny stops himself from saying anything more, for fear of breaking down completely. Because that's exactly what he did last time. Broke down to the point of no return. And whatever happens, I cannot let that happen to him again. Ever.

Hushing him this time, I give his hand an affectionate squeeze. "I'm okay now, Jonny, and that's all that matters."

Shaking his head at himself, he says, "I treated you appallingly yesterday, Lauren. Just walking out on you after we…and then the stuff I said to you…"

"It doesn't matter," I say quietly, trying to make him feel better.

"Of course it fucking matters," he snaps, "it matters a hell of a lot."

"Look, Jonny, yesterday happened and we can't change it now, no matter how much we might want to."

Looking up at me with guilt ridden eyes, Jonny says, "I wouldn't want to change yesterday."

"You wouldn't?" I ask in surprise.

He shakes his head at me, his eyes misting over with some unnamed emotion. "I wouldn't change it for anything…except for the bit afterwards. If I could take all of the shit back that I said to you yesterday then I would do, right now."

I was fearful of getting my hopes up before, wondering if Jonny was here with me out of sheer worry or even duty, nothing more. But now, hearing him say these things to me, seeing the regret in his eyes and the softness of his features as he gazes over at me, I know that he's here for another reason. A reason he can no longer hide from me.

"I still love you, Lauren," he suddenly blurts out, knocking the very wind out of me. Holy shit, I had silently hoped for this moment, to hear Jonny say the words I'd been longing to hear. Words I feared I may never hear him say to me ever again. "I've always loved you. I loved you then, I've loved you every single day in the ten years when I was without you and now, I think I love you even more. So much that it hurts, it physically hurts me."

Oh my god. I thought my world was ending this morning, and now, after having a horrific panic attack, which I'm now secretly grateful for, I've got Jonny back in my life like I wanted him to be, sitting on my bed, declaring his undying love for me. Life really doesn't get any better than this.

"Oh, Jonny," I whisper, tears now swimming around in my eyes, "I love you too."

I throw my arms around his neck, Jonny pulling me hard against him, his strong arms wrapping themselves tightly around me. And then we kiss. We kiss and we kiss and we kiss, both saying sorry for the wrongs that we've done, both telling the other that we really and truly cannot bear to be without the other. Jonny feels warm and safe, his hands gently clasping at my cheeks as he breathes fresh, new life into me. I feel awake again. I feel alive. Truly alive.

"We'll work our shit out together, Lauren," he murmurs

between kisses, "it won't be an easy ride but I want this...I want you."

"And I want you," I whisper, "more than my next breath." That next breath is stolen by Jonny as he seals our promise with a kiss so tender and so meaningful, it makes me want to cry out loud with the feeling.

Pulling his lips slowly from mine, Jonny then lays my head on his shoulder, keeping me close. "You still feeling okay?"

I smile up at him. "I am now."

The smile I receive in response makes my chest ache, because it's the smile from Jonny that I've long missed. The genuinely happy smile that reaches his eyes, his heart, his very soul. I take a moment to drink him in, the dark hair and brown eyes, the long black lashes that frame those very eyes. And that mouth. Oh, that mouth. The mouth that has said and done all manner of things to me in the past. But most of all, out of everything, I take in his smile.

"You know, as much as I'm loving our reunion, I seem to recall that the doctor asked you to pee in a pot," says Jonny, suddenly looking serious.

I chuckle. "You declare your undying love for me and now you're asking me to pee in a pot?"

"No, the doctor has asked you to pee in a pot, so you really need to go and pee in a pot."

Tutting my annoyance, I say, "Fine, although I see no point in testing my pee, my blood sugar is fine, it was a panic attack, nothing more."

Resting me back on my pillows, Jonny raises an eyebrow up at me. "Doctors orders, Lauren, you're peeing in a pot and that's the end of it."

"Oh, I love it when you talk dirty to me." He grins at my suggestive quip. "It might help if I actually needed to pee though," I say, "and my mouth is as dry as a bone, I could do with a drink."

Pressing a soft kiss to my lips, he says, "I'll go and get you a drink of water."

"I'd prefer tea."

"You are one bossy patient," he says, narrowing his eyes on me.

"Hey, I'm just following doctor's orders, Jonny, he said have something sugary and so I'd really like a sugary tea please, if it's not too much trouble?"

With a wry smile, he says, "I'll fetch you a sugary tea *and* a glass of water."

"Fine," I say. He then moves to leave my side but I quickly pull him back. "Don't be long though, eh?" I ask, suddenly anxious about him leaving me.

Brushing a stray curl of my hair to one side, he says, "I'll be five minutes, sweetheart. Okay?"

Feeling relieved, I nod. "Okay."

CHAPTER 13

I do as I'm told and spend the rest of the afternoon in bed, only getting up to pee in my pot and have a quick shower. Other than that, I am ushered back to bed by Jonny every single time, who then has to leave my side anyway to go to the O2 arena for the concert tonight. He makes sure I'm tucked up in bed with a drink and a tray of food to eat before he leaves. Which is sweet. Completely over the top and unnecessary but ever so sweet. And Stacey has been the same. She even phoned up work for me to tell Frankie that I won't be in tonight due to illness and apparently, that went down like a lead balloon.

It went down even better when she then told Frankie that she wouldn't be going into work either because she was the one having to look after me. I insisted she go into work but both Jonny and Stacey agreed between them that somebody should stay with me tonight. And so, they won. Yes, they're ganging up on me already and Jonny and I have only been officially back together for five minutes. Still, I have to admit that I'm kind of enjoying it. In fact, scrap that, I'm loving it.

And speaking of love, I'm already missing Jonny like crazy and he's only been gone for an hour. Stacey kept me company for a short while after he and Ben left but now she's gone for a bath so I suppose I should get some more sleep. Picking up my kindle from my bedside table, I decide to read a bit more of my book before turning in for the night. It's still early and if I fall asleep now, I'll probably be wide awake during the night. Yes, I'll have a good read of my thriller I think, that should keep me awake for a little bit longer....

I wake at some unearthly hour in the morning to find one of Jonny's arms draped over me and my bedroom in complete darkness. Squinting at the alarm clock on my bedside table, I see that it's 3.00 am. I then see that my kindle has been placed on there, alongside a glass of water. Jonny must have put them on there because I certainly didn't. Hell, I must have been tired if I didn't even wake up when Jonny came to bed. And now that I'm awake, I do not want to go back to sleep, especially now that I know Jonny is sleeping right next to me.

Turning slowly over, I gently manoeuvre Jonny's arm so as not to wake him. As tempted as I am to wake him up, I'd rather do this. Just lie in the darkness and watch him sleep. Lying this close to him, watching him intently as he breathes in and out ever so gently, it gives me goosebumps.

He looks so peaceful and relaxed, so beautiful, that it makes me wonder how on earth I survived all these years without him. I can barely breathe right now, consumed by Jonny in a way that I can't even put into words. I can't even form a rational thought around him sometimes, that's how much I love him. And I'll spend the rest of my life making sure he knows that, because nothing and nobody will come between us again. Ever. I'll make damn sure of that this time.

****

It's actually light when I wake up again several hours later, Jonny awake with me this time as he cuddles me close, his chest to my back. "Good morning," he murmurs into my ear.

Placing my arm over his, I smile up at him. "Good morning to you too," I whisper, kissing him lightly on the lips.

"You sleep okay?" he asks, nuzzling his nose against mine. I wonder whether or not to tell him that I spent at least half an hour during the night watching him sleep, but then decide against it. That's my secret all for myself and nobody else. Not even him.

"I slept like a log," I say. Which is true. When I wasn't perving on my boyfriend of course.

"That's good to hear," he says, and then he sighs. And it's a contented sigh, telling me that he really is beginning to relax with me. And after yesterday's events, relaxation is most definitely needed for the pair of us.

"How was the concert last night?" I ask.

"Yeah, it was good. Nowhere near as good as the opening night of course. When a blonde bombshell took to the stage with me in a sing song. But, it was still good."

I grin up at him. "Flatterer."

He kisses me softly on the lips and then gazes down at me. "So, you're feeling okay now?"

"I'm feeling more than okay, Jonny," I say, pressing my bottom into his crotch, "but I think you know that already."

Biting down on a smile, Jonny says, "Am I being that obvious?"

"That you want sex?" I ask with a chuckle, "well, you might have just about got away with the discreet hint had it not been for the fact that your hard on has been digging into my lower back since I woke up two minutes ago."

He belts out a laugh. "What can I say, baby? You have that effect on me. You always did. I was always like a horny fucking teenager around you."

Narrowing my eyes on him, I say, "What is it with you and flattery this morning? You do realise that flattery gets you nowhere, right?"

"And you know damn well that I don't need to flatter you to get what I want. I only need to look at you in the right way to make you wet, we both know that. It was always the same."

"Oh, is that so?" I ask, raising an eyebrow up at him.

"Damn fuckin' right it's so," he murmurs against my lips.

Without warning, Jonny suddenly rolls me on to my front and then lifts up the hem of my satin nightie. Arching up my right leg so that its at an angle, he then slips his fingers between my legs from behind. "Mmm, so wet," he says, his voice all husky, "I think it's fair to say that I've now proved my point."

I let out a muffled moan into my pillow, Jonny's fingers already beginning to work me up into a frenzy. Normally, I would hate the fact that he is right and oh so smug about it, but on this occasion, I am willing to overlook that. "You like that, baby?" he murmurs into my ear.

God, I love how he can go from being all sweet and loving with me one minute to being all hot and dirty with me the next. Leaning my head back against his chest, I let out another soft moan of yes. "You want more? You want my cock in you?"

Biting down on a saucy smile, I whisper, "What do you think?"

Pressing his erection harder against my rear, he then says in a much firmer voice than before, "Then say it. I wanna hear you say it to me."

Gazing up at him through hungry eyes, I say the words, "I want your cock in me, Jonny. Right now."

I watch as his dark eyes suddenly flare to life with that fiery like passion I've long missed. I swear that his stare is so intense, so hot, that it marks me. He is claiming me as his without even saying a single word, and I love it, I love him. And I want him. God, do I want him. I want him so much that I can't bear to wait for him to be inside me for a minute longer. Thankfully, Jonny feels the same way as I do.

Shoving my nightie up even farther, I gasp as Jonny exposes my naked bottom to him. He then yanks down the strap of my nightie, exposing my right breast. Positioning himself behind me, I simply lie there and allow Jonny to take full control of my body, getting me into the spooning position he needs to before entering me from behind. Wrapping his right arm around me, he then squeezes my right breast, pinching the nipple between his thumb and forefinger as he thrusts slowly into me.

We both moan in unison, Jonny holding me close, his lips on my ear, his breath on my cheek. We stay still for a short time, both savouring this precious moment and the deep rooted connection we have to one another. "I love you," Jonny whispers into my ear, "I love you so fuckin' much."

Pressing a soft kiss to my bare shoulder, he then starts to move slowly inside me. Achingly slow. And because of our position, Jonny keeps it slow the entire time. It's both lazy and intensely passionate all rolled into one, Jonny's slow but deep seated thrusts reaching to that part within me that only he can reach. The part of me that was only ever reserved for him and him alone. The part where Jonny's soul intertwines with my own.

Turning my face to look up at him, Jonny's dark browns burn into my blue ones, the intensity of his stare as he continues to thrust slowly into me almost sending me crazy. "I love you too, Jonny," I breathe.

He lets out a small sigh of pleasure at my declaration before kissing me passionately on the lips. Moving his hand from my breast, he then grabs a tight hold of mine. Guiding both our hands together down my body, Jonny then skims the tips of my own fingers over my swollen clit, causing me to moan loudly.

"Oh yeah, that's it baby, feel me," he breathes, his eyes still blazing down into mine. "Feel me inside you. Feel our connection. Feel how fucking amazing we are together." *Oh my god.*

I kiss him this time, almost bruising his lips with my onslaught, our fingers slipping wildly together over my clit as Jonny continues his slow, deep thrusts from behind, gradually building us both up to an overwhelmingly intense climax. We both come together with a loud, measured moan, Jonny stilling deep inside as he empties himself into me.

Burying my face into my pillow afterwards, Jonny clings on to me, beads of sweat from his body mingling with mine in a way that makes me want to do it all over again. *Some things never change.*

Staying inside me, Jonny then plants dozens of little kisses all over my shoulder, my neck, and finally, my cheek. "Just so you know, I'm not going anywhere this time," he murmurs, causing me to smile.

Nuzzling his face into my neck, he then lets out a satisfied sigh. Cuddling his arms around me that little bit more, I then close my eyes, taking a moment to bask in the aftermath of our wonderful love making.

"That was amazing, Jonny," I whisper, "you're amazing."

"No, sweetheart, like I said to you just now, *we're* amazing. Always were. When two people fit together as perfectly as we do, how could it ever be anything else?" He threads his fingers through mine when he says that to me, and I smile up at him.

"You certainly have a way with words, Jonny Mathers." Giving him a quick once over with my eyes, I then say, "Amongst other things."

"And don't you fuckin' well know it," he murmurs, pulling his still hard cock gently out of me before slowly thrusting inside me once more, causing me to gasp.

I swear this man rarely grew tired when it came to sex and that certainly hasn't changed over the years. Mind you, when it came to Jonny, I rarely grew tired of sex either. Only with him though. Only ever with him. Nobody else. No other man ever came close to how I felt about Jonny. So much so that I've only had the grand total of two boyfriends since leaving Jonny ten years ago, and both of them were disastrous relationships.

They were both loveless and somewhat lacking in the physical department, which is why both relationships fizzled out as quickly as they began, leading me to conclude that I would forever be on my own. Until now. When finally, after all this time, fate decided to be nice to me and bring back the love of my life. The love of my life who clearly cannot get enough of me this morning as he starts to make love to me all over again.

Flipping me on to my back this time, he then strips me of my nightie completely and climbs on top of me, burying himself inside me once more, thrusting much harder into me this time. And after several minutes of fast paced, rolling around the bed, headboard banging against the wall type of sex, Jonny brings us both to orgasm for the second time this morning. He collapses on top of me afterwards, the pair of us breathless, sweaty, and, for the time being, well and truly sated. Pulling slowly out of me, he then rests his head on my chest.

We lie in silence for a while afterwards, Jonny's fingers slowly circling their way around my navel before heading gradually south. Glancing up at me, Jonny then slowly shuffles his way down my body, his head coming to rest on my right thigh. I know what he's about to do before he even does it, my eyes already misting over with emotion.

Reaching across, Jonny then places his lips against the horizontal scar on my skin that is just above my pubic bone, the white, barely there reminder of what we once lost. He kisses it softly, his eyes closing for the briefest of moments, before he rests his head on me once more, on my tummy this time.

Jonny doesn't utter a single word to me in that moment, nor me to him. Because words simply aren't needed right now, and they never were. Not when it came to losing him. Our baby. Our son. Not talking about our stillborn son was damaging of course, to the both of us, but no matter how hard I tried, I simply couldn't do it, and so Jonny found his own way to acknowledge what had happened to us. By remembering Oliver in the only way he knew how. By kissing that very part of me that brought our beautiful son into the world, a reminder to us both that Oliver did exist and that we both loved him more than any words could have ever expressed.

A single tear rolls down my cheek but I quickly swipe it away before Jonny notices. Placing my hands in his hair, I then gently brush my fingers through his mussed up sex hair, Jonny revelling in the feel of me touching him, caressing him. He nuzzles his cheek against my stomach and places his right hand against my hip, sighing contentedly. "You know, I spent so long without you, Lauren, that I'd actually forgotten what this was like," he says quietly, finally breaking the silence.

"Yeah, me too," I agree, feeling exactly the same.

Placing a kiss on my tummy, Jonny then says, "I can't even begin to tell you how much I've missed this...missed you..." Gazing up at me, he looks at me longingly. "Because there was only ever you, Lauren, and I want...I need you to know that."

Smiling down at him, I say, "I know." And I do know. Deep down I do, but now that he's said those words out loud to me, it suddenly makes me think about all those missing years that I spent without him in my life. The years he spent without me. In the band, touring the world, becoming rich and famous, women throwing themselves at him. The women. Oh, his many women. And therein starts my paranoia.

"Jonny?"

"Mmm."

Clearing my throat, I think carefully about how to word my question because the last thing I want is for him to think I suddenly don't trust him. "Do you think that it's possible for two people to always be this passionate together? I mean, when couples grow old together? Do you think that we'll still be this passionate when we're old and grey or do you think it will eventually wear off?"

"That's kind of a random question," he says, looking up at me questioningly.

I shrug my shoulder. "I was just curious, that's all."

Not looking entirely convinced with my response, Jonny decides to answer me anyway. "Lauren, my passion for you will never die. It might get less frequent the older we get or the less mobile we get." I can't help but chuckle at that remark. "But, as far as the passion is concerned, you and I will never lose that." He frowns up at me. "Sweetheart, why are you really asking me this question? What's this about?"

Feeling a little embarrassed about my reasoning for asking him this question, I flush pink. "I just…well, I love how passionate we are together. And, like you said just now, I've missed this part of us so much and I just want it to last forever. Call me greedy for you or whatever but I'm scared of it maybe, you know, one day, wearing off. Like, if you get bored of me, or…"

"Bored of you?" he asks in complete surprise. "Fuck me, Lauren, where is this coming from? We were together for four and a half years the first time round and we were steaming hot the entire time and clearly, we still are now." Bracing himself over me, his concerned eyes begin searching mine. "What is it?" he asks, "what's bothering you?"

"Nothing," I say with a shrug.

"Oh come on, Lauren, we've been back together for barely a day, we've just had the most mind blowing sex ever and now you're suddenly paranoid about me getting bored of you or losing interest as we get older? Where the fuck has all this come from?"

I try to act all casual but fail miserably. I wish I hadn't said anything now. It was a genuine wondering to begin with but now that Jonny is digging into the whats and whys of it all, I find myself having to confess to my sudden paranoia. "Well, you've…you know, had a lot of…women over the last few years, and…"

"Hey!" snaps Jonny, actually looking offended. "You can stop right there, right now."

I open my mouth to speak again but instead decide not to, which, looking at Jonny's face right now, is probably the sensible thing to do. No, Lauren, the sensible thing would have been to *not* open your mouth in the first place! Oops, too late now.

"I've said this already but I'll say it again to you, Lauren. Do you honestly think that any one of those other women ever meant a thing to me?"

Feeling stupid for being so paranoid, I look away from him. "No, of course not, but…"

"But what?"

Blowing out a breath from between my lips, I say, "They still had a part of you, Jonny."

He shakes his head at me. "No, Lauren. They had no part of me at all. Yes, I fucked them. Too many of them." I close my eyes at hearing him say it out loud, physical pain flashing across my chest at the very thought of Jonny being with any other woman other than me.

Clasping my hand in his, I open my eyes once more and watch as Jonny places my hand across his chest, over his heart. "But none of them had this," he whispers, "I swear." After a moment, he says, "And you forget, Lauren, you forget what the lost years without you have done to me. The very thought of those men just looking at you in that club you've worked in for so long honestly makes me want to be sick. And as for any ex-boyfriends you've had…well, I can't even bear the thought of that."

Reaching up, I cup his cheek in my hand. "You have nothing to worry about there, Jonny, there are only two ex-boyfriends and no others in between, and neither of those relationships lasted longer than a few months."

He looks shocked at my confession. "Just two men in ten years?"

"What can I say, Jonny? Nobody even came close to you…and nobody ever will."

Nodding gently, he then says, "Even so, it's still two men too many for me. The very thought…" I hush him once more, with my mouth this time, kissing him tenderly. "You see," he whispers between kisses, "we're both the same, Lauren. Both equally wrecked by the other one."

Clinging on to the back of his head, I press his forehead against mine. "That's because we love each other so much," I whisper.

"Too fucking much," he breathes, kissing me again.

We make love for a third time, both intent on proving to the other one yet again of our never ending hunger for one another. It's hot and steamy, wet and wild. Completely wild. And afterwards, we just lie together in bed, all wrapped up under the duvet, talking. About everything. Everything we need to talk about but so far, haven't done.

Jonny tells me all about his mum, opening up his heart to me about everything that's been happening in his life of late, getting everything off his chest and finally out in the open. And to me, that means everything. Because Jonny doesn't wear his heart on his sleeve and never has done. Not to the rest of the world anyway. But to me, he always has. And now, without a shadow of a doubt, I know that this passion between us, this all-consuming love we feel for one another will never end. Because, as Jonny told me himself before, no other woman on this earth has ever had that part of him. His heart, his very soul. And no other woman ever will.

****

"So, you're quitting your job at the club?" asks Stacey, looking surprised, "as in, today? Like, right now?"

Rolling my eyes at the impending inquisition I was expecting from Stacey, I quickly finish putting on a pot of coffee before turning around to face her. "Not right this second, no, but… at some point today…I will be quitting that shithole for good, yes."

To my complete surprise, Stacey lets out a squeal of delight before jumping up and down on the spot and then pulling me in for a hug. I frown, feeling confused at her reaction, but hug her back all the same. "Okaaay, not what I was expecting at all but I'm happy that you're happy."

Pulling back, she frowns. "Well, what were you expecting? Hell, Lauren, I've been waiting for this moment for you for so long! I know how much you hate that place and dare I say it, how much you hate *him*, the Tango Man. Eurgh, if I could, I would quit right along with you, although I have to say, I would miss the whole pole dancing thing, you know how much I love to work that pole." She starts to mimic dancing around a pole and we burst out laughing.

"And fuck do I love to watch you work that pole, babe," says Ben, strolling into the kitchen with a huge grin on his face. Stacey whirls around in surprise. "Hey, babe," he says, pulling her in for a kiss, "don't stop on my account."

Wrapping her arms around the back of his neck, she beams up at him. "I'll never stop dancing for you, Ben Anderson, and you know it."

And then they're off, snogging each other's faces off. I'm just about to make some sort of sarcastic remark when Jonny does it for me.

Breezing into the kitchen, fresh from his morning shower, he says, "Fuck me, get a room."

Pulling apart briefly, Ben says, "We already have one."

Stacey grins. "Actually, we have two…we have your hotel room *and* my bedroom…"

Ben wiggles his eyebrows suggestively. "I know which one I'd prefer to use right now."

She giggles. "Me too." Stacey gives us a little wave before pulling Ben by the hand, leading him back to where they've been all morning.

Mind you, I'm one to talk, both Jonny and I have only been out of my bedroom for about fifteen minutes ourselves. And looking at him right now, with his hair still damp from his shower and dressed only in light grey sweatpants, I think I'd rather like to yank him back into my bedroom and get my tongue to work on those tattoos of his. He's such a distraction to me. Always was.

Circling his arms around my waist, he pulls me against him and kisses me. "Good morning," he murmurs with a grin.

I flash him a suggestive smile. "Oh, it was more than a good morning for me, Jonny, as I hope it was for you too."

"Good isn't a word I'd use to describe how it feels when I'm inside of you, Lauren. In fact, I don't think there is a word that could possibly describe that feeling. With you, there are no words." *Jeez, what is he doing to me?*

Taking his face in my hands, I kiss him hard and deep, unable to hold back from all the feelings he's stirring up inside of me. I feel out of control with him already, completely addicted and head over heels in love with him all over again. And it feels wonderful. Really bloody wonderful.

The coffee pot boiling vigorously brings about an end to our moment, Jonny gently pulling away from me. "I think the coffee's as hot and bothered as I am," he says with a grin.

"You want some?"

"Are you talking about coffee or sex?"

I shrug. "How about both?"

"Now you're talking," he murmurs.

I smile. "I take it that's all we're going to be doing today, then?"

"Each other?" he says, "fuck yes, I've got an entire decade of lost time to make up for with you, remember?" I chuckle. "There is just one other thing that I do want you to do today though, besides me of course."

"Oh?" I say, raising an eyebrow.

Raising an eyebrow right back at me, he says, "What we discussed earlier?" Pretending to forget for a moment, I frown, as if deep in thought. Jonny's face grows slowly serious. "Your job, Lauren, I'm talking about you quitting your job."

Breaking out into a slow grin, I say, "I knew what you were talking about, Jonny Mathers, I was just playing with you."

Narrowing his eyes on me, he says, "You little minx." I giggle. "Oh, you just giggled, Lauren Whittle," warns Jonny. Caging me in against the kitchen worktop, he says, "And you know what happens to me when you giggle." I giggle again before pushing him away and then running off.

Jonny gives chase through my apartment, catching me just as I'm going into my bedroom. Armed with a tea towel in his hand, he twists it and then uses it as a weapon against me in his mission to catch me. Scrambling on to the bed to get away from him, I shriek as the corner of the tea towel cracks against the skin of my right bum cheek, Jonny laughing as I end up rolling off the other side of the bed and onto the floor.

Lying in a crumpled heap on the floor, I roll around laughing, desperately trying to rub my now stinging bum cheek. Jonny towers over me, still clutching the tea towel, grinning like the cat who got the cream. "I don't know whether I'm amused by what just happened or completely turned on by all that ass rubbing you're doing right now."

I chuckle. "Piss off."

Reaching up, I manage to grab one of the pillows from my bed and throw it at him. He bats it out of the way before dropping to the floor himself. I shove at his chest in my last feeble attempt at holding him off but it's no use, he's too strong for me. He wins the fight. This time anyway.

Pinning my hands to the floor above my head, he crawls on top of me. With a mischievous twinkle in his eye, he says, "Do you surrender, baby?"

"Like I have a choice?"

Jonny's face suddenly grows serious. Releasing his grip on my hands, he pulls back slightly. Frowning down at me, he says quietly, "With me, Lauren, you always have a choice."

I feel a pang in my chest when he says that to me, because even now, ten years on, it's clear to me from the look in his eyes and his sudden change in demeanour that Jonny is still wary. Wary of the fact I was violently beaten by my father. He always was. So much so that he used to get stupidly paranoid sometimes that he himself had perhaps said or done something very wrong to me. But Jonny never did a thing wrong to me. And he never could. Ever.

Swallowing down a lump in my throat, I reach up and clasp his face in my hands. "I know I do," I whisper, my voice quivering slightly. Kissing him softly on the lips, I say, "And that's one of the many reasons why I love you so bloody much. Always have done. Always will."

Our eyes lock for a long moment, our mood turning from playful to emotional in a matter of seconds. And then Jonny makes love to me. Right there on my bedroom floor, he makes slow, passionate love to me and I lose my mind all over again.

CHAPTER 14

It's Sunday night, the last night of Reclamation's five night run, and I'm here, side of stage, with the main man. *My* main man. The band are just about to take to the stage for their final show, bringing their UK tour to a close. And what a night it's going to be. I can already feel the buzz of the crowd and I'm not even standing amongst them this time. Oh no, I have the best seat in the house this time, as does Stacey. Although Stacey isn't actually standing next to me at the moment. She's off fraternising with that randy bassist of hers and considering he's due on stage in five minutes, you could say he's cutting it a little fine.

The pair of them have been inseparable since getting it together last week, something that Jonny told me he's never seen before with Ben. In fact, Jonny told me that Ben's never been with the same woman twice since joining the band. Something that both worries and pleases me.

Worried because Ben is leaving the country for good on Wednesday, but pleased because it's Stacey he's chosen to go back to over and over again. He's so smitten with her it's untrue but, smitten or not, that doesn't change the fact that he's in a world famous band and he lives over in LA.

And speaking of LA, that is something else Jonny and I need to fully discuss. Jonny has already made it abundantly clear that he wants me to go back with him to LA on Wednesday. I on the other hand want to leave it at least a month before flying out there to be with him. Not only have I got stuff to sort out with our apartment and our landlord but I've got to consider Stacey in all of this. Stacey is like a sister to me and the only family I've got. Whenever I think of leaving her behind in London my stomach lurches and I feel so sick that I just can't even bear to think about it.

I think I just need time to digest what's happening to me and take it all in really. I mean, it's only been a week since I first saw Jonny after ten entire years and as desperate as I am to be with him, we need to take things at my pace. I just need to work out how to broach the subject with him though, because, like the coward that I am, I've admittedly been putting it off. And I'm still putting it off.

In my mind, I can deal with it later, or maybe tomorrow, or maybe never! Still, he can't really argue with me on the subject. Well, he can, and he most likely will, but, at least I've done the one thing that should really mean something to him in all of this. I've already quit my job!

Yes, I officially quit my job yesterday afternoon and it felt absolutely fantastic! Frankie flew off the handle and almost turned purple when I told him I was leaving and never coming back without even a month's notice, but the buzz I got from telling him to go and fuck himself was immense.

In fact, it was so immense that after I left the club I went straight outside to Jonny in the waiting Range Rover and gave him a hand job in the back of the car as we travelled back to my apartment. And then he returned the favour with those musically talented fingers of his. The privacy screen was up of course, wouldn't want Andy and Tony seeing more of us than we'd like them to see.

Anyway, I digress, back to the here and now. And the here and now is Reclamation's final show, which is about to start in just under five minutes. I therefore have five more minutes of a leather clad Jonny kissing me into a frenzy.

Ready to rock with his electric guitar slung on his back, he's literally pressing me up against the wall, right at the side of the stage where dozens of people are running around like headless chickens. It's all very busy and technical around here but Jonny just doesn't give a shit. How the hell he can be so calm before playing to an audience of thousands I really don't know, but I don't care when he's kissing me as desperately as he is doing right now. His hands are beginning to wander up my stocking clad thighs and I swear he's getting hard. Time to stop I think.

"Baby," I murmur, my lips still beneath his, "can you bring this leather outfit into the bedroom with you later on?" My sexy request works. Pulling away, he bites that delicious bottom lip of his, his eyes darkening. Fuck, I so wish I could ride him right now.

"You suddenly got a penchant for leather, sweetheart?" I bite my lip and then slowly turn the collar of his leather jacket upwards, exactly as he wore it the other night, the first time I saw him on stage.

Reaching up on to my tiptoes, I whisper into his ear, "No, I have a penchant for *you* in leather, baby, there's a vast difference between the two."

Moving his hands away from my thighs, he traps my face in his hands, his nose just touching mine. "Well that works out pretty well then because I have a penchant for you in short black dresses and stockings," he says, in reference to my outfit.

"Meant to be," I whisper.

"Damn fucking right," he growls, before taking my mouth under his again, his tongue sliding against mine in that deliciously filthy way that makes my body go all tingly and my knickers instantly wet. It doesn't help that Jonny is topless beneath this leather jacket of his, my fingers now crawling their way around the many tattoos on his chest. Holy cow, what I would give to run my tongue around them right now.

"Fuck me, put her down, will you? We've got a show to put on!"

Ben's sudden interruption to our little tryst doesn't go down well with me or Jonny, but especially Jonny. Swearing under his breath, he swings round to find Ben grinning like a loved up loon with Stacey standing by his side, running a hand through her now messy hair. The little minx, no prizes for guessing what those two have been up to for the last fifteen minutes.

Jonny shakes his head at the pair of them while I stifle a laugh behind my hand. "You're un-fucking-believable you are! At least I'm ready to go on stage! Talk about cutting it fine!"

Ben winks, pulling Stacey into his side just that little bit tighter. "What can I say, dude? I got distracted." Stacey giggles and then pulls Ben in for a kiss.

Jonny turns to me. Rolling his eyes, he says "Fuck me, I think I preferred him before."

"Oh shut up," I say, hitting him on the arm, "you were practically having me up against this wall just now."

"Erm, carry on with backchat like that, Miss Whittle, and I will have you up against this wall and I don't give a shit about who is or isn't around either, and don't think I'm bluffing."

I giggle as he pushes me up against "our" wall again, his mouth nibbling at my neck. "And stop giggling," he murmurs against my neck, "you know what it does to me, look what happened yesterday." I can feel him smiling against my skin and I can't help but feel all giggly and girly, his playful attack against me giving me the warm fuzzies.

"Jonny, you're on! And Ben, you should already be on stage waiting with the other two! Come on people, get a move on around here, we have a show to put on!"

Okay, whoever that extremely loud man is, I now officially hate him. Because my man is now being taken away from me, but then, he isn't going very far. And he's going on stage. Right next to me. Where I can perv on him to my heart's content for the next three hours. Sounds yummy to me. One last kiss from him and then he pulls away. Swinging his electric guitar around to his front, he winks at me.

"Enjoy the show, sweetheart."

"Oh, I will baby, and as much as I love watching you on stage, I look forward to my own private showing of you later on." I wink in return and he blows me a sexy kiss in response, puckering up those sex hot lips of his especially for me. Jeez, I'm almost drooling.

As he ascends the steps to the stage, I give him a little wave goodbye and then, turning to Stacey, I see she's busy drooling over Ben who has literally just shot off to take his place by the bass guitar. He's so last minute!

The stage fades to black and then, Stacey and I are subjected to the deafening roar of twenty thousand screaming Reclamation fans, waiting desperately for their idols to grace them with their presence.

I feel excited all over again but it's a different kind of excitement this time. The last time I watched Reclamation perform, I wasn't with Jonny. I got up on stage and sang with him but I wasn't *with* him. Now that I am, this whole experience is so much better than I could have ever imagined. I'm practically wetting myself just waiting to hear the first few strings of Jonny's electric guitar intro. Thankfully, I don't have to wait for very long.

Seconds later, the moment I've been waiting for all night is finally happening. My man has started strumming on that electric guitar of his, sending his legions of fans, and me, into an absolute frenzy. The place is still in darkness of course, just like it was the other night. And then…moments later. Bang! There he is, on his platform, bathed in light, standing in the exact same rock star pose that he was standing in just a few nights ago.

But this time, I'm not thinking about "if only" and the "what ifs." This time, I'm not thinking anything. I'm just smiling with happiness. Smiling in the knowledge that Jonny Mathers, musically talented world famous rock star, the one who is now standing on that platform in front of twenty thousand screaming fans, is mine. All mine.

****

Reclamation's official end of tour party is taking place in Lucidity, a top class London bar come nightclub which basically blows Infusion, the club where they held their first after show party on Wednesday night, out of the water.

This club is situated right at the very top of an expensive central London hotel. It spans four entire floors, each floor having a completely different design. The VIP floor is at the top of the building and that's where I'm lucky enough to be tonight. It's all glass and mirrors, the modern décor and plush furnishings really setting this club apart from anything else I've ever seen. Not that I've been in many posh clubs of course.

There's an entire wall of sliding glass doors at the far end of the room. The doors slide open and beyond them is a large rooftop terrace giving their customers the most amazing view of London I've ever seen. You can see the London eye from here and everything. It's breathtaking. Truly breathtaking.

Stacey and I are sitting together in a private booth in the corner, enjoying a bottle of champagne while the boys have gone off to do their post tour interview with Lara. Jonny said he wouldn't be long and I hope to goodness that he isn't because I already hate the fact that he's with Lara instead of me.

He introduced me to her earlier, shortly after we arrived, and she looked at me as though she wanted to squash me. Her smile was forced and she didn't even offer her hand out to me as Jonny made the introduction. I barely smiled back at her, quickly looking to Jonny for support. He soon got the message that I was uncomfortable in her presence and so moved me away, settling me and Stacey into a booth with one hell of a view of London.

"Well, this beats dancing around poles any night of the week," says Stacey, topping up our champagne flutes.

I smile. "Well, thankfully, I don't need to dance around a pole ever again."

"Lucky cow." Stacey shakes her head at me. "Honestly, Lauren, just when I thought I couldn't possibly hate Frankie any more than I already do, I actually do. I swear he nearly didn't give me the night off tonight when I asked if I could book it as a holiday. You leaving has put him in a right mood. He even asked me if I could fill in for you while he finds a replacement."

"He didn't?" I say, horrified.

"Oh yes he did, the tosser. I mean for one, I can't even bloody sing, and for two, like I'd ever take my best friend's job within a day of her leaving…or ever!"

"So, what did you say?"

"I told him to go and fuck himself," she says with a grin.

"Oh my god, and what did he say back to you? He didn't fire you, did he?"

Stacey rolls her eyes at me. "Of course not, the wanker is one girl down already, his *star* attraction, he's hardly going to fire me when he's already shitting himself about telling the big boss at the top about you leaving him in the lurch."

I grimace. "I have kind of left him in the lurch though, haven't I? He could sue me for breach of contract for not working my notice, you know."

Stacey screws up her face in disgust. "Number one, no you haven't left him in the lurch, I was just quoting his pathetic words to me from earlier, and number two, if he even attempted to sue you, Jonny's legal team would be all over him like a rash, as would Jonny."

"I guess you're right," I say with a sigh.

"I am right. Look, Lauren, don't go all soft on him after feeling so great about it all yesterday. Frankie deserves everything he gets for the way he's treated you and the other girls over the years and *you*, my kind, beautiful best friend, you deserve everything that you are currently getting and are going to be getting along life's way with Jonny, and don't ever think otherwise. Okay?"

I give her a reluctant nod. "Okay."

"Good," says Stacey, handing me my champagne flute. "So, here's to new beginnings," she continues, raising her glass.

Raising mine, I clink it gently against hers. "To new beginnings, Stace."

****

Jonny and the boys rejoin us some time later, all six of us nicely squished up together in our booth. It's nice to see Will and Zack again after only meeting them once, very briefly, at Infusion last week. I really hope to get to know all of them better when I move over to LA. Ben is the only one I've started to get to know properly because of how much time he's been spending with Stacey and I have to say, there's a lot more to Ben than I first thought. Jonny doesn't seem to think so but I know that most of the time, he's just saying things in jest.

"So, how did the interview go?" I direct my question at all four of them but it's Jonny who responds.

"Shite, as per the norm."

I roll my eyes at him. "You really don't like being interviewed, do you?"

He shrugs. "Who does? It's just all pointless shit to me. We get asked questions like what did we think of the tour? How do we think the tour went? Well, check the ticket sales and ask the fans and then you'll get the answers. I just hate all this fake shit. All I care about is making music and pleasing our fans. If the fans are happy, I'm happy."

"And the fans are happy when they hear their idols being interviewed after their tour saying how much they enjoyed doing it, so it isn't pointless shit, Jonny. Really it isn't."

Jonny raises his eyebrows up at me in surprise. "Know all about PR all of a sudden, do you?"

"No," I say, "but as Stacey and I are two of your biggest fans, I think I know of what I speak."

The other lads around the table snigger into their beer bottles, Jonny being rendered speechless for once. Clearing his throat, he then tries to offer up some sort of explanation. "Yeah, well, like I said, what my fans think is all that matters to me so if you think interviews are important then maybe… maybe I'll think a little differently the next time I do one."

I smile. "Yeah?"

Jonny breaks out into a slow smile. "Well, after that telling off, how can I not think of you from now on when I get interviewed?" *Aww, sweet.* He leans in for a kiss, the guys whistling loudly as Jonny's lips meet with mine.

"Dude," says Ben, "what the fuck has happened to you? Three days with Lauren and this is what she reduces you to?"

Pulling away from me, Jonny looks over at Ben and says, "This coming from the man who was heard serenading his new girlfriend in the bathroom this morning."

Will and Zack laugh, Ben's cocky smile slowing fading from his face. Stacey turns her face into Ben's shoulder, unable to keep from laughing herself. "Yeah, alright, laugh away mother fuckers but you know what? I don't give a fuck, because yeah, I did sing to Stacey in the bathroom this morning…and then I made her sing in return."

Stacey looks up at Ben in shock, swiping him on the arm for that suggestive remark. "Ben!"

"What?" he asks, holding his arms out in defence, "what did I say?" Stacey shakes her head at him, everybody else around the table laughing at the pair of them now, me included.

"Don't you join in as well," says Stacey, flushing pink.

"Oh come on, Stace, it's to be expected with Ben. Right guys?" I look over at Will and Zack, both of them nodding their heads in agreement.

"That's just the tip of the iceberg where Ben's concerned," says Will, laughing, "believe me."

Ben narrows his eyes on Will. "Hey, knock it off. Stacey doesn't need to know anything else about me other than I'm unbelievable in bed and a great bassist."

"Still trying to find those two things as well, is she?" quips

Jonny, "that could take a while."

"Hey, what is this? Gang up on Ben night or what?" says Ben, actually looking offended.

Leaning across the table, I pinch Ben's cheek playfully. "Aww, are they being mean to you, Benny?" Ben swipes my hand away, Stacey now laughing into her champagne glass.

"Don't pinch my cheek and do not call me Benny."

"Nice one, baby," says Jonny with a grin.

As Ben continues to rant on to Stacey about being the but of everybody's jokes, Jonny suddenly pulls away from me, his hand dipping into the left pocket of his jeans. Plucking out his mobile phone, he looks down at the caller ID and immediately frowns.

Leaning over, I say, "Everything okay? Who is it?"

Staring down at the phone for a moment, he finally says, "It's my dad." *Oh shit.* Jonny stands up from the table. "I need to take this," he says.

"Do you want me to come with you?" I ask, standing up alongside him. He turns to me and shakes his head.

"No, it's okay, baby, you stay here and I'll take this out on the terrace."

"You sure?" I ask, feeling worried. He nods, already walking towards the glass doors.

"What was that about?" asks Stacey, frowning.

Sighing, I reluctantly sit back down. "It's Jonny's dad on the phone," I say quietly.

"Hey," says Will gently. I look over at him. "Don't worry Lauren, there won't be anything wrong with Jonny's mum. Pete always rings him after a show. Well, it's Judy who gets him to ring Jonny actually. Judy is the one who always insists she speaks to Jonny after a show. Jonny can't ring her because he never knows how she's going to be at any given moment, she spends a lot of her time sleeping you see, because of all the medication she's on."

For the first time tonight, our entire table falls silent, each of us suddenly feeling the weight of what Jonny is actually dealing with in his personal life.

My eyes dart over to where Jonny is standing outside on the rooftop terrace. He's pacing up and down and he looks angry. Really angry. Oh hell, this isn't good. This isn't good at all. I need to go out to him and calm him down and find out what the hell is going on.

Standing up, I leave everybody else sitting around the table and head towards the glass doors. Sliding one of the doors open, I step out onto the rooftop terrace and slowly slide the door closed behind me. Jonny looks over at me in surprise and then shakes his head. I start to walk towards him but he holds his hand out to me and then turns away.

"Look, I'm not talking about this now, or ever. If Mum's asleep at the moment then there really wasn't any point in you ringing me, was there?" Jonny sighs heavily down the phone. "That really is none of your fucking business, and it never was." Pete must be talking again because Jonny falls silent once more. Another moment passes before Jonny speaks again. "The next time you ring me, I expect Mum to be on the other end of the phone." Jonny ends the call and then sighs.

I don't really know how to approach him or what to say to him, so instead I say nothing. Jonny stays standing with his back to me, only moving to put his phone away and pull out his packet of cigarettes from the back pocket of his jeans.

Sparking up a fag, he takes a long pull on his cigarette before finally turning to face me again. He looks royally pissed off which in turn makes me sad, especially after the last few happy days we've spent together. I choose my next words carefully.

"I would ask you if you're okay but I know that you aren't, so I won't."

Jonny takes another long drag on his cigarette, inhaling the smoke as though his life depends on it. Blowing out the smoke from between his lips, he says, "Same old story, Lauren. Same shit from my dad, different day."

"So...I take it he knows about us then?"

Jonny nods. "Oh, he knows about us alright. In fact, I'm surprised it's taken him this long to find out to be honest. The papers have been printing stuff about us all week after you got up on stage with me the other night, and my dad always has his nose in the gossip columns. He follows my life in the limelight like a fucking private eye but...I suppose he *is* the band's manager after all."

Jonny sounds so bitter when he says that to me, so very bitter. "I thought he was ringing because my mum wanted to speak to me," he says sadly, "just like she always does after the shows." Jonny takes one last drag of his cigarette before stubbing the end out between his fingers. "But not tonight," he says angrily, "tonight he used my mum as a fucking excuse, Lauren. An excuse to get me on the phone just so he can try and "talk some sense" into me about you." I look down at the floor as Jonny continues. "He wants to talk some sense into me, Lauren! Fucking wanker!"

"Jonny, don't," I say quietly, finally looking up at him. "Please don't."

"Don't what?" he snaps, "don't get angry with him?"

"Precisely, don't get angry with him, Jonny, don't let him get to you! He always got to you!"

"Yeah and he still fucking does!" shouts Jonny, "I've got so much shit going on at the moment with my mum being terminally ill and with the band being on tour and everything, but you've helped me with that, Lauren. Already you've helped me with that. I'm happier than I've been in a long time and yet he still refuses to see it. He still manages to somehow make me feel like this!"

I dash over to him and wrap my arms around his neck, hushing him gently. "Sssh baby," I whisper, "ssshhh."

Jonny presses his forehead against mine. "Why does he always manage to turn my happiness into bitterness, Lauren?" he whispers, "why?"

"The same reason why my own dad did what he did to me, Jonny," I say quietly, "because they both wanted to be in control of their children's lives, one with their fists, the other with his big mouth and wallet full of money. But they aren't in control of our lives anymore, Jonny, and they never will be ever again."

Jonny sighs against my mouth, his eyes closing briefly. "God, I love you," he whispers, "I love you so fucking much…I always did."

Suddenly, he takes my face in his hands and kisses me hard and deep, the burning anger he still holds for his father igniting his never ending passion for me. I cling on to him tightly, kissing him back with everything I have, until the pair of us are breathless, panting and more than wanting.

Taking an unsteady step backwards and trying desperately to compose himself, Jonny says to me quietly, "We're leaving. We're leaving right now."

CHAPTER 15

We're lying on our fronts on Jonny's queen sized bed in his hotel suite, both hugging our pillows tightly against our chests, both naked. The room is in total darkness except for a sliver of light from the moon just peeping through the blinds of the bedroom window.

We are basking in the cosy afterglow of our wonderful lovemaking and enjoying the silence of being locked away in his hotel suite. Just for now, we can be Jonny and Lauren again, away from the outside world and all its troubles.

Jonny brushes the tips of his fingers back and forth along the entire length of my spine, the roughness of his skin against mine giving me goosebumps. "Are you okay?" Jonny asks quietly. Even though it's dark, I can just about make out the slight look of concern in his eyes.

"You've just given me three orgasms in a row, Jonny, okay is hardly the word to describe how I'm feeling right now. In fact, there are no words to describe how I feel when you're inside me. Sound familiar?" He smiles when I say that to him.

Brushing a gentle hand through his mussed up sex hair, I say, "What's with the sudden concern for me, anyway?"

Finding the small of my back, he begins to draw circles with his fingertips around the skin there. It makes me tingle all over. "I was worried that I might have been a bit...rough with you...when we first got back to the hotel, after what happened with my dad's phone call earlier on. I was so angry with him and my head just went and I couldn't even think straight. In fact, I didn't think, that's the point."

Resting my hand against his cheek, I say, "Jonny, you should know by now that I love it when you're rough with me. You and I always loved a bit of the rough stuff together. That certainly hasn't changed."

Trailing his fingers along my spine once more, he says, "Even so, there's such a thing as being too rough, to the point of hurting someone unintentionally."

"Jonny, you could never hurt me. Ever."

Turning his mouth into the palm of my hand, he presses a kiss there. "I'm glad you think so."

Brushing my thumb across his cheek, I say, "I don't think so, Jonny, I *know* so." Leaning up, I plant a soft, reassuring kiss against his lips. "I love every single thing we do together, Jonny Mathers," I whisper, "I love the fast and rough, I love the slow and tender, but most of all, I just love you, with every fibre of my being."

Burying his fingers into my hair, he kisses me softly on the lips before enveloping me in his arms and pulling me against him. Resting my head on his shoulder, I sigh with contentment. "I wish it could be like this forever, Jonny, just us two lying in bed for as long as we want, doing whatever we want, when we want to."

Kissing me on the forehead, he says, "I know, baby, me too." He goes quiet for a moment and then says, "It'll be different when you come over to LA though, Lauren, I promise. We can make a proper life out there together. Live the dream. Just you and me."

The sheer mention of LA brings me back down to earth with a great big bump. Not that I'm not looking forward to starting a new life out there with Jonny. Hell, LA and going over to the States is something that I've always dreamed of, but, and here's the but, I'm terrified of it all not being quite how I imagine and hope it to be. I'm scared of being lonely. Jonny may think that it will be just me and him out there in LA but he's a busy man these days and I'm worried that once I get over there and the newness wears off, I won't see him as often as I would like to. And that's going to hit me hard.

Back when we were first together as young, loved up teenagers, we were inseparable. We spent every waking moment together and didn't see a life outside of that little bubble we created for ourselves. We had a good circle of friends and a great social life touring the pubs of Manchester with his music but other than that, we were mad crazy and only had eyes for each other.

Jonny's life has changed so drastically over the last ten years that it's going to take some huge adjustments on my part. And not only that, I still haven't told Jonny that I won't be flying out with him to LA on Wednesday. It's Monday tomorrow so I'm going to have to tell him soon. Not right now though, because I don't want to spoil this perfect moment between us. Right now, I just want to be with him. Tomorrow…I'll tell him tomorrow…

****

The following morning, Jonny treats us both to breakfast in bed from the room service menu. It's absolutely delicious and there's so much food it's ridiculous but, somehow or other, we manage to eat most of it. I can barely move afterwards, Jonny having his morning shower all on his own while I snuggle back under the duvet for a little bit longer. It isn't long though before Jonny is yanking back the duvet and hauling me out of bed and literally forcing me into the shower, my protests of not wanting to move anywhere for the rest of the day falling on deaf ears.

He's so sprightly this morning and so full of energy whereas I am the exact opposite, absolutely shattered from our late night/early morning sexcapades. Add to that the lethargy I'm suddenly feeling from stuffing myself silly with far too much food this morning and that's my excuse for wanting to do absolutely nothing for the rest of the day.

After my shower, I find myself feeling a little better although the sudden realisation that I don't have any fresh clothes to wear today kind of puts a dampener on things for me. My black dress and underwear from the night before are nowhere to be seen, in the bedroom anyway, and the thought of wearing that outfit right now does not appeal to me at all. I just want comfort, and so I go rummaging through Jonny's wardrobes. I end up stumbling upon a plain white t-shirt and throw that on. Even though it's clearly been washed, I can still smell his aftershave on the material which makes me love it even more.

Walking out of the bedroom and into the lounge area, I stop dead in my tracks as I take in Jonny's luxurious penthouse suite in all its glory. It's the first time I've seen it properly. Funnily enough, I didn't really get chance to see any of it last night. Well, I saw the bedroom and that was about it.

It's all very posh and regal in design, almost palace like. The living area is all open plan, a cosy dining area with seating for two people over in the corner and a nest of ornate looking sofas and chairs in the middle of the room with an antique coffee table at the centre. Hell, this place is like a stately home. All very nice to look at but a bit…stiff, if that's the right word.

Glancing over to my left, I see something I really like, something that's far more welcoming and not at all stiff. A set of French doors leading on to a huge balcony.

Wandering outside, I find Jonny sitting at the table in the

sunshine smoking a cigarette whilst working on his laptop. He glances over, his eyes roaming over me in appreciation. He clearly likes my new outfit then.

"Who'd have thought that a scruffy old t-shirt of mine would look as hot as it does on you right now? Come here." Stubbing out his cigarette in the ashtray, he then grabs a hold of my hand and pulls me down onto his lap so that I'm straddling him.

Wrapping my hands around the back of his neck, I press a quick kiss to his lips. "I'm glad you like it, Jonny."

"I more than like it," he murmurs, his hands skimming up my bare thighs, pushing the t-shirt up along the way.

Batting his hands away, I say, "You can stop that right now, Mathers."

Jonny raises his eyebrows in surprise. "You telling me to stop? That's a first."

Rolling my eyes, I say, "For starters, I'm not wearing any underwear…"

"Really not helping me in the raging hard on department, Lauren."

His hands start to wander again and I grab them this time. Pinning them behind his back, I say, "What I meant was, we're on a balcony in broad daylight and I don't want to give the neighbouring people of London a view that they really don't need to see."

"Never stopped you before, sweetheart. You always were a bit of an exhibitionist."

I shove him in the chest for that remark and then stand up, Jonny still trying to make a grab for me. I manage to dodge out of his way, sitting myself down on a chair on the opposite side of the table.

Sitting back in his chair, he folds his arms and narrows his eyes on me. "How you can expect me to concentrate on anything other than you sitting there in my white t-shirt with no underwear on is beyond me."

"I'm not deliberately teasing you, Jonny, I have no clothes here because we came straight back to your hotel room last night so I haven't been home and the only outfit and underwear I did wear last night is nowhere to be seen."

"They're on the floor next to the coffee table in the lounge."

"Oh, well thanks for returning my clothes to me, Jonny," I say, feeling a bit annoyed.

A sly smile creeps across his lips. "What can I say? Every time I looked at your clothing just lying there on my lounge floor this morning, it brought back memories of every single filthy thing we did to each other last night."

I flush pink with embarrassment. Yes, I know, me embarrassed, who'd have thought it? Jonny continues. "So I left it there, yes, but only because it turned me on so fucking much." Jeez, he really does have a way with words. Such a smooth talker, which is why he always managed to wrap me around his little finger. Well, most of the time anyway.

Shrugging off his flirty manner, I say, "Well, as it happens, I didn't want to wear that outfit from last night anyway, I just wanted something comfy to wear. I can't help it if you find an oversized t-shirt on me a distraction."

Jonny grins. "Baby, on you? Anything would be a distraction."

I smile. "So, what are you working on, then? On the laptop I mean?"

Returning his gaze to the computer screen, he says, "Lara's

just sent me through an email about the flight times to LA on Wednesday." My stomach instantly plummets to the floor. "We can fly out either early afternoon or if you'd prefer to give yourself more time to pack then we can just book the night flight instead. Whatever you want to do, baby."

Jonny looks over at me, his face all happy and excited. And I am about to blow all of that excitement apart in an instant. Oh hell, I feel so guilty about what I'm about to do but surely, once I explain my reasoning, he'll understand...I hope.

"Erm, Jonny," I say, feeling hesitant, "I've been meaning to talk to you about that."

"About what?" he asks, frowning.

"Well, we haven't actually discussed the whole me moving to LA thing properly, have we?"

His frown deepens. "Meaning?"

Clearing my throat nervously, I finally pluck up the courage to tell him what I should have told him a couple of days ago. "Jonny, I can't fly out to LA with you on Wednesday."

Jonny screws up his face in confusion, but before he gets the chance to reply, I cut him off. I need to get all of this out, and fast. "What I mean is that I have things to sort out here in London first before I can move out there with you. One month is all I'll need, just to get stuff sorted out with the landlord and our apartment. I also need to get everything packed up, and then of course there's Stacey to consider..."

I decide to stop rambling. I could go on and on about the reasons for me not wanting to move out there with him immediately, but it wouldn't make a difference, not one little bit.

Sitting back in his chair, he suddenly seems unusually quiet. I expected shouting at first but, as yet, none of that. This is unnerving, and so not like Jonny. Resting his arms on either side of his chair, he fixes me with a long, penetrating stare. "So, let me get this straight, you don't want to come out with me to LA on Wednesday to start our new life together and yet you decided to tell me this today? Monday. Two days beforehand."

"Look, I'm sorry about the timing, Jonny, I know it's shit, but, in my defence, I was worried about how you would react."

Nodding his head at me, his eyes turn angry. "Well, you know what, Lauren? You were right to be worried, because I am angry. In fact, no, I'm not angry, I'm fucking well furious!" Jonny snaps, his calm, quiet demeanour from a moment ago finally going by the wayside.

"Jonny, be fair," I say, trying to keep my voice light.

"Be fair?" says Jonny, a look of disbelief crossing his features, "how the fuck do you expect me to react?" Right, that's it, I'm becoming annoyed with him now. Really annoyed.

"Jonny, as much as I love you and want to spend the rest of my life with you, this is a huge move for me. I need time to get myself sorted out. I mean, only ten days ago, you weren't even back in my life and then suddenly, we're back together again and committing to spending the rest of our lives together, which is wonderful, but…"

"But what?" snaps Jonny in irritation.

"But I need time to get my head around it all and I don't think me coming over to LA in a month's time instead of coming with you this week is being unreasonable."

Jonny laughs humourlessly. "You needing time to get your head around it all is the lamest excuse I've ever heard anybody come up with in my life. You think I can't see that you're already getting cold feet about coming over there with me?"

With an eye roll, I say, "Don't be ridiculous. I've more than committed myself to moving out there with you by quitting my job without even giving them notice. All I need is just time to sort everything out properly and, as I said before, there's Stacey to think about."

"Stacey's a big girl, Lauren, I think she can take care of herself."

Taking offence at his throw away comment about my best friend, I immediately leap to her defence. "Don't you dare start on Stacey, Jonny, Stacey is the only family I've had here in London for the last nine and a half years. She's a huge part of my life and if you think I can just walk away from her and London so damn easily then you're very much mistaken."

"Oh, I'm sorry, I didn't realise that you'd suddenly grown so fond of the life you've been living down here in London as a mere lap dancer."

I feel like he's just slapped me in the face, angry tears now burning at the back of my eyes as the shock of what he just said to me begins to sink in. "You hurtful bastard," I mutter angrily, "you take that back. You take that back right now."

To my horror, he does the exact opposite of that. Shaking his head, eyes wide, he says, "No, Lauren, I won't take it back, and you know why?" Lowering his voice, he looks me straight in the eyes and says, "Because I meant every fucking word of it."

Shoving his chair backwards, he stands up and storms off back inside. I follow him, because if he thinks for a minute that he can say hurtful things to me like that and then just walk away, he's very much mistaken. "Don't you dare walk away from me you bastard!" I yell.

Swinging around to face me, he just holds out his arms and shrugs. "If you're looking for an apology, it isn't going to happen." I'm just about to hurl more abuse at him when he cuts me off. "You know, most women would give their right arm to be in your shoes right now, to be given the opportunity to live out in LA with me for the rest of their days. But not you, Lauren. Not you. I shouldn't be so surprised really, you always did like the simple things in life. Our days together in Manchester are a fine example of that. Only difference back then was that you actually kept your clothes on for a living as opposed to taking them off!"

Anger like never before boils out of me. Stepping forward, I slap him so hard across the face, the palm of my hand stings afterwards. And just as Jonny is coming round from the shock, I slap him again and again and again. "Don't you ever undermine my life down in London ever again, do you hear me, Jonny?!" I scream at him.

Jonny shrinks away from me slightly, his hand on his now reddened cheek. For the first time since this argument between us began, I think I see a slight pang of guilt cross his face. But I'm too far gone to give a shit about whether or not he feels guilty. Right now, I couldn't care less if I never see him again after today.

"And what's so bloody wonderful about your life over in LA then, huh? The money? The fame? The women? You know something, Jonny, my life here in London has had its fair share of ups and downs but for the last nine or so years, I've been happy enough and settled. I have Stacey and we have a good group of friends and I have money and a roof over my head. Okay, so you spoiled me for every other man I ever met after you but you know what? I made a *good* life for myself down here despite all of that. I came down here with hardly anything at all and yet, I made it. I got a job, got a home, and made friends. That was all I ever needed, so don't you bloody dare undermine everything I've fought so hard to get for myself over the last ten years. Don't you bloody dare!"

Jonny's hand drops from his face in shock, my words finally

registering with him. Too late for that though, I can't even bear to look at him right now. And I don't. Pushing past him, I quickly grab my underwear and dress from the floor by the coffee table and then head over to the bedroom to get dressed.

"Lauren...I..." Jonny starts to speak but then thinks better of it and instead falls silent.

I can feel his eyes on me as I go into the bedroom, but I don't turn round to look back at him. Slamming the door behind me, I waste no time in getting dressed. I'm probably going to look like a right state walking through the posh hotel reception this morning, shamefully wearing my dress and underwear from the night before like some high class hooker. But, I don't really care. I just want to get out of here. And fast.

Walking out of the bedroom, I head straight over to the front door of Jonny's suite. Jonny rushes over to me in a panic. "Lauren, I'm sorry, please stay, let's talk this through. Please..."

Glaring up at him, I say, "Sorry is just a word, Jonny." Looking ridden with guilt, Jonny stays silent. "So next time you say sorry to me," I continue, "mean it."

And just like that, I walk away. I open up the door and walk away from him without even looking back. I just need to be away from him. But for how long, I honestly don't know.

After leaving Jonny, I do my walk of shame through the hotel reception area and head straight home. Thankfully, the apartment is empty when I get there. Stacey must have also decided to stay at the hotel last night with Ben instead of coming home and I'm actually grateful for her not being here. The last thing I want or need right now is a full on Stacey inquisition. I meander through to my bedroom and get dressed into a tank top and jeans, throwing my clothing from the night before into the laundry basket.

Slumping down onto my bed, I am just about to lie down

when my mobile phone starts ringing. Reaching over to my bedside cabinet, I pick up my mobile to see Jonny's name flashing up at me. I reject the call and then quickly switch my mobile off. I can't face speaking to him right now.

In fact, now that I've switched off my phone, Jonny will be doing the next best thing to try and talk to me. He'll be coming straight over here. In which case, he leaves me no choice. I'm going out, and I'll make damn sure I'll be out for some time . I could do with clearing my head anyway and London is the ideal place to do that. Yes, time to go for a long walk I think.

****

I walk around London for at least two hours, mostly window shopping and people watching. It's a really good way of clearing my head and it seems to be working, until I decide to pop into a nearby café for a quick sit down and a coffee. And that's when I start thinking. Thinking about whether Jonny and I are even compatible anymore. Clearly, we're still more than compatible in the bedroom, we're combustible in fact in that department, but, putting the physical side of our relationship to one side for the moment, I do wonder whether there really is anything else between us anymore.

My chest constricts in pain at the very thought. Of course there's something more than just physical between us. There's so much love still between us and yet, somehow or other, it doesn't feel quite the same as it once did. Not yet anyway.

Thinking back to our time together in Manchester, I feel a pang of grief for the relationship I once had with Jonny. It was a completely different life we led back then, we were so young and naïve, so in love and so very happy. We had lots of dreams and ambitions. We were going to take on the world together. And then I fell pregnant. It was a huge shock at the time but Jonny and I embraced my pregnancy, both excited about the prospect of a little "us" arriving into our little bubble of love that we had created with each other.

We'd just found out I was expecting a little boy, right before he was cruelly snatched away from us. Our little Oliver didn't even get to take his first breath. I never got to hear his newborn cry or cradle him on my shoulder in the middle of the night as he fell asleep after his midnight feed. I never became a mummy, and Jonny never became a daddy. Something that went on to eventually destroy everything that we ever had together.

And now, here we are, ten years on, both completely different people from who we were back then. Change is to be expected of course. Two people can't possibly be apart for an entire decade and then come back together as if they've never been away from each other. But, Jonny has changed so much that I barely recognised him this morning. The rich and famous lifestyle he leads these days has clearly left its mark on him. He's so used to getting his own way on a daily basis that he almost has a tantrum when he doesn't get it. To the point of behaving like a child and hurting the one woman he says he loves more than anything.

Jonny was always argumentative and stubborn but he was never hurtful to me. I've been on the receiving end of Jonny's nasty tongue one too many times already since our reunion and at first, I put it down to him hating my job, but now, I can see that it isn't just that. It's part of who he is now and, in all honesty, I don't know whether I can live with it. I shouldn't have to live with it, that's the point.

Picking up my cup from the table, I drink the last of my coffee and decide to go for another long walk. To Hyde Park this time. I need to be on the move again because I'm dwelling far too much just sitting here, doing nothing. Maybe going out into the fresh air again will clear my head properly this time. Here's hoping....

****

I while away the hours in Hyde Park for the rest of the afternoon and when tea time arrives, I decide to treat myself to a meal out at one of the local pubs nearer to home. It's another way of avoiding going home and facing the music I suppose, but it's a nice treat for me too.

It's almost 8.00 pm by the time I finally arrive home and what a facing it is when I get there. Walking into the lounge, I find both Jonny and Stacey pacing up and down, the pair of them talking over each other loudly as they fight between themselves over what to do next. Lucky for them they don't need to do anything at all now.

"Lauren!" screeches Stacey, looking royally pissed off with me, "where the hell have you been?!"

Heading over to the kitchen, I place my handbag down on the worktop and say, probably a little too casually, "I've had a day out in London, Stace, am I not allowed to have a day to myself now?"

Placing my hand on my hip, I look over at the pair of them once more. Stacey looks furious whereas Jonny just looks uncomfortable. And quiet. He hasn't said a word to me as yet, which is a good thing. Jonny being sensible for once by keeping his mouth shut tells me that he knows he was in the wrong this morning and still feels guilty for it. Well good, so he should feel guilty.

"One text message!" snaps Stacey, holding up her index finger, "one bloody text message just to tell us where you were and that you were okay, Lauren!" I'm just about to defend myself when Stacey cuts me off. "Eight hours you've been gone! You can't expect us to not start panicking about you when you've been gone for eight hours without any contact whatsoever!"

I frown over at Stacey. "And how would you know I've been gone for eight hours? You weren't even here when I came home this morning."

"Jonny told me of course!" shouts Stacey, gesturing over at Jonny who is looking more uncomfortable by the minute.

"Of course he did," I say with an eye roll.

"Hey!" says Stacey, storming over to me in the kitchen, "whatever is going on with you two, just sort it the hell out but all I ask is that in future? At least just tell me where you are so I don't worry about you!"

Feeling a little guilty about making my best friend worry unnecessarily, I say, "You're right, I'm sorry." Glancing over at Jonny, I then say, "But I'm only sorry for making *you* worry Stace. Nobody else." Jonny rolls his eyes at my little dig at him and then shakes his head, still saying nothing.

Looking between us, Stacey says, "Look, I'm going to work now so you two just sort it out. Whatever it is, just sort it out."

Really not wanting to be left alone with Jonny to "face the music" as it were, I can't help but dig my heels in with him even more. "I'd prefer it if you stayed and Jonny left," I say to Stacey.

With a roll of her eyes, Stacey says, "Sorry, Lauren, work calls and all that." On her way out of the kitchen, Stacey says to Jonny, "Looks like you've got your work cut out with this one tonight. Good luck." One more glance over at me and then Stacey is gone.

The sound of the front door closing fills me with dread because now, Jonny and I are well and truly alone. Something that I've been trying to avoid all day long. Jonny is standing at the opposite end of the kitchen to me, resting against one of the kitchen cupboards with his arms folded. Blowing out a breath from between his lips, he finally speaks. "So, are you going to talk to me or not?" Jonny looks over at me and I immediately avoid his gaze.

"Not," I say firmly. Turning away from him, I set about busying myself in the kitchen, starting with wiping up the pots that have been left on the draining board for the last two days.

With a heavy sigh, Jonny says, "So, that's it? I'm just supposed to accept you not talking to me and walk away then, am I?"

"Not really bothered, Jonny, just do what you want. That's what you normally do, isn't it?"

"Okay, fine, you're unbelievably pissed at me, I get that, but at least give me the chance to apologise for the things I said to you this morning," says Jonny, beginning to sound irate.

Slamming down one of the dishes I'd starting wiping, I finally whirl around to face him properly. "You want to apologise, do you?!" I yell. Placing a hand on my hip, I say, "Well go ahead then, Jonny, apologise away if it makes *you* feel better!"

Pushing himself away from the cupboard, he then stands in the middle of the kitchen. Holding out his arms in surrender, he says, "Okay, I'm a bastard! I'm a hurtful, arrogant bastard who doesn't deserve you! I hate myself for what I said to you this morning, really I do. I've been in turmoil all day long and yes, I deserve to feel that way but please believe me, Lauren, that I am standing here now in front of you, truly sorry for everything that I said."

"You said you meant it this morning," I say bitterly, "you said you wouldn't apologise for what you said because you bloody well meant it!"

"I was angry!" he shouts, "and upset at the thought of being apart from you for an entire month after just getting you back in my life! Yes, I shouldn't have said what I said and yes, it was hurtful, but people say things sometimes when they're angry that they don't really mean."

I shake my head at him. "Being angry is not an excuse for saying what you said to me, Jonny. You belittled my life here in London, you made nasty digs at me again over my former job and not only that, you belittled the life we once shared together in Manchester. A life you once claimed to love..."

"I did love that life with you, Lauren, I loved it so much that I physically ache whenever I think about it," says Jonny, looking desperate. Placing his hand across his heart, he says, "And I want that life with you again. I want it so much that I'll do anything to get it, and if that means living without you for a few weeks while you sort yourself out here in London then I'll do it, Lauren. I'll fucking well do it, because I'm desperate here. I'm desperate to hold on to you and never let go."

Jonny's sorrowful eyes meet with mine, the look of pure panic on his face finally striking a chord with me. I can feel my anger towards him beginning to dissipate, but my uncertainty remains. Uncertainty over whether we can really make a happy life together out there, because, after this morning, I'm not so sure that we can.

"Jonny, I..." I hesitate, trying to find the right words to say to him, "I can see that you're sorry now, and I accept that, but, I've spent a lot of time thinking about us today and in all honesty, I'm not so sure about the whole moving over to LA thing anymore..."

"You're unsure?" asks Jonny, looking even more worried than he did before, "but I thought you wanted to be with me. I thought we were forever..."

"Jonny, I love you more than anything or anyone else in this world but, you've changed so much over the last ten years and with the lifestyle you lead now, it's to be expected…but, this morning, when you said those hurtful things to me, I barely even recognised you."

Jonny shakes his head at me. "Don't write me off yet, Lauren, please. I know I've changed in some ways and not for the better, but I can work on it. I want to work on it. For you. For us. There's still some of the old Jonny left in me, you just have to dig a little deeper to find him. And you have found him, many times already, when we've made love, and you know you have."

Looking down at the floor, I say quietly, "I know I have, and I believe everything that you're saying to me, about working on things and trying harder, really I do, but it's not just about this morning. Like I said before, I've had all day to think about things properly today and I admit that I'm scared. Scared of going over there with you on the promise that everything will be okay and then it isn't. Your life in LA is a completely different world to the one I've been living in London and that scares me, Jonny. It scares the shit out of me."

Jonny approaches me cautiously. "I understand why you feel scared, Lauren, I do, and I understand it's going to take you a long time to adjust to that life out there with me but, our life out there together is going to be what we make it, and if we want it to be like it used to be in Manchester, then it will be. I'll make damn sure of that."

I shake my head at him. "Our life will never be like it once was in Manchester. Never. I have to share you with the entire world now and I don't really like the thought of having to share you at all. With anyone."

Daring to touch me for the first time since this morning, Jonny takes a hold of one of my hands. Squeezing it gently, he says, "My life over there isn't as busy or as crazy as you might think it is. The tours are always mad crazy yes, but, when the tours are over and done with, my life does eventually go back to something that you might call normal. I promise."

Feeling a bit more reassured about things, I nod my head gently. "Okay then," I say quietly.

Looking up into his face, I'm met with uncertain eyes. "Okay? As in, okay you will come out to LA to live with me?"

I nod. "Yes, I'll move out to LA with you, Jonny, but still on the condition that I only move out there in a month's time."

Jonny nods eagerly. "Of course, whatever you want." Taking hold of my other hand, Jonny then says, "And now I have a condition of my own."

Raising a suspicious eyebrow up at him, I say, "Which is?"

Clearing his throat, Jonny says, "I've decided to stay in London for another week, so that we're only apart for three weeks instead of an entire month. If that's okay with you of course?" Jonny looks at me tentatively, trying to gauge my reaction to this sudden announcement.

"Okay," I say, feeling a little unsure about his decision.

Releasing my hands from his grip, Jonny frowns down at me. "Well, you could look a bit more enthusiastic about my decision."

Feeling bad for making him think otherwise, I say, "Sorry, it's not that I'm not enthusiastic about you staying longer, it's just, well, with your mum being terminally ill and the US tour coming up next month, are you sure it's a good idea to stay here longer than you originally planned to?"

He shrugs off all of my worries. "My mum is doing okay at the moment and I speak to her every day so I'm in constant touch with her, and as for the tour, my employees over at the label will take care of all of that and it doesn't start for another five weeks anyway, so there'll be plenty of time for me to catch up on all the preparations when I go home next week." Jonny makes his busy life sound so simple and easy sometimes. I'm fairly sure that it isn't, but, if he says it is, then, who am I to argue?

"Okay, condition accepted," I say.

Jonny smiles with relief. "Well, thank god for that." He falls silent for a moment and then says, "So, am I allowed to kiss you now?"

Still feeling a little vulnerable and unsure after everything that's happened between us today, I say, "Not just yet, Jonny. Why don't we just...have a drink together or something. Cup of coffee?"

Jonny looks a little dejected when I say that, but he quickly recovers. "Sure," he says, nodding, "whatever you want, Lauren."

Smiling, I say, "Coffee it is then."

CHAPTER 16

By the time Wednesday rolls around, I am so relieved when Jonny doesn't have to board that plane back to LA. So relieved in fact that I can't get enough of him, or him of me. We literally spend all of our first day alone together locked away in the bedroom in his hotel suite, only surfacing every now and again to go to the toilet or to have something to eat. It's like being on honeymoon but without the wedding ceremony. And it's bliss. Pure, uninterrupted bliss.

At least, it's pure uninterrupted bliss until Thursday afternoon anyway. When our alone time together comes to an abrupt end when Jonny receives a worrying phone call. A phone call that drags him straight out of the bedroom and onto the balcony outside.

Wrapping the bed sheet around myself to cover my nakedness, I walk out of the bedroom and try to follow Jonny outside onto the balcony, but when I get there, I see he's already closed the French doors behind him. He clearly doesn't want me to hear what's going on. I should be upset that he's keeping me out of the loop but at this moment in time, all I care about is the phone call not being about his mum. Because if anything happens to her while he's over here with me when he should have gone back home yesterday to be by her side, I will never ever forgive myself.

Feeling brave, I dare to open the French doors and step out onto the balcony. Jonny immediately turns round to face me as soon as he hears the doors opening. He looks so angry. As angry as he looked the other night when he was on the phone to his dad. Oh no, this is what the phone call is about. It's about me. I know it is.

Covering over the speaker on his phone with his hand, he shakes his head at me and says, "Go back inside, Lauren."

That sounded more like an order to me, not a request. Feeling a little annoyed at his tone, I stand firm. With a roll of his eyes, he then says to the person on the other end of the phone, "Just hang on a minute." Covering over the speaker once more, he glares over at me. "I said to go inside, Lauren, this doesn't concern you." Doesn't concern me! Who the hell does he think he is?

Folding my arms across my chest, I say firmly, "It concerns me a hell of a lot if something bad has happened to your mum."

Jonny's eyes soften slightly and he suddenly remembers himself. "Of course. I'm sorry. Don't worry, Lauren, my mum is fine."

Well, I'm glad he's at least had the decency to speak to me properly this time and calm my worries over his mum. Even so... "You sure?" I can't help but double check with Jonny, he has a tendency to tell people what they want to hear sometimes instead of telling them the truth. Me included.

With a nod of his head, he says, "I promise."

"Okay," I reply quietly, although I'm still not so sure whether I really believe him or not. But, whether I do or I don't doesn't make any difference to Jonny, who clearly wants to be left alone right now.

"Sweetheart, why don't you ring Stacey and have some girly time together, or something? I just need to sort out some business but I promise not to be too long. Okay?"

Girly time? I wonder whether or not to remind Jonny of the

fact that Stacey is hardly going to be wanting girly time with me when she is currently residing in a suite on the floor below us in the very same hotel with that new found boyfriend of hers.

Ben is so besotted with Stacey that he too decided to stay in London for an extra week along with Jonny. Stacey of course was thrilled at the prospect, which is why she's hardly going to be up for spending any time with me this afternoon. Still, we are best friends after all and soon, we won't be able to spend any time together at all when I move over to LA.

Yes, I'll at least give Stacey a ring and see if she wants to go and do some shopping or something. Maybe Ben will come up here himself and find out what the hell is going on. Or maybe he already knows. Either way, I'll give Jonny the space he needs. The inquisition can wait. For now.

"Okay," I finally say. With a thankful nod of his head, Jonny then turns back to his all-important phone conversation.

Leaving him to it, I close the French doors behind me and head back to the bedroom. As I go about getting myself dressed for the day, my mind starts to work overtime. So much so that it starts giving me a headache. Right, I need a distraction. And that distraction is Stacey. Calling up her number on my mobile, I am surprised when she answers after just two rings.

"Hey, girlfriend," she gushes at me down the phone.

"We need some girly time, Stace, and we need it now... please?"

Stacey doesn't even hesitate with her answer. "Of course we can have some girly time, Lauren. Is everything okay?"

I answer honestly. "I'm not really sure, but one thing I am sure of is, I need a drink."

I can practically hear Stacey smiling at me down the phone.

"When you say drink, I am assuming you are referring to alcohol?"

"Hell yes."

She chuckles. "It's three o'clock in the afternoon and you're in desperate need of alcohol? It must be bad. Have you two fallen out again?"

Snatching my handbag up from the sofa on my way out of the hotel suite, I turn around once more and look over at the French doors. They're still closed. "Not exactly."

Sighing down the phone at me, she says, "Okay, well, as volatile as you two are, I don't need an excuse to go out drinking in the afternoon with my best friend, I'll see you in two minutes."

"Won't Ben be pissed off at me for tearing you away from him for more than just a few minutes?" I ask, feeling suddenly guilty for intruding on their alone time.

Another chuckle and then Stacey says, "Ben is currently fast asleep on the sofa in the living room of our hotel suite, I think I've worn him out this week." I burst out laughing when she says that. "And anyway," Stacey continues, "even if he was awake and pissed off, I couldn't care less, because you are the most important person to me, Lauren Whittle, and don't ever forget that."

Smiling at her down the phone, I say, "I won't, I promise."

"Good, now get your ass down here pronto before he wakes up and finds us out." I laugh.

"I'm on my way."

****

Being with Stacey for the rest of the afternoon is like a breath of fresh air. After giving her a brief rundown of what went on earlier with Jonny's mysterious phone call, we then change the subject and have a right good giggle, not to mention too much alcohol. And as it's Stacey's night off from work tonight, the pair of us decide to really let our hair down and hit the bars of London like we really mean it.

We drink, we chat and we dance the evening away and before we know it, we completely lose track of time. Until one of us finally breaks away from all the gossiping and the drinking to actually check our mobile phone. Oops, it's now 10.00 pm and from my call log, Jonny has tried ringing me at least ten times up to now.

Giving Stacey a gentle nudge with my elbow, she then checks her mobile to discover that Ben has also tried ringing her as many times as Jonny has tried ringing me. Double oops. Oh well, we've been having the best time ever and anyway, this was all Jonny's idea in the first place.

We head outside of the wine bar we're currently drinking in so that we can both check in with our men. Stacey rings Ben first and ends up with an ear bashing down the phone, asking her why she never woke him to tell him where she was going or even leave him a note. Stacey gives him a good ear bashing back and within two minutes, Ben is apologising down the phone to her. Stacey is smiling at him down the phone so I know he's more than saying sorry right now.

It turns out Ben is with Jonny and has been for a while and so Stacey passes her phone over to me so that I can speak to him. Jonny must snatch the phone away from Ben though because Ben has barely said hello to me before Jonny is snapping at me down the phone.

"Where have you been, Lauren? I've been worried sick for hours!"

Oh, here we go again, Jonny being his usual bossy, arrogant

self. I wouldn't mind but this was his idea after all, and with the alcohol now running riot in my system, I more than let him know that.

"From memory, you told me to have some girly time with my best friend, so that's what I've been doing and will continue to do if you speak to me like that again."

I'm met with a heavy sigh down the phone. "You're pissed."

"If you mean I'm pissed as in drunk, then yes, Jonny, I am well and truly on my way to being pissed, that's for sure."

"Where are you?" he asks, sounding impatient.

Turning to Stacey, I flash her a cheeky smile and she grins right back at me. She's as pissed as I am. "We're at some wine bar on the outskirts of London. Want to join us? Bring Ben along too." Stacey nods her head enthusiastically and claps her hands together with excitement. But that excitement is soon dampened, as is mine.

"Really? You expect me and Ben to just pitch up at some bar at ten o'clock at night and walk right in there like we're just normal people? What planet are you on, Lauren?" And that's when I snap. Again!

"Of course," I say, a little too loudly, "sorry, I forgot, you and Ben aren't normal at all, are you? I mean, you and Ben just wanting to go out for a drink with your girls at *some* bar in London must take weeks, no, months of planning, what with your security team permanently needing to be by your side and everything. I mean, this place is crawling with your fans, Jonny, and the paparazzi, well, they're just hiding behind the tables in this place waiting for you both to arrive!"

"Look, I've had a lot on today, Lauren, the last thing I need is for you to start giving me shit over the phone because you're pissed," Jonny snaps.

"And what I need right now is for my boyfriend to tell me what the hell is going on with him?" I snap right back.

I can feel Stacey grimacing next to me. I can also feel about half a dozen pairs of eyes on me right now, fellow customers of the bar who've come outside to enjoy a smoke and a drink in pleasant surroundings and are instead being subjected to this crap, courtesy of me and Jonny.

Oh well, only one way to put a stop to that. "Look, if you don't want to tell me what's been going on with you today, then don't, but I am not coming back to your hotel room just because you're telling me to. Yes, I am a little drunk and gobby, but Stacey and I are enjoying ourselves and that's what you told me to do, Jonny. Remember?"

He goes quiet for a moment, and then sighs. "I guess I did say that, yes."

"So, are you going to join us then?"

I already know the answer to this question but I'm desperate here. Desperate to have some sort of normality with the boyfriend I once knew. Jonny said to me only the other day that the old Jonny is in there somewhere, but boy is it hard finding him at the moment. Finding him in the bedroom isn't the only place I want that man. I want him here with me, now.

Yes, he's famous and yes, I do understand the whole security thing and the constant worry of being recognised and mobbed by over enthusiastic fans or the press but, when all said and done, famous or not, Jonny's life can be lived however he chooses to live it. And if he wants to come down to some unknown bar in London to spend time with his girlfriend and his friends then he should be allowed to do it. But he won't do it. I know he won't. The Jonny I once knew always lived life on the edge, never caring about the consequences of pretty much anything he did but now, well, this life of his has changed him beyond words.

"I can't, Lauren, you know I can't."

Feeling more sad than I expected to feel, I say quietly into the phone, "Okay, maybe next time then."

"Lauren..." Jonny starts to speak but I instead hand Stacey's mobile back to her.

With a roll of her eyes, she awkwardly places her mobile against her ear once more, half expecting Jonny to still be on the other end. "Oh, hey baby," she says in surprise. "Erm...no idea. Look, I'm staying with Lauren tonight. Okay?"

Stacey's phone conversation with Ben is a lot easier and far more pleasant than mine was with Jonny, leading me to wonder yet again if Jonny and I are ever going to last the test of time.

When Stacey hangs up the phone, I say to her, "Are you thirsty?"

Stacey raises her eyebrows up at me. "Seriously? You want more alcohol?"

"After that little chat with Jonny, he's driven me to drink. You can blame him for this, Stace, not me."

Threading her arm through mine, she says, "Okay, a couple more drinks and then I'm taking you home, Lauren Whittle. We'll keep each other company tonight."

Wrapping an arm around my best friend, I pull her tightly against me. "I love you, Stacey Kerr. I'll never be able to live in LA without you, you know."

Stacey forces a smile to her face when I say that. "Let's not do that right now, Lauren. Let's just...live for tonight." I like that saying. I like it a hell of a lot.

With a smile on my face, I say, "Yes, let's live for tonight, Stace."

****

I wake up the following morning in my own bed, all alone, with the mother of all hangovers. It feels as though I have little people hammering away at my skull with chisels, my head is *that* painful. My tongue is so dry, it has literally glued itself to the roof of my mouth. *What the hell was I thinking last night?* I wasn't thinking, I was too busy enjoying, that was the problem. I should have come home when Stacey initially said to. Oh well, too late now. I wonder if Stacey feels as crap as I do.

After ten minutes of attempting to peel myself away from my mattress, I finally get out of bed and shrug into my dressing gown. My head begins to thud as I walk through the hallway and into the living room. To my surprise, Stacey is already up and about. In fact, more than that, she is over in the kitchen cooking us a fry up. Eurgh, food, I can't face food right now, or ever again.

Stacey turns around and grins widely at me. "Good morning," she says, far too breezily for my liking.

With a groan, I slump down into one of the dining chairs. Placing my arms flat on the table, I rest my head on them. "Is it?"

Stacey chuckles. "I would say I told you so, but I won't."

Lifting up my head slowly so as not to encourage the little people currently chiselling away at it, I mumble, "You just did."

Biting down on a smile, Stacey says, "Sorry, couldn't resist."

I groan again in discomfort. "Oh, Stace, I know you're doing a lovely thing cooking us some breakfast but, I really can't face eating anything right now."

Stacey sighs. "The cure to a hangover is food, so you are eating this whether you like it or not. You then need to take some painkillers and drink a pint of water. That should pretty much do it."

Placing my chin in my hands, I say, "How the hell are you so chirpy this morning? You drank nearly as much as I did."

Stacey shrugs. "I don't know why but I'm not complaining. Now come on, get this down you."

Stacey places a plate loaded with what should look like a mouth-watering, hard to resist, cooked breakfast in front of me. To me, the very thought of eating it makes me want to be sick. But Stacey is insistent that I eat something and so, after much deliberation, I do as I'm told.

Sitting opposite me, Stacey starts to tuck into her own cooked breakfast, with far more enthusiasm than me. "Oh, by the way, Tony and Andy are coming to pick us up in an hour," she says, ever so casually.

I almost choke on the mushroom I'm currently chewing. "Erm, what? Why the hell are Jonny's bodyguards coming here to collect us?" I ask, the look on my face probably saying it all.

Stacey pauses with her fork in mid-air. "Because the boys want to see us of course and apparently, the crowds outside the hotel have doubled overnight. It's for our safety."

"For our safety? But why do we even need to go to the hotel? If they want to see us so badly then why don't they come here?"

Stacey sighs. "Lauren, don't be difficult again. Jonny is trying to make nice."

My turn to sigh this time. "You are so easily swayed by Jonny and this lifestyle of his, aren't you? Look, if they are so desperate to stay out of the limelight and away from all the crowds then they need to be well away from that hotel."

"Hey, I am not easily swayed by anything and if you must know, I think the exact opposite to you. Why should they check out of the hotel that they're currently staying in because of all the crowds outside? That's just running away from the issue instead of facing it."

"I'd want to run away from the crowds. I say retreat away from all of that media shit and go and hide under a rock somewhere."

I start to pick at my food. Just as I was beginning to get an appetite, I now feel sick again. Sick at the thought of turning up at the hotel to be faced with crowds of strangers just waiting for a glimpse of my boyfriend. The whole concept of it just messes with my head and in all honesty, I can't bear to think about it at the moment.

"Why have the crowds doubled overnight, anyway? Don't they have anything else to do with their boring lives?"

Swallowing down a mouthful of food, Stacey says, "Because they're wondering why on earth their idol is still residing here in London with the band's bassist while the other half of Reclamation have gone home. There's apparently an article in one of the tabloids this morning saying that some of the fans are fearing the worst, that the band are breaking up now that their European tour has finished and that the US tour is going to be cancelled."

"That's ridiculous!" I yell.

Stacey shrugs. "Yes, *we* know it's ridiculous but if you think about it, they're going to think that until they hear otherwise."

Placing my head in my hands, I say, "Meaning that Jonny or his dad or the label have to make a statement to the press to tell people why he's still over here. Oh shit. Shit shit shit. This is going to piss his dad right off. Even more than he was before."

"Hey," says Stacey, forcing me to look at her, "they could just deny the rumours and not actually give a reason but, as yet, Ben says Jonny is not for saying anything which kind of makes it more difficult for both you and him but, well, you know Jonny."

Sitting back in my chair, I look up at the ceiling and let out a huge, exasperated sigh. "Oh, I know Jonny alright, and if Jonny doesn't want to make a statement to the world's media then he won't. He won't be forced into anything, trust me."

When Stacey stays silent, I speak again. "Jonny and I would probably be married now, if I hadn't have just upped and left him when I did. We would be happily married, perhaps with children, both with normal nine to five jobs and a small two up, two down house in the suburbs of Manchester somewhere. He'd come home every night to find his dinner on the table and his children doing their homework. He'd get up the following morning, kiss his wife and his children goodbye and then go on his merry way to work. Without being followed by people. Without being recognised by anybody other than the people who already know and love him. That's what our life should have been like, Stace, and now, thanks to me, we're faced with this. This nightmare that seems to be his life and I have no fucking idea how to handle it."

"Hey," says Stacey. Taking hold of one of my hands from across the table, she squeezes it gently. "Nothing is worth making you panicky, Lauren, so please take a deep breath and calm down. It'll all work out in the end with Jonny. I promise you it will." God, I hope she's right. I so want her to be right.

With a nod of my head, I say, "You're right, I do need to calm down. And I think when I see Jonny, I'll feel better. Everything was kind of left hanging between us last night and now, the following morning, in the garish light of day and with a hangover to end all hangovers, I just want to make it right with him."

Stacey smiles. "So go and talk to him and make it right with him."

Squeezing her hand right back, I say, "I will. And thanks, Stace. For last night and this morning. For everything."

"That's what best friends are for, Lauren. Now, finish your breakfast and go and get showered and ready, Tony and Andy will be here in an hour to collect us, remember?"

With a roll of my eyes, I say, "How could I forget?"

****

Unsurprisingly, Jonny is on the phone when I arrive at his hotel suite, just as he was a little under twenty four hours ago. He's sitting on the sofa in the living room with his phone pressed to his ear whilst dragging his other hand back and forth through his hair in agitation.

Wearing only a pair of light grey sweatpants and nothing else, my eyes go straight to the tattoos on his arms and chest, the inky works of art already working their magic on me, drawing me in like a magnet that cannot be pulled back, even if it wanted to be. The question is, do I want to be pulled back from Jonny right now? Well, after the hassle of actually getting into the damn hotel without being seen by the crowds – Andy and Tony took us round the back of the hotel and we got in that way – I am just relieved to be here actually, and so, the answer to that question is a definite no. I don't want to be pulled back from Jonny. I just want to be with him. Talking to him would be a start though.

Walking right into the middle of the living room, I deliberately stand on the other side of the coffee table directly in front of him. Folding my arms across my chest, I just stare down at him and wait until he bothers to actually make eye contact with me. He knows I'm here of course, but he's just so involved in whatever is going on at the moment that he's focusing on the phone call and blatantly ignoring me.

"Look, I said I need to think about what to do first...no. Do nothing. I'll handle it. We'll talk later."

Jonny abruptly ends the call and then tosses his mobile on to the coffee table in front of him, almost smashing the expensive looking glass. Looking up at me, he sets me with a serious, but penetrating gaze. Unfortunately, my body is now reacting to that gaze of his, goosebumps now popping up all over my skin. Damn my hormones.

"I missed you last night," he says quietly.

Feeling a pang of guilt for not coming back to his hotel room last night after my drunken antics with Stacey, I say truthfully, "I missed you too." And I did miss him. I especially missed not waking up next to him this morning.

"Are you hungover?" he enquires.

"I was," I say with a shrug, "but one Stacey Kerr breakfast, two pints of water and two painkillers later, I'm feeling much better than I was...look, Jonny, right now, I couldn't care less about me. I'm just worried about you. And I've been worrying about you since yesterday afternoon so please tell me what's going on."

Jonny glances away from me briefly, as if contemplating what to say to me next. "It's nothing you need to worry about, Lauren."

With a heavy sigh, I say, "Why won't you just talk to me? What's wrong?"

Standing up from the sofa, Jonny walks over to where I'm standing. Placing himself deliberately between me and the coffee table, he then cups my face in his hands, taking me completely by surprise. "I don't want to talk," he whispers.

His dark brown eyes are ablaze with heat, his body pressing hard against mine, proving, yet again, how desperately he wants me. And as much as I want to talk to him. As much as I want him to just tell me what the hell is going on, I can't resist the pull of him. And I don't.

I allow him to strip me completely naked. I allow him to throw me onto the sofa and to take me right there and then. I allow him to fuck me until I can't think straight. And then, when he's finished, I beg him to do it to me all over again. And again. And again. Because I need this. I need him. I need all of him and I will stop at nothing to get it.

He gives me orgasm after orgasm, making me scream, making me pant, making my body all wet and slippery. And I do the same to him. It's angry and intense and so hot and wild that I don't want it to end. Because this is us. Jonny and Lauren. We're volatile and passionate, and desperately in love. And in spite of everything, we'll always come back to this. To each other. No matter what stands in our way.

****

Some time later, when we've finally drained each other of absolutely everything we have, we lie back on the bed, fighting to get our breath back. After having me on every surface imaginable, Jonny finally brought me in here, the bedroom, finishing off our hour long sexathon on one unbelievable high. I swear he's like a drug to me, giving me the highest of the highs to the point where I find myself actually *needing* my fix of him. I am well and truly addicted and he knows it. Boy does he know it.

Rolling on to my side, I catch Jonny staring up at the ceiling, still fighting to get his breath back. Propping myself up onto my elbow, I decide to use this post sex opportunity to my advantage before the rosy afterglow of our intimate time together wears off.

"So," I say quietly, "I thought that maybe later on today we could perhaps...go for a walk in Hyde Park or something, or maybe grab some lunch together, you know, like a normal couple."

Jonny sighs heavily, his eyes closing briefly. "Lauren, I told you last night, I can't just do that as easily as you seem to think I can. Plus, I've still got some stuff to sort out back here." Averting his eyes from the ceiling, he finally turns to me and says, "You know this already and yet you still won't let it go, will you?"

Okay, so the rosy afterglow has already upped and gone, if it ever even existed. Rolling away from him in anger, I then sit myself up on the bed and glare down at him. "So this is all I get, is it? You and me locked away within these four walls for an entire week while you're constantly on the bloody phone to LA?"

"Lauren..."

"Is this what you had planned for our week alone together? To do nothing other than each other in between you taking calls from across the Atlantic?"

He scowls up at me. "I didn't see or hear you complaining about any of that just now, Lauren. In fact, you were saying the exact opposite of what you're saying to me now. *Begging* me in fact to do it again, and again, and again after that. And now I'm the one in the wrong?!"

Sitting himself up on the side of the bed, Jonny then turns his back on me and proceeds to get dressed. Something that hurts me that little bit more. Him just turning away from me like I mean nothing more to him than an easy lay he's just had with one of his many women.

"You make it sound so cheap, Jonny," I bite out, "like what we've just done together for the last hour is cheap and sordid and nothing more."

Pulling his sweatpants back on, Jonny turns to me and gives me a look of complete disbelief. "Lauren, what the fuck are you talking about? How is me telling you what you've just clearly enjoyed doing with me in any way cheap?"

Folding my arms across my chest in order to cover up some of my nakedness, I say, "It's not just what you said to me, Jonny, it's how you said it."

Holding out his arms to the sides, he says, "Well it doesn't seem to matter what I say or do to you at the moment, does it? Because, where you're concerned? It's wrong. Everything I fucking do or say at the moment is wrong in your eyes!"

"Oh, that's bullshit!" I snap, "that's bloody bullshit, Jonny, and you know it! I just want you to talk to me like you were doing last week! I just want you to tell me what the hell is going on so I can help you! And yes, I want to do other things with you other than just having sex. As mind blowing as the sex is, we were always about more than that!"

Gripping his hair in anger, he says, "It's manic out there, Lauren! I can't just walk out there holding your hand and take you for a leisurely stroll through a park! And believe me, I want nothing more than that at the moment. But I can't."

"If this is about the tabloids starting the rumour about you guys possibly breaking up because you're still here in London with Ben then just set the record straight, tell them why you're here!"

Jonny shakes his head at me. "And feed you to them? No, Lauren. I will not hand you over to them vultures just yet because believe me, sweetheart, when they get a hold of you, they will not let up and I won't allow that to happen. I won't."

Calming down slightly at seeing how torn up he is over this issue, I lower my voice. "Then don't tell them anything other than the truth, that you're not breaking up and the US tour is going ahead as planned."

Jonny sighs. "It's not as easy as that, it's not as cut and dry as you think it is."

Raising an eyebrow up at him, I press him for more information. "What do you mean?" Jonny hesitates, but before he has the chance to even consider giving me a proper answer this time, his mobile starts ringing. *Oh, here we go again.*

Leaping off the bed, I wrap the bed sheet around me and quickly dash over to him. "Don't answer it, Jonny. Please. Just talk to me....please?"

Jonny is torn between answering the phone or finally talking to me. Jonny looks at the screen flashing up at him, his face deadly serious. Looking back to me, he says, "I'm sorry, Lauren, I really need to take this call."

And just like that, we're back to square one all over again. I don't even bother to argue with him this time. I'm too bone weary to argue with him anymore and anyway, it's clear to me that Jonny will do what Jonny wants to do, no matter what.

"Fine," I whisper, before turning away from him. Jonny leaves the bedroom then, closing the door shut behind him.

I emerge some time later, fully dressed and ready to leave Jonny to it. I'm not hanging around here for a minute longer. I feel like Rapunzel being trapped in that tall tower with no means of escape, until she uses her beautiful long locks to her advantage and gets the hell out of there.

Well, my hair might not be anywhere near as long as Rapunzel's but, I do need to get the hell out of here. Once and for all. And yes, I know I am partly to blame for all of this, the sex with Jonny pulling me in every single time. I am weak around him and I know it, but I also know that deep down, this relationship of ours that we've rekindled together isn't healthy. We've either been arguing or having sex, without much else in between, and it can't carry on like this.

Walking out of the bedroom and into the living room, I find Jonny pacing up and down angrily whilst swearing at the person on the other end of the phone. He glances over at me and I give him a quick nod, before heading towards the door.

He panics then, knowing my intention is to just leave without saying a proper goodbye. "Look, I'll call you back," he snaps, quickly ending the phone call.

I have just about opened the front door to his suite when he slams it shut again. "Don't go, Lauren...please." Looking up at him, I try to ignore his pleading eyes. I need to stay focused.

"Tell me what's going on, Jonny, or I walk out of here right now."

With a heavy sigh, he says, "I'm just trying to protect you, that's all."

"Protect me from what?" I ask, feeling alarmed.

Taking a step backwards, he says, "Somebody somewhere has cancelled five of the thirty shows we had booked for our US tour. Five venues Lauren. The biggest venues of the lot." *What the actual hell?*

"Holy shit, Jonny...who would...who would...I mean who would do that?" I'm so shocked that I'm almost speechless.

"That's what I'm trying to find out, but at this moment in

time, I'm more bothered about how the fuck they managed to do it, the why they did it is fucking obvious."

Looking down at the floor, it doesn't take me long to work that bit out for myself. "Because you're here in London with me when you should have gone home on Wednesday," I whisper. That makes me sad. So sad for Jonny that somebody would actually do this to him.

"Exactly," says Jonny, "which is why I've been trying to keep it from you. Imagine telling the woman that you love that some evil person out there has done something as damaging as this to the band because they want him away from her that badly."

It all makes perfect sense to me now. No wonder he didn't want to share this with me. Hell, this is a lot to take in, and because it's so much to take in, I end up bursting into tears.

"Hey," says Jonny, quickly coming to my aid. Wrapping his arms around me, he holds me tightly against him. "Sssh, baby, it isn't worth the tears. *They're* not worth the tears." He kisses the top of my head and then rests his chin there.

"Who would do this to you, Jonny?" I say, my voice all wobbly, "who would be so cruel to do this to you and the band?"

Jonny falls silent for a moment and then says, "I'm not sure, although I'd be lying if I said that my dad doing this to us hadn't crossed my mind."

Pulling away from him, I look up at Jonny in shock. "No way."

"No way?" Jonny raises a questioning eyebrow up at me. "After his reaction to you being back in my life and you really don't think my dad had the means or the motive to do this?"

"The means, yes, he's the band's manager after all and is in the ideal position to be able to pull off something like this but the motive? Even your dad wouldn't do this to you and I think you know that."

"Do I?" asks Jonny, not looking convinced.

"Jonny, you and the band have been your dad's obsession for years, he prides himself on your reputation and your music, no way would he ruin that just because of me."

Thinking about it for a moment, Jonny then says, "Maybe I am taking my suspicions a little too far but, whoever did it knew all about the venues and the planning behind it all, they were meticulous in their timing of it too. This bastard fucking works for me, I'm sure of it, and when I find out who is behind it, they'll regret they ever crossed me."

"So, what are you going to do? About the cancelled shows?"

"That's what I've been trying to figure out. I've been ringing the venues myself trying to get them to come up with alternative dates in the hope that they can somehow tag on the dates at the end of the tour or something but so far, none of the venues have come up with anything because they're all fully booked. I'm so fucked off with this entire thing that I can't even think straight anymore. No matter what I do, the fans will lose out and our reputation will be tarnished as a result. Add the bullshit press story about the band breaking up to all of that and Reclamation are well and truly fucked."

"Hey," I say, reaching out to him, "the fans will understand once you tell them the truth, Jonny."

"The truth?" He looks mortified.

Clasping his face between my hands, I say, "Yes, the truth. Tell them about why you are still here in London. Tell them about the cancelled shows and the sabotage you've experienced. Tell them all of that and they will rally behind you. In fact, the fans will probably find the bastard behind this before you do."

"Really? You think I should just release a statement telling them everything?"

I nod. "Yes, I do, and if you're still unsure about what to do regarding the cancelled shows, set up a forum on your website or Facebook page or something and ask the fans for their help and their suggestions. Communicate with them, Jonny, it goes a hell of a long way and believe me when I say, it will mean the world to them. I should know, I am your biggest fan after all."

Jonny gazes down at me in wonder, his yearning eyes making the breath catch in my throat. "All this time, all this stress, twenty four hours of trying to keep this shit from you to try and protect you, when all along, you were the one who had the answer the entire time."

Brushing a tender hand through his hair, I say, "A problem shared is a problem halved, that's what I've been trying to tell you."

Pressing his forehead against mine, he says, "I know, but I thought I was doing the right thing by you, and I couldn't bear the thought of seeing you upset because of some bastard who is clearly trying to keep me away from you for whatever reason."

A chill runs down my spine when he says that, my mind automatically going back to Jonny's dad and the possibility of it really being him who's behind this. No, he wouldn't damage Jonny's reputation like this. Would he? No, I think in spite of everything, it's a step too far, even for him.

Reaching up, I press a soft, lingering kiss to Jonny's lips. "Hmm, that's much better," Jonny murmurs.

Smiling up at him, I say, "There's something else I think you really need to do as well."

"Oh?"

"I think you need to move out of this hotel and go into hiding, or at least, stay under the radar and away from the limelight anyway. What Ben chooses to do is up to him but I really want you to move into my apartment with me for the remainder of your time here, Jonny."

Raising his eyebrows up at me, he says, "You want me to move in with you, do you?"

Biting down on a smile, I say, "Yes, I do, but on the condition that you release that statement to the press and put an end to this constant phone line you have going on with LA, apart from when you're talking to your mum of course. But, other than that, I want us to spend some proper quality time together and if it means dressing incognito and going out for that walk in the park we both really want to do, then we're going to do it. But you have to be willing, Jonny. You can't hide away forever, it isn't normal and it certainly isn't healthy."

Narrowing his eyes on me, he says, "I forgot just how bossy you can be."

"Takes one to know one, Jonny Mathers."

CHAPTER 17

The next two days pass by in a blur of Jonny finally leaving his hotel suite behind him and moving into my apartment, the pair of us dressing incognito and having a picnic lunch in the park in broad daylight and a trip to the cinema. Yes, would you believe it, we even managed a trip to the cinema without being seen. It was wonderful to be out like a normal couple.

However, that whole normal couple thing is already beginning to wear off because, as of yesterday afternoon, when Jonny finally released his statement to the press about the sabotage and the reason for him still being here in London, both fans and tabloids alike went even more nuts than they already were. As Jonny predicted, they're out for me now too and want to know absolutely everything about me and no doubt they will go to extreme lengths to get any information they can get their grubby hands on.

It's too early as yet to get any sort of feedback from their fans regarding the whole sabotage issue and the cancelling of five shows but, from what Jonny's PA, Lara, has been saying, feedback is mainly positive. Only time will tell though and of course, not everybody agreed with Jonny's decision to tell the truth. Well, Jonny's dad mainly.

No surprises there though and Jonny was prepared for the barrage of abuse from his father that came after the press release. And boy did it come. He must have been on the phone to his dad for over an hour last night. I left him to it in the end and we haven't really spoken about it since. I didn't want to pry and so I've left the whole subject alone – for now.

Anyway, back to my lazy Sunday morning in bed with my rock star. Well, he was in bed with me the first time I woke up earlier on. Rolling over to automatically reach for him now, I find the bed to be empty. I pout. Well, how very dare he leave me alone in my bed? I must have dozed off again after my early morning wake up call.

I smile at the memory of Jonny going down on me this morning, rousing me from my slumber. Or should I say, *arousing* me. Honestly, I could get used to being woken up like that every single day. Hopefully, when I move over to LA, that's exactly what will be happening....

Getting out of bed, I decide to not bother getting dressed into my clothes for the day, instead pulling on my new favourite t-shirt. Jonny's t-shirt. The plain white t-shirt that I sort of borrowed from him last week has kind of become a more permanent fixture of mine since he moved in here. It's big and comfy but more than that, I'm just addicted to the smell of him. And while I can, I will wear it.

It isn't as if I have to worry about what I'm wearing around my apartment at the moment anyway. Stacey and Ben decided to stay in the hotel instead of staying here. They said it would be cramped with the four of us and anyway, Stacey loves that whole posh hotel suite stuff so it's right up her street. Unlike me. I don't care where I am, as long as Jonny is right here with me.

And speaking of Jonny, I end up finding him sitting on the sofa in the living room engrossed in his laptop with a mug of coffee on the table in front of him. He's still in his pyjama shorts and nothing else and that suits me down to the ground. He looks so much more relaxed and casual since moving in here, and after that press release yesterday, it's wonderful to see.

Glancing up at me from his laptop, he smiles. "Hey, baby." Joining him on the sofa, I immediately thread my arms around his neck and plant a soft, sweet kiss to his lips.

"Hey to you too," I whisper, "but I have a bone to pick with you, Mathers."

"You do?" he asks, raising his eyebrows in mock horror.

"Yes, you left me all alone in my bed. I hate waking up without you being next to me."

Raking his eyes over my face, he says, "Well, you fell asleep again and you looked so beautiful and relaxed that I just didn't want to wake you."

I pretend to contemplate his answer for a moment. "Hmm, good answer, you're forgiven."

He grins widely and then kisses me on the lips before lying us both down on the sofa, me on top of him. Looking down, he says, "You've stolen my t-shirt again I see?" His gaze drifts back up to mine, his eyes twinkling mischievously.

Smiling, I say, "I wouldn't quite say stolen, Jonny, more like borrowed."

"Well, you can borrow anything you like of mine, sweetheart."

"Just this t-shirt will do, but thank you all the same."

Running his fingers along my back, he then grips the material of his t-shirt lightly in his fingers. "So, tell me, what makes this t-shirt of mine so special then?"

Placing my hand on his chest, I avert my gaze from his for a moment and instead focus on his tattoos, slowly working my fingertips around the inky edges. "It's *your* t-shirt, Jonny, which means it smells of you, and the smell of you makes me feel warm and cosy and loved but most of all…it makes me feel safe." I look up at him once more, my hand now motionless, my fingers spread eagled across his chest, over his heart.

Jonny gazes at me longingly, his fingers now raking their way gently through my hair. "I love that even now, after all these years, I can still make you feel safe. You don't know what it means to me to hear you say that."

"Oh, I think I do," I whisper, reaching up to kiss him again.

Jonny then rests my head against his chest. I take comfort in hearing the steady rhythm of his heart, the feeling of him breathing in and out beneath me. I inhale deeply and take a mental picture of this moment. It's one of those perfect moments that I don't want to ever forget. Just us two in the peace and quiet of our surroundings, both relaxed and content with each other and nobody else bothering us. No arguing, no outside aggravation, just us being together as a couple.

This is what I've wanted all week and it took a while to get here but now it is here, I don't want it to end. And whenever I'm alone with Jonny, I never want it to end. The more I have of him to myself, the more greedy I become for him and the less I want to share him. That isn't normal of course. It's just, the last time we were together, that's all I knew. Just us two against the world and nobody else. We had our circle of friends but really and truly, we only existed for each other. But now, now I have to start trying to handle Jonny's fame and it's going to be a long road for me, that's for sure.

"You know, since speaking with my dad on the phone last night, it got me thinking again," says Jonny, finally breaking the silence.

Feeling a little unnerved about what Jonny is perhaps going to say next, I can't help but cling on to him that little bit tighter. "How do you mean?" I ask quietly.

"Well, I ended up accusing him of being the one behind the sabotage."

"What the hell?"

Pulling out of Jonny's hold, I sit up in shock. Jonny pulls a face and holds up his hands. "Whoa, okay, calm down and don't overreact, will you?"

"Calm down!" I say, slightly higher pitched than I intended it to come out, "Jonny, what were you thinking?"

Resting his head back on the sofa cushion, he looks up at the ceiling. "Yeah, I know, I took it too far," he says with a sigh, "but he pushed my buttons, Lauren, and I flipped." He looks over at me and I give him an eye roll.

"No surprise there then. Your dad pushing your buttons? So what else is new?"

Pushing himself up into a sitting position, Jonny says, "Look, it's been bugging me, Lauren. I mean, who else out there would do this to us? Who else would sabotage the tour in the hope that it would get me straight back over to LA and away from you?"

I must admit, it's the exact same thing that has been whirling around in my mind since it all happened but I've just tried to push all such thoughts away. I want to believe that Pete would never go to those extreme lengths to rid me from his son's life all over again but if Jonny is even beginning to think it, without any knowledge of what happened the first time round, then maybe I'm right to be thinking it too.

"So, what did your dad say? When you asked him?"

I'm trying to play it cool here. I don't want Jonny getting wind of me being overly suspicious of his dad in case he starts asking me questions about why I'm so suspicious. Because if

Jonny starts asking questions, I'll start to panic, and then he'll see right through me and then everything will come out and I can't allow that to happen. Ever.

"How do you think he reacted?" Jonny sighs. "I think I actually hurt him, for the first time ever. He sounded so wounded on the phone and then I tried to explain why I asked him and then he started tearing into you again and raking up our past and that's when it all got ugly. Needless to say we ended the phone call on bad terms. It's been going round in my head all night since then though, did he do it? Didn't he do it? But now, talking to you about it all, it seems such a low thing for me to have done. Accuse my own dad of sabotaging our tour. He's literally dedicated most of his life to me and my music career, not to mention getting Reclamation off the ground. He may have been a shit dad in so many areas and I hate how he speaks about you and how he can't see what I see in you but, and here's the but, really and truly, when I think about it, he wouldn't jeopardise everything he's ever worked for...would he?"

Jonny is clearly feeling a mixture of both guilt and uncertainty over this issue and is now looking to me for reassurance. And of course, I'm going to give him that reassurance. In spite of my own uncertainties and suspicions, I have to do what's right, for Jonny's sake.

Shaking my head, I say, "No, Jonny, I really don't think he would do something like this to his only son." *Even though he ripped me away from you ten years ago, leaving you in that awful rehabilitation centre in Manchester all on your own.* I am screaming inside. Screaming to say it out loud and tell him everything. But, I don't. I just wrap my arms around him and give him the reassurance he needs.

"Thank you," says Jonny, giving me a gentle squeeze.

"You don't need to thank me, Jonny, that's what I'm here for.

I'm just glad you're talking to me and telling me things."

Jonny smiles down at me. "Yeah, me too." He kisses me. "And speaking of telling you things," he says, with a cheeky glint in his eye, "I had an idea this morning."

"Was that before or after you left me in bed all alone?" I pout. He grins wickedly.

"Oh, it was definitely after I left you, baby, believe me." I swipe him on the arm for that remark.

"This is going to involve sex isn't it? This idea of yours?"

He frowns. "Actually, it doesn't…although, well, we will be having sex there, that's a given, if you agree to come of course…pun intended." He winks at me.

"Jonny, what the hell are you going on about?"

I have to say, he has my curiosity piqued now, that's for sure, although he better be quick at telling me because I can't take much more of this talking in riddles nonsense.

"Well, how about we…go away for a couple of nights, in the countryside somewhere? Completely off the grid, no security guards, no mobile phones, no communication with the outside world at all, apart from me keeping in touch with my mum, obviously, but, other than that, we just go away for a couple of nights and go under the radar. What do you say?"

I don't even need to think about my answer to that amazing question. "Oh my god I say yes yes yes!" I squeal with delight, throwing myself at him.

Jonny laughs. "Hang on, you haven't heard the rest of my idea yet."

Pulling back, I eye him suspiciously. "Go on."

"How would you feel about Ben and Stacey coming with us?

We'd be in separate accommodation, obviously, but I thought it would be nice to spend some time with them and maybe, you know, do the whole double date thing you keep going on about?"

"Oh my god I think I love you even more now!" Unable to contain my excitement, I throw myself at him for a second time, kissing him all over his face.

"I'll take that as a yes then," he says, laughing. "Which is a good job really because I've already asked them, and of course they already said yes."

"So Stacey managed to get the time off work to come?" I ask excitedly.

Jonny nods. "She managed to wangle the time off apparently."

"Bloody hell, just how long was I asleep for this morning? You've arranged a break away for us and somehow managed to speak to and organise it with our friends as well? Are there no limits to your talents, Jonny Mathers?"

He grins down at me. "Nope, and you know it."

Threading my hands together around the back of his neck, I say, "So, Mr Mathers, where are you whisking me away to?"

Pulling back, he hesitates slightly. "Well, we're going to be staying in one of those...camping pods...over in Yorkshire somewhere." He's looking at me tentatively, trying to gauge my reaction to this camping idea of his. Well, he doesn't need to worry on that front. Not where I'm concerned.

"That sounds perfect to me. I haven't been camping since we went together as teenagers, Jonny."

He smiles. "Well, back then, it really was camping, but this?" He spins the laptop round to show me the website he's been looking on. "This is what they call *glamping*, baby."

I stare at the computer screen, one of those really fancy looking camping pods staring right back at me. Scrolling through the many photographs, it looks amazing inside. It comes equipped with a double sized bed, modern furniture and décor, electric and gas hook up, the works. It looks all snug and cosy and it's literally in the middle of a field with about five other pods in the middle of nowhere, which sounds like absolute heaven to me.

"I love it," I say, giving him a huge smile, "although, I have to be honest and say that I'm not so sure if Stacey will love it. She's more of a, shall we say, creature comforts type of girl, you know, central heating, city living, noise everywhere she goes sort of thing."

Jonny chuckles. "Ben's the same, which is why I haven't told them about the glamping side of it. We'll just break it to them gently when we get there."

I giggle. "Oh my god, they're going to kill us."

"Oh, they'll get over it," he says with a shrug.

"Hmm, not so sure about that, Jonny, but it's going to be fun finding out."

****

"What the actual fuck is *that*?"

Snatching his sunglasses away from his face, Ben glares over at Jonny. Stacey is standing next to Ben, her mouth open in shock as she looks over at the camping pods. The very camping pods that are going to be our home for the next two nights. Well, it'll be home for me and Jonny anyway, not so sure about Ben and Stacey looking at their reaction. Jonny can't help but snigger at their reaction to his little surprise.

"They're *camping* pods, Ben."

"Camping what?" asks Ben, screwing up his face in disgust.

Stacey sighs. "Camping pods, you know, as opposed to a tent?" Stacey turns to look at Ben who just shrugs his shoulders at her.

"And what the fuck am I supposed to do in one of these pods then?"

"Enjoy the silence?" suggests Jonny, his sarcastic remark going down like a lead balloon. Ben glances over at the pods once more before looking back to Jonny, his face one of complete and utter disbelief.

"In what world would you think I would enjoy the fucking silence?"

"Hey," says Stacey, slapping him on the arm, "don't be so ungrateful." Turning back to Jonny, she gives him a sheepish apology. "Sorry." I can tell she's bitterly disappointed at the whole camping idea but at least she isn't saying it out loud. Unlike Ben of course.

"It's okay," Jonny says to Stacey, "because I know that deep down, Ben is just as grateful as I am to get away from the glare of the cameras and the fans. Right Ben?"

Dropping his bag on to the floor, Ben sighs. "Look, dude, just quit with the joking around and show me where the fucking hotel is."

Stacey rolls her eyes at him. "Seriously? Do you see a hotel anywhere in this field in Yorkshire?"

Trying to stifle my laughter, I quickly turn away from the pair of them, instead burying my face into Jonny's leather jacket.

"You're seriously telling me that we drove for over four hours so that we could spend the next two nights living in a fucking field?" says Ben, looking horrified.

"Well, you won't technically be living *in* the field," says Jonny sarcastically, "the camping pods are *in* the field. You'll be *in* the pod."

"He will be living in the bloody field if he carries on like this," says Stacey, throwing her bag over at Ben. It hits him in the stomach before dropping to the floor like a sack of spuds. He winces.

"Hey! What was that for?"

She tuts her annoyance at him. "Why don't you make yourself useful and bring the bags."

Pulling a face, Ben finally relents and picks up Stacey's bag. "Fuck me, babe, what's in this thing? We're staying for two nights not two fucking weeks."

Stacey scowls over at him. "You wanna stay in the field? Keep talking!" Looking at both me and Jonny, Stacey says, "Sorry again for Ben and...thank you, Jonny, for bringing us away with you. It was a lovely idea." Stacey starts walking towards the pod. "Come on, Anderson!"

Sighing, Ben then reluctantly decides to follow her. Clutching at both of their bags, he scowls over at us as he walks past. Jonny can't help but make another quip. "Oh by the way, I probably should warn you before you go in, there's no television or radio in the pods."

Dropping the bags to the floor again, Ben says, "What the fuck, man?!" Glancing over at Stacey who's now standing just outside the front door to their pod, I see her grimace.

"Seriously? No TV?" she asks, looking desperate.

"Sorry, kids," says Jonny, "I just wanted us all to switch off from the outside world for a couple of days so I asked the owner to remove them." Ben just shakes his head in disbelief, muttering to himself under his breath.

"Look, there's a docking station if you want to play music on your Iphones," says Jonny.

"Oh, thanks for that," says Ben, snatching his bags back up from the floor again, "thanks a fucking lot." Ben walks off in a huff towards his camping pod, Jonny grinning over at him like a Cheshire cat.

"Well, that went well," I say, unable to keep the sarcasm from my voice.

"Better than I expected, actually," says Jonny. Looking down at me, he smiles. "Admit it, you loved watching that scene unfold just now."

"I'd be lying if I said I didn't enjoy it, although I do feel sorry for Stacey, being stuck in a camping pod for the next two days with bouncing Benjamin over there."

Jonny chuckles. "Nice nickname, baby." Pulling me against him, he kisses me on the head. "Don't worry, he'll soon get over it."

"You think?"

"I don't think, baby, I know he will, because that best friend of yours won't allow him to sulk like the baby that he is for too long. One way or another, she'll tell him to get over himself, and because he's mad crazy about her, he will."

I smile up at him. "He is mad crazy about her, isn't he?"

Leaning down, Jonny presses his nose against mine, nuzzling it gently. "He is. In the same maddening way that I am bat shit crazy about you, Lauren Whittle."

I grin. "You must be bat shit crazy about me if you've brought me all the way up here to Yorkshire to stay in a camping pod in the middle of a field."

"Nothing wrong with a camping pod, sweetheart, it's what the people do while they're living in the camping pod that counts." Hmm, I like his thinking.

"Let's not waste another second of our time standing here then!" I say excitedly. Pulling out of his grip, I run off towards the pod. "Last one in the pod has to cook tea tonight!"

****

Despite Jonny being the last one in the pod earlier, I still end up cooking tea for us, and when I say us, I mean just us two. I offered to cook for Ben and Stacey too but Ben was still being his grumpy self so we decided to leave them to it for the rest of the night. We'll be going out with them tomorrow anyway, Ben's mood pending of course.

"Well, I have to say it, sweetheart, you've still got what it takes in the kitchen as well as the bedroom, that dinner you cooked for us tonight was sublime, Ben and Stacey have missed out for sure."

Jonny slips his arms around my waist from behind and pulls me against him. Turning the tap on the kitchen sink, I start running the hot water to wash the dishes.

"Oh, it was only a quick thrown together thing from the bits I picked up from the supermarket on the way here, Jonny, it wasn't exactly what I would call one of my better dishes. Still, it was meant to be an easy tea, we are camping after all." I squeeze the washing up liquid into the sink and swirl it into the water, creating bubbles.

Jonny chuckles at me. "Glamping, baby, remember?"

"I doubt Ben and Stacey are thinking that right now," I say with a smile.

"Oh, Ben will have got over it by now, in fact, he's probably getting his leg over Stacey as we speak." I elbow him in the ribs. "Erm…ouch," he protests, pretending to be injured.

"Stop with all the suggestive comments then," I say, "and stop taking the piss out of our best friends please."

Grinning against my cheek, he says, "Sorry, can't help it where Ben's concerned, but I'll try harder. Promise."

Turning round in his arms, I then flick water up into his face, causing him to pull back from me in protest. "Now that was uncalled for," he says, making a quick grab for me.

I dodge out of his way and instead dash over to the sofa in the living area of our pod. It's all open plan in here and very modern but ever so cosy and warm, almost like we're cocooned inside a really large egg. It's fabulous. I love it.

Sitting down on the sofa, I lay back and grin over at Jonny. "It was more than called for, Jonny, and your punishment is doing the washing up."

Rolling his eyes at me, he then reluctantly sets about washing up all the pots. I take delight in watching him do something that he probably hasn't done in very many years. "So, how long has it been since you washed up the pots then, Jonny?" I tease.

He pauses, casting a quick glare in my direction. "Oh, very funny, baby, hilarious in fact."

"I'm actually being serious."

Pinning me with a serious stare, he says, "What? You think washing and wiping the pots is beneath me these days? Seriously?" Oops, Jonny seems suddenly offended at something that was only supposed to be a joke.

"I was only joking," I say.

"Were you?" he asks, raising an eyebrow up at me.

Breaking eye contact with him, I find the nearest sofa cushion and start to pluck at the edge of the material with my fingers. "I made it into a joke but I guess that maybe I did think that something as trivial as washing the pots would be something that you bypassed these days. I mean, most people I know own a dishwasher."

"Except you," says Jonny.

Glancing up at him, I see a ghost of a smile playing across his lips. "Except me *and* Stacey, yes. Why waste all that water on two people who hardly use any pots?"

"I couldn't agree with you more, baby, but I have to admit to you that I do own one but in my defence, I hardly use it."

Shrugging, I say, "I wouldn't care if you did use it. Honestly, I was joking, it's no big deal."

Focusing back on the job in hand, Jonny says quietly, "I know you were…I guess I just…well, I want you to see more of the old Jonny standing before you…instead of the new one…"

I frown over at him. I don't like hearing him speak about himself like that and I'm ashamed to say that I feel as though I'm partly to blame for that. Getting up from the sofa, I wander back over to where Jonny is standing in the kitchen.

"Hey." Jonny looks down at me. Placing my hand on his arm, I say, "I love the man standing in front of me, Jonny Mathers. I love everything about him, the old and the new."

He looks away from me again, instead scrubbing away at one of the plates in the sink. "But not all of the new," he says, as if he's stating a fact.

Immersing my hands into the warm soapy water along with his, I gently pull Jonny's hands out of the sink and force him to turn and look down at me. "I said I love everything about you, Jonny. Yes, you have changed in some ways and some of those changes are proving to be a little hard to adapt to, but…I've changed too, and not necessarily for the better."

Suddenly clasping my face in his wet hands, he frowns. "You talk like that again and I may have to fall out with you."

"Just stating a fact," I say with a shrug.

Scowling down at me, he then takes me completely by surprise by leaning down to plant a hell of a smacker on my lips. Wrapping my wet hands around the back of his neck, I hum my approval at his lips moving slowly over mine, his wet hands on my face. And then suddenly, without warning, Jonny picks me up off the floor and starts spinning me slowly around on the spot, making me smile.

"You fancy a dance with me then, or what?" he murmurs.

I giggle. "We're already dancing."

Jonny presses another soft kiss to my lips and then says, "I'd hardly call what we're doing right now dancing. And there's me thinking you were a pro at this sort of thing."

Narrowing my eyes on him, I say, "You know full well what I meant, Jonny Mathers."

He spins me around one last time before setting me back down on the floor again. Grabbing his mobile phone from the kitchen worktop behind me, he then heads over to the living area, straight for the docking station. "Of course I knew what you meant, sweetheart." Glancing over at me, he flashes me a cheeky wink. "But where's the romance in dancing without the music?"

My stomach flips with excitement, the little butterflies now taking flight in there and going absolutely wild at the prospect of dancing with my man in the privacy of our own little world. Jonny and I used to dance together often once upon a time.

Depending on our mood, our dancing could range from slow, sweet and romantic to fast paced, sweaty and sexy as hell. Sometimes I would dance only for him while he watched me for what felt like hours. I used to tease the hell out of him, getting him so worked up to the point where he couldn't bear to keep his hands off me for a minute longer. I bite my lip at the memories of those times together. I remember them so vividly, almost like they only happened between us yesterday.

"Any special requests?" asks Jonny, snapping me out of my reverie.

I wander over to where Jonny is standing by the docking station. He's swiping through the music on his phone. He looks over at me expectantly.

"What music do you think I want to listen to, Jonny?" I say with a smile.

"Well, I don't know, that's why I'm asking."

With an eye roll, I say, "*You* Jonny, I want to listen to *you*."

"I knew what you meant, baby," he says with a wry smile, "I just wanted to hear you say it."

I give him a gentle shove on the arm. "Conceited idiot."

He chuckles. "So, which album of ours do you want to listen to then?"

Brushing a tender hand through his hair, I say quietly, "Your first album, Jonny. Take me back to where it all began for Reclamation." Jonny nods, his face turning slowly serious as he scrolls through his phone to find their first ever album,

Blazing Inferno.

Clicking on the first song, Jonny then takes hold of both my hands, pulling me into the centre of the living room along with him. Placing one arm around my waist, he pulls me close against him, his other hand firmly in mine. Gazing down into my eyes like nothing else in the room or even the world exists, Jonny then starts to sway gently along with me as the first song on the album begins to play.

It's a track called Forsaken Eyes, a beautiful piano and electric guitar piece that bagged Reclamation their second number one hit over here in the UK. Much slower and less rocky, Forsaken Eyes was a surprise release for a band whose first number one single had been heavy on the suggestive lyrics as well as heavy on the guitars. But knowing Jonny so well, inside and out, it didn't actually come as much of a surprise to me at the time. He was always so versatile when it came to writing his music and I could never put Jonny into one particular genre. To me, Jonny is his own genre and he always will be.

Looking up into Jonny's eyes as I sway gently against him, the lyrics of his song start to wrap themselves around me, the meaning behind the lyrics starting to really strike a chord with me like never before.

'Now I see the truth behind my oppressive ways, got to keep the faith to build a better day, I've still to find me some peace of mind, but will I see the light in your forsaken eyes, in your forsaken eyes. You and me, we're not the same, only you have the faith I've got to gain, I'm alone out here with all my fears but will I cry my final tears, got to find a way out of this, solitude is a near miss...'

I stop dancing, the lyrics bringing tears to my eyes as I suddenly realise what this song is about. Jonny stops dancing too, his eyes never leaving mine. "Lauren…" Jonny starts to speak but then stops himself.

"This song is about how you felt after I left you, isn't it?" I whisper, my voice a little wobbly.

A moment passes before Jonny reluctantly nods. "I'm sorry, Lauren."

I shake my head at him. "No, Jonny, I'm the one who's sorry." Clinging on to his arms, I look up into his sorrowful face and say, "I'm so sorry for what me leaving did to you. I'm so so sorry." The tears that have been threatening to fall finally break free from my eyes, rolling down my cheeks. Jonny wipes them gently away with his thumbs.

"I'm sorry I wrote about us, Lauren, I'm sorry I put us out there."

I shake my head once more. "I'm not sorry for that, Jonny. You wrote how you felt at the time and lyrically, it's amazing and beautiful but so heart wrenching. But only for me. Nobody else. You were always so clever like that. Nobody else out there would have ever known you were writing about your own personal experience of something like that. I didn't even know…well, I thought that maybe Blazing Inferno might have been about us but I never thought for a minute that this song was, until now…"

Cupping my face in his hands, Jonny then presses his forehead against mine. "Blazing Inferno was about us, Lauren."

"It was?" I ask, still slightly surprised even though I had suspected it.

Jonny sighs. "Of course it was," he says. "Baby, I had to get you out of my system. Somehow or other, I had to work you out of me and music was the only way. You'd left me in Manchester and fuck, I missed you like the air that I breathed. Coming down from you was worse than coming down from the fucking drugs I'd been hooked on, and when I did finally get clean and out of rehab, I started writing. About you. About us. And once I started writing, I couldn't fucking stop. I wrote half the album before the band even came to be and part of me is sorry for that but the other part of me isn't. The other part of me was so angry with you, so fucking angry and desperate to be with you again that the only solace I could find was in my music and…well, the rest is history…ancient history."

Holding on to his face, I press a soft, tender kiss to his lips. "I'm sorry," I whisper, feeling wretched.

Jonny hushes me quietly before wrapping his arms around me once more. "No more talk about the past, baby," he whispers into my hair, "let's stay in the present. And the present is me and you dancing the night away in our camping pod."

In spite of my tears, I manage to smile up at him when he says that to me. "I love you, Jonny Mathers."

Smiling down at me, he says, "I love you too, Lauren Whittle. More than you'll ever know."

We start to sway to the music once more, Jonny's hand pressing gently against my lower back. I bite down on my bottom lip as I feel the rough edges of his fingertips slowly working their way beneath the hem of my top, just above the waistline of my jeans.

"Still your soft spot then," says Jonny, noticing my reaction to him, his fingers now circling around the bare skin of my lower back, the sensation driving me nuts.

Closing my eyes, I bite back a moan. "God yes," I breathe.

Jonny then dips his fingers that little bit further, reaching into my jeans, within touching distance of my g-string. "And how about now?" Jonny murmurs quietly into my ear.

"Yes," I whisper, "hell yes."

Opening my eyes once more, I look up to find Jonny's eyes blazing down into mine. Our eyes stay locked together as we continue to sway along to the music, Jonny's fingers beginning to slowly trail their way down to my g-string. Jonny wraps the top of my g-string around his index finger before suddenly releasing it, allowing the material to snap loudly against the top of my bum cheek.

I gasp at the sensation, heat pooling between my legs. Jonny's eyes then drop to my mouth as his fingers continue their journey, reaching around to between my legs this time. "Oh god," I moan softly, throwing my head back.

Undoing the zipper of my jeans with his other hand so he can get better access, Jonny then shoves my g-string to one side and begins to swirl his fingers around my clit as I cling on to his arms in desperation. The rockier tones of Reclamation begin to fill the room as the next song starts to play and as the bassline of their song becomes harder and louder, Jonny and I become harder and louder too. We are in unison with the music, Jonny's fingers pounding into me over and over as I stand there in the middle of the room and grind down shamelessly against them, greedy for more and aching for release.

Right now, in this moment, I am surrounded by so much Jonny that I don't know what to do with it all. The euphoria of being completely immersed in both Jonny musically, as his rocky vocals echo all around me, and sexually, as Jonny himself takes me once more to the dizzying heights of yet another earth shattering orgasm, is almost too much to bear. So much so that when I come, I burst into tears. I let out a mournful sob as I bury my face into his neck, riding out the rest of my orgasm, an orgasm so intense that my legs almost give way afterwards.

Pulling his fingers out of me, Jonny then gently prises my face away from his neck, a look of concern crossing his features. "Lauren? Fuck, are you okay? Did I hurt you?"

I am quick to reassure him. With a shake of my head, I say, "No, baby." Reaching up, I kiss him hard on the lips, but Jonny pulls back.

"So, what's wrong? Why the tears?"

Letting out a shaky sigh, I then rest my wet cheek against his shoulder. "Sometimes, Jonny, with you, it becomes...too much."

Jonny frowns. "Too much?"

I gently trail my index finger along his right cheek. "What I mean is that sometimes, my feelings for you are so overwhelming that I don't know what to do with them all."

Jonny gazes down at me for a long moment before pressing a gentle kiss to my forehead. "Right back at you with that one, sweetheart," Jonny whispers against my skin.

I close my eyes on a sigh. "Make love to me, Jonny. Please make love to me."

Jonny leads me over to the sofa where he slowly strips me naked, taking the time over me and then pleasuring me once more, with his mouth this time. As Reclamation continue to play in the background, Jonny and I make slow, passionate love on the sofa. I sit on top of him, riding him slowly, deeply.

Our eyes lock together in a steamy haze of lust and love as our bodies meld together to become one. I feel more naked right now than I have ever done with Jonny before, because he can see me so clearly, so deeply, right through to my very soul. That very thought alone is overwhelming in itself and I find myself reaching out for him, kissing him hard on the lips as his hands find their way into my long blonde locks, his fingers tangling through my curls as I continue to slowly ride him.

As Jonny tugs gently on my hair, I let out a breathy moan, throwing my head back as Jonny's mouth finds my neck. He plants a trail of kisses all the way along to the hollow of my neck before moving across to my collarbone.

Grabbing a gentle hold of his head, I then guide Jonny's mouth to my breasts, his tongue instantly darting out to lick my left nipple. I cry out in pleasure, tugging on Jonny's hair hard as he sucks the entire nipple into his mouth before releasing it again with a loud pop. He then goes to work on my right nipple, swirling his tongue over and around, sucking and nipping gently before pulling it into his mouth and releasing it with another pop.

I clasp onto Jonny for dear life as he continues to worship my breasts, his tongue laving wildly against my nipples as I push myself down harder on his cock. Jonny groans loudly, his hands now on my hips, willing me to move faster, harder.

Releasing Jonny's hair from my grip, I then reach behind him to grab a tight hold of the sofa before slamming myself down on to his cock over and over and over again. Jonny licks greedily at my breasts as they bounce in his face, his fingernails digging into the skin of my hips as we begin to climb towards our ultimate high.

"Oh, god," I groan, as Jonny sucks hard on my right nipple, "oh fuck...Jonny..."

Making a grab for his face, I kiss him harder than I've ever kissed him in my life, my teeth clacking against his as we both finally lose all sense of control with each other.

"Holy fuuuuuck...Lauren!" Jonny groans loudly against my mouth as he comes hard inside me, slamming himself up into me as I slam down on to him.

I come with a loud scream, my body convulsing around him, milking him for all his worth. But I don't stop moving. I can't stop. I just need him over and over again until I have nothing else left.

"Baby, you're insatiable," whispers Jonny, breathlessly. Placing his fingers on my clit, Jonny then starts to make me climb all over again, his cock still hard and still buried deep. So deep.

"Ah," I moan, throwing my head back once more.

"Oh, Lauren," breathes Jonny, "you were made for me, baby."

"Ah…Jonny," I gasp, feeling the deliciously familiar sensation build up within me all over again.

"That's it, baby, come for me again. And when you're done, I'll make you come again and again and again, until you're begging me to stop."

"I'll never beg you to stop," I pant, "never."

Sweeping his fingers over my clit once more, he says, "You're in for a hell of a long night then, baby."

CHAPTER 18

The following day, all four of us are up super early and out of our camping pods by 9.00 am, which is surprising for both me and Jonny, considering the late night we had last night....

Anyway, back to the present, and both Stacey and I are super excited about the day ahead and even though Ben is still a little unenthused by the whole camping trip idea, he's a bit more enthusiastic than he was yesterday.

At the breakfast table this morning, Jonny suggested a spontaneous road trip, where we all just take off in the car together and land wherever the four wheels of the Range Rover takes us. Ben seemed to like the idea of being anywhere other than in the middle of a field and so he agreed instantly. So that's exactly what we're doing.

We are going on a road trip and I was so excited about it that I even packed up a huge picnic hamper full of stuff in the hope that we could perhaps lay down on an abandoned beach somewhere and chill out for a while. Even though it's cooler and a little windier up here in Yorkshire than it is down in London, the weather is still fairly warm and sunny, so I'm confident that we'll find somewhere to enjoy our picnic at least.

"We really are in the middle of nowhere out here, Jonny," I say, peering through the car window at the beautiful heather covered North York Moors. It's like a sea of purple as far as the eye can see and having never been to Yorkshire before, it's like a whole new world to me. A peaceful haven well away from the hustle and bustle of the city living in London that I'm used to.

"I know, beautiful isn't it?" replies Jonny.

He looks as enraptured with the countryside as I am. Sitting in the driver's seat of the Range Rover, Jonny is clearly enjoying being in control of driving the car for a change. In fact, he looks the most relaxed I've seen him since we got back together. Being away from the glare of the paparazzi and the fans is really doing him the world of good so far, and hopefully, it can only get better from here.

Reaching over to where Jonny's hand is resting on the gear stick, I rest my hand on top of his before giving it a gentle squeeze. Jonny glances over at me and smiles before giving me his trademark wink. I mouth the words 'I love you' to him and he just shakes his head at me, chuckling to himself before focusing his attention back on the road ahead.

"Any chance you could go a bit faster? You know, ideally so we get to where ever we're supposed to be going to at some point today?" says Ben, finally coming up for air.

Both he and Stacey have been snogging each other's faces off in the back of the car for the past ten minutes, maybe more. Jonny and I didn't know where to put ourselves at first, but our embarrassment quickly wore off when we realised that we were enjoying the silence. After spending four hours in the car driving up here with Ben yesterday, we were dreading getting back in the car with him today. Until our saving grace Stacey came to the rescue. Well, she rescued us for ten minutes anyway.

"Oh," says Jonny, pretending to act surprised, "it speaks." I laugh.

"Very fuckin' funny," says Ben with a sigh, "look, just put your foot down, Jonny, and get us there, will you?"

"Get us where exactly?" Jonny asks Ben with a frown.

Turning round in my seat, I'm met with the oh so familiar Ben scowl. Nodding towards Jonny, Ben says to me, "Hilarious he is."

Smiling over at Jonny, I say, "A proper comedian, isn't he?"

Jonny grins. "Look, we're on a road trip to nowhere so just sit back, relax, and either listen to the music or carry on where you left off with Stacey." Jonny flashes Stacey a cheeky smile through the rear view mirror.

Shaking her head at him, Stacey smiles back at Jonny. "Hey, I've more than played my part this morning in getting him to shut up. He's all yours from now on."

"Hey!" snaps Ben, looking offended, "what's that supposed to mean?"

"Exactly how it sounds," says Stacey, deadpan.

Leaning back in his car seat, Ben narrows his eyes on Stacey. "So, you're telling me you just allowed me to stick my tongue down your throat for the last five minutes just so you could keep me quiet?"

"Yeah, pretty much," says Stacey, trying her best not to laugh.

"It was ten minutes actually," I jest. Both Stacey and I burst out laughing.

"Nice," says Jonny, grimacing, "real nice."

"Oh, it was more than nice, Jonny," quips Ben, "in fact, maybe I should take over driving for a bit so you and Lauren can hop into the back seat instead. You know, take a leaf out of my book and loosen up a bit."

"I'm already loosened up thank you very much, Lauren made sure of that early this morning."

"Oh, I bet she did," says Ben, breaking out into a slow, suggestive smile before flashing a cheeky wink in my direction.

I slap Jonny on the thigh for that smutty remark. "What?" asks Jonny defensively, "I'm paying you a compliment."

"Yeah but you're also filling the already filthy mind of Ben and let's face it, he hardly needs any encouragement on that front now, does he?"

Jonny smirks. "I wouldn't worry about it, sweetheart, Ben's mind isn't big enough to retain thoughts about anything for very long, sex included. He'll have forgotten about it in a minute." Both Stacey and I burst out laughing again at Jonny's quick wit, but of course, Ben hits back straight away.

"Who needs a big mind when I have a big dick?"

Stacey's eyes look up to the heavens. "Oh my god, could you be any more crass?"

Ben's face screws up in confusion. "Crass? What the fuck does that mean?"

Biting back a laugh, Stacey just looks over at me and shakes her head in exasperation. Jonny glances down at me and says, "I think I've just proven my point."

Ben scowls over at Jonny. "Oh, there he is, Mr Comedian is at it again." Jonny just laughs. "Oh fuck off," Ben mutters, folding his arms in annoyance.

Finally feeling a little bit sorry for Ben, Stacey leans over towards him, trying to be affectionate like they were earlier, but he isn't for having any of it. "Ah, we don't mean it really," says Stacey in her mushiest voice.

"*We* mean it," says Jonny, chuckling proudly to himself, "Stacey doesn't."

I roll my eyes at him. Honestly, Jonny and Ben are like two little boys in a playground at school sometimes. Hilarious to watch I admit but at times, they can be trying. *Very* trying. But, as trying as they are, I wouldn't have them any other way because without them, this trip would be a very quiet trip indeed....

****

"Well, I have to hand it to you, Jonny, this is perfect, truly perfect."

Kicking off my trainers, I step on to the sand alongside Jonny before doing a little excitable dance on the spot. "You found us an empty beach!" I squeal, before throwing myself into his arms. Picking me up off the sandy beach, Jonny laughs in delight as he spins me around in his arms, just like he was doing in our camping pod last night.

"You're crazy," he says, still laughing.

"Why am I crazy?"

"Because it's fucking freezing," says Jonny.

"It's still sunny," I say, not caring about the weather.

"It's sunny, baby, but it's still freezing on this beach. It's supposed to be summer, remember?"

I grin. "We're in Yorkshire now, Jonny, not London or LA, but Yorkshire."

Nuzzling his nose against mine, he says, "I know where we are, Lauren, I booked it, remember?"

"Of course I remember, silly."

We both giggle before Jonny finally sets me back down on my feet. I squeal at the feel of the sand between my toes. "What is it?" asks Jonny.

"The sand," I say, glancing down at my feet. Deliberately sinking my toes into the golden grains, I say, "It's been a long time since I've felt the sand beneath my feet or between my toes. Over eleven years actually."

Jonny looks surprised at my confession. "You haven't been on a beach since we went to Newquay together?" Jonny catches me completely off guard with that remark. In fact, I'm so bowled over that I don't know what to say to him at first. "What?" he asks, frowning down at me. "Are you okay?"

Placing my hands on his chest, I look up at him and say, "I can't believe you remembered, Jonny."

Brushing his knuckles across my right cheek, he says quietly, "Like I could ever forget that holiday." Feeling a sudden pang of emotion for what came out of that last holiday we had together, I try to quell my tears of sadness over something that was actually our happiest time.

"Hey," whispers Jonny, clasping my face in his hands. "Please don't be sad. You were so happy a moment ago and I don't want anything to change that."

Shaking away my emotions, I say, "I'm not sad, Jonny, I'm just...reflecting."

"Reflecting on all the amazing sex we had in the back of that cramped up Volkswagen camper van we borrowed from my friend for the week?" says Jonny, trying to lighten the mood. And it works. I let out a small laugh.

"How the hell that old thing even got us down to Newquay was a miracle in itself."

Jonny chuckles. "It was pretty battered but, somehow or other, I fell in love with it." Slipping his arms around my waist, he pulls me closer to him. "And boy did I fall in love with you all over again in the back of that battered old camper van."

Biting back another wave of emotion, I can't help but blurt out the very thing I was trying to avoid saying a moment ago. "Newquay will always hold a special place in my heart, Jonny. We made...Oliver there, and...I don't know, maybe one day, when I'm ready, or when we're both ready, if you want to, I think I might like to go back down there...to perhaps...scatter his ashes..."

Jonny looks down at me in shock. "You still have...Oliver's ashes? After all this time?"

Swiping away an errant tear from my cheek, I deliberately break eye contact with Jonny, instead looking out at the beach, towards the sea. Unable to find my voice, I simply nod, blinking back more tears as I do.

"Oh, Lauren," whispers Jonny. Pulling me against him once more, Jonny folds me into his warm embrace, his arms wrapping tightly around me. His lips find the top of my head and they stay there, Jonny just holding on to me for as long as I need him to, for as long as he needs.

It's the first time we've mentioned our stillborn son since getting back together and in all honesty, it isn't something we ever talked about in great depth after it happened. Jonny wanted to talk about it initially as he thought it might help us, but I didn't. Because talking about it would have meant accepting that what had happened to us had been real.

In my eyes, if we didn't talk about it, it wasn't real. I even went as far as locking Oliver's ashes away in a wooden box. A small wooden box that I hid away in the back of our wardrobe, pretending from that moment onwards that it had never ever happened to us. And Jonny allowed me to do that. He allowed me to do it because he felt he had no choice. And that was when our relationship became toxic. So toxic that by the time Jonny got admitted into rehab for his crippling drug addiction, we were literally shells of the people we once were before we lost our baby boy.

I don't know how our future would have played out had I stayed in Manchester with Jonny, but what I do now know is that there is no way on earth I will allow anything like that to happen to us ever again. I won't allow our hurtful past to control our future. A happy future. Filled with endless opportunities and memories to be made. Starting now, on this freezing cold beach somewhere near Bridlington.

Looking up at Jonny through teary eyes, I say, "Time to start making new memories, Jonny."

Clearly struggling with his own emotions, Jonny tries his best efforts to put a brave face on it, but I know he's hurting. He's hurting as badly as I am. "New memories," he says, his voice trembling slightly.

Reaching for his hand, I give it a gentle squeeze before pulling him along with me. We saunter slowly along the beach towards the sea in silence, the waves crashing on to the shore and the cries of the many seagulls overhead the only sounds to be heard. It's both relaxing and comforting and in a way, healing too.

When we finally get to the water's edge, Jonny says, "There hasn't been a single day when I haven't thought about Oliver, you know. I know you're probably surprised to hear that, considering the lifestyle I've led over these last few years with the band but…I swear to you, Lauren, I've thought about him every single day since he…left us. Even when we never spoke about him…couldn't speak about him…he was always in my head…and my heart…and he always will be."

Swallowing down a lump in my throat, I whisper, "Me too, Jonny…me too."

"You know I never told one single person about him," Jonny

continues, "not one single person…in all these years."

With a shake of my head, I say quietly, "Me neither."

Jonny sighs. "Sounds awful, doesn't it? That we once had a son together and we never spoke about him to anyone. Like he never even existed."

"We told your mum and dad about him, they knew he existed…"

"Only because we had to tell them," Jonny says bitterly, "after everything that happened."

Squeezing his hand that little bit harder, I deliberately keep my eyes on the horizon ahead of us. If I look at Jonny now, I really will break down and cry and I don't want to do that. Not today.

Another moment of silence ticks by before we hear laughing in the distance. A couple of minutes later and Ben and Stacey are gracing us with their presence. I'm first to greet the happy pair while Jonny takes a moment to compose himself first, keeping his eyes on the horizon out to sea.

"Lauren, you have to come and take a look at this cave we've just found," says Stacey, excitedly, "not only is it huge but the entire rock face surrounding this cave is so beautiful, it's definitely the perfect place to lay our blanket and enjoy our picnic."

"Erm, who found the cave, babe?" says Ben, pointing to himself.

"Okay, *you* found the cave," says Stacey, giving him the usual eye roll.

"Yeah I did," Ben says, pulling Stacey in for a quick kiss. Slinging his arm around Stacey's shoulders, Ben then says to Jonny, "You coming, dude, or what?"

Turning back to Jonny, I slip my hand into his once more, silently coaxing him to turn around and be happy with our friends. Thankfully, it works, Jonny slowly peeling his gaze away from the sea at last. Both Stacey and Ben exchange worried glances.

"You okay, dude?" asks Ben, showing concern for his best friend. Surprising for Ben I know but, every now and again he does appear to show some sort of feelings towards his friends. Not very often but, when he does show his feelings, it's usually when they are really needed the most. Jonny nods.

"Yeah, course, I was just…it doesn't matter."

"You sure?" asks Ben, not looking entirely convinced.

Jonny looks down at me with uncertain eyes, as if he's suddenly unsure of himself, something you don't see very often where Jonny is concerned. Giving his hand another big squeeze, I smile up at him, showing him that no matter what, we will smile through our pain and enjoy our time away with our friends.

Today has been a revelation for us as a couple, a happy day out with our friends suddenly raking up the heartbreaking memories of our painful past, taking us both completely by surprise. But we've faced those painful memories now, we've faced them together and started talking about them and that in itself is a step forward for us. A huge step. And one that I'm secretly grateful for.

Looking back to Ben, Jonny says, "So, where's this cave you were talking about?"

And just like that, Jonny's mask slips right back into place, normality finding the pair of us once again. And we welcome that normality. We welcome it with open arms and hold on to it for dear life.

****

That evening, we dine out at a country pub about half a mile down the road from where we are staying. It's the perfect place to eat out because it's literally in the middle of nowhere meaning that not one person in the entire pub even bats an eyelid when both Jonny and Ben walk through the door. And whether anybody actually recognises them or not is irrelevant. The point is that they treat them like normal, everyday human beings which is a far cry from what they've had to grow accustomed to over the years.

Jonny can barely step out of a vehicle or a building without being photographed or mobbed and that's why he was so desperate to get away from it all and have a break. Ben may still be missing the buzz of being in the limelight in some ways but I think even he is enjoying this mini break. Okay, so he isn't keen on the whole camping in a field thing but I actually think that being away from the band and spending some quality time with his friends is something he's beginning to really enjoy.

We've had an amazing day together so far and I really want to enjoy these last few hours together tonight. We're going home tomorrow morning and both Jonny and Ben are flying back to LA the day after that so I just want to soak up these last couple of days with them as much as I can.

"So, how did you two meet, anyway?" Ben takes a swig of his beer and then leans back in his seat. Draping his right arm casually around Stacey's shoulders, he pulls her gently against him and she smiles.

Raising my eyebrows in surprise at Jonny, I then look over at Ben and say, "Jonny didn't tell you how we met then?"

Ben sniggers into his beer bottle. "Yeah right. He's been nothing but secretive about you two since you pole danced back into his life, Lauren."

I feel Jonny instantly tense up next to me, Ben's quip about my pole dancing provoking an instantaneous reaction from him. "No need to mention the whole pole dancing thing, Ben. We're all well aware of how we reunited."

Jonny snatches his bottle up from the table and chugs down his beer, the happy atmosphere around the table suddenly turning a little frosty.

Placing a reassuring hand on Jonny's knee beneath the table, I swiftly change the subject in a bid to restore the happy vibes from just a moment ago. "Believe it or not, Jonny and I met at opposing school bus stops when we were just fifteen years old."

"You were only fifteen?" asks Ben, raising his eyebrows in genuine surprise.

Placing his beer bottle back down on the table, Jonny says, "You look surprised, Ben."

Ben shrugs his shoulders. "Dude, I've only ever known you in the band. I know nothing of your life before the band so this is a complete shock to me. You two really met at fifteen?"

Jonny turns to me and smiles. "Yeah we did," he says quietly, his eyes gazing down at me longingly. My stomach flips, just as it did the very first time I laid eyes on him all those years ago.

Looking back over at Ben and Stacey, I continue with my story. "Jonny was waiting for his school bus on one side of the road with his friends and I was waiting for my school bus on the opposite side of the road to him and, when our eyes met and we saw each other for the first ever time, it was like something in the pair of us clicked. It took him two weeks to approach me though."

Stacey laughs out loud, having never heard this story before either. Apart from telling her that Jonny and I were actually a couple, the story of how we met each other hasn't really come up in any of our conversations so far but, now that it has, I can see that she's loving hearing about it.

"So, you didn't talk to her for two entire weeks?" she says to Jonny, "*you*, Jonny Mathers, didn't dare approach a female?" She laughs again and Jonny rolls his eyes in response.

"Ah come on, Stace, he was only fifteen when he met me, all young, sweet and innocent." I grab at one of Jonny's cheeks, giving it a quick squeeze, but he gently bats my hand away.

"Very fucking funny," he mutters, swigging more of his beer down.

"Well, this is all new to me," Ben says with a grin, "and don't stop there."

I'm about to open my mouth to respond to Ben when Jonny turns to me and scowls. "I don't think Ben needs any more ammunition against me, sweetheart."

"Oh come on, I'm not giving him any ammunition, I'm just telling our friends about how and when we met. What's wrong with that?"

"Nothing's wrong with that when you're telling that story to anybody else on the planet *other* than Ben."

Ben breaks out into a sly grin. "I would say I'm offended by that remark, but I'm not."

"You see?" says Jonny, gesturing over at Ben, "he doesn't even deny what he is." We all laugh.

"Seriously though," continues Ben, "I can't imagine the Jonny Mathers that I know ever being a shy fifteen year old."

Flashing a knowing smile up at Jonny, I say, "Oh believe me, the shyness wore off pretty quickly. In fact, I think it was all for show, a way of reeling me in."

Jonny grins down at me, his eyes twinkling mischievously. "It worked though, didn't it?"

I bump shoulders with him. "It certainly did."

Leaning down, Jonny plants a soft kiss on my lips, causing Ben to protest loudly. "Fuck me, save it for later, will you?"

Pulling his lips swiftly away from mine, Jonny turns back to Ben and says, "I'll remind you to do the same thing tomorrow on the drive home when poor Stacey is trying her best to keep *you* quiet again."

"Touché," says Ben, raising his beer bottle in the air.

It isn't long before we're tucking into our delicious home cooked pub meals and downing even more alcohol, the atmosphere in the pub around us becoming livelier by the minute.

By the time we've finished our food, the pub is packed out to the rafters and over in the corner, I notice a karaoke system being set up. Feeling excited at the prospect of getting up in a sing song, I shout across the table to my best friend. "Hey, Stace, looks like it's karaoke night in here tonight. Fancy it?"

She pulls a face at me. "Me? Sing? Yeah right! Not unless you want to clear this pub out completely!" She laughs.

"Oh come on, we love karaoke!"

Stacey waggles her finger in the air at me. "Uh uh, *you* love karaoke, Lauren, not me. And you have the voice of an angel whereas I sound like a cat being strangled so no. On this occasion I will decline."

I pout. "Oh come on, we've done karaoke loads of times before!"

"Yeah, in London. In bars and pubs that expect people like me who can't sing to get up and make fools of themselves. I am not getting up in the middle of a country pub in Yorkshire and making an idiot of myself."

"You clearly haven't had enough to drink then."

Jonny and Ben suddenly arrive back at our table with another round of drinks, a bottle of prosecco for both me and Stacey and bottles of beer for them. "Great timing," I say, grinning over at Stacey. "That girl over there needs more booze in her."

"Oh, she does, does she?" asks Jonny with a grin. Slipping back into his seat next to me, he looks between us and says, "And why does she need more booze?"

"So she can get her ass up off that seat and come and sing on that karaoke machine over there with me."

Jonny raises an eyebrow up at me. "There's a karaoke machine?"

I roll my eyes at him. "Like you didn't notice that being set up on your way back in from having your *tenth* cigarette tonight."

He narrows his eyes on me. "Actually, it was my ninth cigarette."

We both burst out laughing and then Jonny pulls me against him. Kissing me on the top of my head, he then says, "To be fair, we didn't notice the whole karaoke set up because me and Ben instead made a beeline for the bar when we came back in. You know, getting our priorities right for you ladies and all that."

"You're so full of shit sometimes, Jonny Mathers."

"But somehow, it works, because you fucking love it." I smile. "Anyway," he says, turning back to Stacey, "back to this karaoke set up. What's the problem? Why won't you sing?"

"Hey, don't you go siding with her just because you're all in love with her blah blah blah," says Stacey. "Just trust me on this, Jonny, that you really do not want to hear me sing. In fact, it wouldn't even be singing, it would sound more like a cat being strangled."

Jonny chuckles. "I'm sure you're not that bad, Stacey. You can't be any worse than Ben anyway."

"Hey, I'm a bass guitarist, Jonny, I ain't no singer."

"Stating the obvious," says Jonny, his face deadpan.

Turning to Stacey, Ben says, "Look, you getting up there to sing or what?"

Stacey shakes her head. "Absolutely not."

Feeling a little disappointed about having to sing on my own, I then have an idea. Turning to Jonny, I flash him a sickeningly sweet smile.

Jonny catches on very quickly to my thinking. With a firm shake of his head, Jonny says, "No."

"Oh come on," I say, beginning to sound a little whiny.

"No, Lauren, I'm not doing it."

"What? You don't mean you want Jonny to get up there and sing with you, do you?" asks Stacey, looking appalled.

"What?" I shrug.

Leaning across the table, Stacey says to me, "You can't come away for a couple of days to deliberately get away from the limelight and then expect Jonny to just jump up on some karaoke machine and start belting out songs in a pub full of people who may seem like they don't know who he is but probably know exactly who he is. And even if they don't, they will know after about ten seconds of hearing him sing."

Honestly, Stacey goes so over the top sometimes, it's

ridiculous. I love her to bits but seriously, this is beginning to get my back up.

Turning to Jonny, I say, "You used to sing on the karaoke with me all the time when we lived in Manchester, so what's changed?"

Stacey looks over at Jonny and then at Ben. "Am I talking in riddles or something? Or is my best friend more pissed than I first thought?"

Placing his bottle of beer back down on the table, Jonny ignores Stacey and instead turns to me. "A lot has changed since then, Lauren, and Stacey's right, we've come away to be away from the limelight and just for the last few hours of our time away together, I'd really like it to stay that way."

Feeling dejected, I pick up my glass and down some more bubbles. If I'm going to be doing this karaoke thing on my own then I'm going to need some more Dutch courage for sure.

Placing my glass back down on the table, I pick up the bottle of prosecco and proceed to refill my glass. "And now you're pissed off with me," says Jonny with a sigh.

"Hell yeah she is," says Ben with a chuckle.

"Oh shut it you," snaps Stacey, slapping him on the arm.

"Hey! Less of the violence, babe," Ben protests.

Reaching for my glass to drink more prosecco, Jonny catches my hand part way, gently forcing me to put my glass back down on the table. "Hey," says Jonny, taking a hold of my hand. "You know how much I loved singing on the karaoke with you back in Manchester, but…"

"But what?" I ask, frowning at him.

"Things are different now," he says, "and you know they are."

"Oh, enough of this bullshit, Jonny, you've lost your nerve and you know it."

"Lost my nerve?"

"Yes, you've lost your nerve for doing anything out of the ordinary that is in actual fact so bloody ordinary to us people living a normal life that you've forgotten what normal is. I mean, you play to stadiums filled with thousands upon thousands of people and yet you won't get up in a tiny pub in the middle of nowhere and enjoy a sing song with your girlfriend on the karaoke because you're too afraid of being recognised? Seriously? The Jonny Mathers I once knew was afraid of nothing and nobody. What happened to that man, Jonny? Is he still here or has he upped and left for good?"

Our entire table descends into silence, both Stacey and Ben so shocked at my outburst that I've rendered them both speechless. Oh shit, I've taken it too far. I know I have. And I have the alcohol in my system to thank for that. I always get a bit gobby when I've had too much to drink and tonight, it seems, is no exception.

"Erm, I'm...I..." I start to stutter my way through some sort of pathetic apology but apparently, an apology isn't needed right now.

"So, you think I've lost my nerve, do you?" snaps Jonny.

"Look, I didn't mean..."

"Yes you did," says Jonny, cutting me off, "but you know what? You're wrong, and I'll prove that to you right now. If you haven't lost your nerve for singing in public of course?"

I see a slight smile pulling at the corner of Jonny's mouth. Oh, so he's turning the tables on me now, is he? Laying down the gauntlet to me in the hope that I'll be the one to back out instead of him. I don't think so.

Standing up, I say, "Challenge accepted, Mathers. Let's go."

I feel the eyes of Ben and Stacey on me as I walk away from the table, Ben muttering things such as feisty and minx which I assume are the words he is choosing to describe me right now. Well, bring it on I say. I don't know about the minx part, but feisty? Hell yes, I feel feisty. And a little more drunk than I first thought. Oh well, too late now because I am about to approach the poor young man who is in charge of the karaoke set up tonight. The poor young man named Bryan who not only has to deal with me chewing his ear off about the fact that I'm here on a mini holiday, but who also has to deal with my jealous ass of a boyfriend who can't intervene quick enough.

Deliberately placing himself between me and Bryan, Jonny glares over at him. Instantly recognising who Jonny is, Bryan suddenly goes to shit in front of us. "You're? Are you him? You are, aren't you?" Before he gets the chance to say anything else, Jonny holds his hand up to silence poor Bryan.

"No, I'm not whoever you think I am. Tonight, I'm just Jonny. Jonny from Manchester." Turning to me, he pulls me against him and then says, "And this is my girlfriend, Lauren. We're looking at singing a duet, probably something along the lines of River Deep Mountain High or…"

"I Got You Babe?" I suggest, hoping Jonny won't cringe at my request. He never was keen on that song but I always adored it. Yes, it's cheesy, but it's a great duet.

Nodding reluctantly, Jonny says, "Or, I Got You Babe?"

Nodding probably a little too enthusiastically, Bryan finally recovers from the shock of having a world famous rock star standing in front of him, long enough to confirm that he does in fact have both of those duets, along with a whole lot more to choose from.

Jonny finally agrees on the song made famous by Sonny and Cher and after only getting a very brief moment to prepare ourselves for what's coming, the karaoke system suddenly blares to life and we start singing. And boy do we sing. We sing our bloody hearts out.

Our nerves about this entire karaoke idea soon melt away, both of us firmly accepting the challenge laid down by the other one and both of us really enjoying it. Jonny especially. Not only is he smiling at me but in typical Jonny Mathers fashion, he's smiling at his audience, seducing them in a way like only he can.

The entire pub has come to a complete standstill, every single person standing there watching our performance. People are taking photographs on their mobile phones, some are whistling while others are cheering. Their reaction to our little performance is what spurs us on for more, the pair of us now dancing and encouraging our audience to join in with us. And they do. So we sing another song. And another one after that. In fact, we end up singing the grand total of six songs, ending with the song choice that Jonny originally wanted, River Deep Mountain High.

The rapturous applause we get at the end of our performance is immense. So immense that I'm beginning to feel inside how Jonny must feel whenever he performs to a live audience. And this is only the second time I've ever felt like that, the first being only recently. On that amazing night when Jonny pulled me on stage at the O2 arena in London to perform to twenty thousand screaming Reclamation fans.

Now, this isn't anywhere near the scale of performing at the O2 arena but the feeling is much the same. It's like a high. A high that I seriously do not want to come down from. My body is buzzing with so much life and energy that I don't know what to do with it all.

Looking over at Jonny, I see that he's still smiling. Smiling and nodding his thanks to the wonderful crowd of people here in this pub tonight. And he's so grateful to them for receiving us so wonderfully that he offers to pay for drinks for every single one of them. And they accept his offer wholeheartedly, cheering loudly for him as we walk back to our table over in the corner.

Well, we certainly made our mark here in Yorkshire tonight, and we had one hell of an amazing time in the process. Sitting back down at our table, we are greeted by one very excited looking Stacey. "You two were amazing!" screeches Stacey, "like, seriously amazing!"

"Amazingly stupid," says Ben, "you do realise that that little performance of yours will have gone viral within the hour?"

Taking a firm hold of my hand, Jonny smiles down at me and then looks back over at Ben. Shrugging his shoulders, he says, "And?"

"And you wanted to be under some rock away from the glare of the world, remember?"

"Well fuck it, I enjoyed it tonight. And so did they." Jonny points over to the crowd of people behind us, still buzzing loudly from what they've just witnessed. "And Lauren enjoyed it too," Jonny says, looking over at me, "and that's all I care about right now."

Giving his hand a gentle squeeze, I say, "Me too, Jonny. Me too."

CHAPTER 19

We set off for London the following morning after having the most wonderful two days away. I am sad to leave Yorkshire behind and find myself feeling a little down in the dumps by the time we arrive home later that afternoon.

My low mood takes a turn for the worse that evening as I am forced to watch Jonny beginning to pack up his belongings ready for his flight back to LA tomorrow morning. So much so that I can't bear to watch him for a minute longer, instead taking myself off for a long soak in the bath.

After about an hour, Jonny comes knocking on the bathroom door. "Lauren? Are you okay? Or have you got lost down the plughole?" Normally, I would laugh at something like that, but not tonight. Tonight my sense of humour has all but gone.

"I'm having a bath, Jonny. That okay with you?"

I suddenly see the door handle turn, Jonny attempting to get into the bathroom to speak to me properly but he fails, because yes, I admit I locked the door behind me. Cruel I know.

"So, not only are you clearly pissed at me for some reason, you're now locking me out of the bathroom as well? What have I done?" *Nothing* I want to say to him. Only I don't.

"So I'm not allowed to take a bath on my own now?"

Oh my god, what the hell is wrong with me and my big fat mouth? It's our last night together before he leaves me for three entire weeks and I'm suddenly acting like a first class bitch with him. I so need to get a grip on my mood. I hear a loud sigh come from behind the door.

"Fine, take a bath on your own then, see if I care."

I think about shouting him back but I don't. I instead stew in the bath for a little bit longer before finally dragging myself out of the water and into my fluffy white bathrobe. Even that does little to comfort me. Jeez, if Jonny sees me like this then it'll set him off and he'll feel awful when he gets on that plane tomorrow morning. The last thing I want is to make him feel guilty about leaving me when it was my choice to stay behind here in London in the first place.

Walking into the living room, I find Jonny placing his guitar case on the floor next to the sofa, alongside his suitcase and bags in readiness for tomorrow. My stomach lurches, that feeling of uneasiness settling inside of me deeper than ever before.

I don't know what it is but something about him going home tomorrow is really bothering me, far more than the obvious me missing him like crazy for three weeks stuff. I feel anxious and unsettled, a feeling I've had since I woke up this morning. A feeling that is becoming so deep rooted within me that I just don't know what to do with it.

Jonny casts a brief glance over in my direction before turning back to sorting out his baggage. I suppose I deserve to be ignored after the way I spoke to him before. Feeling a little awkward, I take a tentative couple of steps towards him. "Hey," I say quietly.

Zipping up one of his bags, Jonny then stands up and glares over at me. "So you're talking to me now?"

Deliberately breaking eye contact with him, I stare down at the floor and simply shrug. "I was never not talking to you, Jonny, I was just...taking a bath, that's all."

Clearing his throat, Jonny then says, "Okay, so you were taking a bath and being oh so polite about it. Sorry, my mistake."

Looking up at him, I'm met with another scowl before he stalks past me, presumably heading for my bedroom. I sigh heavily. Shit, this is not how tonight was supposed to go but no matter what I say or do, I can't shake this feeling away. It's like a huge blanket of darkness has been thrown over me and I feel like I'm suffocating beneath it. I feel like I can hardly breathe and if I carry on feeling like this, I will have a panic attack. *No, Lauren, not tonight, not ever again. Get a grip on your feelings, Lauren, get a bloody grip.*

Taking a deep breath, I decide to be brave and follow Jonny along the hallway and into my bedroom. He has just about closed the door on me by the time I get there. Pushing the door against him, I walk into my bedroom like I mean business. "Don't close the door on me, Jonny," I say, slamming it shut behind me.

Whirling around to face me, he says, "I wasn't closing the door on you, Lauren, you appeared from nowhere just as I was closing the door so get your facts right first before you start sounding off at me, won't you?" Folding my arms across my chest, I let out another heavy sigh. "Just what the fuck is wrong with you? You've been quiet since we left Yorkshire this morning and now you're snapping at me? Have I done something? Or is this about me leaving tomorrow?"

I shake my head furiously at him. I don't want to admit to him about how I am feeling and so I say nothing. Jonny raises his eyebrows up at me. "So, that's all I get? A fucking head shake?" Furious at my silence, he turns away from me. Brushing an angry hand through his hair, he says, "We had an amazing couple of days away together, I'm leaving for LA in the morning, and this is what I get tonight?" Turning back round to face me, he says, "You fucking raging at me for no reason!"

"I'm not raging at you, I'm just…"

"Just what?" he snaps, "are you getting your period or something?"

I take offence at that. "Oh, so just because I'm being a bit off, I have to be getting my period, do I?" I snap back at him. Hell, maybe I am getting my period after all.

"A *bit* off?" Jonny laughs humourlessly. "Oh come on, Lauren, you've been acting odd all day and you damn well know it." Jonny starts to brush his way past me but I grab at his arm, pulling him back from storming away from me again.

"Look, I'm sorry, okay?"

Jonny sighs heavily and then looks down at me. "This is about tomorrow, isn't it? I don't know why you won't just admit it. I'm feeling it too, you know, the thought of being without you for the next three weeks…it's fucking killing me."

I bite down on the insides of my mouth to stop myself from bursting into floods of tears when I hear him say that. I can't handle feeling like this. I feel as though something is gnawing away at my insides and I don't know how to get rid of it.

"Lauren?" My lack of an answer is making Jonny impatient again. "Lauren, will you just talk to me please?" he says with a sigh.

When I finally look up at Jonny and his eyes meet mine, I almost crumble. I almost tell him the truth about how I'm really feeling. But it wouldn't help him, or me, at all. It would make him feel worse about leaving me, he'd then try and convince me to go back with him tomorrow as he had originally wanted me to and it would all become messy. Really messy. No, I have to make things right with Jonny before he gets on that plane tomorrow morning. And I have to make things right in the only way I know how.

Reaching up, I gently cup Jonny's face in my hands and kiss him softly on the lips. He seems hesitant to kiss me back at first. Pulling away slightly, he frowns down at me and says, "Lauren, what are you…"

I kiss him again before he gets the chance to finish that question, harder this time, silencing him with such force that by the time we pull apart, he looks completely taken aback. "Lauren, what is going on with you at the moment?"

Taking a step back from him, I grab a hold of the belt around my bathrobe and untie the knot. Slowly, and very deliberately, I push the bathrobe over my shoulders and down my arms before finally letting it drop to the floor in a heap around my feet.

Sweeping his eyes slowly over me, Jonny then says, "So, now you want sex? After being strangely quiet all day and then going off at me just now, you suddenly want sex?"

Not exactly the response I was hoping for but I can't say I blame him after the way I've been behaving today. Still, he didn't have to say it *quite* like that.

"Fine," I say with a sigh, "if you don't want to bother then I'll just get dressed."

Feeling suddenly teary at the rejection, I reach down to the floor for my bathrobe. Hell, I seriously am touchy today. My head is all over the place and I just can't get a hold on it.

"Jesus, Lauren, it was a joke," says Jonny. As I begin to wrap my bathrobe back around me, I look up at Jonny and am met with an eye roll. "For fuck's sake, now you're being ridiculous," he mutters.

"Oh, so I'm ridiculous as well as premenstrual now, am I?" I snap at him.

Feeling stupidly mad, deeply upset and completely unwanted, I wrap my bathrobe around myself even tighter. Reaching for the belt, I set about re-tying it when Jonny suddenly snatches my hands away.

"What are you doing?" I say, my voice coming out all screechy and high pitched. When I reach for the belt again, Jonny grabs a tight hold of my hands and doesn't let go of them this time.

Backing me up towards the bed, he says in a firm voice, "I'm about to give you what you so clearly need."

Before I have time to even react to that statement, Jonny is throwing open my bathrobe. Pushing it over my shoulders, it drops to the floor once more, Jonny then hauling me up into his arms before throwing me on to the bed. My back hits the mattress with a thud, Jonny quickly stripping himself naked in front of me. *Holy shit, this is hot. Really hot.*

Without warning, Jonny then crawls on top of me before yanking my legs wide open. He then kisses me hard on the lips as his fingers tangle their way into my damp hair. He tugs hard on the long strands and I let out a load moan.

Jonny smiles against my mouth. "Is this what you want?" he murmurs, as he presses the tip of his cock against my entrance. "Is this what you need?" *God yes*, I think to myself. This is probably what I've needed all day long. Jonny. I need Jonny to fuck whatever it is out of me. I need him to fuck all of my fear and anxiety away.

Tugging at my hair once more, Jonny insists on an answer. "Is this what you need, sweetheart?"

Reaching up, I give a slow, deliberate lick of his lips with my tongue. Jonny's eyes darken, his grip on my hair tightening. "Yes, Jonny," I whisper against his mouth, "I want you to fuck me, I *need* you to fuck me. You're all I'll ever need."

Jonny's lust filled gaze lingers on me for a moment before he suddenly plunges himself deep inside of me, taking me completely by surprise. I cry out loudly in pleasure, Jonny quickly drowning out my cries with his mouth before slowly pulling out of me and slamming into me once more.

I cry out again but Jonny gives me no time to come round this time. He starts to thrust into me so hard and so fast that I find myself clawing at his back in a desperate bid to hold on to something. Anything. Scoring my nails into his flesh, Jonny growls loudly against my lips, his thrusts coming thick and fast.

Wrapping my legs tightly around his waist, I squeeze hard, pulling him into me even further. Jonny lets out a loud groan of pleasure as his hand finds my right breast and squeezes it hard. "Oh god…Jonny," I moan, throwing my head back.

"That's it, baby," Jonny breathes, pinching my nipple between his fingers, "take all you need from me and let go."

Jonny continues to slam his cock into me over and over and over again, to the point where I can barely take any more. Placing his mouth against my ear, Jonny says in a husky voice, "Let go, sweetheart, come for me and take me with you." Moving his hand between us, Jonny places his magical fingers against my clit. Sliding them over my wet mound of flesh, he then says in awe, "Fuck, you're so wet. I don't think I've ever seen you this wet." *Oh. My. God.*

My orgasm tears through me like a tornado, ravaging everything in its wake, draining the very life out of me as he fucks every last shred of my fears and anxieties about him leaving tomorrow away.

Seconds later, Jonny comes with a loud groan of release before collapsing on top of me and burying his face into my neck. Wrapping my hands tightly around the back of his head, I cling on to him desperately, his body heaving against mine as he fights to get his breath back.

We lie there in silence for a short while before Jonny finally speaks. "Better?" he asks, before nuzzling his nose into my neck. I can't help but smile at him.

"You're such an idiot." Slipping his hand beneath my upper thigh, Jonny then makes a grab for my bum. I squeal like a teenager. "Okay, okay, yes, I'm much better now, thank you."

I can feel Jonny smile oh so smugly against my neck. "Baby, you are so welcome."

I laugh. "And you are so bloody arrogant, Jonny Mathers."

Positioning himself above me once more, Jonny deliberately pulls his cock out of me before slowly thrusting back into me, causing me to gasp. "I'm entitled to be arrogant when my dick is still as hard as it is for you after that fast paced session."

Biting down on a suggestive smile, I say, "Then maybe I should be the arrogant one, Jonny, you know, for being the one who keeps your dick hard and all that."

Jonny smiles. "I couldn't agree with you more, baby, and speaking of keeping my dick hard." Thrusting himself into me again, Jonny then rolls us over so that I'm on top of him this time. "I thought you could ride out the rest of your anger by doing what you do best."

"And what's that, Jonny?"

He smiles up at me. "Me of course."

I burst out laughing. "How can I possibly resist?"

Narrowing his eyes on me, he says, "Cheeky."

Smiling, I plant a quick kiss on his lips. "I wasn't angry before by the way," I say, offering up some sort of explanation.

"You weren't?" asks Jonny in mock surprise.

"Oh, very funny," I say, scowling down at him. Jonny smiles. "Look, what I'm trying to say is that I'm sorry for being weird today, I've just been feeling...a little..."

Jonny silences me by placing his index finger over my lips. Gazing deep into my eyes, he then whispers, "I know."

"You do?" I ask, surprised.

Running a hand through my hair, he says, "I know, because... I feel it too, Lauren...I feel it too."

Jonny lifts his mouth up to mine, our lips meeting in a slow, tender dance, our tongues sliding together as Jonny's hands find my hips. Urging me forwards, Jonny starts to move me back and forth slowly on his cock, the gentle, tender motion of his thrusts making my heart soar and my throat thicken with emotion. God, do I love this man. I love him more than my next breath.

"I love you, Jonny," I whisper breathlessly, "don't ever forget how much I love you."

Jonny's mouth falls open on the next thrust, his eyes raking over my face like I'm the only thing in the entire world that exists to him. "I love you too, Lauren," he breathes, "so fucking much that I ache with the feeling. I physically ache with it."

Clasping his face in my hands, I kiss him hard and deep, pouring every ounce of love that I have for him into that kiss, telling him that I don't want him to leave tomorrow, that I want him to stay by my side and never leave me again. I thrust Jonny deeper into me, harder, but it still isn't enough. Hell, I just want to dive into him, seep into his skin, into his very blood, and remain there. Forever.

"Three weeks, baby," Jonny whispers against my lips, as if reading my mind, "just three weeks apart and then we'll have this forever, I promise."

Three weeks, I think to myself, *we just need to get through the next three weeks.*

CHAPTER 20

My apartment is quiet. Deathly quiet. And it's only been two hours. *Two* hours. That's all. Two hours since Jonny left me to go to the airport and I can safely say that they have been the longest two hours of my life. I wanted to go to the airport to see him off properly but, it was too much, not only for me, but for him too.

Being under the glare of the paparazzi as he left London for good was also something that Jonny did not want to subject me to and so, we said our emotional goodbyes in the privacy of these four walls. Jonny seemed a lot stronger than I had expected him to be this morning whereas I was a complete mess. Inside. I kept it all locked away and then let it all out after he had gone. I crumpled to the hallway floor in a heap and didn't move for the first half an hour. I then found my way back to bed and haven't moved since.

Grabbing a gentle hold of the neckline of my t-shirt, I lift it up to my nose and inhale deeply. My eyes close on a sigh. Jonny's white t-shirt which I *borrowed* from him whilst he's been staying here with me is officially mine now, and I'm so glad that it is because whenever I smell it, I can see him in my mind's eye. *Three weeks Lauren, you just need to get through the next three weeks.*

I gulp back my tears and try to keep that positive thought in my mind. Trying to stay positive though is still proving a little too difficult for me at the moment. My fears and anxieties over being separated from Jonny are still gnawing away at me but I have to stay focused. I have to stay focused on the life we are going to be building together over in LA and if I keep that in my mind then my fears will eventually diminish. I hope.

My mobile phone ringing on my bedside table suddenly pulls me out of my tearful reverie. Rolling over on to my side, I quickly snatch it up from the bedside table, stupidly thinking for a minute that it might be Jonny even though I know for a fact that he'll be on board the plane by now.

I smile through my tears when I see Stacey's name flashing up at me. Bless her, she went to the airport to see Ben off properly this morning. Unlike Jonny and I, both her and Ben couldn't care less about the paparazzi and so off she went along with them.

"Hey, Stace," I say, in as cheery a voice as I can possibly muster.

"He's gone, Lauren," replies Stacey, clearly blubbering away on the other end of the phone. Oh hell, now I need to be the strong one of the two of us. Normally I can rely on Stacey to be the strong one.

"Oh, Stace," I say, my voice quivering slightly, "just get yourself back here and we can hug each other better."

She sighs down the phone. "I'm sorry I didn't come straight home after seeing them off. I got a taxi back from the airport but then I just couldn't face coming back to the apartment straight away and so I got the driver to drop me off on Oxford Street."

"Oxford Street?" I ask, surprised at Stacey's sudden extravagance.

"Well I was so down in the dumps that I got the taxi driver to drop me off somewhere with enough shops to keep my mind occupied."

"And did it work?"

"Oxford Street doesn't have anywhere near enough shops to keep me from thinking about how much I'm already missing Ben." Stacey sighs once more. "I know you're no doubt feeling shit too but at least you know for a fact that you're going to be seeing Jonny again soon, and that you're going to be making a life out in LA with him. What have I got to look forward to?"

My stomach lurches, the thought of leaving my best friend behind in London on her own kicking me in the guts all over again. "Come home, Stace, and we can have a proper talk."

"I'm already on my way home, Lauren, so don't worry, I won't be long."

"Okay, see you soon."

****

"So, Ben hinted at wanting you to go over to LA to be with him?" I ask, completely shell shocked.

Stacey nods gently as she wipes away the last of her tears. We're sitting on the sofa in the living room with a bottle of wine sitting between us on the coffee table. It's barely even midday and we've already drunk half of the bottle. It is a one off though and boy do we need it.

"So, what did he say exactly?"

Stacey shrugs her shoulders. "It's a bit blurry now really. It was in the heat of the moment you see, last night, when we were in the middle of…"

"Sex?" I flash her a suggestive smile and finally, after all her tears, she smiles back at me.

"Okay, yes, it was in the middle of sex, so…after all that it probably means nothing…right?"

Taking a sip of my wine, I think about what she's saying for a moment and then reply honestly. "In my experience, with Jonny anyway, I find that sex is when he's at his most honest. Most vulnerable. Not that he isn't honest with me normally but, what I mean is that Jonny can hide nothing from me in those moments of intimacy and that is how I know one hundred percent that he is the one for me, my absolute soul mate."

"Yeah but it's different with you two, Lauren, you and Jonny were teenage sweethearts and fell head over heels in love. Ben and I are different. We were just…having fun, and I knew that from the outset and it's fine…"

"But he hinted at you going over to LA so tell me exactly what he said."

Stacey takes a huge gulp of her wine before answering me. "Okay, well, he was on top of me…his hands were in my hair, his mouth was on my ear and he was about to…"

"Come?" I say with another suggestive smile.

Stacey rolls her eyes at me, her cheeks flushing a light shade of pink. "Yes, when he was about to…do that, he groaned into my ear, something along the lines of 'I don't want this to end' and then something about 'come with me' which of course, could have a double meaning. In fact, now that I've heard myself saying it out loud to you, I think that both of those statements could have a double meaning which points to the conclusion that it was all in actual fact in the moment and was all sex related. I mean, let's face it, where Ben is concerned, everything is sex related." Resting her head against the back of the sofa, Stacey lets out a huge sigh.

"Not necessarily," I say, trying to remain positive, "what did he say after that?"

Stacey sighs once more. "Nothing, he fell asleep." I burst out laughing. Glaring over at me, Stacey says, "Hey! You're supposed to be cheering me up, not making fun of my situation!"

"Oh come on, Stace, it is kind of funny if you think about it."

Slowly but surely, Stacey begins to smile. "I suppose it is a bit funny, him falling asleep on me. Mind you, we'd had sex three times by that point so I think I'd worn him out."

I chuckle. "Stacey Kerr, you are one filthy little minx."

"You're one to talk," quips Stacey.

"So, I take it you haven't actually asked him about what he might have meant then? Either last night or this morning?"

Stacey shakes her head. "Like I said, he fell asleep last night and then, this morning, it was such a rush to get to the airport and by that point it seemed really stupid to bring it up with him and when he didn't bring it up, I assumed I'd made a mistake and got it all wrong." She sighs. "Which clearly I did."

I give her shoulder a gentle squeeze. "Oh, Stace."

"It wasn't just sex for me, you know," she says quietly, suddenly looking wistful, "it was so much more for me than it ever was for him." Stacey looks down into her half empty wine glass before gulping the rest of it down in one go. She then refills her glass before topping up mine, draining the rest of the bottle. "We're going to need more wine," she says.

"Erm, you do realise it's only midday and that you're working tonight?"

Taking another slurp of alcohol, Stacey says, "Well fuck it, I feel like shit and I certainly can't face work tonight. I'll ring in sick or something."

Picking up my glass, I clink it gently against Stacey's. "I'll drink to that." We both take a sip of our drinks. "Look, Stace, I may be wrong here but, hand on heart, I really honestly believe that Ben feels something more for you than just sex."

"You do?" She doesn't look convinced.

"Yes, I do, because otherwise, why on earth did he just want to be with you while he was over here? He could have slept with you just the once and then moved on to all the other females in London, but he didn't, he stuck with you and believe me, that is a first for Ben."

"I...suppose it is," Stacey says, giving the matter some thought.

"Suppose? Stace, Jonny told me so. He also told me that for as long as he's known him, Ben has never been with the same woman twice. Fact."

Now I've got her attention. "Are you being serious?" She looks shocked.

"Deadly serious," I say. Reaching for her hand, I squeeze it gently. "So don't give up on Ben just yet. He may not have said it in so many words but I think that this whole being apart from you will make him realise what he's missing."

"God, I hope so," she says with a sigh, "I really do hope so."

****

I wake from my slumber to the shrill ringing of my mobile phone blaring loudly at me from its position on my bedside table. My bedroom is in complete darkness and my head is swimming thanks to my all day drinking binge with Stacey.

Turning over to reach for my mobile, I realise just how drunk I still am when I accidentally knock my alarm clock on to the floor. "Oh shit," I mumble. By the time I've reached for my clock from the floor, which tells me it's an unearthly 3.00 am, I end up missing the damn call.

Swiping at the screen, I am delighted to see Jonny's name on my missed calls list. Five missed calls to be exact, three of those calls from over an hour ago. Shit, I really must have been out for the count if I haven't heard my mobile ringing. Well, missed calls or not, I'm just so thankful that he's landed safely. However, I am not so thankful for being so bloody drunk that I've ended up missing his calls.

I pout, wondering whether to call him back or to perhaps text him to ask him to call me back. The call to LA will cost me a small fortune, but it's a small price to pay to speak to the man I love. I am just about to dial his number when Jonny's name flashes up at me on the screen. My stomach flips. Smiling down at the screen, I answer quickly.

"Hey, baby," I say excitedly.

"Well, thank fuck for that," says Jonny, breathing a sigh of relief down the phone.

"Are you okay?" I ask, suddenly worried.

"Well, I am now," he says, "when I couldn't get hold of you, I started to panic."

I smile down the phone at him. "Jonny, it's three o'clock in the morning over here, I was asleep."

"I know that, Lauren, but you're normally a light sleeper so I thought you would have answered your phone straight away and I know it's early hours over there but I just couldn't wait any longer to speak to you."

Lying back down on my pillow to try and stave off any more dizziness, I say, "Sorry I missed your calls, I admittedly got pissed this afternoon with Stacey, we started on the wine at midday and didn't stop drinking until around nine o'clock when we both staggered our way to bed. We were both feeling a bit shitty and so alcohol seemed like the only answer at the time. Doesn't seem like the answer right now though." I grimace as another bout of dizziness hits me.

Jonny chuckles at me down the phone. "Missing us both that much, are you?"

"Too right we are. In fact, missing you is an understatement."

"Me too, baby," he says, "these next three weeks can't go quick enough, believe me."

"So, how's your mum? Have you been to see her yet?"

Jonny falls silent for a moment before answering me. "I'm here with her now at the hospital, she's just fallen asleep so I've nipped outside to call you, but she's…she's not good, Lauren, not good at all. They're talking about stopping her chemo because of how ill it's making her. The doctors said, and my mum agreed, that it's pointless putting her through more chemo when she won't be better at the end of it. Palliative care is the only thing they can offer to her now, anything to just keep her as comfortable as we possibly can."

Jonny's voice is quiet and sombre, his heart silently breaking on the other end of the phone as I try desperately not to break down and cry for him. I should be over there with him, supporting him while he's going through the most horrific time of his life. Instead, I've been moping around the apartment all day with Stacey, getting stupidly drunk on wine and feeling sorry for myself because Jonny has gone back to LA without me.

"I'm sorry for not coming with you, Jonny," I whisper down the phone to him, "I'm so so sorry for staying behind in London without you while you're going through this hell. I feel so…helpless, and shit. I'm a shit person for not coming with you…"

"Hey, that's the wine talking, Lauren. You're the kindest most supportive woman I've ever met and I understand you had to stay to get stuff sorted out so don't let me hear you talk about yourself like that again, okay?"

"Okay," I say quietly.

"Okay," says Jonny, "so tomorrow, you start getting things organised and start planning, because LA is just a stepping stone away for you, sweetheart, I promise." I smile, but it's only brief, my stomach doing its usual roil again as I think back to the many conversations I had with Stacey today. "Lauren? Are you okay?"

Clearing my throat, I finally decide to just bite the bullet and broach the subject with Jonny. "Stacey and I were talking today and she seemed to think that Ben may have said something to her that would suggest he might want her to…join him over in LA?"

I am dreading the answer, absolutely terrified of it actually, and, as Stacey asked me not to say a word to Jonny, I'm kind of fearful of facing Stacey's wrath tomorrow morning. Oh well, too late now.

"Look, Lauren, I'll be honest with you, men don't really talk in depth about feelings and relationships and shit, but, if you want my honest opinion, I think Ben does have deeper feelings for Stacey than he's letting on. He was quiet on the plane back over here and Ben's never quiet. He went straight home without any suggestion of going for a drink with the lads down town which again, is unknown for him, and lastly, he broke his infamous rule over in London of being with the same woman not just the once, but many many times, so Ben told me repeatedly."

"So, you two do talk about relationship stuff then?"

"I'd hardly call what Ben has told me about him and Stacey deep relationship stuff, Lauren. I mean, let's face it, he only has one brain cell that works, remember?" I chuckle down the phone.

Jonny continues. "Look, I know you're going to miss Stacey terribly and I know that she's more like family to you than a friend and...to be honest, I'm not all that comfortable with bringing you out here without her coming with you." Now that gets my attention. I bolt upright in bed when Jonny says that to me, my drunken head immediately spinning at the shock of being forced upright so suddenly.

"What did you just say to me?" I ask in shock.

Jonny chuckles. "I said I want you to bring your best friend to LA to be with you, to be with us. Whatever happens between her and Ben is their business and it's up to them if they want to try and make a go of it together but that aside, Stacey is your family and she belongs with you."

Oh my god, could he be any more perfect? But as wonderful as his idea is, Stacey couldn't possibly afford to move to LA. The savings she's been stashing away over the last few years combined with mine would barely get her through the first few months over there, that's how expensive it is.

"As wonderful as you are for even suggesting it, Stacey wouldn't be able to afford to move over to LA, Jonny. Even with her savings and mine, she'd still..."

"I've got a little house in the hills not far from where I live now," Jonny says, cutting me off, "it was the first house I ever bought out here. I've been renting it out on the cheap to one of my employees for the last few years. Well, I was renting it out to him until recently, when he just suddenly decided one day to fuck off to another music label and leave me in the lurch. Anyway, that's not important, the point is, there's a nice house over here for Stacey if she wants it, rent free, for as long as she needs. When she does eventually get herself a job out here and decides that she wants to pay me any rent at some point then we could come to some sort of arrangement but, as you well know, I don't want or need the money." *Oh. My. God.*

Suddenly overcome with emotion, I can barely get my words out to thank him. "Just when I thought I couldn't possibly love you any more, Jonny Mathers, you go and make a gesture as grand as that and bloody hell I do, god I do."

Hell, if I could pounce on him right now and show him my gratitude then I would. God, I just want to kiss him and hold him and make love to him…badly. So very badly. Lying back down on the bed, I find myself clinging on to my phone for dear life. "I so wish you were here with me right now," I whisper, "I'm missing you so much…too much. And what you're doing for me? For Stacey…you…you're…"

My words are lost as the tears I've been desperately trying to push away finally break their way through, rolling down my cheeks. I cry silently, holding on to the phone as if I am holding on to Jonny.

As if sensing my spiralling emotions, Jonny says quietly, "There isn't anything in this world that I wouldn't do for you, Lauren, and you know that."

Sniffing loudly, I say, "I do know that. I've always known that, Jonny."

"So talk to Stacey about it tomorrow and we can get things in motion."

"She'll be ecstatic," I say with a smile.

"Well, I'm glad," says Jonny, "now, I'm sorry to have to say it but I'm going to have to say bye to you now because I really need to get back inside the hospital to be with my mum. She may be asleep but I haven't seen her in so long that I really need to spend as much time with her as I can before I go on tour again in a few weeks."

"Of course you do," I whisper, "give her my love, won't you?"

"I will do," says Jonny.

"Oh, Jonny?"

"Yeah?"

"Any luck with re-booking those five dates that got cancelled on your US tour?"

"No," Jonny says with a sigh, "it's looking like we're going to have to refund the fans and do those five shows at a later date at a reduced price. From the online forums it looks as though the fans are anticipating this outcome anyway so hopefully, not much damage will be done."

Breathing a sigh of relief down the phone, I say, "Thank god for that."

"Yeah, and I have you to thank for that. You make me honest and you make me a better person. Inside and out. You always did. And fuck do I love you all the more for it."

"I love you too, Jonny," I whisper.

"Night, baby," says Jonny, "sleep tight, and I'll speak to you tomorrow."

"Night, Jonny, speak tomorrow."

****

Stacey can barely believe her ears the next day when I tell her about Jonny's offer. She's speechless at first. Shell shocked in fact. "Jonny actually…he actually offered these things? He…really?" I nod my head at her. "I mean…really?" asks Stacey again, still unsure whether to believe me or not. I nod madly at her before breaking out into a huge grin. "Oh my god!" Stacey screeches before leaping up and down on the spot with excitement. "Like, seriously?"

I laugh at her. "Yes, seriously!"

"Arghhh!!" screams Stacey before grabbing me by the neck and yanking me against her. The pair of us then start jumping up and down together, screeching at the top of our voices as we get lost in the excitement of it all.

This really is the most amazing gesture anybody has ever done for me and part of me is still in disbelief that this is actually happening. But it is happening, and boy are Stacey and I going to enjoy it. We deserve to finally have some happiness in our lives and this is it, our moment to be excited and look forward instead of looking back. After about five minutes of bouncing up and down together, Stacey suddenly says, "Oh, what about Ben? Does he know? Does he even want me over there?"

I hold up my hands and say, "Jonny admittedly said that what happens between you and Ben is your business but he does think that Ben has stronger feelings for you than he's letting on. He said he's never seen Ben like this over a woman before but, before you decide on anything, Stace, I think you should talk to him. Whatever happens between you two though, I really hope it won't stop you coming over there with me…if you want to come over there of course?"

Stacey places a hand on her hip and raises her eyebrows up at me. "Did you seriously just ask me that question? Hell, wild horses couldn't keep me away from moving over to LA with my best friend! Whether I end up with Ben or not, that has absolutely no bearing on my decision whatsoever. I am coming over there with you, girl, and nothing on this earth is going to stop me."

She pulls me in for a proper hug this time and I sag against her with relief. "Well, thank god for that," I say, my voice a little wobbly with emotion, "because I was honestly beginning to wonder how I was going to cope without you over there."

Pulling back slightly, Stacey smiles down at me with teary eyes. "Well, now, thanks to your wonderful boyfriend, you'll never have to find that out, because you can't get rid of me that easily, Lauren Whittle."

"Wouldn't want to," I say quietly, "best friends forever, remember? No matter what."

Stacey cuddles me against her once more. "Best friends forever, Lauren," she says, whispering my words back to me, "no matter what."

****

As it turns out, Stacey needn't have worried about Ben's reaction to her moving out there along with me. He's all for the idea and apparently is missing her like crazy already. So finally, after all this time, it feels as though everything is falling into place for us. I've got Jonny back in my life, something I used to dream about often but thought would never ever happen, and Stacey has finally met a man who could possibly be the one for her.

Obviously, it's still early days for the pair of them, but things are certainly looking positive and to top it all off, I am going over to live the life that dreams are made of over in LA with my boyfriend *and* my best friend. Life really doesn't get much better than that. Which is why Stacey and I end up hitting the city of London that night to celebrate our good news.

Stacey rings in work sick for the second night running, too excited and care free to give a shit whether or not Frankie suspects she is bluffing about being ill or not. She'll soon be leaving that crappy lap dancing club behind anyway and so, off we go into London city, dolled up to the nines, ready to party the night away together. Time to celebrate life to its fullest by doing what we do best. Drinking and dancing. I only hope London is ready for us....

CHAPTER 21

It's funny how life can change in an instant, how one minute you can be riding the highest of highs before suddenly skittering off the edge of a precipice and falling into the abyss once more.

For me, in these last two days since Jonny left, I've felt as though I've been riding on one constant, unbelievable high. My fears and anxieties over being separated from Jonny have finally diminished, replaced only with excitement, laughter and a whole heap of fun being had with my best friend, Stacey. Two days of planning our big move over to LA so far and the pair of us just can't stop smiling. It's like we've been walking on air, floating through life as though we're being carried along on a breeze, and it's felt amazing. So amazing that Stacey even left to go to work at the club with a huge smile on her face tonight. I swear I've never seen her look so happy and most probably, Stacey has never seen me looking so happy either.

After checking in with Jonny over the phone, the call lasting at least an hour, I then settle down on the sofa for the night to watch a rom com. It's the first night I've been on my own since Jonny left and now that Stacey has finally gone back to work, I suddenly feel very aware that I'm on my own tonight. Something that has never bothered me ever before. I suppose I've grown used to being in the company of so many people since reuniting with Jonny that now I'm finally getting some time to myself, I don't much like it. Oh well, it won't be for long. Stacey will be home after 2.00 am although I'll most likely be tucked up in bed fast asleep by then.

A sudden knock to the front door of my apartment almost makes me jump out of my skin, causing me to spill wine down my pyjama top. "Oh shit," I mutter, plonking my wine glass back down on to the coffee table. I swipe my hand over the wet patch on my top. *Oh great, right across my left nipple.* And my top is white. And right now, very much see through. Just great!

Grabbing my dressing gown from the sofa, I stand up and wrap it around me to cover up my wet mess. What the hell is all this then? And more to the point, who the hell is it? Checking my watch I see it's just gone 9.00 pm.

As I wander slowly through my living room towards my hallway, there comes a second knock to the door, a much firmer one this time, and then silence. As I arrive in the hallway and stand stock still right behind the front door, I begin to panic.

Should I answer the door at this late hour? What if it's somebody who knows I'm in all on my own and has come to attack me or worse still, rape and murder me. *Yeah Lauren, get a grip of yourself, that only happens in the movies.*

Trouble is, it doesn't just happen in the movies. It happens in real life too. In this city no less. Goddamnit I wish we had one of those peep holes in the door so that I could see who is standing on the other side. This is the second time in as many days when I've wished for one of those.

The first time I'd wished for the peep hole, Jonny had been standing on the other side of this door. Maybe it is Jonny. Maybe he's surprising me by coming back to London to help me and Stacey with the move. No, I spoke to him earlier and he was definitely in LA because I could hear Ben and the other lads in the background. No, this definitely isn't Jonny. *So who the hell is it?*

A third knock to the door and I back up against my hallway

wall in fear. My heart is beginning to pound in my chest and my hands are shaking. I am terrified and in all honesty, not really sure what to do. I could ring 999 but this isn't an emergency. Yet. I could always ring Stacey to tell her to get back here now but then, she wouldn't have her phone on her while dancing. Oh hell, maybe I should speak. Speak to whoever is on the other side of that door. Yes, that's what I need to do.

Taking a long, deep breath in, I exhale slowly and, closing my eyes, finally dare to speak to the stranger on the other side of the door. "Who...who is it?"

I'm met with silence, which does absolutely nothing to calm my nerves. Swallowing down the lump in my throat, I somehow find my voice again. "I said, who is it?"

I hear somebody cough, as though clearing their throat to speak, but then they fall silent again. Something that really gets my back up. Finding some courage from somewhere, I finally push myself away from the wall and walk over to my door. "Look, if you don't tell me who you are or better still, go away, I will be calling the police." I hear a low rumble of laughter from behind the door.

"Oh, I've flown a long way to talk to you face to face, Lauren, so I won't be going anywhere. Not until we've spoken to each other anyway. I can promise you though that involving the police will not be necessary."

My blood runs cold, the hairs on the back of my neck standing to attention at hearing that male voice. A voice that sounds scarily familiar to me. A voice that belongs to a man who clearly knows who I am. A man who is amused at my fear and is getting some sort of perverse pleasure out of it. And there were only ever two men in my life who got pleasure from my fear. One of those men was my father. And the other....

My mouth runs dry, my body going into instant panic. *No, Lauren, don't show him your fear. Do not panic. You can do this. You've got this. Show him you're stronger than you've ever been.*

Yes, I can do this. I have to do this. Taking another deep breath in, I slowly and very cautiously, unlock the front door. I turn the handle and, with a shaky hand, I finally open the door. And there, on the other side, is my worst fear realised. "Hello, Lauren," says Pete Mathers, a sly smile plastered across his face, "long time no see."

****

I feel numb with shock, panic and fear taking a firm hold of me once more. This cannot be happening. Jonny's father, Pete Mathers, cannot really be standing on the other side of my front door. This has to be a nightmare. A nightmare I am surely about to wake up from.

Folding my arms across my chest as if I am feeling far more confident than I actually am, I discreetly move my fingers beneath the sleeve of my dressing gown. Taking a firm grip of the skin on my wrist, I pinch it hard in the hope that somehow or other, the pain will wake me up from this nightmare I am suddenly finding myself in. But sadly, it doesn't wake me up. And it doesn't wake me up because Pete Mathers is really standing here in front of me, smiling down at me in that overly imperious way he used to.

I start to fidget on the spot, averting my gaze from his, because he's doing it to me already. Making me feel like I am nothing more than a piece of shit on the bottom of his shoe that he's come to wipe off and dispose of. Somehow or other, this man always managed to make me feel like that.

He is like my own father in so many ways. The only difference between the two of them is that my father made me feel worthless by beating me with his fists. Pete made me feel worthless with his words. Well, I am not going to fall to pieces in front of him. Not like last time. I have to stand up to him. I have to fight for the man I love and if it means taking Pete Mathers head on then so be it.

"What do you want?" I ask firmly, straightening my back in an attempt to look as though I really mean business.

Pete simply shrugs, as if he hasn't just flown over five thousand miles across the Atlantic Ocean *just* to talk to me. More like he'll be warning me off, just like he did the first time round. "It's in your best interests, Lauren, that you let me in so we can talk properly. Wouldn't want to disturb your neighbours at this late hour now, would we?"

Pete's accent has more of an American drawl to it these days I notice, and looking at the expensive light beige designer suit he's wearing and his tanned skin, I would say that life over in LA is more than agreeing with him.

Standing my ground, I say, "We would only be disturbing my neighbours if our voices were raised. You planning on raising your voice at me, Pete? You planning on getting angry with me?"

Pete flashes his pearly white teeth at me as he chuckles to himself, clearly amused at the effect he's already having on me. It makes my skin crawl. I swear, he is getting off on this, loving the fact that he is taunting me by just being here, never mind what he's actually here for.

Pete sweeps his eyes around the corridor he's standing in, almost like he's checking his surroundings before resting his steely gaze back on me again. "I want to be nice to you, Lauren, and I want to keep this as friendly as possible, so I suggest you let me in."

"And if I don't?"

With a firm shake of his head, Pete says, "Don't test me, Lauren."

But I just can't help myself. I refuse to be bullied by this man all over again. "How the hell do you even know where I live, Pete? More to the point, how the hell have you got here without arousing suspicion with Jonny about where you've gone? I'll call him you know, I'll call him and tell him everything..."

Pete turns nasty then, slamming his hand against my front door as I try to close it shut against him. "Get the hell out of my apartment!" I yell, hoping against hope that my neighbours will hear me and come to my rescue.

Pete pushes his way into my hallway, forcing me to stumble backwards against the wall. Somehow, I quickly manage to recover myself and am just about to go up against him and scream the place down when he slams the door shut behind him and grabs at my arm. "You don't want to scream, Lauren, trust me."

"Get the hell off of me!" I try wrenching my arm from his vice like grip but it's no use, he has a firm hold of me and is not about to let me go any time soon.

"One call is all I have to make, Lauren. One phone call and your past will be all over the tabloids and the internet by tomorrow morning." *My past?* What the hell?

I stop struggling for a moment, my eyes widening in horror as I look up into the angry face of the man who took everything I ever had away from me. And now, here he is, ten years later, taking it all away from me all over again. "What...what are you talking about? My past?"

Finally releasing his grip from around my arm, he then takes a step back from me, dusting his suit off as though he's been touched by something dirty. That something dirty being me.

"Like I said, I want to be nice to you, so let's just get this over with, shall we?" He then whisks off down the hallway and into my living room, leaving me behind to slowly follow him, like I'm a naughty child who's done something wrong.

When I eventually join him in the living room, I see him closely scrutinising his surroundings, as though he has been sent to carry out some sort of inspection around the place. I swear, if he didn't have some sort of apparent hold over me, I would swing for him right now.

Coming to a halt in the middle of my living room, Pete continues to look around my home. "Not as bad as I thought...for a lap dancer."

Pete's cruel words are already beginning to seep their way into my skin but that's exactly what he wants. He wants me to crumble in front of him and back down, but I will not go down without a fight, no matter what sort of hold he thinks he has over me.

"So, what is it that's all so important to you, Pete, that you thought you would fly over to London in secret to talk with me while your loving wife is gravely ill back home in hospital with your son by her bedside?"

I almost feel bad for playing the guilt card against Pete by using Judy in this way but where Pete is concerned, I have to pull out the big guns.

Pete frowns over at me. "Judy is perfectly comfortable and Jonny thinks I'm off on a very brief business trip. I'll be gone all of twenty four hours, if that, so if you think the whole guilt thing is going to work on me, Lauren, then you're very much mistaken."

"I highly doubt you could ever feel guilty about anything you do in your life. That's what makes you so good at your job as the band's manager after all. What is it that the papers call you again? Ruthless Pete?" I pretend to think about it for a moment. "Or is it Pitiless Pete? I can't quite remember now."

"Enough!" snaps Pete, raising his voice slightly.

"Touch a nerve, did I?" I snap back at him.

I know I'm probably pushing him a little too far but right now, pushing him to his absolute limit is all I've got left. Taking a step closer, Pete narrows his eyes on me, his dark browns almost a direct copy of Jonny's. In many ways, Pete is a clone of Jonny, or should I say, Jonny is a clone of his father. I'm just thankful that that is where the similarity between them ends, because, as I am finding out once again, Jonny is absolutely nothing like his father.

His father is hurtful and cruel and above all, selfish. He will stop at nothing and nobody to get what he wants and he is about to prove that point to me all over again.

"You are not going to ruin my son's life again, you got that? I will not stand by and watch him fall from the top of his game back to the bottom again because of being associated with some whore like you."

I am about to cut him off and shout back at him but he continues to threaten me, walking towards me like some sort of predator about to pounce on his prey. I walk backwards towards my kitchen, fearful of what he may say or do to me next.

"You're bad for him, Lauren," he mutters, "you always were, and from the look of the papers recently, you still are. You need cutting out of his life for good and I'm going to be the one to do that." I find myself backed into a corner against my kitchen worktop, Pete's face literally only inches from mine. "And if you don't leave him alone and instead decide to continue this... relationship..." He struggles to even say the word relationship, almost like he's gagging on the word. "...then I'll have no choice but to put your story out there for the world to see."

Pete takes a small step backwards, finally giving me a little bit of breathing space. Not that I can breathe at all right now. In fact, I think I'm beginning to panic. Really panic. *No Lauren, don't give Pete the satisfaction, don't let him bring you down.*

With a shake of my head, I say, "You can't do this to Jonny, not again. This will break him, Pete. He loves me. I love him. And I'm good for him. Can't you see that I'm good for him?"

Pete sneers at my words. "Scum is what you are, Lauren. You came from the scums of Manchester and you'll always be from the scums of Manchester. You and your father were almost the downfall of my son and I will not allow you back in his life to do that all over again." He points an angry finger over at me. "And it was all because of the power you held over him! And that power is still there! He's crazy when he's around you and I cannot and will not allow you to have that hold over him all over again. He's at the pinnacle of his career and he's worked hard to get where he is so you need to go quietly through the back door and never come back into his life ever again, you hear me?"

Pete's cruel words do their work, tears now brimming at the back of my eyes as I finally find myself unable to hide my emotions from him any longer. "You just can't stand the thought of Jonny ever being happy, can you? So come on, Pete? What hold do you have over me then? What sordid little details do you know about my past that you're going to blackmail me with?"

Pete looks at me with disdain. "If you don't do as I have asked, I will release a story to the papers."

"No story you release to the papers could ever stop me from being with Jonny."

"I beg to differ," says Pete. "Because think of how Jonny would feel if he woke up one morning to see the story of your past together plastered across the front of the tabloids. More to the point, Lauren, think how you would feel?"

Oh my god, just when I thought that Pete Mathers couldn't stoop any lower than he already has, I am proven wrong yet again.

"You mean? Surely you don't mean…"

"Oh, I mean everything about your past together, Lauren. The good, the bad, and the fucking ugly…"

"No you wouldn't," I say, shaking my head at him, "even you wouldn't do that to your own son."

Pete steps toward me again. Putting his face within inches of mine he says, "I would do anything to protect my son from you and if this is my leverage against you then so be it."

I shove him away, storming over to the other side of the kitchen as the reality of my situation begins to sink in. "So, you don't want me to be with Jonny because you think I'll somehow bring his life crashing down around him but you're prepared to do that anyway yourself?!" I scream at him, "by putting our entire history out there to the world for every man and his dog to read about?!"

Tears begin to stream down my cheeks and I swipe angrily at them as Pete stands there and sneers over at me. "You're honestly prepared to tell the world and all his fans about the baby we lost and what my dad did?"

I start to pace up and down the kitchen floor in anger. I swear my entire body is shaking right now. I feel so angry and hurt, but most of all, fearful. Fearful of Pete and how far he really is prepared to go just to get me out of Jonny's life once and for all.

Glaring over at him, I say, "Jonny's mum, your wife, is terminally ill with cancer, and you're prepared to just wrench me away from him in the cruellest of ways at what is currently the worst time of his life?!"

Pete simply shrugs. "Cruel or not, if it's the only way I can get you to walk away from him for good this time then I'll do it, believe me I'll do it."

"Jonny needs me!" I yell at him, "he needs me to support him through this rough time and if I'm not there for him, what then? When Judy finally passes away and I'm not there to support him through it, what then, Pete?" I storm over to him and get right into his face. "What then?!" I scream up at him.

Pete's face darkens and as he takes a menacing step towards me, I suddenly think I've pushed him too far. So far in fact that I wouldn't be surprised if he raised his hand to swipe me across the face with it. But Pete is too clever for that. Pete knows that if he harmed me physically then I wouldn't think twice about reporting him to the police, and where Pete is concerned, reputation is everything.

Swallowing down his anger, Pete remembers himself and instead shrinks back a little. "Tomorrow morning, a news story is going to be printed in the tabloids. The story is going to be the cause of your break up with my son..."

"Nothing a tabloid prints about Jonny would ever cause me to break up with your son!" I bite out at him.

Slamming his hand down on the kitchen worktop, Pete begins to get angry with me again. "You'll do it, Lauren, and I know you'll do it. You'll do anything to protect Jonny from that painful part of your past, the past that you caused..."

"I caused nothing..."

"You and your scumbag of a father caused everything. If

it wasn't for meeting you, Jonny would never have got into drugs. I blame you for that drug addiction, an addiction he'll silently have for the rest of his life. If only I'd have found out about your violent father sooner than I did, I could have prevented all of that from happening."

I look up at him in sheer disbelief. "I didn't ask to have an abusive father. None of what happened was my fault."

Pete looks away from me for a moment, reaching into his pocket for his mobile phone. Glancing up at me, he says, "When I leave here, I'll be making the call for that story to go to print tomorrow morning. The rest is up to you."

Oh my god, he really is insane. Hasn't he heard anything I've just said? With a heavy sigh, I turn away from him. Placing my hands in my hair, I close my eyes and try not to imagine what my life will be like without Jonny in it. Of course I've done it before, survived ten years living without him, but this time is different. Because I don't think I could survive losing Jonny for a second time. If I really and truly have no choice but to do as Pete says, then my life is over for good.

Taking a deep breath in, I say quietly, "What is this bullshit story you're releasing to the tabloids tomorrow, then? Something you've cooked up on the flight over here no doubt?"

"You may be surprised to learn that for once, the story I am selling to the papers about my son is actually all true. Right down to every last sordid detail." I squeeze my eyes shut, as if that could somehow drown out what Pete is about to tell me. "But I won't put you through the mill right now, Lauren, I owe you that much at least. Plus, I think the element of surprise tomorrow morning when you switch on the television or log on to social media will make your reaction to the story more believable."

Right, that's it, Pete has said more than enough and gone way past the point of insanity. Whirling around to face him once more, I point over towards the hallway. "Get out!" I scream. When he doesn't move, I stalk over to him and practically shove him out of my kitchen. "I said get the fuck out of my apartment!!"

Pete raises his arms to defend himself. "Take heed of my advice, Lauren," he says, as he starts to finally back away from me. "You break up with Jonny following the tabloid story tomorrow and nothing else needs to get leaked to the papers."

I practically chase him out of my apartment, screaming at the top of my lungs, my body shaking with anger and fear as I finally slam the door on the evil bastard. I lock the door quickly and then, placing my palms flat against it, I start to cry. I cry and I cry and I cry. Crying soon turns to sobbing and a moment later, I find myself too weak to stand up for a minute longer.

Dropping to the floor on my knees, I start to howl like a baby in the hope that somehow or other, the howling might put a stop to the horrific pain I am currently in. But it doesn't work. Nothing will work. Because Pete has ruined my life all over again. And despite my protests tonight of never leaving Jonny, despite my endless promises to Jonny of never leaving him ever again, Pete already knows that I will give him exactly what he wants. And I know it too. Because I will do anything and everything to protect the man I love. And Jonny needs protecting from our past. And if leaving him all over again is the only way I can do that then I have no choice. Where Pete Mathers is concerned, I never had a choice, and I never ever will.

CHAPTER 22

I wake with a start, Stacey hammering on my bedroom door and then suddenly bursting into my room before I even have the chance to open my eyes properly. "Lauren, you need to see this…well…I say you need to see it, but…you won't like it."

My stomach plummets to the floor, the god awful memory of last night slowly floating its way back to the surface of my mind once more. With a loud, discontented groan, I pull my duvet up and over my head and turn away from Stacey. I can't face this right now. And I certainly can't face my best friend being the one to tell me what the papers have printed about my boyfriend. Especially when, according to Pete, every sordid detail is apparently true.

I haven't even seen Stacey since she returned home from work late last night. After Pete left, I got pissed on two bottles of wine I found in the fridge and then stumbled my way to bed well before Stacey got home. I figured that was the only way to blot out the hell of last night and the one thing that would get me to sleep. Trouble is, I've slept so deeply because of the alcohol that I haven't even had the chance to properly process what happened to me last night, never mind decide about whether or not I am going to tell Stacey about Pete turning up at our door.

Of course I'm not going to tell Stacey about Pete turning up at our door. She'd be on the phone to Jonny within seconds and then Pete would see through his threat and then…the world would know everything about our past.

Pain sears through my chest at the very thought and I clutch at my duvet, pulling it against myself so tightly that my knuckles turn white. "Lauren? Are you okay?" asks Stacey quietly. She touches my shoulder through the duvet. "Have you seen the article already? Is that why you're upset?"

Okay, I can't avoid this any longer, time to face whatever the hell Pete Mathers has thrown at me and deal with it head on. With a huge sigh, I pull the duvet back down and roll over to face Stacey who is now sitting on the edge of my bed looking really worried. "You look...have you been crying?"

"No," I say, a little harsher than I intended to, "I just feel a little...off this morning, and to be honest, a little shaken up at how you burst into my room just now. Talk about an early morning wake up call!"

"It's actually midday, Lauren, you over slept."

"And?" I ask with a shrug, "can't a girl enjoy a lie in anymore?"

Stacey frowns. "What is with you?"

Shit, I'm already snapping at my best friend, not a good start when I'm supposed to be trying my utmost to act as normal as I possibly can. If nobody is to find out about this then I seriously need to keep my shit together.

With a heavy sigh, I say, "Sorry, Stace, I'm just...over tired. I shouldn't have snapped at you. Now, tell me what's going on, you sound worried. Everything okay?"

Stacey looks away from me, her eyes briefly darting to the duvet before finding my gaze once more. I wait with baited breath for her to speak but before she says anything, she pulls out her mobile phone.

"I...I need to show you something, Lauren. Something that

went viral on the social media sites earlier this morning. Something that has most likely been printed in the tabloids too, although, I haven't been out to the shops to check that as yet but...well, social media is the news these days and, well, this is the stuff they love...and it involves Jonny."

I already feel as though I have been punched in the gut. I feel sick. So sick with anxiety over what the story is about and even more sick at the who is behind the story, not to mention the why. Clearing my throat nervously, I then say quietly, "Show me the story, Stace."

Stacey puts down her mobile for a moment. "Look, Lauren, before you read the article, I really think that you should remember that it's most likely all bullshit anyway, and not only that, you really need to hear Jonny's side of things before believing any of this crap that they write all over social media. I mean..."

"Just give me the damn phone," I snap, cutting her off.

I reach for Stacey's phone but she snatches it away from my grip. "Lauren..."

"Fine, I'll get my own phone instead..."

"Okay okay, here, have mine," says Stacey, swiping at her screen. "I just wanted to give you a moment before you read it, that's all."

"Jesus, Stacey, how bad can it be? Just give me the bloody phone!" I'm getting panicky now. If Stacey is hesitant at allowing me to read the article then it must be bad. I'm even beginning to wonder whether she believes the story herself.

Stacey slowly places her mobile into the palm of my hand and then says, "Just remember that everything in that article, true or not, is in Jonny's past, as ugly as it is." She almost grimaces when she says that. Hell, if Stacey is grimacing then what the hell am I going to think?

Okay, no use in putting off the inevitable, time to read what Pete has taken delight in releasing to the newspapers this morning. Time to find out what ugliness from Jonny's past will be used as the ultimate tool in breaking us up all over again.

My eyes flick down to the small screen lying flat in the palm of my hand. The headline reads, *"Jonny Mathers in drug fuelled orgies fest – rock star photographed naked on week long binge of parties, drugs and women."*

That headline alone is enough to turn my stomach but as I scroll down further, it gets worse. So much worse. Because those photographs that they refer to in the headline are now staring up at me from my best friend's mobile phone. Photographs of Jonny sitting naked on some chair in the middle of a room looking worse for wear with at least three semi naked women leaning over him, sat on him, rubbing their tits in his face, blah blah fucking blah. Oh my god, this is so much worse than I envisioned it to be last night.

When Pete said he was releasing some story to the papers, I expected it to be bullshit. Something about some bust up from his past or some usual past flings with women or something pretty much standard that I've read about before, but this? Oh my god, this is horrific.

Seeing Jonny in the photographs not only proves one hundred percent that it is him but knowing that he took part in things like this? It changes my opinion of him completely. I mean, I know he's been with hundreds of women over the years since he became rich and famous and oh so bloody well loved, but orgies? And doing drugs while he was at these orgies? And god knows what else too.

Holy shit, this article is going into too much detail for me.

Sexual details of what the women got up to with Jonny and the stuff he did to them. The things he said to them in bed and how he made them feel. How dirty he was and stuff he asked them to do for him.

Clearly, Pete has got some minion of his to approach a couple of these women and has then offered them money to sell this juicy story on his son. How the hell any father can do that to their own son, I just don't know, but I'm certain of one thing to come out of all this. Pete has successfully managed to make me seriously doubt my future with Jonny.

Before reading this article, I thought nothing and nobody could ever do that but, somehow or other, that bastard of a man has managed it. He's managed to plant the small seed of doubt in my mind that I thought he could never ever do. And I hate that I am doubting the man I love because of something wicked that his own father has done. But Jonny will never get to know about that act of wickedness. And I'll have to be the one to make sure of that.

After reading a couple more sentences within the article, I can't face reading it anymore, instead practically throwing Stacey's mobile at her before scrambling off the bed and running towards the bathroom.

I just about make it to the toilet before spilling my entire guts up, most of which is water and bile as my stomach is empty. I clutch the toilet bowl tightly as I continue to wretch for several minutes, my stomach muscles protesting loudly as my body tries desperately to rid itself of all the hurt and pain that Pete Mathers has caused me.

Stacey suddenly joins me by the side of the toilet bowl, pulling my hair back from my face and rubbing a soothing hand along my back. "It's okay, Lauren, I've got you."

I wipe my mouth with the back of my hand, quickly flush the

toilet and then sit back on my heels. "Before I read that article, you said I needed to get Jonny's side of the story…"

Stacey frowns over at me. "Lauren…"

"And then you said the words, true or not…"

"I was just trying…"

"To what?!" I snap, "fucking defend him? Jesus, Stace, you could see it was him in the bloody photographs! Hell, the entire fucking world can see that it's Jonny! So why say those things to me knowing full well that the article is all true?!"

Stacey pulls her hand away from my back and shrinks away from me. "I wasn't defending him, I was just trying to…"

"Ease the blow?!" I yell, "while in a roundabout Stacey way trying to defend him, just like you always do, like you've done from the moment I reunited with him!"

Hell, I feel so angry. At Pete for starting all of this. At Jonny for doing what he did with all of those women. And at Stacey for bloody well defending him all of the time. Considering I was supposed to be acting my way through all of this, the surge of anger I'm now feeling is suddenly becoming very real to me.

Standing up from the floor, I decide to have a shower. "I need a shower, can you leave me alone please?"

Slowly standing up, Stacey then says, "Lauren, I really think you should ring Jonny and talk to him….."

"Right now, I'm going for a shower, so if you could leave me alone please."

"Lauren…please…"

"I said leave!" I snap, glaring over at her.

Stacey finally holds up her hands in defeat. "Fine, have your shower and be on your own then."

She slams the bathroom door behind her and it's only then that I crumble. I crumple to the floor in a great big heap and start to cry quietly. Just twenty four hours ago, my life was finally perfect, I was riding the highest of the highs and I was finally looking forward to a happy future with the man I love. And now, here I am, only a day later, reduced to this. A great big heap of hurt and pain and tears.

I'm teetering along the knife edge of my life and am about to fall off into the huge black hole of abyss just waiting for me at the bottom. But before I hit rock bottom, I have to do the very thing that I swore I would never ever do in my life again. I have to break up with Jonny. I have to hurt him and push him away and lie to him so that he will believe our break up to be real. Hell, I need to believe that our break up is going to be real because, as angry and as hurt as I am right now after reading that article, I still can't bear the thought of living the rest of my life without him.

I don't want to live the rest of my life without him. But I have to. I have to leave him in order to protect him from our past. And I have to do it soon. Like ripping off a plaster, I need to do this quickly. *Today Lauren, you have to do it today....*

CHAPTER 23

Later that afternoon, I receive the phone call from Jonny that I have been dreading all day long. I almost don't answer his call, too afraid to face the shitstorm that his own father has created. But I have to face it, and I have to face it sooner rather than later.

Swiping the screen to answer his call, I simply place my mobile phone against my ear and say nothing, not even so much as a greeting. It almost kills me inside to do that to him but I have no choice, I have to stand my ground and stay angry with him because my anger is the only thing I am depending on right now to get me through this.

"Lauren? Are you there?" says Jonny, sounding panic stricken.

I sigh at him down the phone. "You know I'm here, Jonny, so just say what you have to say and then leave me alone." I grimace, pain slicing through my heart at hearing myself actually saying those words out loud to him.

"Leave you alone? Lauren? What the fuck?"

"What the fuck?" I snap, feeling angry, for real this time, "are you being serious?"

"Look, Lauren, I am so sorry about that article…"

"You're *sorry* about the article? What part are you sorry for exactly? The fact that it got printed? Or the fact that it's all true?"

Jonny sighs heavily down the phone. "It was…look, Lauren, it was well over a year ago…."

"So you think the passage of time makes reading this filth easier to accept, do you?"

I'm met with another sigh. "No, of course not. I'm…disgusted with myself, you have to believe that I am…and I was…then…after it happened…"

I squeeze my eyes shut in a desperate attempt to blot out the devastating images of Jonny and those women from my mind, but it's no use, they keep swirling around and around in my mind's eye, taunting me in the cruellest of ways. I feel sick to the pit of my stomach all over again.

"You were disgusted with yourself after your week of drug fuelled orgies, were you? How very remorseful of you, Jonny."

"It wasn't a fucking week, the papers have exaggerated all of that. It was a couple of nights when I went on an absolute bender because of…"

"Because of?"

"Look, it was when my mum first got diagnosed with breast cancer, okay?"

Jonny then falls silent and I am left feeling guilty. But I can't be allowed to feel any sort of guilt right now because if I let my guard down with Jonny just a tiny bit, I will crumble.

"Okay, so your mum got diagnosed with breast cancer and instead of being supportive, you went out on a two night bender doing drugs and god knows what else?"

"It sounds bad when you say it out loud," he says quietly.

"That's because it is bad, Jonny! It's screwed up! I mean, how often have you partaken in orgies for god's sake? Just how many more women are going to come out of the woodwork after this?"

"Hey!" he finally snaps, "that's the one and only time I have ever fucking lost it and done something like that and I instantly regretted it. In fact, I don't even fucking remember most of it!"

"Oh, this just gets better and better!"

"What the fuck do you want me to say, Lauren? Would you prefer it if I did remember it? All of it? Every last sordid detail?"

I lose it with him then, big time lose it. "I don't want you to bloody remember it, Jonny! I want it to never have happened! And the fact that you barely remember it at all means that you could have picked up anything! Just how stupid were you to do something like that?!"

"I hit an all-time low again because of my mum's breast cancer diagnosis and I went to shit, like I always do…"

"And how about now?" I bite out, "how about now with your mum's cancer being terminal? How did you react to that news when you found out?"

Jonny goes quiet for a moment, and then says, "Lauren, as you well know, I only found out about my mum's terminal diagnosis just before we headed over to the UK from France so I've barely had time to properly process it…"

"What did you do when you found out?" I think it's a fair question to ask of him, however Jonny thinks otherwise.

"What the fuck does it matter? It was before we got back together…"

"Jonny, did you? In France…did you…were you with women?"

"Jesus Christ, Lauren, it was before we got back together…"

"So you were with women?"

Jonny sighs loudly. "I was on tour and the night I got the news about my mum's cancer being terminal...I admit that I lost it and did a couple of lines of coke with a woman I hooked up with that night, but that was it, I swear."

I can't believe I'm hearing this. If reading the article wasn't bad enough, now I have a whole load of other shit to deal with from Jonny on top of all of that. "So, after just telling me that you instantly regretted your behaviour last year, you then go and tell me that you've gone and done it again? Recently?"

"That one night in France was nothing like what I did last year! Yes, I had a slip and did a bit of coke again but I fucked one woman, Lauren. Just one woman for one night, that was it."

Placing my forehead in my hand, I sigh heavily down the phone at him. "You talk about fucking a woman as though you've just been to play a tennis match or something, like it's some recreational activity that you partake in and then move on to the next match the following night. You make it all sound so bloody cheap and sordid and I hate that you're making me feel like this."

"Like what, exactly?" says Jonny, his voice accusatory.

"Ashamed of you, disgusted with you, upset and hurt by you. I mean, I know you have a past and I realise that none of us can change our pasts but this is all a bit too much for me to handle right now, Jonny..."

"Whoa! You can stop talking like that right now, Lauren. What I did before you came back into my life is exactly what you just said, it's in my past. I love you more than anything in this world and you know that. I respect you and I worship the very ground that you fucking walk on..."

"Worship the ground that I walk on? And yet you slept

with me the first moment you got and allowed me to have unprotected sex with you over and over again knowing that you could be passing on some sort of disease to me? I mean, let's face it, Jonny, you could be carrying all sorts and you wouldn't even know!"

"I fucking well resent that!" he shouts. "And for your information, I got checked only recently, and after last year, when I finally woke up and realised what I'd done, I got every test done under the sun and lucky for me I was clean. And I've always played it safe ever since then, including the woman in France. I may have been high at the time but I used protection, Lauren. Since that wakeup call last year, I have used protection. Except with you. You wanted me without protection and I hesitated, you know I hesitated, but with you…I just couldn't say no. And I trusted you, Lauren. I trusted you without a moment's thought and despite my past, you can trust me, I swear."

God, I just want this to be over with because, as angry and upset as I am, I still wouldn't walk away from him for what he's done. Yes, my anger with him is very real right now and I'm disgusted at him for what he's done but my love for him could overcome that. Hell, my love for him could overcome pretty much anything. All except for one thing. One person. Pete Mathers.

"I'm sorry, Jonny, but I don't think I can trust you anymore," I say quietly, my voice wavering slightly.

"Are you being fucking serious? Lauren, somebody out there has deliberately sought out and paid these women to come forward and talk to the press about me. The same person who cancelled five of our shows. The same person who wants to rip you away from me. Why can't you see that?"

Holy shit, the shows. The shows that got cancelled. They were the work of Jonny's dad after all! Jonny was right all along. And yet he doubted himself. Jonny doubted himself for doubting his father and yet he had good reason to. But I convinced him otherwise. I was the one to convince him and now look at the mess that I'm in.

I could tell him. I could tell Jonny right now and get it all out in the open so we could move forward. But his mum is gravely ill and he's about to go on tour again and then Pete will release the story of our past to the newspapers and then…and then everybody will know what happened to us. And nobody can ever know that. There are some things in life that aren't meant to be shared and that part of our past is one of them.

"I'm sorry, Jonny, but I can't be with you anymore, not after this. I don't trust you anymore and if two people don't have trust in their relationship, then…"

"Bullshit, Lauren!" he snaps, "this is all fucking bullshit and I don't believe for a minute that you would finish with me over this! What happened to riding through all the shit together no matter how hard it got, huh? What the fuck happened to you staying by my side no matter what life threw at us? You're telling me you're seriously going to bail on us already?"

I fall silent for a moment, tears glistening in my eyes as I fight to hold on to some sort of control. If I break down and cry now, he will see right through me. He will know that I'm lying and he will force the truth out of me. I'm only thankful that I'm doing this over the phone because if I was sitting here face to face with him, I would most definitely crumble. Finishing with him over the phone is cruel and cowardly but I have no choice.

"I can't live that life with you over in LA, Jonny. I had doubts before you even left to go back home…you know I did…"

"So you thought you'd take the coward's way out and finish with me over the phone instead?"

"Jonny…"

"You would have finished with me anyway, wouldn't you? If this article hadn't even have been printed, you would have fucking finished with me anyway? Because let's face it, you never wanted to come out here with me really. Which is exactly why I wanted you to come over with me instead of staying in London. Because I knew that deep down, somehow or other, you would do this to me again."

Now that hurts. And it hurts because it is so far from the truth that I can't even begin to tell him how far away it is. "No, I wanted to come out there with you, I wanted to be with you… but all of this has just reminded me that…"

"That you can't handle the life I lead now? That you can't handle the fame and the fortune and the fact that I've got an unsavoury past?"

"Jonny…"

"Well, you know something, Lauren? If you can't handle it and your love for me isn't *strong* enough to overcome all of the above, then fuck you."

My mouth drops open in horror. "Jonny! Don't talk to me like that! If you would just understand…"

"Understand?!" he shouts, "I can't even begin to understand just what the fuck is going on with you, Lauren! And I don't think I'll ever fully understand the why. Why you left me then." He pauses for a moment, his voice wavering slightly, "And why you're leaving me now."

"Jonny…"

"But know this, Lauren. Know this, because it's the last thing I am ever going to say to you…"

"Jonny, please…"

"This will be the last time you ever leave me because I will never allow you to do this to me ever again."

"Jonny, I'm sorry, please..."

But it's too late, Jonny has already cut the call dead and severed all ties. Instantly regretting my decision, I try to call him back but he rejects my call. So I try again and again and again but he rejects all of my calls before finally switching his phone off.

Oh my god this is so much worse than I ever imagined it to be. So bad in fact that I feel like I'm beginning to go mad. Why did I give in to Pete and his demands? Why didn't I stand up to him and tell Jonny everything so that we could face it together? *Because you're a coward, Lauren. And you're weak.* I am weak. And where Pete and my dad were concerned, I always was.

Throwing my phone on to my bedside table, I then curl myself up into a ball and pull the duvet up and over my head and begin to cry. Two minutes later, Stacey is knocking on my bedroom door asking if she can come in.

"Not now, Stace!" I shout from under the duvet, "I just need to be alone right now."

"Okay," she shouts through the door, "but whatever just happened between you and Jonny, remember I'm here for you when you're ready."

Biting back a sob, I shout, "I know you are...thanks, Stace."

****

"You finished with him?!" Stacey screeches. "You're seriously telling me you finished with him? Please tell me you are joking!"

Pouring myself a large glass of wine, I raise my eyes heavenward before sighing loudly. "Aren't you supposed to be leaving for work round about now?" I ask through gritted teeth.

I expected this reaction from Stacey of course because in her eyes, Jonny can do no wrong, however, on this occasion, she is bang on the money. I just can't allow her to know that.

"I'm not leaving for anywhere until you tell me what the hell is going on with you?"

"I finished with my boyfriend, that's the new hell I am currently living in."

"A hell of your own doing!" she snaps. *No it isn't of my own doing at all,* is what I really want to say to her.

"It's of Jonny's own doing actually, not mine," I snap back at her, before slamming the wine bottle back down on the kitchen worktop. Picking up my glass, I down the entire glass of wine within seconds before refilling it again.

"And you think getting pissed on wine is going to make it all go away, do you?" says Stacey, continuing to provoke me.

"No, but I'm hoping it may just send you away for a short while to give me a bloody break!" I down more wine which only adds to the fuel in Stacey's anger right now.

"Give *you* a bloody break?" she scoffs, "Lauren, what the hell is wrong with you? You've been locked away in your bedroom all afternoon without saying a single word to me and then when you do finally surface, right before I am due to go out to work I notice, you tell me about your break up with Jonny as though it was something that I expected to hear…"

Slamming my wine glass down on the worktop this time, I finally turn around to face Stacey head on. "And what did you expect to hear, exactly? That I'd been talked around by Jonny into forgiving him for something so sordid and cheap that I can't even think about it never mind talk about it..."

Stacey shakes her head and starts to do that whole finger wagging thing at me like she normally does when she's about to give me a good telling off. "Oh no, I'm not having it, this isn't you talking here, Lauren Whittle. I know how much you love Jonny and I have seen first hand how you are around him and how you were together and you love him unconditionally, no matter what, so this act that you're putting on for me right now? Utter bullshit is what it is, so cut the crap and start talking because I'm not going anywhere until you tell me what the hell is going on with you?"

I admit that I think about it. About telling her. For a split second I do honestly think about telling her everything. That we could maybe work it all out together and come up with some sort of plan...but then Pete Mathers' face flashes up in my mind and I'm instantly reminded of the potential consequences that my actions could cause.

"I am telling you the truth, Stace, and the truth is I can't be with Jonny because of both his sordid past and the potential life I could be living out there with him. I can't handle the life he leads and I'll never be able to..."

"This coming from the woman who's been doing nothing but plan our life over in LA with me for the last two days!"

"That was before the article got released!" I yell, "and anyway, just because my plans with Jonny have come to a screeching halt doesn't mean your plans with Ben have to! I mean, that's why you're really pissed at me, isn't it? Because your dreams of an LA life with Ben are in tatters now because of me?! Well I'm sorry I've wrecked everything for you, Stace, but I can't stay with Jonny for the sake of you and your new found boyfriend, okay?"

As soon as the words are out of my mouth, I know I've gone too far. Stacey's face drops, her fiery like anger from just a moment ago completely doused out now thanks to me and my big mouth. "Oh, Stace, I'm sorry, I didn't mean..."

"Of course you meant it, Lauren, you meant every word," says Stacey, hurt now swirling around in her eyes, "trouble is, I just don't understand why."

I shake my head at her. "I didn't mean it, I swear I didn't..."

"Just like Jonny didn't mean to do that stuff last year with those women because of course, he didn't have a crystal ball and therefore couldn't predict that he was going to reunite with you just twelve months later..."

"Stacey, please, try to understand..."

"I don't think I'll ever understand this, Lauren. Unless of course you finally decide to tell me the truth."

With a weary sigh, I say, "I am telling you the truth, and if you can't see that, then..."

"I'm late for work," says Stacey, suddenly cutting me off.

"Stacey, please, don't go to work and leave things like this between us."

Grabbing her bag from the kitchen worktop, she throws it over her shoulder and then turns to leave. "Don't bother waiting up for me, Lauren. I'll see you tomorrow...maybe."

"Stace..." I start to follow her out of the kitchen and through the living room towards the hallway but she just walks off without so much as a backward glance. She slams the front door shut behind her and suddenly, I'm alone all over again. Well and truly alone. And I deserve to be.

CHAPTER 24

"Thought you could do to take a look at the latest newspaper article printed today," says Stacey, tossing said newspaper on to the coffee table in our living room.

With a heavy sigh, I say, "Will you stop buying the bloody newspaper please?"

"Not until you get it through your head that you need to make things right with Jonny. You need to contact him, Lauren."

Snatching up the tabloid from the coffee table, I am met with yet another photograph of Jonny out on the town in LA somewhere, looking drunk and disorderly. He isn't alone in the photograph I notice. Oh no, he has two women hanging off his arms this time. As opposed to just the one woman in the last photograph that got splashed across the tabloids just two days ago.

Two weeks since I broke up with Jonny and this is what I've been subjected to. Daily. Stacey's never ending attempts at getting me to contact Jonny by buying me a bloody tabloid every day with the latest updates on his welfare. Well, from the looks of things, Jonny is doing just fine. He might be out getting pissed regularly and getting into some scrapes along the way but surprise surprise, he certainly isn't lacking in the companionship department.

"If you think that showing me newspaper articles of Jonny with other women is somehow going to entice me into getting back together with him, then you're mistaken, and anyway, Jonny is well and truly over me by now and he's making that statement crystal clear."

I throw the tabloid back on to the coffee table and turn my attention back to the television programme I was watching.

Stacey sighs. "I've had enough of this shit." Strutting over to where the television is in the corner, she switches it off at the plug and then glares over at me. "This has to stop," she says firmly.

I simply shrug my shoulders at her. "What has to stop exactly?"

"This!" she screeches, gesturing wildly with her hands, "you sitting here on your backside watching the bloody television twenty four seven!"

I take offence at that. "Excuse me? I'm not sitting here twenty four seven!"

"Oh my god, you haven't left our apartment for two weeks!" she snaps, finally losing her temper.

"I have," I say, defensively. Although as soon as I say it I quickly realise that Stacey is in fact correct. I haven't left the apartment in two weeks. Meaning that I haven't seen the light of day or surfaced from within these four walls for two entire weeks. A fortnight. Holy shit, that's bad.

Biting down on my bottom lip, I mumble quietly, "Okay, you're right, I haven't."

Stacey looks up to the heavens. "Finally, you're admitting to something."

"Look, I don't know how you expect me to be after what happened…" I say to her, feeling annoyed.

"Oh my god, Lauren, you broke up with him, remember? And

since breaking up with him you've done nothing but mourn for him!"

"Mourn for him?"

"Yes, you're mourning for him. For Jonny. You're grieving for the love you once had and you clearly can't live without him and yet you pushed him away again…"

"Hey!" I snap, "what do you mean *again*? I didn't push him away the first time round, he was wrenched away from me, remember?!"

"Yes of course I remember!" she yells, "But then you were lucky enough to have a second chance with him and now you've gone and thrown it all away!"

Standing up from the sofa, I decide to end this conversation once and for all. "I haven't thrown anything away, okay? I couldn't handle his fame and his past and so I chose to walk away and that's it."

"That's it?" asks Stacey, raising her eyebrows up at me.

"Yes," I state, "now for goodness sake, stop buying the bloody tabloids and leave it the hell alone!" I start to walk out of the living room but Stacey calls me back.

"And where do you go from here then, Lauren? Huh? Are you going to spend the rest of your life in mourning or are you actually going to get up off your ass and maybe, I don't know, start living your life again? Maybe even get yourself a new job? You know, earn some money like the rest of us have to?"

Turning back round to face her, I say, "You know full well I've had my savings to fall back on so don't start making out like I haven't been paying my way when you know full well that I have."

Stacey simply shrugs her shoulders at me. "I'm just saying

that if you're so over Jonny and out of mourning then you should go back out there and get yourself a job. You know, start living again."

"Fine!" I snap, "I'll start looking for bar work."

"Bar work?" Stacey looks surprised.

"Yes, bar work," I sigh, "I've worked in pubs and bars before, back when I lived in Manchester with…with Jonny."

"You know, Lauren, I may have been friends with you for almost ten years but recently, since all this shit with Jonny started, I sometimes feel like I hardly know you at all."

"Well, maybe that's a good thing," I say, sadly.

"You know what? For once? I think I agree with you." Pushing her way past me, she then says, "Oh, and one last thing, please god have a bloody shower and get dressed into something that resembles anything other than your pyjamas or dressing gown."

I think about responding to that snide remark but instead say nothing, allowing Stacey to leave the room quietly for once.

I can't remember a time in my life when Stacey and I have ever fallen out with each other as badly as this. And it's all my fault. Everything that's shit in my life right now is all my fault. And all because I am weak. And frightened. Frightened of a man who has a hold over me and always has done.

The thing is, I want to tell Stacey everything. Everything about my past with Jonny and all the bad stuff that happened to me. I want to tell her everything that's happening to me now and why I left Jonny all over again. But I can't. I swear I've never felt more trapped in my life than I do right now and worse still, I am hurting my best friend in the process. A best friend who is more like a sister to me.

Tears begin to well up in my eyes but I blink them quickly away. I can't allow my emotions to cloud my head right now. I need to stay focused and turn my attention elsewhere. Starting with getting myself a new job. Yes, that's what I need to do. Stacey is right. I need to sort myself out and get myself back out there. And it starts now.

****

Eight weeks later and I have thrown myself into my new job working behind a bar five nights a week in some nightclub in the middle of London. The money is crap and the tips are practically non-existent but it's so busy that I don't have much time to think about anything else.

At least, I don't have much time to think about anything else in the evenings anyway. During the day is different. Because everywhere I go, I see Jonny. Either on the television or in the newspapers, his life going from bad to worse in front of the watchful eyes of the world's media.

My heart broke for him three weeks ago as I woke to the news that his beloved mum, Judy Mathers, had finally passed away after her long battle with cancer. Jonny was only into the second week of Reclamation's US tour when it happened. He postponed the tour straight away to return home following her death and hasn't been out of the news since. For all the wrong reasons. Because after his mum's funeral, which literally took place only two weeks ago, Jonny went straight back on tour with the rest of the band. Which was a huge mistake. Not only for Jonny, who has clearly gone back into the limelight far too soon after suffering such a terrible loss, but for the rest of the band too. Because Jonny has gone so far off the rails since losing his mum that I can't even bear to log on to my phone or switch on the television anymore for fear of seeing what may happen to him next. In fact, it's become so bad that I don't even so much as glance over at the newspaper stands anymore, never mind actually buy one.

I was so cut up for him after his mum died that I even sent Jonny a few text messages. Messages telling him how sorry I was to hear about his mum and how sorry I was for hurting him so badly again. Of course he didn't respond to any of them. I thought about ringing him to speak to him but then decided against it. He never wants to see or hear from me ever again and I don't blame him. His dad got exactly what he wanted and there will be no going back from any of it ever again.

Stacey and I are also still at odds with each other, mostly due to the fact that she's still in touch with Ben over the phone. Only yesterday she took great delight in telling me how Ben, Will and Zack hold me wholly responsible for Jonny going off the rails and I of course thanked her for her unending support right before I slammed my bedroom door in her face.

Things at the moment are bad. Really bad. Jonny's life is in tatters and in all honesty, so is mine. Was protecting Jonny from our past really worth all of this pain? I let out a weary sigh as I scroll through the photographs of me and Jonny on my mobile phone. I pause on the one where we're both smiling up at the camera from my bed. It's one of the many I took after we'd just made love. Jonny is smiling against my cheek and I'm grinning up at my phone like a loved up teenager. *God, I miss him.* I miss him so much that I can barely breathe whenever I think about him.

Placing my index finger over the photograph of Jonny's smiling face, I close my eyes and whisper the words, "I love you, Jonny. Always have. Always will."

****

I go through the rest of the week in a haze, just going about my work and trying my best not to pay attention to anything else that is going on around me. I keep my head down and lay low, going out to work at the bar in the evenings and then returning home again, without doing much else in between. Except when I get to Thursday. Thursday morning to be exact. When Stacey comes bursting into my bedroom in a panic about yet another news story about Jonny.

I groan my annoyance. "Stacey, I told you, I don't want to hear..."

"Look at him!" she yells, before pushing her mobile phone into my face. "Just bloody look at him, Lauren!"

Squinting down at Stacey's phone, I can barely make out the photographs at first. "What am I looking at, Stacey?" Stacey scrolls down a bit further, to the headline just under the photographs. It reads, *Jonny Mathers storms off stage – fans outraged*. What the actual hell?

Grabbing Stacey's phone from her hand, I scroll back up to the photographs again. *Oh my god*. Now I realise why I couldn't make out the photographs properly before. Because most of the photographs have been partially blocked out. And for good reason. Because Jonny is partially nude in these photographs. On stage. Whilst on tour with his band last night in Chicago. Oh my god, he got his manhood out while on stage with the band, what the hell was he even thinking?

"Oh my god, this can't be...I mean, Jonny wouldn't..." As I start to read the article, I begin to feel sick. "Stacey, this says that he...got himself out of his pants and started dancing and laughing at the audience...he then got booed at and...stormed off stage...oh shit this can't be happening. Stacey, please tell me that this isn't happening."

Prising the phone out of my grip, Stacey places it face down on my bed and looks over at me. For the first time in weeks, she actually looks as though she feels sorry for me. "I'm sorry I had to show you that, Lauren, but...I couldn't keep something like that from you…I just couldn't." I start to cry. "Oh, Lauren," says Stacey, reaching out for me. I stop her from getting anywhere near me.

"No, don't hug me, Stacey, I don't deserve to be comforted right now. If Jonny isn't getting comfort then I don't deserve to be comforted either."

"Lauren…"

"Have you spoken to Ben about what happened?" I ask, cutting her off.

"No," she says, shaking her head, "it only happened last night and it's too early to ring him now, and, to be honest, after this? I'd be surprised if he ever wanted to speak to me ever again."

Raising my eyebrows up at her, I say, "Hey, none of this is your fault. This is all my doing, Stace, not yours. Ben, Zack and Will have every right to be angry at me but not you…not you."

Stacey reaches across for my hand and gives it a gentle squeeze. "I'm sorry for being a cow with you over these last few weeks…"

"Don't apologise to me, Stacey. Please don't. I should be the one apologising to you. For putting you through all of this…I…I'm sorry."

"Sssh, Lauren, it's okay, you've been through a lot…"

I shake my head at her, anger beginning to rise from within me like a bubbling volcano about to erupt. "No, Jonny is the one who's been through a lot. And it's all down to me…if I wasn't so weak…none of this would have happened…"

"What do you mean?" asks Stacey, suddenly looking suspicious.

Tell her, Lauren. Just tell her and get it all out in the open.
"Stace…I…"

"What?" she asks, looking concerned. "What is it, Lauren?"

"I need to tell you something."

"Tell me what?"

"But before I tell you, you have to promise me that you will say nothing to anybody else. That you will keep it to yourself and yourself alone. As my best friend in the whole world I think you owe me that much."

Stacey frowns. "But what if the something you are about to tell me requires me to do something. To do something or to tell somebody in order to help you…"

I shake my head at her. "No. And if you can't promise me your silence then…I can't tell you."

Closing her eyes briefly, as if warring with herself, Stacey sighs. "Okay, I promise, but only because I love you so bloody much."

Breathing a sigh of relief, I take hold of Stacey's hands. "I need to warn you that some of what you're about to hear is ugly. Really ugly. Okay?"

Stacey nods. "Okay. Hit me with it."

****

A few hours later and Stacey and I are sitting on the grass under a huge oak tree on Hyde Park. After breaking down and telling her absolutely everything about my past, as well as finally telling her the real reason behind my break up with Jonny, we both had to just get out of our apartment and get some fresh air. And it was a good decision.

Since moving to London, Hyde Park quickly became one of my favourite places. Even on the darkest of days, this park somehow always managed to make me feel a little more at peace with the world, even if only for a short time. And Hyde Park is even more beautiful at this time of year. As it's now early October, the leaves on the trees are finally beginning to change colour, the lush greens finally giving way to vivid golds and vibrant reds. It's a warm and sunny autumn afternoon out here and I'm already beginning to feel a little calmer about things.

Finally sharing everything with Stacey has really helped with that too. I've literally shared over a decade of my life with her today and I feel so much lighter, freer, almost like a snake shedding its skin. Like I've rid myself of all my hurtful past and finally got it out in the open to be dealt with. Well, sort of. I don't think it's quite as simple as that but at least I have finally opened up to somebody about it all. And there is nobody else in the world who I would have shared it all with other than Stacey. It just needed to be the right time. And today was definitely that time.

"So," says Stacey, plucking a daisy out of the grass, "where do you go from here?" My sigh is a huge giveaway to Stacey. I don't have a bloody clue, and for once in her life, I don't think Stacey has a clue either. "I don't suppose there's any point in suggesting you speak to Jonny now, is there? About his dad I mean?"

Glancing over at Stacey, I deliberately side step the question when I see she is making a daisy chain. I can't help but smile at her. "Is that for you or for me?" I ask, secretly hoping that it's for me.

Returning my smile, she says, "This one is definitely for you, Lauren."

"You think I need brightening up?" I ask, raising my eyebrows.

Casting her eyes downwards, she says, "I think that would be putting it mildly."

As she continues to make her daisy chain, we fall into a lengthy silence. My thoughts start to drift to Jonny again and the current state he's in. God damn the drugs he's got himself hooked on all over again. God damn it all to hell.

"Stupid question I know but, are you okay?" asks Stacey, noticing my sudden mood change. Hell, the worry and anxiety really must be etched all over my face. Either that or Stacey can read my mind. Probably the latter actually.

Picking at a blade of grass, I say, "I was thinking about Jonny's crippling drug addiction and how I'm so angry with him for being so weak, but…"

"But?"

I exhale loudly. "I can't help but feel partly responsible for his drug addiction. After we lost…Oliver…" I gulp back the huge lump in my throat that forms whenever I say his name out loud. "After we lost our son…both Jonny and I turned away from each other. Well, I turned away from him because I didn't want to talk about it, and…well…he then turned away from me."

Swiping away an errant tear, I suddenly feel Stacey's arm wrapping its way around my shoulders. "It wasn't your fault, Lauren. You were both dealing with your loss in the only way you felt you could deal with it."

I sniff loudly, trying desperately to force back my tears. "But I pushed him away and he couldn't handle it. After everything that happened, losing our son, and then…all the stuff that happened after that, with Jonny and my dad…Jonny's head went and I should have let him talk to me. I should have talked to him…but I didn't…" Stacey hushes me gently. "You know, we lasted six months after Oliver died before Jonny went into rehab, before I left Manchester. And when I think back to those last six months of our relationship...it makes me feel so ashamed..."

"Ashamed?" asks Stacey with a frown, "what do you have to feel ashamed about for what happened back then?"

Blowing out a shaky breath, I say, "Because I left it far too long before getting Jonny the help he so clearly needed. As soon as I found out about his drug addiction, I should have got him help...but I didn't..."

"Lauren, you had your own demons to deal with. You were grieving over your stillborn son for god's sake."

I shake my head at her. "That's just it though, isn't it? I wasn't grieving, Stace. I wasn't really grieving at all. I was just existing. Like a hollow shell. Floating through my life from one day to the next like a ghost, and I felt absolutely nothing inside...unless Jonny and I were making love. Then, and only then, did I feel something again. Which is why I was so selfish. Selfish because I couldn't bear the thought of Jonny going into rehab and being away from me and therefore I just allowed him to carry on. I used to go on at him of course, all the time, about kicking his addiction, about joining one of those anonymous groups where addicts go to get the help and support they need. But of course, Jonny wouldn't go, because Jonny never did something that somebody told him to do. He always did the exact opposite. Which is why we argued so much. Some of the rows we used to have were so bad sometimes that Jonny would leave the flat for hours on end, making me stew and worry and agonise so badly over him that by the time he came home, hours later, usually in the middle of the night when I was asleep in bed, I'd forgive him instantly."

I pause momentarily, Stacey's arm still wrapped tightly around me, keeping me warm, keeping me safe. "And then we'd make love. Every single night for however long this shit went on for. Knowing he was as high as a kite on cocaine, I still let him make love to me. And all because I loved him so deeply, so desperately. Because Jonny was like my own drug. I needed my fix of him as badly as he needed his fix of cocaine. He was the high I needed to numb the pain I was feeling inside over the baby we'd lost. It was only years later when I thought back to those last six months with Jonny in Manchester that I realised just how toxic our relationship had become. I couldn't see it at the time. I was so blinded by my grief that I just couldn't see it…and neither could he."

Unable to keep my tears at bay for a minute longer, I allow Stacey to curl me into her embrace. She strokes my hair as I sob quietly against her chest, the last decade of hurt, grief and pain finally clawing their way out of me. "It's okay, Lauren," she whispers into my hair, "it's all going to be okay. I promise."

"But what if it isn't?" I manage to splutter between sobs, "what if…"

"Sssh, now," she says gently, "let's not do that right now, eh? Not right now."

****

A short while later, Stacey and I begin our stroll back through Hyde Park, towards the tube station. "I know I keep repeating myself," says Stacey, "but I think Jonny needs to know the truth about everything."

I shake my head sadly. "He's way off the rails now to even think about telling him something so upsetting. And if I try to get anywhere near him, Pete will release the story of our past to the papers, and as you now know, I don't want that story coming out to anybody. Ever."

"So the bastard wins again," Stacey mutters angrily.

"I guess he does," I say with a heavy sigh.

Linking her arm through mine, Stacey says, "What if I talked to Ben? Without actually telling him any details I mean. Tell him to speak to Jonny when they're alone and maybe, I don't know, come up with a plan to…"

I stop walking and Stacey falls silent beside me. As I turn to look at her, her burst of enthusiasm soon fades, quickly giving way to disappointment once more. "You don't want me to help you at all, do you?"

Giving her a sympathetic smile, I say quietly, "Stace, I love you, and I love how desperate you are to help me out but you must understand, you *have* to understand my situation. The consequences of the story of our past being released to the world is unthinkable. It would dredge up all sorts of painful memories that are best left behind us in Manchester…"

"If you're referring to something coming out about Jonny coming to blows with your dad after what happened, I hardly think you need to worry about what people would think about that. Hell, if anything, they would sympathise with both you and Jonny. In fact, I think your dad got off lightly. Way too lightly. He should have gone to prison for life after what he did. And to think that that bastard is still out there somewhere…"

"Exactly. The last time I checked up on his whereabouts, he was still living and breathing, which is why I want to keep all of our past well under wraps. The last thing I need is him crawling back out from which ever rock he's hidden under. I'd rather he stayed under said rock and rotted away…"

I start to feel dizzy and sick at the very thought of my dad and what he did to me that day, and Stacey reaches out to steady me.

"Lauren, don't think about it now. Any of it. Just calm down, look at your surroundings and take a deep breath in."

I do as she says, taking in the calming scene in front of me, the autumnal leaves falling from the trees on to the gravel path in front of us, the children nearby, laughing with their parents as they play football together. With Stacey's help and support, I manage to ground myself again, remembering to leave the past in the past and focus on the present.

"Come on, Lauren," says Stacey softly, "let's get you home."

****

The next few days are a living hell. I feel utterly helpless as I literally have to stand by and watch the love of my life shatter to pieces in front of the entire world. With the future of the band now in jeopardy thanks to Jonny's drug fuelled antics both on and off stage, their US tour has had to be postponed for a second time. Maybe even cancelled altogether if things continue as they are. And to make matters worse, Ben and Stacey have also officially split up after Ben started laying into Stacey about me.

That was two days ago, and they haven't spoken to each other since. All in all I have made a right bloody mess of everybody's lives and I can't really blame Ben or the rest of the lads for feeling so angry with me. If it wasn't for me, Jonny wouldn't be in the mess that he's currently in. Yes, he'd still be grieving badly over his mum, he'd even possibly be back on the drugs, but if I'd have stuck by him like I promised I would do, he wouldn't have hit rock bottom like he has done.

The way I see it, I've run out of every option. Neither Stacey nor I can come up with anything other than having to just sit back and watch events unfold. And it's torture. Sheer torture. Imagine watching the one person you love the most in the world go through the worst pain imaginable whilst being unable to comfort them as they go through it. And knowing you were the one that put that person in pain in the first place. *No, Lauren, his own dad put him there, not you.*

Well, if Pete thinks that things are working out well for his son now that I'm out of Jonny's life then he is very much mistaken. I only wonder where Pete will take things from here. Check Jonny into rehab most likely, if Jonny will go of course. Looking at how far gone he is at the moment, I would say that Jonny will not go quietly. If he goes at all.

More days tick by, days soon roll into weeks, and then one day, at the beginning of November, out of nowhere, Stacey receives a phone call from Ben. I know that something is seriously wrong when Stacey answers the phone, her face blanching within a minute of Ben speaking to her.

"He what?" she asks, her face aghast. Oh shit, now I really am worried.

Walking over to where she is standing in our kitchen, I say, "What is it? What's happened?"

Stacey's eyes slowly come to rest on me as Ben continues to talk to her urgently down the phone. Oh my god, she looks as though she's about to burst into tears. A chill runs down the length of my spine, my stomach beginning to roil as a strange feeling of unease begins to settle in my gut. I can't take this not knowing anymore. I need to know what the hell is going on and I need to know now.

Stepping as close to Stacey as I can possibly get, I say, "What the hell is it? What's going on, Stace?"

Stacey shakes her head at me so I make a grab for the phone but she yanks it away. "I'll call you back," she says quickly to Ben before hanging up the call.

"What the hell was that?!" I practically screech at her, "why did you cut him off without letting me speak to him?!"

Placing her hands on my shoulders, Stacey says, "Lauren, I think it's best you sit down…"

Smacking her hands away in anger, I shout, "I don't want to

sit down! Just tell me what the fuck is going on before I lose my mind!"

Stacey closes her eyes for the briefest of moments, as if building herself up for something huge, something terrible. I swear it feels like an eternity before she finally opens her mouth to speak to me. To tell me the worst news imaginable. "Jonny's in hospital, Lauren. He's been admitted into intensive care." What the actual hell?

"In hospital? What with? What's happened? Is he okay?" Stacey's expression remains grim. "Stacey, just bloody tell me!" I yell, feeling panic stricken.

"He's taken an overdose," Stacey says, "a concoction of both drugs and alcohol…Ben went round to Jonny's house early this morning to check on him after he went on an absolute bender last night and when he didn't answer, he got Jonny's dad round so they could unlock the door and get in, and when they did finally get in they…found him on his bedroom floor unconscious…"

The room suddenly starts to swim in front of me, my eyes losing focus as I try to take in exactly what she's saying. Jonny has taken an overdose? A deliberate overdose?

Making a grab for the kitchen counter, I suddenly find myself unable to breathe properly. "Lauren, are you okay?" asks Stacey. She tries to reach for me to help me but I bat her hands away.

"So are you saying that Jonny…tried to kill himself?"

The words are like acid on my tongue and I refuse to believe that I'm even thinking something like this, never mind saying it out loud. Because Jonny has done this before, but last time it was an accidental overdose. Surely this is the same thing. Surely? When Stacey doesn't answer me, I begin to panic. "Stacey, did Jonny try to kill himself?"

"It would appear so, yes," she says sombrely.

Well there it is, my worst fear realised. Jonny Mathers, the love of my life, has tried to take his own life. He felt so unhappy and alone, and so consumed with grief over his mum dying that he felt there was no way out. No way out other than to end it all so that he could put an end to his unbearable pain.

Oh god, I can't handle this. This was never my intention. I wanted to be with Jonny forever and stand by him through anything and everything. This wasn't how it was supposed to be. This wasn't how our story was supposed to end.

I just about manage to stagger forwards towards Stacey. Gripping her arms tightly, I say, "Jonny's going to be okay, isn't he?" Stacey's sorrowful eyes meet my gaze and when she doesn't answer me, I start to shake the words out of her. "I said Jonny's going to be okay, isn't he?!" I screech.

Stacey takes a firm grip of my shoulders and says, "I don't know, Lauren." Her voice is barely audible. "I'm sorry but I honestly don't know."

I let out a piercing howl, almost like an animal in pain, before dropping to the kitchen floor. I curl myself into a tight ball and start to rock back and forth, images of Jonny lying lifeless in a hospital bed in LA wired up to god knows what now whirring around in my mind. I scream and I cry, punching at our floor tiles with my fists in anger.

Stacey crouches down in front of me, trying her best efforts to comfort me, but I don't want comforting right now. I only want Jonny. I need to see Jonny and I need to tell him I love him. I need to tell him everything. Looking up at Stacey, tears now streaming down my cheeks, I say, "You need to ring Ben and find out more, because I'm flying out there to be with Jonny as soon as possible."

Brushing my hair out of my face, Stacey says, "You're absolutely sure you want to do that?" Is she for bloody real or what?

"Of course I'm sure!" I screech, "I couldn't give a fuck about Pete or any of that anymore because none of that matters! Jonny's lying in hospital seriously ill after trying to kill himself, Stacey! Do you honestly think I'm going to just sit back over here in London and wait for him to get better, or, worse still, die?!" I almost gag on the last word, my throat slowly closing up as my panic really starts to set in.

Stacey hushes me gently. "Okay, I'm sorry I asked that of you, Lauren. Of course I'll ring Ben now and sort out everything... but you're not going alone. I'm coming with you."

I nod, the action causing my head to spin even more. Shit, I can't breathe properly. I need air. I need to get out of here so I can get some air. "Stacey, I need..." I make a grab for Stacey's arm, my chest feeling tighter by the second, almost like my ribcage is closing in around my lungs, squeezing the very air out of them.

"Lauren?" she asks, sounding worried. "Lauren...Lauren..." Stacey's voice slowly gives way to the loud ringing in my ears and then suddenly, everything goes black....

To be continued...find out what happens next when Jonny and Lauren's story continues in Blazing Inferno - Book 2 of the Reclamation Rock Star Series.

ACKNOWLEDGEMENT

Thank you for purchasing and reading this book. I truly hope you have enjoyed Lauren and Jonny's story so far and are desperate to find out what happens in their next instalment, Blazing Inferno, which is told from the point of view of them both.

If you did enjoy the story then if you would please leave me a review on Amazon or Goodreads, I would be most grateful. Reviews are so important for authors and most especially, for self-published authors like myself who are trying to build their audience.

For more up to date news and further releases, you can follow me on Amazon, Tik Tok and Instagram, by following JFrances81author.

Thank you for reading. J x

Printed in Dunstable, United Kingdom